Valiant

Aralot's Keepers Book One

Amanda Heit

This is a work of fiction. All similarities to real life are coincidental and unintentional. Names, characters, places, and incidents are products of the author's imagination and used fictitiously. Enjoy the story!

Heit, Amanda.

Valiant / by Amanda Heit.

1st edition.

Paperback   978-1-949858-10-5

eBook   978-1-949858-11-2

Printed in the United States of America

September 2020

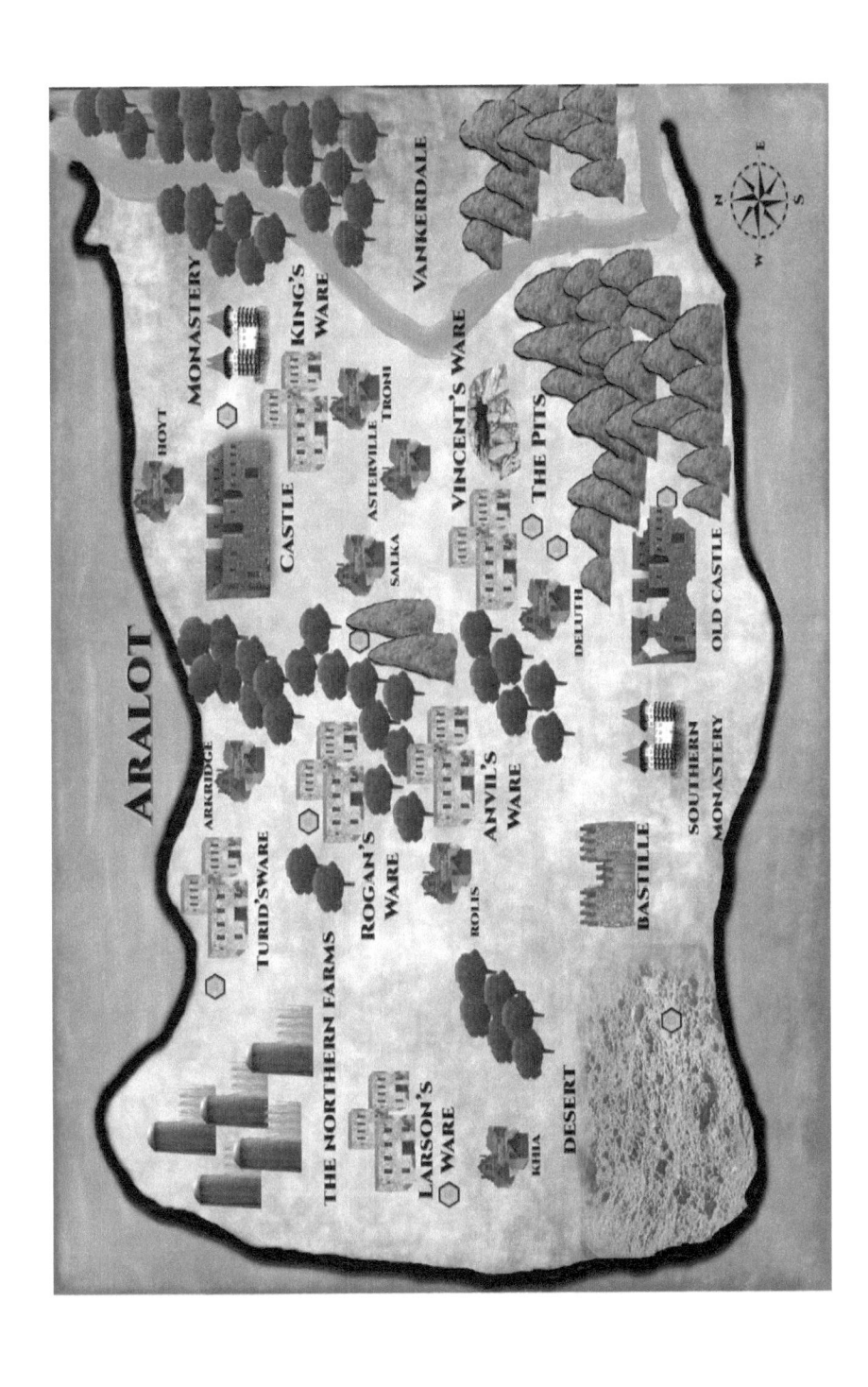

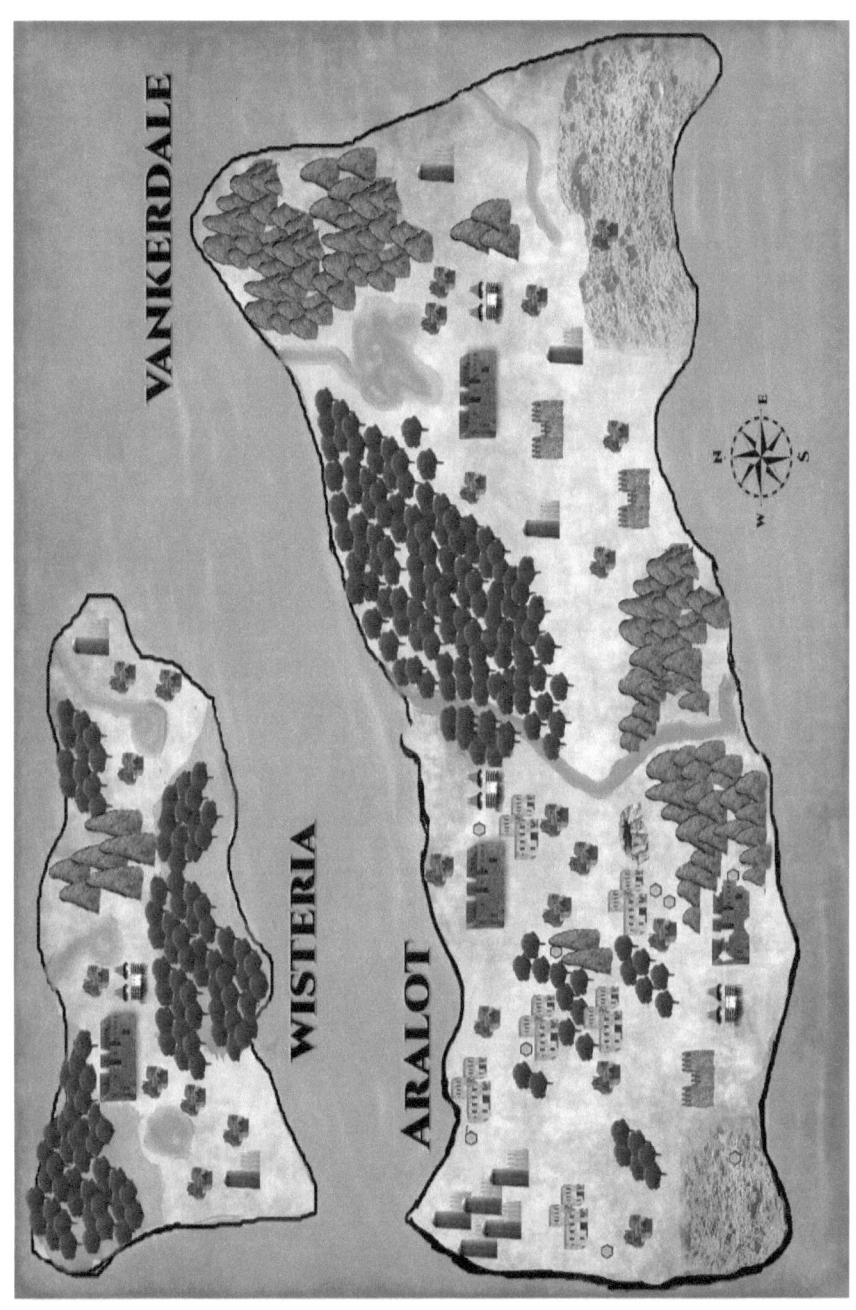

VANKERDALE

WISTERIA

ARALOT

Chapters

Dragon Eyes

Kayla

For most people, dreaming was a restorative and relaxing activity. For Kayla Brixton, it was a time to fight. She fought against the past trying to suppress important lessons that she still hadn't figured out. Lessons that she didn't want to get into. Lessons that she had already corrected ages ago…

Jack Brixton with his scraggly brown hair had his back to his six-year-old daughter as he smiled at the sight of the empty calf-high magical orb shattered open on the ground. If this scene had come from Kayla with human eyes, that would have been all she cared to note, but the images came into her dreams from the eyes of a dragon. She could make out each hair on her father's head, the stitches of his leather clothing, the shadows beneath his arms, and the magical red glow that always surrounded him due to the protective spell his king dragon had given him. Jack had been bonded by a red fire-breathing dragon named Pyro rather illegally.

Since dragon eyes viewed two-hundred and seventy degrees, Kayla could tell exactly which dragon's memories she was currently trapped inside, because she could see the white scales from the corner of the domed eyes. Kayla was being Sparkle, her mother Tia's bonded non-magical ice dragon.

Sparkle was currently feeling a sense of satisfaction for having cut through the magic orb. She preened slightly for all the other nearby dragons to see. The container of magic was made from ice so thick and so strong that it took the exquisite force of an ice dragon tail to pierce it open. Either that or a specially crafted cauldron that could melt the ice.

Magical orbs were crafted inside the belly of special ice dragons, although the dragon who had gifted the blue power of this orb was nowhere around. Everyone called the old ice dragon Mr. Grumpy even if his real name was Bantin. He was an antisocial creature because both his bonding fangs had been cut out shortly after his birth to prevent him from claiming multiple humans with his fangs. Ice dragons were the only ones that could bond more than one person at a time, and they loved the mental chatter in their minds. They were typically lovers of mankind except for when their heads were refused any sort of mental connection at all like Mr. Grumpy's brain.

Sparkle was forbidden from bonding anyone other than her rider Tia, but Tia was a keeper, a rare individual who could link to multiple dragon's thoughts without needing a physical bond. Tia Felding's inherited magical blood kept Sparkle entertained by extra dragon voices instead of human ones.

Mr. Grumpy couldn't bond a rider, but he could be bribed quite well to share his magical talents. It was written in Aralot's laws that the small kingdom would merge again with the neighboring kingdom of Vankerdale if they didn't have magic to sustain them, so Mr. Grumpy's magic was well appreciated. Currently, his orb of ice was melting into the forest floor, while the blue magic that had been within had moved into the ruby ring on Jack's hand.

Kayla took a step closer keeping her eyes on the ground so she didn't have to engage with the curious dragons that flocked around her father. Her downward gaze was a blast of annoyance to Sparkle as the dragon eyes viewed the young girls knotted red-brown hair despite Tia chasing her child around the house with a comb that morning. Kayla had found it a fun game to escape outside. Now it was even more fun because her dad had told her she was old enough to touch magic. She wanted to help.

Jack looked away from the broken ball of ice to a stack of heavy crates that had bold black letters stamped on the side. Kayla finally looked up, but only so she could squint at the boxes and try her best at reading the word "Cutlery." She slowly got closer and closer to her dad. The crates had just been delivered directly to Jack's home, and instead of setting up a wagon to transport the items to the nearby beach so the trade goods could reach Wisteria, Jack was going to use magic to send the boxes over.

Jack let the blue force of magic travel the short distance from his ring to the palm of his hand sending out into the air the warm scent of fire and smoke with a hint of licorice. Dragons loved that particular spell and more than just Sparkle inhaled to savor the scent. A few dragons hummed in pleasure as one of the crates started to move upward.

Then they all screamed as knives exploded outward bouncing off their hard hides and slicing through the delicate nature of their wings. In the center of the commotion was Kayla's small hand grasping onto her father's stronger one.

Six-year-old Kayla cried as Jack yelled at her. Fifteen-year-old Kayla struggled to wake herself up in bed because she was upset too. Did she have to see this *again*? She got it. She shouldn't have jumped at her father's hand and tried to help him control the magic to move the boxes. That was nine years ago. What other lesson was she supposed to learn from this nightmare? Her father had healed all the dragons she refused to acknowledge, and she had spent a full week searching the woods for slivers from the crates.

It was lessons like this that reminded Kayla why she was so avoidant toward dragons. When they got angry and hurt, they flamed things. Their tails knocked over trees. Their cries brought out her dragon warrior mother, and flattened Kayla to the ground. Kayla wished she could avoid dragons as well as everyone thought she did, but her dreams refused to release her from their images.

If the dream wouldn't let go, she would release herself. Kayla shifted her mental focus into her legs attempting to make them move only to find her dream shifting into another one that she didn't like reliving. Probably the only thing she had accomplished so far was to disrupt her blankets with a useless twitch.

She was seven and short with her red-brown hair long and loose trailing down the back of the pink sweater with the hood. She had loved that sweater when she was seven. She wore it every single day for two years until it ripped apart. Now she hated bright colors preferring gray over pink. Pink only made it easier for dragons to spot her in a field of tan leather-clad dragon riders.

It was among those riders that her younger self walked. Her location was Uncle Anvil's dragon training ware. The grass beneath her feet was green and well fertilized. The surrounding trees were cultivated and planted for their healing properties to dragon and rider alike. Massive stone buildings rose into the air although not as high as the dragons.

The smells of sweat, dirt, metal, and dragon dung prevailed no matter which direction one turned, and Sparkle's dragon eyes were turning taking Kayla along in her sleep. The eyes scanned over all the other dragons that were avidly watching Kayla prance. With a swift motion, Sparkle moved in closer, always the protective shield against other dragon fangs that might want to slip into "her baby" and take the human from her. As an ice dragon, Sparkle viewed Kayla as already claimed.

No, no, no. Kayla really didn't want to see this dream. There was nothing new to learn! She fought with her mind to release her back into the present time getting the odd sense that she was already upright instead of laying down. Kayla struggled to move in her current time against her captured mind. She failed.

Most people didn't experience looking through dragon eyes until they bonded their own dragon and the dragon turned a year old so that the rider and dragon could sightshare. Sightsharing took place when a dragon and rider swapped souls for a while, existing inside the other's body. King Klavian called it ugly possession. Riders called it special. Kayla called it dreaming.

At the time of this past event, Kayla was entering the ware alone, except for the wild dragon guard that Tia Felding always had hovering over her child's head. It was a brown male dragon that now flew rather high to avoid the training warrior dragons below him. Tia herself had ridden Sparkle over to the ware for Uncle Clark's birthday, but Kayla refused to touch dragons, and had taken the longer way of traveling through a magical portal and repelling down a mountain.

The bad moment was getting closer. Kayla struggled again to regain her consciousness and might have bonked her shins on something, because she felt a slight throb before the dream sucked her back under. She wasn't always looking out of Sparkle's eyes in these nightmares, but when she was, it was always extra frustrating because she could feel the dragon's emotions as her own, and it was strange to feel so restrictive over herself.

Unlike her parents, she couldn't love dragons the same way they did. Kayla rode none of them. Talked to none of them. Looked at none of them. This was the day that Kayla had been contemplating a nasty word for her emotional condition.

Depression.

She was skipping across the field not because she was feeling happy, but because she was trying to prove that the word didn't define her at all. She hadn't enjoyed reading that term, but she had finished the section on it all the same and was now going to prove that it wasn't what she had.

Chirp.

The curious sound had Kayla groaning in her sleep. If only she could stop it! It happened eight years ago and she still couldn't stop it! Kayla tried to raise her current hands to slap herself awake only her arms were not moving. She knew the feelings were coming, and when possible, Kayla still avoided them every single time.

Sparkle's eyes zoomed away from the young Kayla who was pulling her pink hood over her head so that the dragon could see another creature of pink. Galivant. He was a pink-scaled dragon, a rare bred creature that came from Vincent's Ware. Since Galivant had refused to bond upon hatching, the notoriously skilled ice dragon trainer Shilo had sent Galivant to Anvil who was also good with nearly-there ice dragons. Shilo's goal in life was to create a real ice dragon one day. When Vladimir had died, he had taken his ice dragon secrets with him, leaving behind Sparkle, who couldn't create magic because of the strange events of her birth, and Mr. Grumpy, who was getting old, as the only two white-scaled dragons in existence.

Pink dragons were people pleasers, aggressive toward other dragons if they didn't get the right rider and team. They didn't shoot ice but fire like most of the other dragons around them, and Sparkle was starting to churn up ice in her stomach to remind Galivant that he wasn't as brilliant as she was.

Since Kayla couldn't hear her own thoughts in the dream, she could only remember them. Regardless of the disconnect, Kayla felt her past emotions exceptionally well having suffered through this nightmare again and again. The avalanche had reached her. Her emotions started to mix inside of her stronger and stronger. Kayla saw herself stop moving and freeze on the field.

Chirp, chirp, chirp.

Galivant's cries were getting more insistent toward Kayla, but Sparkle didn't snarl because real ice dragons attacked silently without any thought of ever backing down. Since Kayla never looked at dragons except in her dreams while she reviewed her failures, she had trained her ears to learn their language. When she was seven, she hadn't understood these words. Now she knew them by heart. They stabbed. Every time.

"Hey, hey, hey! Look at me!"

Kayla tried arching her back to wake herself up next. Perhaps if her spine developed an impingement she would wake up. No such luck. She even avoided the impingement.

Seven was too young to bond a dragon, but there was no denying that Galivant had been interested in her enough to give it a try at the time. The pink dragon winged in closer. Kayla's mother, Tia, smelled fabulous to ice dragons. Kayla wasn't surprised that she did too. Dragon's picked their riders by instinct and scent. However, Kayla never wanted a dragon of her own, unlike her mother who had fifty.

Born a keeper through the hereditary Felding line, Tia was bonded to one dragon called her gatekeeper. In her case, that was Sparkle. Sparkle sorted through all the other dragon thoughts linked to Tia's mind and picked which ones to send to her bonded rider. Kayla always thought it would be really hard to be a gatekeeper like Sparkle. Keepers were known to have up to seventy dragons in a bond at a time. How did the gatekeeper dragon think anything for themselves when seventy other voices chatted away? Sparkle had been easily distractible as a hatchling since she wanted to play with everyone. Now she had figured out how to handle the mental comments and she *still* wanted to play with everyone. It wasn't all bad though. Sparkle could get messages from all over the kingdom from connected dragons and share important news with Tia instantly. Tia was a fantastic spy that way.

Kayla was nothing but in trouble. She pulled the hood down farther as the next command sprang up.

"Hey, gorgeous! Come here!"

The emotions flooded through her little body. Sadness. Depression. It coursed through her making her knees shake while her eyes filled. Sparkle's dragon eyes settled onto Galivant, and the defending shriek from the white-scaled ice dragon Sparkle testified that Tia had been alerted to the problem at hand and was mentally coaching Sparkle through using words to solve the problem instead of ice.

"You leave my baby alone!" Sparkle screamed.

That's what Kayla was to Sparkle. The baby. Kayla was nearly sixteen now and the dragon still called her the baby. Little child Kayla grabbed at the hood and ran for the edge of the field trying to escape. The dream skipped over the fight this time, but Kayla had been made to watch it plenty of times before as Sparkle came against Galivant with her experienced team. Sparkle had the black night dragon Midnight, the pink dragon Duchess, the green Fang, the bronze Lightning, the brown Hemp, the red Darkwing, and the brown Fern on her personal attack force. Since they were in Tia's keeper bond, their attacks were coordinated through instant thought. They were fast. Deadly. Brutal.

Since then, Galivant had been moved to Turid's Ware where he had bonded an older rider who had lost his dragon a few years before. It worked out best all around, and Galivant was content with his place far away from Kayla. While Turid's Ware was the closest one to her house, Kayla avoided it when she could. Her avoidance centered around this depression thing.

As if her subconscious was reviewing if the term "depression" was still correct after all these years, the dream continued. Feldings were known for having strange mental disorders. Sure, that normally attributed to being poisoned by people who feared their abilities as keepers, but Kayla hadn't escaped the early onset of those mental issues.

"Why are you causing fights, Kayla!?"

Fights yes. She was going to keep fighting this. She would not see it out to the end. She would escape before her younger body exploded. Kayla tried biting her tongue in her sleep. She felt the short stab and remained snoozing.

The legs of a green dragon landed before her and the depression hit at her young form so strong that she dropped to her knees. She didn't need to look to know who was screaming at her. This was Fang after the fight with his rider Achilles. All the people in her mother's rider team thought they could boss her around. They always let their dragons get too close!

Breathe! She had to breathe! Her emotions had taken over her again, filling her with despair and instant tears that she failed to hold back. Still trapped in the dream, Kayla could make out all of Fang's green hide. Green dragons had curved scales like raindrops. Fang copied the norm. Kayla could trace scale patterns in her sleep. She could mimic dragon speech in her sleep too. Once her father had woken her up asking her why she was talking about five hundred sheep using dragon speech. She had no idea.

"Can't you at least make an effort to promote peace?" Achilles screamed again.

Make an effort? Like, look at the new pink dragon and smile at it? No way! That would have Sparkle trying to rip Galivant's head off after she dislocated his tail. Ice dragons were territorial. They never shared riders, and Kayla had ridden on Sparkle for the first five years of her life while her mother held Kayla in her arms.

She had done the right thing—at least that time. If only that was the end of her nightmare, it still would have dragged Kayla down to an uncomfortable level, but fighting dragons wasn't the topic of the night. It was her avoidance to look at the scaled animals. She ignored them because of these emotions. Kayla was supposed to be a keeper like her mother was. She was supposed to have inherited special blood that let her talk with more than one dragon inside her head. She'd keep them all out of her head if she could. She simply couldn't... breathe! Kayla gasped for air, which let out the strained wail she had been retaining by holding her breath. She felt her breath in real life mimic the sound.

"I made it fourteen seconds on Tripper last night!" The young male voice of a kid shouted in her direction. Caleb Andrade. If it wasn't a dragon trying to get her attention it was this kid. She had conflicting feelings about that too. She'd never looked at him, had no idea what this kid looked like, but he had a habit of making distracting comments that saved her from bad situations. He had good timing. He was probably a rider that was destined to be the next ware leader or something despite his tendency to get himself in trouble.

Distracted away from her inability to inhale, Kayla jumped to her feet and ran for Uncle Anvil who had come toward the field at the first sound of clashing dragons. He had always been a tall man with a good sense of humor. Anvil had blond hair and earrings. One ruby earring in particular he never took off because it gave him magical protection and had saved his life multiple times. Unlike her parents, Uncle Anvil had gotten the hint to not ask her to look at dragons.

"Nasty stuff isn't it?" Uncle Anvil replied tucking her safely into his side as she reached him. "I suppose in this case our normally impartial parties are too partial to handle a cool-down session. Clawson will go shoot steam up Galivant's nose. Don't worry. Galivant will figure it out soon. You did the right thing not increasing the tension between ice dragons and partial ice dragons."

Kayla had pressed her pink hooded self in closer to Anvil, and he had scooped her into his arms like he was the sole giver of her personal comfort. Sparkle snorted, still feeling the rage of fighting off another dragon that had chirped at her human baby. She didn't care if Anvil held Kayla like this, even if her father Jack did, so Kayla was very familiar with the shape of Anvil's arms, the soothing nature of his voice, and the hard planes of his chest. Anvil was the first person Kayla always ran to.

Kayla stopped trying to wake herself up. Why bother now? She had already passed the bad part, and she'd take being cradled by Uncle Anvil any time of the day or night.

With her larger eyes, Sparkle noted Jack running to reach his daughter. Uncle Anvil's green dragon, who was named Clawson, was also inside of Tia's mentally linked keeper bond. Clawson gave Anvil the heads up whenever Jack was around, and he did so again in the dream like he had done every other time it played out. Anvil dropped the pink Kayla in the dirt right as Kayla's heart had started to even out. Feeling unloved, she had curled up in a ball before she realized why she had been discarded. Anvil cut off all affection whenever her father was around as if to give it out was illegal.

"Kayla are you okay?" Jack Brixton had asked. He was always one to ask questions first and judge last, but even he couldn't understand why she wouldn't look at dragons. She tried to tell him once and failed. Maybe she just couldn't explain. She didn't have the right words. Was the right word depression? That couldn't be it. Depression didn't have a set external cause. It was a mental and emotional unbalance.

Okay there. See, she didn't have depression. She didn't need to keep watching this dream to remind her of that. Her sadness was caused by a trigger instead of a mental imbalance. It wasn't depression. She had a weird anxiety disorder toward dragons although her parents wouldn't like that decision either.

All at once, Kayla felt her mental focus shift back inside her living body, finally free of the nightmare. She shifted her arms and legs around happy to find them respond, but since she was at a good part, Kayla kept the dream going from memory just a little bit longer.

"She's fine," Anvil had answered for her.

"It wasn't her fault. Kayla didn't do anything but walk. She's got a mighty fine walk!" Caleb had called out having followed her. Kayla had heard Anvil shift his feet which meant that he probably gave Caleb the rider signal to get lost because the kid laughed. She didn't hear him run off, but she did hear Anvil grunt at her dad.

Something silent passed between her dad and her adoptive uncle. Both of their dragons, Pyro and Clawson, could trade mental thoughts with each other since they were linked to Tia. So many times Anvil and Jack talked to each other through their mental connection bouncing words between their dragons to swap things they didn't want to say out loud. To everyone else, it looked like they spent a lot of time staring at each other. To them, they shared secret, personal conversations.

"Can you get up?" Her father had knelt beside her, scanning Kayla over before he started to rub her back. "Don't blame yourself. That was bound to happen sometime. You're just too irresistible to dragons. You get it from me."

Kayla had rolled her eyes. Pyro had fanged her father in the woods illegally, but it was her mother that dragons always cooed at.

"Yup. Way too cute." Her father had continued gaining the one thing the other dragons couldn't get from her—a glance. Kayla looked up at him to catch his smile. It was warm, something that her mother wouldn't echo if any of her dragons got hurt in the scuffle. Tia was the same as Sparkle when it came to her favorite creatures—always defensive.

"You did remember to bring the birthday present, right?"

This was the reason Kayla kept this memory going. She wanted to see her father's smiling face again. He had been missing for three months. Yes, people were lost for longer periods of time, but not her father. Everyone was worried to have Aralot's magical spellcaster missing.

"That's my girl. Don't tell Uncle Anvil what it is. He'll confiscate it."

Kayla recalled her father's famous smirk. Jack had brown scruffy hair on the top of his head. When he did let his beard grow out, it was the same red-brown as Kayla's hair. Jack had mesmerizing starburst brown eyes. Kayla's eyes were blue like the rest of the Felding line. When Jack had a challenge on his lips, they perked to the side, a combination of cocky and amused. Jack had looked at Uncle Anvil in that way. Uncle Anvil had walked off disregarding that he was the ware leader and needed to confiscate illegal items.

They had gotten Clark fireworks. It was true that he wasn't allowed to shoot them off into the air. Such things could confuse dragons, especially at a ware that had dragons flying all over the place all the time, but Clark had been overdue for his hard-earned vacation. He had refused to take his leave until his wife Rosa could. They had a trip planned for the ocean, and Kayla had helped them launch off all those fireworks watching the beautiful colors burst to life and then fizzle into a watery grave.

It was a beautiful memory marred by the grating sound of dragon laughter near Kayla's bedroom window that jolted Kayla awake. Oh sure, her kicking her legs, biting her tongue, trying to slap herself, and fall out of bed had done nothing at all. It was the dragons always winning out against her fears. But she could, and would, win out against them eventually. Sparkle laughed again and Kayla moaned consciously aware that she wasn't in the same position she had laid down in last night.

There went her mom telling Sparkle some kind of joke that filled the outside woods with the familiar sound of the dragon's soprano. Kayla found her pillow, which was on the opposite end of the bed since she was now backward on her mattress. She stuffed the pillow over her head.

Most people she knew would smile at the sound of dragon laughter. For one, it meant that the dragon wasn't angry or feeling up to attacking anything. For another, most people that Kayla knew loved dragons more than their own lives. Kayla didn't fit with their category at all. She preferred her life away from the scales and flame. She preferred being able to sleep in because despite going to bed earlier than normal last night, she felt tired today. It had been like this all week.

Sparkle hit the side of the house with her tail and then her tones of controlled laughter tried to pin the blame on the wild dragon Luna, who had shown up some time yesterday whining about missing her brother Pyro. Kayla didn't mind that Pyro was lost, but since he was her father's dragon, and her father was lost too, Kayla felt the loss just as keenly. What she wouldn't give for her dad to come home! He at least *tried* to understand why Kayla refused to interact with dragons. Her mother, Tia, didn't even try anymore. Just yesterday she had given Kayla "the look" when Kayla walked past Sparkle without a single glance.

Looking at dragons was hard! Trying to interact with Sparkle was the worst, and Kayla hadn't done anything with the dragon since she was five, so why did her mom think she was going to change now? Turning sixteen next week wasn't going to make a remarkable difference in her life. All her other birthdays had come and gone without her becoming like her mother. She had no desire to protect dragons or have them inside her head. Kayla didn't think she was ever going to be a keeper like the other Feldings. She was born a Brixton.

Pg. 14

The dragon Luna from outside whined at Tia as the woman cranked open a window and told Luna to stop hitting the house. Sparkle couldn't contain her laughter, and it was with another dose of annoying dragon behavior that had Kayla tugging the pillow down deeper.

"Sparkle is the one who did it," Luna barked out in dragon speech.

More laughter from Sparkle as Tia didn't understand the muttered words. Kayla's mother could read tail speech in a flash far better than anyone else in the kingdom, but picking out the words from verbal dragon speech wasn't her forte. Kayla didn't know of anyone that could interpret the dragon language the same way that Kayla could. The best speech scholars could recognize the top one-thousand words used. Most riders only learned the top fifty. Kayla knew all the sounds since it was her main device to avoid dragons.

Most dragons, with the exception of Sparkle since she was an ice dragon, would always voice their deeds and brag about them verbally before doing them. That gave Kayla loads of time to dodge sneaking tails, scamper under bushes away from pestering eyes, and clear the field before talons sharper than cleavers came down beside her body. She never had to look at dragons if she could pick them out from their sounds.

"Kayla! Breakfast is ready!"

Kayla pulled the pillow down even more, but it was no good. She was awake, and Sparkle and Luna were chatting outside at full volume about how Pyro and Jack were not located halfway into the ocean. Why would her father try to go into the ocean? Pyro was not a water dragon. He would need to land on something eventually, and Kayla doubted that with the dragon king's size, he would be able to keep a boat steady when he landed instead of capsizing the thing.

They were all wasting their time looking in the wrong places, although Kayla couldn't come up with a better spot to search either. Jack left on an ordinary morning without mentioning that he had dangerous plans. He hadn't come back home for three months. Her mother would have been in a worse panic if she wasn't connected to Pyro's thoughts through her keeper abilities. Pyro kept claiming that Jack was fine. He wasn't off flirting with another woman. He wasn't dead or injured. He was doing something important, but Pyro wouldn't say what or where.

Kayla put her pillow back on the bed and sat up. She groaned again spotting the reason for why she was tired. She had papers all over her desk—the worst of the worst. She couldn't remember getting up in the night to draw images. It was like another human took over her physical form at night and possessed her.

The first time her father had mentioned possession spells, Kayla had jumped on the idea of learning everything she could about this particular evil. There was no way that a possession spell would ever be able to take her down and control her the same way it had once gotten her mother. Jack thought that Kayla's avid interest was because of her mother's past incident with being possessed, but it wasn't. Kayla's interest was because of these blasted pictures! She would go to bed and wake up in the morning having completed intricate drawings that she never had any recollection of making. She had been doing this for years and had checked herself over carefully for signs of possession. She wasn't possessed. She simply had a very bad habit of moving in her sleep. Moving and not waking up when she wanted to.

Apart from casting spells on herself to ward off evil, Kayla had cast spells to prevent anything from getting into her room be it spell or person. Nothing. Her room was fine. Her father was the spellcaster for the entire kingdom of Aralot. He was the only man allowed to dabble in magic, although Kayla knew of a few other people who touched the substance. Anyway, with his books and being able to pick his brain, Kayla had exhausted every angle to her nighttime drawing except that she had an overactive imagination. What were the pictures this time?

Kayla slowly moved to her desk trying to not see what she had drawn last night. She remembered having a bad dream about her mother being dead, and then she thought she'd slept just fine after that until the dream of her slicing dragon wings and then feeling the depression. How wrong she was.

Dragons! Kayla shrieked and used her arm to push the papers off the desk onto the floor. She had been drawing dragons! She hadn't done that in a while, and she didn't want to have done it again today. It was the worst when she started drawing dragons. She had the unfortunate habit of knowing who each dragon was even if she had never seen any of them before with her mortal eyes. Why couldn't she claim she was possessed and make this whole thing easier?

The papers slowly descended from her push, and not all of them conveniently turned upside down. Kayla scrambled to pick them up so she could burn them in the fireplace downstairs. The first upright picture was of Luna. Kayla had never looked at Luna. How then did she know what Luna looked like? Irritating.

Another picture was Sparkle and another was of Pyro. Kayla paused on the picture of Pyro, but only because her father was standing beside him in the picture. Jack Brixton came up to the animal's side when Pyro was kneeling. Behind them in the picture was a random castle. Jack was pointing inside. It wasn't Aralot's castle. Kayla knew that place well since King Klavian was good friends with her parents and she had been going to visit the castle since before she could walk. The castle in this picture had to be someplace else.

Seeing her missing dad had her tearing up, so Kayla grabbed up the pictures and tucked them to her chest. She ran down the stairs already hearing her mother humming a song. Tia Brixton had been composing one this week about Jack. It was sort of sad that Tia thought her husband would come home when she finished the melody so that he could hear it.

Kayla ran across the front room to the unlit fireplace. She knew she wasn't supposed to waste magic since they had a limited supply from Bantin, but it was very important to get rid of the pictures before her mom saw them and asked her if she was taking an interest in dragons. She wasn't.

Kayla tossed in the pictures and used her magical keychain to blast the papers into cinder and ash.

"Did you sleep in that?" Tia arrived with her blond hair in a bun, already wearing her dark-brown leather from Rogan's Ware where she had completed her first three years of training. Tia gave her daughter a hug from behind.

Kayla smiled. She had gotten rid of the pictures just in time. If her mom had seen the one of Sparkle, she was likely to frame it. Kayla never let her parents see her pictures for that reason. She did not want another reminder that she had strange night habits. At least she didn't have to share a room. Her parents hadn't been able to have another child after her. Tia had complications at Kayla's birth, and even if the midwives claimed she should be able to have more kids, she couldn't. So Kayla got a room all to herself, and she didn't have to tell anyone what she dealt with. Some people's inner demon was a fear of public speaking. Tia feared losing one of her dragons or riders. Jack feared people using magic in an evil way. Kayla feared her pictures because they never felt like her own.

"You need to change your clothes," Tia demanded.

"Mom, it's fine." Kayla slipped out of her mother's embrace and tried to block out the chattering dragons outside. The window was still open, and their voices shoved their way in. Slasher, one of Tia's wild dragons, had arrived with Luna. They were talking about how they failed to hunt down some really big fish and nearly drowned.

"I changed the sweater before going to bed."

That was a lie; one really big lie. She had been wearing this same sweater for the last four days straight, although Kayla had changed her shirt. Her mom wouldn't know for sure because Kayla had three copies of this same sweater.

"I will ask Pewter to search the ocean further," Sparkle said from outside.

Pewter was her Aunt Rosa's water dragon. Water dragons were very good at long-distance flying. Pewter was kept in top shape protecting supply ships across the ocean between Aralot and Wisteria. He was pretty much in charge of all things to do with Wisterian trade.

"Is breakfast any good today?" Kayla asked before she could shout outside that everyone was wasting their time. Her father wasn't going to be found in the ocean! Maybe he was at that strange castle in her picture.

"We have grits."

"I'll eat at Uncle Anvil's," Kayla replied earning a sigh from Tia. Then she pulled off another trick on her mom. "Any news on Dad?"

Tia shook her head as the melancholy hit at her. Kayla felt a little bad about tampering with her mother's emotions. She normally avoided asking her mother about Dad, because she didn't like to see the look it produced. However, since Sparkle was connected to Tia's thoughts, the dragon stopped talking abruptly and yapped at the other dragons to do the same. They went silent waiting for Sparkle to be done mentally communicating with her bonded rider. Sparkle loved to be happy. If Tia wasn't happy, she would do everything she could do to change that. The dragon would be offering encouragement about where they were going to search next for Jack and how.

Kayla pulled up the hood on her gray sweater and rushed out the door. Now was her perfect chance to get away from the dragons without them trying to talk to her since she had gotten them all busy without needing to talk to any of them herself. Luna and Slasher gave her a short grunt as she rushed from the home that her father, Jack, had built.

Homework Boy

Tyler

It was hard being thought of as the homework boy still. That's not who Tyler was, but he still found himself going along with it. Old habits were just too hard to kill. Prince Evan still handed him the assignments he didn't want to do, even if the man was near forty years old. The prince used to give them to Tyler's older brother Narl, but Narl had grown up and moved out of the servitude of the castle grounds. Tyler was still here. He was almost ready to put behind him his required years to serve the king, and then he really would make everyone proud. He was going to do something fantastic: something that was more than just reading books and answering questions for Prince Evan.

It was a wonder that the man could pass his own tests with how often he sloughed his homework off to others. However, Prince Evan had a sharp mind and could memorize answers easily. What he didn't have was the ability to sit down and read a book.

Tyler glanced at his assignment today and adjusted his glasses on his rounded nose. Then he rubbed at the dark-brown facial hair that circled around his mouth and chin. The book was so old that the cover didn't have a title. He glanced at the paper in his hand and read the assignment. Book report. Tyler wished his feet could stomp the floor, but the floor was lined with thick rugs everywhere he went. Tyler stomped a little in the hallway anyway as he made his way down to his favorite homework location. The rugs were left over from when Vankerdale was plunged into fifty years of perpetual winter. The kingdom's resources were gravely used up during that time. Things were looking better now that the curse of eternal winter had been lifted by their great ruler, King Peyton.

Tyler tried to like the king, but he had trouble doing so. The king was very much like his son Prince Evan, and took credit for other people's work. The dragon bonding curse was the prime example. During the first session of the curse, all bonded dragons that lived in Vankerdale couldn't bond humans to share their thoughts. The curse had been lifted for a few short months before coming back on the land harder than ever. Now any dragon that lived or even entered the kingdom suffered a broken bond. It made entering Vankerdale a very undesirable thing to do.

Tyler saw the additional stipulations to the curse as a harsher punishment of an already nasty piece of magic. It screamed rather loudly that a wrong doing had occurred for Aralot to put it back up like this. King Peyton claimed no association, but it was Aralot's King Gladius who had first put the curse on their land, and it had to be Aralot's spellcasters taking it down and putting it back up soon after. Tyler guessed that the real person responsible for saving Vankerdale was the neighboring kingdom's spellcaster, Jack Brixton. King Peyton had done something to make Aralot's king mad. Mad enough to get Jack to seal off Vankerdale's border and recurse them all. The peace with Aralot hadn't lasted too long.

King Peyton and Prince Evan were always whispering plans on how to abduct the man's wife so that they could force Jack to remove the curses. Jack had put up a very effective border control spell which prevented people from Vankerdale entering Aralot and taking anything back with them that they weren't allowed to have. Merchants from both sides could still transport legally sold goods and verbal information, but no resources or people that belonged in Aralot could traverse the borderline otherwise. Dragons from either side couldn't cross the border at all.

Vankerdale didn't have magic to use as Aralot did. Aralot had ignored their struggles until Jack came around placing King Klavian on the throne. Vankerdale was doing much better now that trade between Aralot, Wisteria, and Vankerdale was alive and thriving. That was Jack's blessing as well. He had ended the curse that the wicked King Gladius of Aralot had placed on the ocean making it impossible for ships to sail. Now with winter gone and ships sailing, all three kingdoms had gained their glory back.

Well, most of the glory. There was that one problem with Vankerdale's dragons not being able to bond humans. Since they couldn't bond, they couldn't mind-speak with man. Dragon wares were nonexistent after fifty years of snow that prevented dragons from mating. A lot of dragons had died leaving the kingdom with young hatchlings who knew nothing of the respect the older dragons held between man and beast.

Then there was the one dragon who knew only what Tyler could tell him. Almost sixteen years ago to the date, Valiant had been located and locked up as a resource to use against Aralot. He was a spellbinding dragon, an animal with silver wingtips, blue-gray scales, and the ability to shoot out magic spells if he could suck up magic first. Vankerdale had no magic for Valiant to eat, but Aralot did.

Jack's wife had that ice dragon named Sparkle, another reason for King Peyton and Prince Evan to kidnap the woman, even if Sparkle was said to not produce magic. Sparkle would still be a good catch, because she was the offspring of the magic producing dragon that everyone called Mr. Grumpy. Kidnapping Tia got her dragon, which got the magic. Or since that idea was still failing, there was Valiant.

The dragon had not been born in Vankerdale but was born in Wisteria. He was brought into Vankerdale right after winter had started to thaw, when dragons didn't mate. Stealing dragons was the only way that Vankerdale could get a new supply of them. Valiant was the very last dragon to be stolen from the kingdom across the ocean.

He was special because the only way to properly breed a magical ice dragon was to mate it with a spellbinding dragon. One day Aralot would realize that the reason they only got pink-scaled dragons that shot fire was because they didn't have a spellbinding dragon to give an ice dragon the ability to create magic. When that day came, Vankerdale had the dragon they needed. Aralot's short supply of ice dragons would be transported into Vankerdale, and all the eggs produced from the magical union would no doubt be hoarded by King Peyton. It was his trap to steal magic.

So far Aralot had not come calling. It was like someone over there knew of the trap and had decided that Valiant was better off left as collateral, instead of giving Vankerdale's rulers the means to start casting out nasty curses.

Tyler unlocked the door to Valiant's caged room and let himself in. He had no idea what the dragon did to entertain himself being locked away for so many years. When the dragon was first brought in, he had been chained into the room. He wasn't now. The dragon was too large to fit through the door, and he couldn't escape on his own. Valiant had no fire to burn the walls. He had no magic from an ice dragon mate to help him cast spells. Valiant was as trapped as he had been for sixteen years. He couldn't even knock down the walls, because if he did, the standing guard on duty would stab him. He had been trained to not hit walls.

Tyler always felt bad about that too. If he was a dragon, he would build up his tail strength until he burst through the walls and took flight. He hoped Valiant could fly. The dragon had been locked up for so long that Tyler feared he would be flightless if he ever did get out of the

Pg. 24

prison, and then his chances of actually mating with an ice dragon would be slim. Ice dragons loved flying, and icing things, and making things generally cold and uncomfortable. There would be no way to impress an ice dragon if Valiant couldn't fly. Keeping him locked away for the sole purpose of impressing an ice dragon to steal Aralot's magic sounded so pointless.

Tyler stepped into the large room and nodded to the guard who was on duty. The guards were all older than him, and they ignored his presence for the most part. Tyler never made an effort to befriend the guards. He was more fascinated with the dragon.

Valiant was sitting on the tip of his tail. His silver-tipped wings were folded, and his steel-blue scales hadn't been shined up in years. Yesterday, Tyler had spotted King Peyton's own spellbinding dragon named SilverWings with a coat of wax. Valiant had his eyes closed, which was a regular occurrence. There was nothing to see other than the dull stone walls he had been looking at for sixteen years. Tyler would have been screaming if this was him, but Valiant was the most patient dragon he had ever met.

When Tyler got assignments from Prince Evan, he took after his brother's example and brought them down here to complete them next to Valiant. Narl had used the dragon room when he worked here because he liked to think in a quiet place. Tyler used it because he thought the dragon needed a friend desperately.

"Hi, Valiant," Tyler said, sitting down at the edge of the room. Narl had named the dragon Smasher when he first met him trying to encourage him to break free. Prince Evan called the dragon MSD, for Mopey Spell Dragon. Tyler preferred to call him Valiant. The blue-gray dragon didn't open his eyes. Tyler only knew he was awake because of the way Valiant sniffed him to catch his scent. If he was asleep, he was too lazy to even do that.

"I have a book report on an old book. It's going to be a doozy. You want to read the whole book with me or should I only read out loud the important parts?"

Tyler couldn't decide which way the guard would rather he complete the assignment. He had no idea how long the guard had been standing there doing nothing but watching a dragon that kept his eyes closed. Tyler liked to pretend that Valiant had really good dreams. Sometimes the dragon would open his eyes to look at his surroundings. He often opened his eyes to eat.

"It's going to be so dry," Tyler fretted as he started to read the first page. "The rules of Aralot when it was first founded," Tyler read. He smiled at Valiant when his eyes snapped open. "You know they'll be looking for some new loophole trying to get into the place. I suppose you're interested?" Tyler asked because Valiant had stood up. He had never once stood up around Tyler before.

The dragon breathed him in again, and then put his head really close to the book and smelled that next. Tyler felt impressed that Valiant might know why he was stuck in the room for the last sixteen years. He was waiting for Aralot to send an ice dragon. If that could be accomplished, he could be set free. But Aralot was incredibly hard to get into now that Jack was there.

Valiant hooted. The sound was so close and loud that Tyler had to cover his ears.

"You want me to read you the whole thing?" Tyler asked.

Valiant pranced on his feet, which was another thing that Tyler had never seen before.

"Awesome! Here comes entertainment for a bored dragon. You can keep me awake."

Tyler didn't expect himself to fall asleep. This was the most awake he had ever seen Valiant. Tyler started to read through the old book looking for anything that Prince Evan might use to trick Aralot. He didn't expect to find anything at all. These rules were set down when Aralot was first founded. A lot had changed since then. The kingdom had gone through fourteen kings including Gladius who everyone knew as a hateful man who ruined the lives of everyone around him. He was so horrible that his own kingdom had killed him.

After about an hour of reading, the watching guard started to snore even though he was upright leaning against the wall. Tyler chuckled at him.

"Now if only we could put them all to sleep to get you out of here," Tyler remarked.

Valiant looked at the sleeping guard too before he gave Tyler a bow. Tyler voiced his surprise. King Peyton's spellbinding dragon would bow to humans and dragons that he tried to flatter and impress, but Tyler had never heard of Valiant doing the same thing. As far as he knew, the dragon had given up on impressing anyone. He wished that Vankerdale's dragons were not cursed. Tyler would have asked Valiant to bond him. Then he would hear the animal's thoughts and encourage him to break free.

"I am deeply honored, Valiant. I would love to be your friend."

Valiant hummed at him, such a startling sound that Tyler felt joy shoot through his core. Unfortunately, the sound was enough to wake the guard. He opened his eyes and Tyler went back to reading the old rule book until he fell asleep again. When he did, Valiant grinned and his stomach shook with silent laughter. Tyler grinned too.

"Would you go to Wisteria if you got out?" Tyler asked, glad that this guard was so tired today.

Valiant surprised him by shaking his head no. Instinctively he should want to return home. Choosing to live in Aralot was dangerous as it gave one kingdom full control of any available magic. At least in Jack's case, he wasn't cruel with it, but other rulers would spring up. Tyler couldn't picture Valiant wanting to live in Vankerdale where he'd been abused his whole life so that left only one choice.

"Aralot then."

Valiant gave off a short hum and then thought better of it. His eye closest to the guard zoomed in on the man to make sure that he was still asleep. Valiant stood up as tall as he could get and started to press his weight into one of the stone walls as if he hadn't really given up all hope of escape. It didn't budge. Valiant eyed the door that was much too small for him and tried to poke his tail at it. The guard sprang to his feet and poked him. Valiant gave off a shuddering cry as he retreated as far back as he could get. Tyler was kicked out of the room in case Valiant did anything more to break free.

Tyler stepped from the room, but not before giving Valiant a conspiring wink. The dragon *did* have it in him to escape. All he needed to do was gain an immense amount of strength. Tyler finished reading the book on his own and wrote up what he could about it. There was not much there that Prince Evan could be interested in. Tyler had read through a copy of the more recent laws in Aralot, and most of the things in the old rules didn't even hold true still. When he gave his report to Prince Evan, the man skimmed the words with a large frown. The frown matched the temperament of Evan's red hair. His growling voice was always deep.

"Do better, Tyler Valeron," Evan snarled. He shoved the book back into Tyler's hands. "I refuse to release you from your service to the kingdom until you find a way to get through those border spells. I need that girl!"

"What girl?" Tyler asked. They tried to capture Tia, but she

Pg. 28

wasn't a girl. She was a woman.

"The blood heir to Aralot, of course. Now get going!"

Tyler backed out of Prince Evan's room confused. Aralot was ruled by King Klavian and his heir was Prince Tristan who was a man. Tyler was very sure of the fact. Prince Evan stormed past Tyler somehow managing to stomp his feet despite the thick rugs that lined the castle floors. Tyler watched the upset man feeling discouraged too. No one could take things out of Aralot that Jack didn't want them to have. There had been hundreds of people who had tried and they had all failed. He would be serving Prince Evan forever!

Tyler tapped the old book in his hands as Prince Evan pulled open the same door Tyler had just come through and went inside. Tyler looked both directions to make sure the prince was not being followed by anyone else and started to follow him. He was heading toward Valiant. Tyler never liked it when that happened.

"Wake up you MSD!" Prince Evan shouted at Valiant as he yanked open the door to the prison. Valiant wasn't really a mopey spell dragon. He had just hummed at Tyler. The animal had it in him to be happy if only he could get out.

"You are going to bring me your rider. She has to be able to hear you by now. You're going to scream until she comes. Do you understand?!"

Tyler stared at the door in horror as it closed back up. Valiant had a rider?! He could only be mentally linked to a person if that person was a keeper. Bonds didn't work in Vankerdale. There was no other way that Valiant could scream for a human unless the person didn't need the physical bond of Valiant's dragon venom to hear him. Aralot was the only kingdom with keepers. Such people were really lucky and rare.

Tia was a keeper, but she was insanely defensive of her dragons.

Tyler wasn't quite sure if Valiant was hers. The other keeper in Aralot was Tia's younger sister named Rosa. However, Rosa wasn't the blood heir to the throne. Tyler was missing something. In any case, Valiant wasn't as lonely as Tyler thought he was if he had keeper dragons in his head to keep him company.

Valiant screamed. Tyler covered his ears. Prince Evan was hurting his friend! The dragon screamed again causing Tyler to drop the book he was holding and cringe. Someone had to defend Valiant. The dragon couldn't do it himself.

Tyler pushed open the door to find Prince Evan holding the guard's weapon and using it on Valiant's face. The dragon was backed up as far as he could get against the wall. His eyes were shut, but Tyler knew that Valiant had smelled Tyler when he stepped into the room.

"I will get past that spell," Tyler told the prince. He had no idea how he was going to manage this, but he had to help Valiant. "I can't do that if you hurt the dragon. I will need him to get us in there."

Prince Evan scowled at Tyler. "You know how to trick the border?"

"I will know really soon," Tyler promised.

"You've got two weeks. If you fail me, you both get it."

Prince Evan dropped the weapon and rubbed at his shoulder. Tyler didn't need to ask him why he was so angry. Prince Evan's dragon had fanged him again. His dragon had tried to connect their thoughts, but the curse prevented fangs from working. Prince Evan was desperate to bond his dragon. The only way to do that was to break the kingdom's curse by using Jack.

Pounding feet launched into the hallway as a group of sweaty guards swept through the area. Tyler and Prince Evan looked into the hallway to watch. Most of the men ran past Prince Evan, but one returned the prince's glare.

"The prisoner broke out!"

The prince's face turned red and furious. Tyler looked at the guard and the prince curiously. They had a prisoner? They hadn't locked anyone up inside the castle ever. Did Aralot have a spy over here looking for Valiant, or was Tyler thinking about this way too hard?

"If you don't get him back, I'll crush your head!" Prince Evan screamed before he shoved past Tyler to continue nursing his stabbed shoulder. Even though Tyler lived in this castle, there were a lot of things that he didn't know. A prisoner! He turned back to Valiant.

"I'm going to help you, Valiant," Tyler told the dragon. "I'll think of something."

The Departure

Kayla

Kayla looked before her at one of her father's famous signs. "You're going the wrong way to the house. Turn around."

She had done this so many times before, but she did it again. Kayla spun around and looked at the next sign that could only be seen from this location. "What did you believe me for? Now you're really going the wrong way."

Her eyes teared up. Her father had the quirkiest sense of humor. He'd put up signs like this for his Colt buddies to discover all over the place. It was rather helpful. When a new Colt stopped by and tried to find her father, Kayla could tell where they were when the new voices started laughing hysterically. She missed him. He always made her laugh too.

Kayla went past those signs and stopped beside the one that claimed it would grant a magical wish if the person dropped a coin in the nearby bucket. She had tried it out loads of times. With her father being the spellcaster of the kingdom it was possible that he knew a spell to grant wishes. What really happened when a coin was dropped in the bucket was a magical message popped up that said, "I hope you wished to lighten your pockets."

It was another spot that made Colts laugh. She had giggled at it many times herself but she had one memory that had changed her reaction to this spot.

"It is fascinating how people don't need wishes granted to be happy," a voice had spoken right after she had dropped in a coin to see the magical message.

Kayla had spun around to find the speaker. Having encountered many Colts here, she wasn't scared. None of them had ever hurt her, and she knew that if they ever tried, her dad would get them back good. She smiled at the man who had spoken. He had brilliant blue eyes, blond hair, and wisdom that reminded her of being aged when he didn't look too old.

"What makes you happy?" Kayla asked the man.

"Right now? Talking with you."

Kayla had smiled at him as she glanced at the flashing message. That time it didn't make her laugh because she was thinking about how talking could make this man happy. She wasn't talking. She had turned back around almost expecting him to have vanished from sight, but he was still there. She had smiled again.

"Guess who I am," he had challenged.

Kayla looked him over again and shrugged trying to puzzle it out. Most Colts didn't ask her this question unless she was supposed to know who they were. She already knew most of her dad's best friends, and his Colt family.

"Are we related?" All of her relatives on her father's side were Colts. She thought that she had met them all, but she could have missed one. She had perked up when she thought she had the answer.

"Uncle Conner?"

Pg. 34

He was the one relative that was talked about that she had never met. He was a Colt. He was also missing, so if he had shown up this would be really fun news to tell her parents. The man tilted his head to the side and then laughed at her. She was guessing that was a no.

"Amusing. You're talking with Ritz."

"Prove it." She had demanded from the leader of the Colts. "Show me that necklace you wear."

Ritz had laughed at her again for the random tidbits of information she knew about him. He wore a replica of a real necklace that had caused her poisoned grandfather, Herb Felding, to fear dragons and turn against them. Her parents had been responsible for ending Herb's terror on the land after he had wiped out a good portion of the Colts, trapped all the ware dragons, and tried to kill off Kayla's mother.

Ritz had pulled out the necklace. Even scarier, he took it off his neck and passed it to her. She never would have handled the real thing. The real item had turned her grandfather Herb insane. Kayla had held the replica and regarded it. Her father, Jack, had told her that Ritz could not be trusted with anything. She was to never take anything from the leader of the Colts. They were renegades and rebels. Jack had been born a Colt, but she was to never turn into one. Kayla was to never tell Ritz any information at all.

Tia, on the other hand, always commented that she liked Ritz when the topic came up. She said there was something good and bright about him that Jack simply couldn't see growing up the way he had. Kayla saw Ritz both ways.

The necklace had been as expected. It had a silver flower with a red ruby in the center. The real necklace gave out a nightmare of a demon dragon. This particular necklace was harmless. She had passed the item back.

"You know where it came from?" Kayla had asked, bursting with being young and talkative and trying to hold back all her other mental comments that might give out information. Asking questions was a good way to learn things without giving anything away. That would make her father happy.

"Your father's friends Ian and August had it created." Ritz nodded. "I know. It's not the real necklace, but it reminds me of the person who first made the real one."

"King Gladius," Kayla had answered. He was her great-grandfather, and he had been worse than Herb. Gladius had cursed everything, tortured dragons, made a large mess out of the kingdom of Aralot that they were still trying to patch back up after he died. His curses stuck everywhere and got into everything.

Ritz had smiled at her and Kayla knew exactly what her mother meant when she said there was something good about Ritz. He was charming. Kayla felt herself relax until her father's voice was back in her head reminding her never to let her guard down around a Colt. They were always after something. Always.

"You don't sound scared of Gladius, but one day you might be," Ritz mentioned.

"Not me! My dad takes down his spells."

"He tries. I'll give Jack that, but there are some places that Jack won't ever be able to reach. You could though. Want to see the spot, Kayla?"

"Into kidnapping today? She won't go with you."

Jack's voice coming down upon them had Kayla jumping and Ritz laughing. Ritz was after her! Either that or Ritz was trying to see how gullible she was. He wanted to see how far she would venture away from the house for his own amusement. Whatever the real reason, Kayla hadn't gone, and Ritz had shooed her away so he could talk with her dad as if that was his goal the whole time.

Kayla walked to the spot where she had first met Ritz and kept going. She had seen him since then, and if they were alone, she teased him about the Uncle Conner comment. She had asked him where her uncle was several times, since Ritz was supposed to know everything. He often kept his information to himself, but he knew things. Her mother had gone to see the Colt leader trying to find Jack when he disappeared the same way that Kayla had turned to Ritz trying to find Uncle Conner. Nowhere. Conner had never turned up yet, and her father was still missing. Thinking of them brought Kayla back to the present of missing her dad. She let out a sigh briefly thinking about that castle picture she had drawn last night.

"You forgot to drop the coin for the fake happiness."

Kayla froze. Was she thinking of Ritz because she had heard him? With most people, she could pick out when they arrived around her. She never got it right with Ritz. He was more silent than the very word.

"Still haven't found my dad?" Kayla asked, hoping that Ritz had stopped by the house because he had found something.

"Ah. Is that what has you down this week? The kingdom of Aralot can feel your moods."

So he said. Anyway, Ritz's silent feet was a feature that made her father twitch too. Now that he was here, Kayla looked at Ritz, comparing him with the image she had of him from her childhood. He hadn't changed one single thing about him. His hair had not turned gray. His bones were not brittle from age. He was blond with dazzling blue eyes.

Stories always said the same thing about Ritz. He had been this same way when her father was a child and before. Since she knew that there had been a Cluster spellcaster once stuck inside of an aging spell that used to guard Aralot's crown, Kayla knew that it was possible to be ageless. She wondered what it was that Ritz guarded, since their one example of an ageless trapped man had been a guardian.

"Aralot feels my moods?" Kayla challenged, not believing Ritz. He said lots of things to mess with people's heads. As old as he was, he had to do something to entertain himself. Jack knew Ritz was stuck in a spell, but he couldn't decide what kind. Magic was picky. Without the right words, intentions, and conditions, it couldn't change. Jack had tried for a few years to solve the mystery of Ritz's age and then gave up. Kayla hadn't tried, but the mystery intrigued her just the same.

"Are you Aralot then? Your agelessness has been noticed. Do you change your name every few generations and watch over all of us?"

"I watch with you," Ritz replied.

"What do you want, Ritz?" Kayla asked, not in the mood to swap mind games with him today. She turned her attention to the air hearing her mother's dragon guard who would have already told Tia that Ritz was here and talking with her. Kayla could never get away from dragons. Her mother always had at least one of the beasts watching her. It was one of the most annoying parts of Kayla's life, given that her mother was a keeper.

"Confirm a rumor for me? The last place your father was seen was at Anvil's Ware. Am I correct?"

Kayla kicked at the ground. No one had new information.

"Yeah, but it can't be right. It's not like he could have up and vanished…" Kayla trailed off and then tilted her head when the guard dragon overhead shifted closer. There was a way Jack could have vanished from that location.

"Uh-huh." Ritz smiled. "Now you're getting it. He's no doubt moseying around portals. He probably got himself stuck out in the

Pg. 38

distance."

"Like he found a way to get into Wisteria or something?" Kayla asked. Ritz gave her a shrug. Assuming Jack was over there, it could take him a good few weeks to get back. But he had been gone for three months!

"He gets himself out of everything, Kayla," Ritz said. "That kid was born a slipknot. However, I agree that his timing is starting to feel long. I could go look for him for you. You just tell me how to slither through portals as easily as he does, and I swear that I'll get your father back home."

Kayla opened her mouth and then closed it. Ritz was trying to trick her. He had come here hoping that she would give him the secret of how to become immune to portals. She couldn't give that out! There were only a handful of people who knew the information that Ritz was after, and Kayla was guessing that out of the handful, she was the easiest target.

King Klavian had sat in a dungeon for five years sheltering the information on portals, refusing to talk. Getting him to start blabbing wouldn't be easy. Her parents had discovered the secrets using their special dragons and because they worked closely with King Klavian. Prince Tristan used portals, but he was a Colt and always denied Ritz that kind of information. Tia had an army of dragons that would back up her refusal to talk, and her father was gone. Then there was her.

"No."

"Someone needs to find your father. You can't do it. You've got so many curses on you that you can't go anywhere."

Didn't she know it? She was always stuck and spied on, but she couldn't give up the secret of immunity to the leader of the largest rebel group in the land. She wished she could. She could hear Ritz's unspoken arguments. He was the best at locating hard to find things apart from her dad. He was crafty and well versed in the world. If her father was trapped someplace, Ritz had an army of spies behind him that would mobilize and launch into any attack at his flowery words.

For Ritz to be coming to her trying to find Jack had to mean that her father was really really stuck this time. Ritz believed that her dad was out of the kingdom. That left two other kingdoms to search: Wisteria and Vankerdale. Combined they were larger than Aralot!

"I can't. I won't talk to you about portals."

"When you change your mind over what's more important to you, you come see me. I'll get our spellcaster back. Aralot needs Jack. He left too many things unfinished. What's one secret compared to your father's life?"

With that, Ritz headed away letting his words linger in the air. They taunted her. Made her want to chase after Ritz and tell him everything. It was only one small thing that he needed. Getting it though... He couldn't. Ritz would need ice dragon venom in order to become immune to portals. Sparkle would never fang him, and Bantin had his bonding fangs cut out. Those were the only two living ice dragons. Ritz would have to storm the castle to get reserved old ice dragon venom from dragons past dead. Colts were not welcome stealing things from the castle. She couldn't send Ritz into that. She couldn't give up the information, and she'd be locked up for the rest of her life if she stole the venom for him. Either that or Ritz would be hunted down while the Clusters tried to kill him.

Kayla let Ritz leave alone, but her mother didn't. Wild guard dragons sprang up from around the area, their wings beating out the message of where Ritz was walking away with his short stab of hope.

"Gah!" Kayla screamed, letting her frustration pour through the surrounding woods into the ears of anything listening. She had searched before, but perhaps her father had left some hint as to where he was going. Kayla ran back to the house, finding it empty. Her mother had left a note on the top of the table stating that she had gone to Turid's Ware. It was the ware closest to their house, but it had been ages since Kayla went there herself.

Kayla turned over the house searching for a note from her dad. She rifled her parent's room, her room, the kitchen, the entry room, her dad's magic room. Nothing! Maybe she could find something at Anvil's Ware? She'd avoid the dragon ware if she could due to the dragons, but it contained her favorite people, like Uncle Anvil.

Kayla made her way to the closest magical portal. It was a gigantic vertical stone slab with hexagonal bricks protruding from it. The slab was tall enough to fit a fifteen-foot tall dragon. Turned on, it swirled with purple and blue magical mist. When she stepped through the gateway, she would move from her home in the north into the middle of Aralot in an instant. One of the first things she ever learned was how portals worked. Most people couldn't use them because portals required magic to work and magic was not handed out. She only had it because her parents were the best dragon riders ever to exist and her father was the spellcaster for the king.

Her long walk to the portal was spent with Kayla's ears working overtime, trying to hear if Ritz was still around. When she reached Anvil's Ware, she let herself down out of the accompanying portal by using the extra-long rope that waited for her there.

Her mother had been a part of the creation of this portal. It was constructed back when she had Misty as her ice dragon instead of Sparkle. Misty was Sparkle's mother, and had been a magical ice dragon unlike her offspring. The portal was set into a cave in a mountain so high up that the most practical way to reach it was to use a dragon. It was dangerous to repel down the mountain face, but Kayla was skilled at repelling. She could get down the mountain through rain or snow. She was good at climbing back up too.

She walked into Anvil's Ware and around the dragons who called out greetings to her. Her mother had a special name in the dragon language and Kayla did too. There was no way to avoid getting her own dragon name when both her parents loved dragons so much. The dragons around her had known her for her entire life. Even with Kayla's known avoidance, there was a brown dragon rolling around on the ground to impress her instead of paying attention to his class. There was a blue dragon stalking behind her flapping her wings. There was a green dragon singing her a song. There was a red dragon hooting out love phrases that kept trying to sneak in front of her. Kayla didn't look at any of them thanks to the memorized path and her sweater's hood.

She reached the eastern field and located Uncle Clark. He was in the process of sharpening a dozen or more prongs. These were a dragon rider's best tool. A prong had three forked ends with fishhook tips for catching dragon scales. Uncle Clark always kept his black hair cut short and had a smile for Kayla. She had to say hello to either him or her Aunt Rosa when she stopped by or they would get on her case. Aunt Rosa was a miniature version of her sister, Tia, with her blond hair and charming blue eyes, but in Aunt Rosa's case, she didn't always keep her blond hair tucked into a bun. She copied her sister in being a keeper though.

"Hi, munchkin!" Uncle Clark waved. "On summer break yet?"

"I wish! Everyone else is on summer break. Mom keeps finding ways to give me more homework."

"It's good for you," Uncle Clark laughed. He put down the prong he was working on and started to say something else. Kayla watched as his mouth suddenly became blurred. His words stopped coming. All she heard was a buzz, and she hated it when this happened to her.

One moment she would be holding a conversation, and the next moment the conversation would come to a sudden dead stop because she couldn't hear it anymore. She couldn't even lipread what the other person was telling her. There was some subject that she was very forbidden from hearing. She had talked Aunt Rosa into writing it down for her once, but even then, she couldn't read it. The words blurred too.

While her random dreams and nighttime drawing couldn't be the result of a curse, this spell right here most certainly was. No one had been able to cure her from it yet. No one had been able to identify who had given it to her despite there only being a handful of people who used magic.

Magic users included Kayla, her parents, Uncle Anvil in secret, King Klavian, Prince Tristan, King Peyton of Vankerdale, and his son Prince Evan. With that list, she would think that someone would have found the cure by now. Sometimes she thought it was Vankerdale's fault. Maybe her dad was in Vankerdale because he thought the same thing?

"Which would be awesome," Uncle Clark's voice cut back in.

"I didn't hear a word you just said," Kayla pouted. "See you later."

Greeting task completed, Kayla left the field aware that some dragons thought she wasn't done saying hello. They continued to chirp at her. She paid only enough attention to know that they were not following her.

When she reached the first of the buildings to the ware, Kayla groaned. Drawings! They were everywhere today! Days like this were hard to handle even if the dragons had been reserved. Maybe the dragons weren't so bad because they were pacified looking at all these pictures of her posted all over the walls. She knew who made those pictures. Caleb Andrade. It was totally his style casting her mostly in shadows, but the strange thing about these was that there were no dragons in any of them. If there had been a dragon that would be the end of her looking.

It was just her walking, rock climbing, and drinking with the hood up. There was one exception, and Kayla stole the picture off the wall as she went past it so she could scan it better. The reason why she hadn't seen a hood on this was because it wasn't of any real event she had ever done. She was standing on top of a ship stuck to the top of a mountain as if a strong wave or spell had stranded her there. In her hand was a flag. On her face was an eye patch and a bandana was tied over her hair. Beside her was the shadow image of a man, presumably Caleb, that had a spyglass up to his eye. Her imaginary pirate was talking.

"Arr you going to be my friend yet?"

She shoved the picture into her pocket as her throat constricted. Blast this guy! She did want a friend today. She wanted someone she could complain to Ritz about. She wanted someone who would tell her that her father was fine. Caleb wanted to be her friend. Too bad she had no idea what he really looked like. She could pick him out by his walk and the sound of his voice. She could pick him out by the sound of his fists flying behind her and the sound of his breathing.

Friend. Yes, she wanted friends! Who didn't want friends? The only problem with being friends with riders is that they had a habit of talking about their dragons. It would be a short-lived friendship the instant he brought up his dragon. She was doing them both a favor by keeping to herself. It was better to leave the guy with no answer than crush any spark of friendship he had for her.

Her eyes prickled. Why was her life so unfair!? Wouldn't it be nice to have a friend her own age for once? The Colts didn't count. They weren't exactly on the got-your-back forever friends category. All she had was Anvil who never talked about Clawson around her. Caleb hadn't mentioned his dragon to her, but she knew his dragon was Warner. He was a brown dragon, and he had done his share of hooting at her. It was only a matter of time before a rider would introduce their dragon to be polite. And why wouldn't they? The dragon was their other half, their very best friend.

"This has got to stop, Caleb!" A kid named Aiden screamed at him. Kayla hadn't heard Caleb yet, but of course he was around. If there was a chance that she would look at his artwork, he was so there. He cut class, ditched assignments, and spied on her. It wasn't hard really. All the dragons knew when she showed up, so riders always knew when she showed up too.

"She's never going to look at you and your ugly face! You're wasting paper on all this drivel of childish fantasies. Grow up!"

"Sounds like you're having a bad day," Caleb replied, while Kayla sucked in her breath. She heard Warner zooming over and the slight strain of Caleb's voice. She could tell Caleb's moods through any intonation. He was angry, which meant that if Aiden pushed him a little bit more, fists were going to start flying—again. She hated causing the fights. Anvil had told her over and over that it wasn't her fault. It still felt like her fault.

"You've got to move on, dude. The Brixton's want nothing to do with you."

Caleb had this level of calm that he gave out. He could take insults about himself just fine. He usually laughed them all off or came up with some retort that left everyone else laughing. There was one type of insult that he couldn't ignore. Everyone knew what it was.

"It's people like you that drive the Brixton's into hiding. Jack's probably gone because he got tired of your pictures getting all over the place like the disease they are."

Kayla felt her stomach clench, and she couldn't help the half turn of her head. Aiden almost got her. He almost caused her to turn around and see Caleb for the first time in her entire life so she could glare. She almost asked Aiden to stop talking about her dad like that, but she didn't, because if Caleb knew she had been bothered by the comment, it was going to get bad. She turned back to the front again, pinching her eyes shut as she took a few steps away. Hopefully, Caleb could walk away from this one too. He'd make it as long as no one said her name.

"Jealous that you can't draw?" Caleb asked.

"No, because I can see this for what it is, unlike you. You're the reason Kayla hides from us all. If you stopped, she might take that hood down. You turn her into a wraith—"

Crack! The sound of Caleb's fists connecting with Aiden made Kayla run. She didn't want to hear this. She couldn't hear this. Not today. Screams and dragon shouts followed the blow along with a whistle that came from the south field probably where Caleb's section leader was as he heard from his dragon that his student was fighting again.

"You know nothing!" Caleb screamed as the scuffle continued on behind her. "That hood is not for me! It's so she doesn't see her mother's dragons!"

Kayla faltered in her steps. He knew. Caleb knew what the hood was for. She wondered if he noticed her stagger wanting to turn around and ask him how he knew. She didn't turn because turning around right now would make her first image of Caleb Andrade one of him fighting.

This was the second person today that had made her want to turn to them to heal part of her aching heart. Ritz wanted to find her dad, and Caleb had stopped drawing dragons just for her. Kayla picked up her speed, racing away before she could hear the punishment Caleb got for his actions. It was going to be harsh. He might change his mind about wanting to be her friend after this. Aiden could have finally gotten to him, made him decide that she wasn't worth all those pictures, right when she finally started to like them.

Kayla stomped her feet down to Uncle Anvil's office and

pounded on the door. She heard a harsh dragon bark behind her. Anvil's green dragon, Clawson, was sitting on top of the study. She kept her gaze down as she realized this. Even knowing how structurally sound each building was, Kayla still didn't like having a dragon on top. Ware buildings were built from stone. They sat on stone foundations that stretched really far under the ground making them strong enough to hold a sitting dragon on top. However, Kayla could still picture the building collapsing on top of her head with the twelve-ton dragon coming down next.

Clawson swished his tail over the side of the study and pointed to the door with the tip to tell her that Anvil was in the study and not in his office. Kayla waited until the tail was back out of the way before she headed over. The door opened before she reached it as Uncle Anvil opened it up. His blond hair was looking sharp today. His ruby earring was shining, and his height made him duck just a tad as he peeked out the door.

"Life is so unfair!" Kayla shouted.

"At times," Anvil agreed.

He stepped from his study and grabbed her arm to pull her inside knowing that she wouldn't enter the room if Clawson was on top otherwise. Things like this made her feel like a pansy. Everyone else around her was brave enough to have a dragon sitting on their head. She simply couldn't! Kayla slid onto one of the stools in the room with her shoulders hunched knowing what was out there.

Anvil's study room was very clean and tidy with books neatly organized on shining redwood shelves. Most people never set foot inside, since Anvil kept his secret books here which included his books on magic that he wasn't supposed to have.

"Why can't my mom stop staring at me all the time? Sometimes it makes me hate her."

If only Kayla could get a reprieve from all the dragons in her life guarding her, her mood could improve some. She could get a little space, a little respect. It wasn't like she was going to get herself lost like her father had done. She knew where she was.

Kayla had seen her mother's nightmares too many times, and the reason for the dragon guard came down to the moment when Herb Felding tried to kill his daughter by having his wife, Alice Felding, light Tia's chainmail shirt on fire. It was Tia's parents turning on her, trying to kill her off, that made Tia so clingy with her own child. She didn't want Kayla going anywhere without protection in case anyone turned on her. The sentiment was nice, but it was really the most aggravating thing in the world.

Kayla couldn't go anywhere without dragons following her. There was never an escape from the spying. There was never the trust that she could handle her own life just fine. If there was one thing Kayla could go back and change in time, that moment would be it. Her mother never would have been burned disfiguring her skin. Tia wouldn't turn cynical that people she loved could betray her.

"Hmm. I've hated your dad plenty of times, but not your mother."

Anvil shrugged as he shut the door behind them and locked it. Kayla couldn't picture it. Anvil and Jack were always on good terms with each other. They played cards together once a month and had dinner every week. Anvil became her father whenever her real father was away, like right now. That's why she called him her uncle even though they were not related.

"Jack and I came to blows a few times." Anvil laughed at Kayla's confused expression. He reached over and plunked down her hood so he could see her better. "I can't decide which one of us felt more satisfied that we got to punch each other. It got us in a lot of trouble. Reminds me of Caleb in a way." Anvil laughed again. "These days we tiptoe around the area we clash on."

"Which is...?"

"I loved your mother. I still do actually, but don't tell anyone, Kayla. She could only love Jack."

"You and my mom?!" Kayla exploded, while Anvil laughed at her again. She had a nightmare that revealed this very thing to her only she had never understood it until right now. Anvil and Jack competed with each other for Tia's attention. Kayla was a newborn at the time of the dream, and her father had accused Kayla of really being Anvil's child. She wasn't. There was too much of her father in her appearance to be anything but Jack's. However, this explained why Uncle Anvil dropped all affectionate ties with Kayla when Jack was around. He didn't want Jack thinking that he was overstepping their friendship.

"Oh, don't look like that. Tia wouldn't so much as dance with me. There was nothing toward me on her part except for friendship. As I said, we were younger back then, and it was very easy to be impressed with your mother."

"I'm not impressed," Kayla pouted. "I'm tired of the dragon guard. I'm tired of people's words blurring in front of my face. Why can't I hear that one forbidden topic? Uncle Clark said something about it today and it only adds to my bad mood."

"Let's try again then. Hold your hand up if anything I say to you gets blurred, alright?" Anvil said.

Kayla shifted forward in her seat. She knew she could count on him. He would find a way around the curse to let her know what she was missing. Then he would tell her that her father was findable and that the dragon guard could vanish. Maybe she was hoping for too much, but Caleb had made dragons vanish in his pictures of her, so perhaps she was getting lucky today. It would be nice to have inherited her father's sense of luck.

"I didn't curse you with this. I don't believe your parents cursed you. I've talked to them both about the matter extensively. What you can't hear is something they both want you to know. We've all tried to take the curse off you, Kayla. There's something else in the way preventing you from hearing the truth. It's not a matter of being old enough to understand. It's a truth you can't hear."

"I've been lied to?" Kayla asked, excited that she was getting some sort of answer about her most annoying curse.

"No. You can't hear lies or truths about it. It's…" Anvil's words became a mumble of sound and his mouth a blurred line. Kayla pouted again and held her hand up. It wasn't fair! What kind of truth was she prevented from learning?

"Sorry. I didn't think that would count as telling you," Anvil apologized. "It's very tricky. I wish you could know it too. I've tried to figure out who else would have put the curse on you. I've run through everyone. It can't be the…"

Kayla sighed. She didn't bother to raise her hand. Her look alone told Anvil that she couldn't understand him.

"You can't hear me name the people I suspect?" Anvil asked. Kayla shook her head but would it matter? She knew all the magic users too.

"It might not even be someone who lives in this kingdom who cursed you. If it was, your father would have fixed it by now. He's an amazing spellcaster but don't tell him I said that."

"It's not fair," Kayla wailed.

"No. It's really not fair. It's sabotage of the worst kind. We could go to war over it."

"War?" Kayla shivered on her stool. She hated fighting. In that regard she was like her mother, except her mother could put aside her dislike of the activity and partake in it when she felt justified to do so. Kayla couldn't hurt anything.

"You heard that?" Anvil asked, scooting forward on his stool too. His expression was eager as he tried to find more ways to tell Kayla what she couldn't hear or read.

"Yes, you knowing about this could cause a war. That's why you're cursed not to know it. I'm surprised you heard me say that. You've been told that before. Perhaps you could hear it this time because of some lingering magical residue in the room." Anvil looked behind him at a book that was left open on his desk. He started talking rapidly after that and Kayla groaned. Everything else he said she couldn't hear. She held up her hand and waved it around to get him to stop talking. It was strange that her forbidden topic could cause a war. People talked about this all the time so casually. There was nothing casual about war. Anvil tried talking to her for a few more minutes regardless of her arms waving.

"Well at least you got one clue about it," Anvil relented. "Don't blame your parents. They're doing the best they can for you."

Kayla sighed and brought up the real reason for why she had come here.

"I know everyone has been over this hundreds of times, but I saw Ritz today, and he was asking after my dad. It's getting serious if he's sniffing around. Can't you tell me what my dad did when he was here on the day he got lost? There has to be some sort of clue. What happened?"

Uncle Anvil slouched on his stool, but he did tell her something new.

"Clawson got this out of your dad's dragon, Pyro. Jack had a list of things to do that day including checking on the royal ports to make sure that the silk was being bought at a fair price and Wisteria wasn't trying to cheat us again. He was going to swing by the castle to visit Merlock, you know the dwarf dragon that guards the secret underground passages, and get a book the animal was guarding. He wanted to check on a few wild dragon territory squabbles and repair the roofing on the guest housing on your property. For that he would need magic, so Jack was going to visit Mr. Grumpy to get a magical ice dragon orb. However, you didn't leave a note describing where you had gone that morning and rather than ask Tia for the information, Jack came here to ask me if you were around."

Kayla felt her throat clench. This was why no one had told her this before. The adults in her life didn't want her to think that her father going missing was her fault. He couldn't still be looking for her. Pyro could talk directly to Sparkle and all the other dragons in her mother's keeper bond. All of them had seen her since that day. They knew she wasn't missing.

"Jack wasn't here long. A rider got his leg sliced up rather badly. I was in the area and started to stitch it up myself. Then Jack asked me, 'Do you think his scar will be as gruesome as the one Kayla got when she was a month old?' I was there the day you were born to mysterious circumstances, Kayla, and you already had the scar on your leg when you were born."

Kayla nearly forgot that Clawson was sitting over her head as Anvil told her this and she started to sit up taller until she remembered. She sunk even lower. She could get information out of Uncle Anvil that she wasn't supposed to hear if she could get him alone. He always treated her like an adult, capable of understanding anything. Her parents did too, except for certain topics. While Anvil might tell her what her father had said, she knew he wouldn't talk about the mysterious circumstances of her birth, so she didn't bother asking him. As for the scar on her left leg, it really was quite gruesome, all slashes and torn up skin that had never healed into fine scars. The flesh on her lower left leg was a mess so she hardly ever wore shorts.

"My dad thought my scar came when I was a month old?" Kayla asked.

Anvil nodded. "I asked the same thing. I told Jack that you had the scar at birth. I try not to bring that day up with your father. He was very angry that I was the one with Tia instead of him when you were born. I couldn't decide if you or Tia were bleeding more when I arrived. It was terrifying. I thought your leg was broken. So, Jack did what he does when we hit these uncomfortable topics. He gave me a short smile, said thanks, and walked off. No one has seen him since. Don't blame yourself, Kayla. It's not your fault."

Kayla opened her mouth in surprise because there was only one person who would have told Jack about her leg. That person was Tia who had not let anyone touch Kayla until she was three months old. Tia never let Kayla move more than a few inches away from her in that time. Tia had lied to her husband, and Jack hadn't been home for the last three months once he figured that out. Was this a marital fit?

"But my parents forgive each other all the time!" Kayla burst. "Tell Clawson to tell Pyro to bring him home!"

Uncle Anvil gave her a sad smile and Kayla sighed dramatically. This couldn't be the result of a marital fit. Her father was a Colt. He had trained himself to spot out information and lies. For Tia to have withheld the date of Kayla's leg accident meant that it was very important. Her father had figured out something more about the day she was born and it had caused him to go missing. No wonder her mother hadn't said anything before if that was the result. Tia probably thought she was saving Jack from whatever fate had come upon him by lying to him. If only someone would tell her what happened when she was born!

"You told everyone else this?" Kayla asked.

"No! I am in your mother's keeper bond. I can't betray her by telling everyone that she lied. You're the only one I've told. Don't go telling anyone else and getting me in trouble. I'm trusting you here, Kayla."

Kayla nodded. This was hard on Anvil to tell her what he had, knowing that it meant something more. His dragon Clawson was incapable of betraying Tia at all. Riders could get around the magic in dragon blood to lie, but a dragon couldn't. Therefore, Pyro and Sparkle and all the other dragons that might know what the real issue was couldn't say anything about the lie. That was why Pyro could only pass along that Jack was fine.

"What happened when I was born that—"

"I don't have all the details either. Now go on." Anvil ordered, looking pained to talk about it. "We're done here."

Kayla stood up and moved to the door, looking over her shoulder long enough to pull the hood back up before she left the study. There was no sense in pestering Anvil so that he wouldn't tell her secrets in the future. She couldn't get anything out of her mother about her birth, especially not since the woman was lying to her own husband about it. Where could Kayla go to learn what happened?

Kayla pictured the scar on her leg in her head. There were the streaks and the one deep indentation from the stab. If Kayla had a guess, she would think that the stab came first and then the clawing. So what had gotten her? It had been so long ago that signs of the scuffle would be long gone.

Kayla strained her ears trying to hear if Caleb had stopped

fighting. She didn't hear any sort of nearby brawl, but she could still see a few of the pictures posted on the walls that hadn't been torn down. Caleb wanted her as a friend. She hid the sting of her eyes wishing for the same thing and then left the ware.

Friendly Offer

Tyler

Tyler thanked the merchant politely even though the woman was getting way more money from him than he felt he should have paid her. She rambled off the answers to his questions so easily he was sure it was common knowledge that had passed him over. Most likely it had passed him on purpose because Prince Evan didn't want Tyler making certain connections.

The rulers of Aralot were exactly who he thought they were. There was King Klavian Cluster with his wife Aria who was a Colt instead of a noble. Their son was Prince Tristan. He had been designated the heir to the throne by his father. But when Tia, the kingdom's keeper, had married Jack, the kingdom's spellcaster, the abbot had given them the rights to the kingdom because it rightfully belonged to Tia through her blood. They had signed a document on their wedding night that left Klavian in place as their steward. Because of that, everyone still called Klavian the king, even if the rightful king was Jack.

Jack and Tia had produced a single daughter shortly after getting married. There was some dark evil deed that happened on the night of the girl's birth that prevented Tia from being able to produce more children. She had tried a few times and miscarried them all. Their living daughter's name was Kayla. She was sixteen, four years younger than

Tyler, the blood heir to the throne that Prince Evan wanted, and cursed. Kayla Brixton had no idea that her parents were the king and queen of the land, or that she could rule Aralot one day. The girl thought the same as Tyler had, that Prince Tristan was going to get that role.

When Tyler heard this revelation, he had felt even worse for Valiant. Valiant's keeper rider had never saved him because she had been a baby. Her parents should have come to save her dragon long ago. Surely some simple spell would have done the trick to take the animal back, even if that would have incited a war with Vankerdale. Vankerdale's dragons were no match for Aralot's trained ware dragons who were all bonded. But instead of the fight, they had all been left in a mysterious silence delaying the inevitable.

Tyler was even more certain that Vankerdale's dragons had been recursed because of what had happened in Aralot. Somehow King Peyton and Prince Evan had stolen away the dragon to the rightful heir's baby. How could Valiant have bonded a baby? Dragons usually appreciated a person that could walk and were capable enough to hold a mental conversation. This was dark indeed.

Tyler slipped into Valiant's room. The guard gave him a nod as Tyler passed him a bribe to keep quiet. There were so many things Tyler wished to communicate with the dragon. He hoped the amount of money was large enough to convince the guard that he didn't need to tell Prince Evan what Tyler needed to ask, because he was siding with Aralot. Vankerdale had wronged that kingdom. Vankerdale should not still be standing.

"Her name is Kayla, isn't it?" Tyler asked to Valiant's closed eyes. The dragon had not opened them even to eat since Prince Evan had threatened to torture him to make his rider show up. Tyler had tried several times to get the creature in a better mood and failed.

"I know you don't want to betray her, Valiant, but if we're both to live through this you have to answer my questions. We can't help her if you don't help me understand what happened."

Valiant growled his reply. The guard readied his weapon and Tyler sighed.

"I want to help you. If you don't work with me then Prince Evan will find some other way to get into Aralot and kidnap her. At least this way you could be around to defend her."

Valiant growled again and flashed his tail over his head angrily.

"I just need you to answer my questions. Are the two of you bonded?"

There was another growl during which Tyler took a few steps back. Valiant stopped his growl to open his eyes. He looked right into Tyler's face and sniffed in a deep hungry sound. Tyler reached out and pet Valiant on the nose. King Peyton's dragon, SilverWings, would inhale like that when he was trying to suck in magic.

"Vankerdale doesn't have any magic. What kind of a spell are you trying to cast on me?"

Valiant blinked his eyes and tilted his head to the side confused. Tyler laughed at him. "What? You didn't know? That feeling to draw something in is you trying to suck in magic. Haven't you ever wondered why you don't shoot fire or water or ice? You shoot spells. You're a spellbinding dragon. You won't be able to find any magic until you locate an ice dragon that has some, and the only ice dragons that we know of are in Aralot. Of course, Sparkle, the ice dragon there, wasn't bred with a spellbinding dragon so she doesn't produce magic either, only ice. If you mated Sparkle, your hatchling would produce magic and you could suck that up. It sounds really twisted doesn't it?" Tyler rubbed the dragon's nose again. "You need the magic from your future offspring. I've been figuring out that everything is a lot more twisted than I had thought before."

Valiant took a few deeper sucking breaths in testing out his ability to inhale magic and grinned. He hummed and blew warm air over Tyler. Tyler smiled back at him, amazed that after all this time, Valiant hadn't figured out what kind of dragon he was. The poor thing. He probably thought his lack of fire was a curse.

"So, my spellbinding dragon, are you bonded?" Tyler asked again. He nodded when Valiant chirped out a yes. "Is she a keeper?" Again there was another yes. "Does she have a lot of other dragons?"

Valiant pulled his head away from Tyler's touch and growled while he dug his claws into the stone floor beneath him.

"It's alright," Tyler assured the trapped animal. "You don't have to tell me that, but you do have to help me figure out how we can get you into Aralot. Dragons can't get in because there are tons of magical spells keeping everyone out. The only one who's ever managed to break through is SilverWings when he sucks up the spells for a time."

Tyler listened to his own words echo around the confining room. Then he laughed. He knew how to break past the border spells! He just needed to convince Prince Evan to release Valiant. The dragon could suck up the magical spells long enough to let them slip through. SilverWings had enough room in his stomach to let small groups slip through the magical defenses, but not a full army. That was how Vankderale sent in spies and kidnapping attempts toward Tia. However, the dragon couldn't take Tia back out, but perhaps Valiant could get around that particular spell because he wouldn't be stealing. He'd be going over the border with his own rider. He'd be taking what was already his.

"We can get in there, Valiant, and the first thing you should do with magic is use it fix your wings so you can fly."

Valiant stretched out his wings and hooted before he hummed at Tyler and bowed to him.

"We'll have to be clever. You know what Prince Evan wants."

He didn't dare say more than that. Hopefully Valiant would realize that Tyler was on his side and he would help him break away from Prince Evan. After that, Tyler wasn't sure what he was going to do. He wanted Valiant free, but he got the sinking feeling that releasing the dragon was going to start the long-delayed war.

Sacked

Kayla

Kayla could hear the creaking of the porch swing that resided in front of her house. She felt warm and happy snuggled up in her mother's arms. She opened her eyes only to realize that she was a tiny baby, and the only thing she could make out were blurry shapes. Her eyesight was horrible, but her hearing was still fine.

This was the one single dream where the images came from her instead of coming from outward-looking dragon eyes. Kayla knew this dream instantly and wasn't surprised that her subconscious was reviewing it when she had been thinking about it the day before. This was the dream where Jack revealed what he really thought about Uncle Anvil's interest in his wife. It revealed what he really thought of Uncle Anvil being her second dad too. Kayla wondered if her dad had changed his mind after the sixteen years since this incident.

"I want to hold her," Jack's voice demanded.

Kayla had felt confused. This wasn't the first time people had asked to hold her, but she knew that this was her father's voice. He had asked to hold her before and her mother always refused. There wasn't anywhere better to be safe and warm except perhaps with her father.

"No, Jack." Tia's voice had lashed back just as harsh if not harsher.

"You said she's mine!" Jack had shouted. "Why can't I hold my baby, Tia? You don't let anyone hold her. I know it almost killed you, but the only reason I can think of for why you keep her away from me is because she's not mine. She had better not be Anvil's."

"This has nothing to do with Anvil!"

The cry was so loud that Kayla had tried to roll over. She was sleepy. She had been happy before. Now she wasn't sure what was happening.

"You can't blame him for this. He had nothing to do with this. If he did, I would have killed him! I don't care if he is a ware leader or not. I would have—"

"Woah! Okay, sorry," Jack had interrupted. "I'm sorry. I do believe you. Perhaps if you could just explain what happened…"

"No!"

Kayla felt herself get a little squished. She had tried to roll back the other direction as her face was pressed up against her mother. She couldn't roll since she was swaddled. A drop of water landed on her face, and she pinched her eyes tighter trying to stay asleep. A few more drops landed on her face from her mother's tears.

"I'm sorry," Jack had said again. "Don't hurt Anvil. I just… I'm really confused. I don't want to end up like my father and take a back seat in this. I want to help you with the baby."

"You are helping. You've already named her." Tia didn't sound excited. She sounded degrading. Kayla heard Jack stand up from the porch swing and walk a few steps away.

"I just… Okay, yes. I named her. Did Pyro tell you? I love the both of you. If you don't like the name, we don't have to use it."

Pg. 64

"The name is fine. I love it."

"Who did this to us?" Jack had questioned. "I understand if you didn't want to say anything while at Anvil's Ware, but I really should know."

"You'll be so mad. You can't retaliate. I'm scared, Jack. You'll do something drastic and ruin the entire kingdom. It's not just us that will be affected. It's everyone."

"Who hurt us?" Jack had used his steely voice. The one that suggested he meant business and he was going to get an answer.

"He betrayed *me*. I already cursed him again for this. I can't see that there's much more you could really do without causing a war. He didn't take her."

"*He* nearly killed you and it was Anvil who came to rescue you." Jack had retorted skipping over the name of the evil doer that they had both guessed or shared mentally.

Jack's words came out with a lot of distaste. Since it had been a while since Kayla had watched this dream from her infanthood, she thought over the killing part. Who would betray her mother enough to try to kill her? Who had Tia cursed? What war was it that everyone was talking about?

"Anvil just happened to be the closest person around. Please don't be mad at him. He didn't do it. He was just as mad as you. I fear what he will do as well. I've tried to talk him out of doing anything harrowing. I think he's already gone to see Klav about it."

"I want to hold my baby." Jack had sounded very pained to be asking for the privilege again.

"Later, Jack. I promise you can hold Kayla later. Where are you going?"

"To bury fifteen hundred knives!"

Kayla could hear Jack stomping away and then the tears were falling back on her baby face until her mother noticed and brushed them off. She felt safe physically but also sad.

The first time she had seen this dream, Kayla had wondered if she was sad all the time because she had been sad as a baby. She was born of tears and blood. She was born of betrayal. However, since she got older, she learned that her parents' actions were not her actions, and she could change the fate of her own life regardless of the circumstances that she had been born into.

That was the life of a Colt in a nutshell. They made themselves better than the hovels they lived inside. They rose above their circumstances, becoming smarter, braver, and stronger. They were a force of progress just as long as they didn't let their egos get in the way. Kayla was banned by her mother from ever fully joining the Colts and getting a wild stallion tattoo for earning her rank like her father had, but it didn't matter too much. She had a lot of uncles and cousins that saw that she got in all their training anyway.

Kayla yawned, prying her eyes open as she slowly looked at her desk. Nothing. Not a single picture. She gave a sigh of relief and did as her mother had suggested the day before and changed her clothes. Yesterday when she had left Anvil's Ware, she had gone to check on the state of the visitor buildings on their property. Anvil had said that Pyro claimed the roofs needed fixing. Kayla didn't want to waste the limited magic she had in her keychain on the task, so she had climbed up and replaced the broken roof tiles by hand all by herself. Her mother's dragon guard of the day took the lazy approach of sunbathing on the ground nearby.

She now felt like her mother who was composing a song for her husband. Kayla had fixed roof tiles hoping her father would come home to see how she had helped him. There were six wooden buildings available for visitors. They had first been constructed to house Shilo and his family in the early years of Sparkle's training since ice dragons had special needs.

After Sparkle was trained, most of Shilo's family had moved back to the desert and established the Desert Ware. Shilo had joined back up with his old ware after the ware leader changed to Vincent. Charles was in charge of the ware closest to the king's castle. Niles led the ware that used to be Larson's. Rogan, Anvil, and Turid still ran their wares with pride.

Her parents didn't keep track of everyone who stopped by, so the empty buildings were now used by Colts and travelers alike. Inside one of the buildings had been a few supplies indicating that they currently had a visitor or that the items were left for the next one.

The Colt mentality was such that they would steal, borrow, and trade with each other all the time. Items were left a lot for the general community when they were outgrown or not needed anymore. There was always someone else that would end up using it for something. If you wanted to keep something safe, you had to hide it.

Most Colts despised dragons, although her immediate cousins and four uncles were much better around the animals now that Jack had bonded one. They didn't engage with the animals personally, but that didn't stop them from teasing her about never looking at them. Colts could be ruthless with their snide comments. Kayla had run away from them in tears plenty of times. Uncle Kyle did his best to not drag her spirits down, but Uncle Steve, Bret, and Fenix were very negative in their opinions of her.

Kayla was prepared for their remarks though. Her father had taught her to be prepared. She could put a mental box around her feelings and tried to not let her Colt relatives know how much they affected her. She thanked them for trying to teach her, but some Colt teachings were easier learned from her much kinder father. Kayla knew that these men had been through some very hard things. They had dragons burn their homes and friends down. They were enslaved in The Pits as stone cutters while they slept out on the ground chained down. She knew their lives had been hard, but that didn't mean that they had to make *her* life hard.

Kayla finished getting dressed before she checked her drawers just in case there were pictures hiding inside of them. All clear! She had her usual belongs, but her rock collection had been sorted. She had either done it in her sleep, or her mother had gotten into her things trying to decide if she had really changed her clothes recently. Kayla grinned about that and then skipped down the stairs.

Tia's golden hair was down today. That was a rare occurrence and usually only happened when the woman didn't plan on going anywhere. She turned when she heard her daughter and gave Kayla a large smile. Kayla gave her mom a hug.

"It was one of your nights where you sleep well so I hope that means you will turn in your homework today."

"Oh, sure," Kayla replied inhaling the scent of a wonderful breakfast. Maybe because she had skipped the grits yesterday Tia had made scones and opened a new jar of jam. Kayla helped herself.

"You don't sound very convincing." Tia laughed as she sat down beside her. "What do you dream about? There was one time where Vermelo asked me if I was having strange dreams. It means something, and I was wondering if it could possibly be related to where your father went."

Kayla swallowed forcing a hard lump to go down uncomfortably. Vermelo was the Captain of the Guard who worked to protect King Klavian and his royal family. The man was always nice to Kayla. He was very busy, but he would play board games with her when she came to visit. He was likewise joyful when Jack and Tia showed up at the castle and would make funny comments about them to Kayla to make her giggle. One time, Vermelo told her that Tia had a large debate with her dragon over if Jack looked cuter shaved or not. Kayla thought her father was handsome all the time with his brown hair spiky and reddish-brown stubble on his chin. It was adorable that her parents still cared about each other enough to worry about looking cute.

Tia kept looking at her, and Kayla squirmed. She never talked about her dreams because she didn't want to explain the unreal sightsharing. What it meant was that she looked at dragons when everyone else thought that she didn't. It meant that she was forced to face her fears every night because she couldn't face them during the day. It meant that she had seen terrifying events from her parents' lives. Yes. She would mention that instead of the dragon thing.

"I sometimes dream about your and dad's nightmares," Kayla replied. "I've seen the moment when your chainmail burned you and when Hilton turned his ware against you. I've seen when you broke the orb that your father was using to control dragons. I see Dad's nightmares too. I've felt his terror when dragons burned his best friends to death. I've seen him fighting my grandfather Herb and how he thought he was going to fail. I saw him fighting off Herb's spellcaster and how exhausted he was. Sometimes Dad has nightmares about losing you to various things. Random Colts in the woods, drowning at sea, the ultra-dragon king."

Kayla shivered. She was trying so hard not to use that scaly word! She could remember meeting that dragon king herself and the words gushed out of her.

"Dad calls that black dragon Pansy in his sleep. I've called him Reaper. I don't think you have nightmares about the stalking wicked thing with gleaming green eyes and crescent-shaped talons, so I don't

Pg. 69

know what you call him."

"Kayla, I've visited that dragon before. He's not going to hurt you."

"Sure, Mom." Kayla shrugged.

The dragon was terrible. He routinely broke through ware defenses and burnt things. He destroyed towns. He harmed people. He had come after her once.

She was nine years old and she had been sent outside to grab some firewood. Her mother was busy dashing around the kitchen to make cookies since her father was returning from one of his expeditions. Kayla could hear her mother's dragons chatting with each other in the distance excited as she had reached the woodpile. Kayla had frozen.

There was something wrong with the woodpile. She had run through the checklist of things she needed to think about when she felt something was wrong. First, she needed to be aware of everything around her. She could not see any humans. She could not hear the cry of a wolf or other hungry nighttime creature. There was nothing on the woodpile.

Second, she needed to turn to her own feelings. Was she making up her own fear because it was dark, or was there a general feeling of magic and evil around her? Evil magic being around her was silly to consider because her father was the kingdom's spellcaster. He had put up so many spells around the house that Kayla couldn't even scrape her knee when she was around it. The first time she had cut a knee was when she was away at school. It surprised her how much it stung.

Third, she needed to consider instinct. Her father told her he had excellent instincts that had kept him alive even when his own feelings contradicted them. Kayla hadn't understood him until this night. What was the difference between instinct and a feeling when both of them were felt?

She had decided that there was nothing wrong with the woodpile and took a few steps closer only to be wrong. Her instinct was right. A pair of large green glowing eyes had opened right behind the wood.

Kayla's scream brought not only her mother but her mother's horde of wild dragons. The black dragon before her continued to stare. It gave her a harsh barking command before it growled at her for not understanding. Oh, she understood. Reaper had told her to come with him and her answer was no. The dragon didn't move until Sparkle started shooting ice at him. Then he had roared a cry that was dark and dangerous and started to attack Sparkle. Kayla was put back in the house, and her mother had risen to the sky to chase the black dragon away.

It was the first time Kayla had ever felt abandoned. Both of her parents were gone. The only things with her were large dominant dragons that wouldn't listen to her if she ordered them about. They were her mother's, not hers. Trusting a dragon was difficult when all the ones around belonged to someone else. She had heard way too many stories about the tricks dragons played on people.

That night her parents had argued over the existence of an ultra-dragon king, because the dragon's attack was beastly and not the usual way a fire-breathing dragon would fight although Reaper did shoot fire. They had left to search through Herb Felding's old farmstead looking for evidence that Kayla's grandfather had tried to breed such an animal. Kayla had been left in the house again surrounded by dragon guards. Whenever she looked out the window to tell if her parents were back, the only thing she could see was a mass of scales and glowing eyes. It had been terrifying.

"Kayla, you shouldn't have my nightmares. Those are my concerns and not yours," Tia said putting an arm around Kayla's shoulders for finally talking about what scared her at night.

"Don't feel bad, Mom. It's not just you. I've seen Herb and Gladius and Troy and Shane too."

"Who?" Tia asked, glancing out the window where Kayla guessed Sparkle was standing digesting all of this new information. Her mother knew Herb and Gladius, but Kayla forgot that she didn't know as much history as Kayla absorbed in her sleep.

"They were past keepers, Mom. You know what? It's not important. The dreams are just history lessons."

"This *is* important!" Tia cried. "You see scary things about past keepers, so you think that a keeper's life is all about these bad things."

"No, I don't," Kayla tried to promote, but her mother wasn't listening. Kayla continued eating her breakfast wishing she had kept her mouth shut just a little bit more.

"This is why you don't like dragons, isn't it? Every night they scare you. Kayla, dragons are so much more than these events. Scary things can happen to everyone, but if you only dwell on the fear, you forget how to live in the joy. There are so many wonderful things in the world to experience. Dragons really want to love us, and when they act up otherwise, it's because other humans or strenuous circumstances have come upon them giving them little choice. Please rethink this."

"I do. Every day," Kayla assured. Her mother didn't look pleased with the answer. Kayla needed a change in subject quick. Her mouth was moving before she had even realized that she was going to try to talk about Anvil's secret and her mother's lie.

"How did I get the scar on my leg?"

"When you were a month old, I dropped —"

Kayla had heard this excuse before. Her mother claimed to be practicing a training technique with her baby at her feet. She had dropped the knives on accident resulting in the scar.

"You favor prongs," Kayla interrupted. "Dad favors knives."

"I was rather sleep deprived. One day you will have a child and you'll understand what I mean."

Kayla could only laugh. Her mother opened her mouth to make a witty retort before remembering that Kayla lived off being sleep deprived. She grinned back and rubbed the back of her neck.

"How did I get the scar?" Kayla tried again.

"Why do you want to know? Are you hearing voices?"

"No," Kayla replied and grabbed a few scones to stuff into her backpack. Riders always wore a backpack with their equipment too. Kayla's equipment contained tools for rock climbing and daytime excursions to visit her cousins or Anvil's kids. It also had her homework.

Her mother was trying to cut her off from this topic and was doing a fabulous job. When Tia asked if Kayla heard voices, she was asking Kayla if she had suddenly turned into a keeper and a dragon was talking directly into her thoughts. Kayla hated this question. Her mother asked it all the time, and Kayla's answer always made her feel like she was disappointing everyone even if to keep her head quiet was satisfying herself.

"Where are you going?" Tia asked grabbing at her blond hair and pulling it into a bun. Kayla raised her eyebrows at her mother and didn't answer. It looked like her mother had decided to go out too, and Kayla didn't need to answer her mother. Tia was going to spy regardless and know exactly where Kayla was headed.

"I'm still your mother and would like to know."

"Troni," Kayla answered. That was the town beside the castle.

Most people never used the town's real name but referred to it by location. "To search for clues about Dad."

"I've searched a hundred times."

Kayla shrugged. "Great. So now I'll search a hundred times. While I do my homework," Kayla added. She moved toward the door with her mother close behind her.

"Thanks for fixing the roofing yesterday. You are a real treasure to have around. How did I ever get lucky enough to have a daughter like you?"

"You married Dad?" Kayla asked. "Where are you headed today?"

"None of your business."

Kayla laughed at her mom. None of her business meant one of three places. Her mother was either going to the castle, to Anvil's Ware, or to the secret cave near the castle to read through Great-Grandfather Gladius's journal entries. Kayla wasn't supposed to know the journal was there, but she had seen dreams about it because Gladius talked about murdering dragons. Of the three, Kayla was guessing that her mom was heading toward the journal. Her mother would want to search for vague references that might tell her why Kayla got nightmares from keepers.

"Dad's not a keeper so my dreams can't only be keeper related," Kayla added to be helpful.

Tia gave Kayla a helpful push out the door. Kayla grabbed for her hood, pulled it over her face, and ran for the nearest portal. Sure enough, she could hear Sparkle flying her mother the same direction and reaching the portal long before Kayla ever would. But she didn't mind. She was building up her leg powers. Uncle Conner was said to have been the fastest runner of his time. One day when Kayla met him, she would challenge him to a race and beat him.

Until that day, she was going to take herself places and not cheat by riding on a dragon. Not that she could get herself to even climb on the dragon to start with, but she liked to give herself other excuses for why she avoided the creatures instead of dwelling on her anxiety disorder. Was it really an anxiety disorder like the fear of spiders or public speaking or failing a test? Kayla thought on the question as she reached the portal.

Each portal was a tall stone slab with hexagonal bricks sticking out from it. The bottom left hexagon was the one that activated the portal and turned it on. When magic was placed there, the portal swirled blue and purple opening up a magical doorway. The swirling mist could be sped up or slowed down through dragon spit. Any dragon would do. The portal destination could be changed by tapping the activating hexagon the correct number of times. She tapped it once to reach Troni instead of the usual nine times to reach Anvil's Ware. Kayla stepped through and came out through a dark cave in the woods.

The best place to look for clues about her dad would be beneath the castle where Merlock, the brown dwarf dragon, lived. He was an aged animal that had been trapped in his tar-covered tunnels to guard treasure and magic for King Gladius. Jack had released Merlock from that spell, but since the animal preferred the dark, he stayed where he was. He would sometimes poke his head up but it was rare to see him. The short waist-high dragon couldn't hunt since Gladius had sliced the tendons on his wings, rendering him flightless, so Merlock relied on the people in the castle and in the monastery to feed him. Jack spent a lot of time with Merlock who had once been forgotten and abandoned but was now loved by Aralot's spellcaster. Kayla had never met the dragon, but she had seen him in dreams before where Jack took down nasty curses that Gladius had left beneath the castle he built. For a dragon, Merlock was cute.

She was going to leave the tar tunnels to her parents. Her

preferred choice today was Joss who was her father's best friend. If her dad was going to knowingly go someplace that he didn't want to tell his wife about, he would probably tell Joss. Ritz had no doubt already tried the man, but Kayla wondered if Joss would tell her anything useful since she was asking after her father.

She stepped on the tar paved roads of the castle town. To her left were the grey stone walls of Gladius's castle now lived in by King Klavian. To her right was the monastery that her father avoided due to the monks. Her mother, though, didn't mind visiting the place for its beauty. Kayla found the place boring. The only thing pretty about the monastery was the stained-glass windows. The town made a much more pleasant scene. Buildings here were squished together like a candy rainbow. They were bright and cheerful in every color.

Shops flew Aralot's white flag with the yellow border proudly displaying the blue mystique flower in the middle. On festival days, Troni was so crowded that no one could walk anywhere and the only way to get around the celebrating people was to fly a dragon or hop across rooftops. Kayla always chose the rooftop method.

Last year for the summer festival, Kayla had been able to spend the entire day with Anvil's family. She had taught her two fake cousins how to jump around buildings. Anvil had been all for it. Anvil's wife Annaliese had been terrified. Kayla found the whole thing funny. She could never be scared of heights unless she was dangling from a dragon. Being up high was wonderful otherwise. She could see so much more when she wasn't stuck on the ground. That was one of the reasons she liked rock climbing so much.

Today the town was unusually quiet making Kayla question if something was going on. Sure there were people walking around, but the voices were lacking against her practiced ears. Kayla turned the corner between the bookstore and the printing press and bumped into a man who grabbed her arm to steady her.

Pg. 76

"Aha. Progress at last. Where is your mother, Kayla?"

"Excuse me?" Kayla asked instantly drawing on her Colt teachings to question everyone back.

It wasn't new to her that everyone knew her parents. It wasn't new that random people asked her to meet her parents either, but she had never seen this well-groomed man before. He looked rather important. He was wearing rich clothes and his red hair was neatly combed. He was probably noble. Her mother had made her meet all the nobles around, and as a Colt, part of the requirement to being politically active was to spy on all the nobles. Kayla hadn't ever spied on this one. She knew how she was supposed to talk to nobles, but since her mother never heeded the lessons on proper etiquette, Kayla never really did either.

"Where is your overprotective mother, Tia Felding? Err... What is Jack's last name again?"

"Brixton."

Kayla rolled her eyes, but she was rather uneasy now. Maybe this person wasn't a real noble but some Colt she didn't know trying to dress up as one and pretend that he was clever. He was already failing his test in her case. Everyone knew her last name. Tia's maiden name of Felding was hardly mentioned at all. That name came along with the mention of Gladius's curses.

Since this faker was still holding her arm, Kayla narrowed her eyes. She considered knocking him to the ground. She could do it easy enough. Her parents spent way too much time teaching her how to defend herself, but Kayla never needed to use any of those lessons because no one ever picked on her physically. They'd hit at her emotions, but with Tia's host of mind-linked dragons following Kayla, bullies stayed away from her. Come to think of it, perhaps that was why she didn't have any real friends that were not either her parent's friends or related to her. One of these days, she needed to find a way to ditch the dragon guard. No one wanted to be spied on all the time. King Klavian had made Tia his royal dragon tamer, which meant that Tia oversaw all the dragon ware problems because King Klavian didn't want to deal with those. It was the one thing Kayla had in common with the king.

"That's it. Tia Brixton. She has been avoiding me for quite some time. When's the last time you saw your father?" the stranger asked next as if testing to see how protected Kayla currently was. She was starting to feel more edgy. The grip on her arm was pressing in.

"No one has seen Jack in the last three months," Kayla replied as she yanked her arm out of that grip. This had to be some phony Colt that wanted to make a nuisance of himself. He was succeeding.

"No one but me then. Perfect."

This guy had her dad? What kind of a liar was this? There was no way this guy had her dad captured if he couldn't remember Jack's last name. This guy was looney. Kayla realized that she was letting her disbelieving expression show on her face, which was bad Colt training. Colts prided themselves and keeping straight faces when under interrogation. Kayla had always been bad at that part. She was a person with personality, not a stone façade that hid the intricate musings of her mind.

A strong wind blew through the town which took away the rest of the regular sounds of people that should have been there. Kayla took a step back looking around and what she saw had her screaming for her mom. The people that had been moving before stood still, not blinking, not breathing, not talking.

"Mom!"

Kayla took back her earlier assumption. Whoever this stranger was, he couldn't be the kind of crazy that she first thought. He was a worse kind that used magic. Kayla had never done this before, but she found herself glancing into the air searching for her mother's guardian dragon of the day. It was always there, only she couldn't hear it. She couldn't see it either, producing a wave of panic that swept through her nerves. This guy had knocked away her defenses! With no outside help, Kayla reached for her magical keychain.

Too slow! Another man jumped on her back with a rope in hand and tied her up so she was separated from her magic before she could reach it. Her father taught her magic spells, but he wasn't the most trusting when it came to giving a child unlimited power. Her magical keychain had limits on it that prevented her from using large amounts of magic at a time. It also prevented her from calling upon the warm blue substance unless she was physically touching the keychain itself. Her life had too many rules! She couldn't get herself out of this on her own!

Kayla searched the blank sky again. Where had all the dragons gone? The King's Ware was right beside her. There should be dragon scouts over her head!

"Not there," the evil new spellcaster said. "Your dragon knows perfectly well how to distract everyone away from you."

"I don't have a dragon," Kayla retorted.

Then she groaned. Now would be a good time to tell some other living creature that cared about her that she was being kidnapped. She'd do that if she had a dragon. What did this man want from her? She hoped it wasn't torture in front of her dad until he snapped and gave the madman some spell he was after. She could picture her father all too well tied up, angry, yet reserved to not draw his family into a magical battle that he wanted to win himself. The image of the picture from two nights ago floated back into Kayla's memory. Her father had been pointing into a castle. Vankerdale's castle? Were her nightmares really things her father wanted to tell her but didn't want to say out loud? No. They couldn't be. He wouldn't want her seeing Gladius hurt dragons.

"What do you want?" Kayla trembled thinking how everything was going to get messed up now. Her mother would go crazy when Kayla couldn't be found. Kayla had heard every version possible of her mother's past adventures, and the woman could get insanely defensive. The word war flashed across her mind next.

"I want redemption."

Where was her mom?! Kayla hadn't spotted her when she stepped from the portal, but then again, her mother expected her to be going to it so she would have grabbed the journal and taken it to a place where Kayla wouldn't interrupt her. Tia was probably inside the magic library or sitting around in the hot desert, in which case she wouldn't be close enough to hear Kayla scream. Sparkle would hear her if Tia was here! Dragon's had exquisite hearing.

"Help!"

The crazy redhead kneed her in the stomach, cutting off her air supply while she gasped. Behind her, the person who had tied her up muttered under his breath while she wheezed.

"Don't fuss. I only want one…"

Her kidnapper's mouth blurred. His words came out as a buzz. Kayla held her breath once she got it back. This was probably the very event her mother had been trying to prevent her from experiencing her whole life. The man before her was talking about her taboo topic *and* kidnapping her. So if it was her mother trying to keep Kayla out of this, that had to mean that Tia was responsible for cursing her so Kayla couldn't hear what everyone was saying. Why was her mother lying to her family?! She was the absolute worst!

"Don't look at me like that! Don't you know who I am?" the angry red-haired man asked her.

Pg. 80

Kayla shook her head. "Not a clue. Are you going to tell me, because if you start talking about my cursed subject again, I won't be able to hear a word you say."

"I got a spy to tell me that Kayla is cursed and can't hear anyone talk about..." The man behind her started to buzz out too.

She was tied up well, but she managed to strain her neck to see who this other man was. He was unfortunately cute with glasses and a dark-brown beard that oddly missed his cheeks. There was no way she had ever seen this guy before either because she would have remembered the strange choice in facial hair.

Kayla wasn't sure about his age, but it was close to her own unlike the redhead who could be her parent's age. The redhead had a deep voice, but the younger guy, probably the evil mastermind's lackey, had a mellow mid-range tone to him.

"Hurry up," the red-haired rich man told his accomplice. Lackey shoved a sack over her head as Kayla screamed again. Perhaps if the sack was a bit shorter, she could have found a way to kick him, but it was large, and she was cinched up like a bundle of potatoes. She had to hold out hope for that assisted rescue or she might really be in trouble here. After all, this was the castle town. There was always someone around. Her mind fought for ideas on escape as she was moved toward the sounds of an unknown dragon.

In most cases, Kayla could guess the dragons scale color by the way it breathed and talked and flew. For this animal, she was drawing a blank, and her imagination was taking off, painting the creature in hard black lines with green piercing eyes. Reaper.

"Help!" Kayla screamed again only to earn a short "of course" grunt from the mystery dragon.

She no longer wanted help from dragons. If she was a keeper, she could ask a dragon for help, but then she would be stuck with the responsibility of taking care of the giant hulking beast for the rest of her life. She couldn't look at dragons without tearing up. There was no way she could send a mental plea into the unknown for a dragon's help. She wanted people.

There had to be a Colt around that could save her. Never mind, they didn't engage in dragon business, and she was being lifted on top of one. A rider would save her. She wasn't special on her own, but she was the kid of the spellcaster and the royal dragon tamer. That had to count for something. Someone needed to stop her from riding this dragon, because she'd not touched a dragon since she was five.

"Get me down!"

The dragon hummed instead, and Kayla screamed louder. So far, she wasn't being hit by the overpowering sadness she got when a dragon took interest in her, but it didn't matter. She still knew very well what that feeling felt like, and she expected it to hit her, cascading tears down her face and across the sack on her body at any moment.

"I can't ride the dragon!" Kayla screamed. "Stop! Please stop! I'll walk. I promise!"

Oh wow. That would never win her a wild stallion tattoo. Colts didn't walk off with their kidnappers and riders didn't either. They fought. They all fought. She had to do something! Kayla squirmed and then a beam of light hit at her face as the top of the sack was opened. The lackey gagged her, leaving her with an aching jaw and her tongue uncomfortable. Kayla choked and fought the sensation while she pushed against the rag in her mouth with her tongue. If she was anything like the rest of her family, she would have freed herself by now. She wished that she wasn't such a failure to them as the dragon's feet took off in a shaky run.

This dragon was overworked. It shouldn't still be out and about, but it was probably driven onward by the evil cranky man who could be into torture. The dragon's feet picked up some speed and gave a short hop. Kayla held her breath. Not yet! It wasn't ready to fly yet! It didn't have enough speed. Luckily the dragon realized the same thing because it went back to running before testing the hop again. Now it was ready. Kayla released her breath as they ascended toward the clouds glad that the tired animal hadn't face-planted them all into the ground. That's where they would have been if it had tried that first jump.

She hoped they didn't have far to go. As the dragon's wings flapped, Kayla still had no idea what kind it was. She did know one thing though. It wasn't a water dragon. This animal wasn't fit for long-distance travel like her Aunt Rosa's dragon, Pewter. This animal had to be a special breed. Maybe some variation of a blotched ice dragon or something.

Beneath her, the dragon gave off an annoyed snort. Kayla wished she could see where she was going even if it did mean that she would get a glimpse of the dragon she was riding, which would turn her body into a lake of tears.

There! Finally the sound of other rescuing dragons! Kayla continued to scream only because it felt better than allowing herself to be carried off. She quieted down a little when she heard the angry cries of dragons giving chase.

There was a blue dragon to her left. There was a bronze dragon to the right. There was a brown wild dragon that didn't like them flying overhead. She could tell that at least one of the dragons was from Charles's Ware, the place that should have already seen her kidnapping.

Kayla felt a horrible sensation in her stomach as the dragon she was on swooped low. There was a loud sucking sound, and she felt the air tingle—more magic. She tried to make out the spell by the way it felt. It was a movement spell of some sort. Her eyes grew wide when the dragon's speed increased beyond anything she had ever experienced before. This dragon knew how to kick up the speed.

Still in the sack, she heard the cries of the man who had tied her up telling the dragon not to let them all slip off. After that, she felt more magic tingle around her, and she was trapped inside a spell that stuck her to the back of the dragon like a suction cup. Nothing was going to get her off the dragon even if the creature spun upside down, which it did.

Her two kidnappers screamed. Kayla held her breath. She could release herself from this spell only if she could move her hands and reach the keychain jewel that she kept clipped on her belt. Over the years, she had gone through several methods of keeping magic on her. She had tried rings, necklaces, and earrings, but with each item, there was always something that bothered her about it. Earrings were too heavy. Rings were too bulky. Necklaces were dangerous when rock climbing. She had ended up with her keychain, and she liked the way it could be hooked to her belt and tucked out of sight. It didn't get in the way of anything. This was the first time she had ever considered the disadvantages of a magical keychain. If her hands couldn't reach it, she couldn't use it.

The dragon continued to fly at its abnormally fast speed until Kayla heard another sucking sound. This was met with a rumble from inside the dragon's stomach. The dragon slowed down and Kayla felt her ears pop as the spell that adhered her to the back of the dragon eased up. She was going to take back some of her previous assumption that the man with her was a new evil spellcaster. He was pulling off spells that were advanced. This wasn't going to end well. Kayla listened to the sounds around her trying to gather clues about where she was.

Birds, the breathing of the men beside her, the sounds of the moving dragon, and rushing water. There was only one place close to the castle that had rushing river water and that was the border river between Aralot and Vankerdale.

Pg. 84

Her nightmarish drawings *were* a clue from her dad. For the first time ever, she started to think of them as such. What other things had she drawn in her sleep, and what could it all mean? A lot of the time she drew fictitious places of people living on clouds or unreal sea creatures. Then there were the dragon pictures teaching her what dragons looked like when she couldn't stand to look at them.

Sometimes she would draw events that happened to her mom like finding rare magical artifacts that had been hidden around Aralot. Sometimes she got double spooky and her drawings matched the dreams she had had from the day before. She'd drawn her younger parents out on their adventures. She'd drawn Tia meeting King Klavian for the first time when he looked like a hobo. She had drawn her parents exploring the mine caves and secret locations of Herb Felding. That sort of stuff. She could walk the layout of the underground tunnels beneath King Klavian's castle without ever having been there. She should have paid more attention to what it all meant instead of being scared that it was happening. Nah. It was still scary that it kept happening.

"Here's the final test," the redhaired man whispered.

"I told you. It can't count as stealing this way," Lackey replied. "We'll make it through the border spell."

She couldn't leave Aralot! She didn't know her way back into the kingdom from other places. She had not studied maps of other kingdoms very thoroughly, and her father's spells made returning very difficult.

"There have to be spells against Kayla leaving, genius," the noble argued. "Her mother can't be kidnapped. Once Tia reaches a border she's thrown backward. It will be the same with Kayla."

That sounded good to her except for the part of the throwing. She was tied up in a sack. Kayla had a sudden image of herself being blasted off the back of the dragon and falling into the rushing river only to drown because she couldn't swim to save herself. For that matter, she really couldn't swim. She had another curse that prevented her going too deep into the water. So what might happen is that she would float harmlessly downstream until some dragon snagged her up because she couldn't go under. Did this mean that her mother cursed her to not be able to hear her forbidden topic, and her father was responsible for the no swimming curse?

"Well if we don't break through you can use Kayla right here."

"If we don't break through, I'll injure you both and go back for Tia. She's the one who knows how to break the spell. She'd end it to get Kayla back in one piece."

This whole thing was about a spell. Kayla sincerely hoped that her studies had prepared her for this sort of thing, because she couldn't hear any approaching dragon that was close enough to do anything to help her.

The dragon below them shivered. The next thing she knew, Kayla felt herself surrounded by a horrible pull of magic. She could feel the forces straining against her trying to keep her inside Aralot. She felt herself start to slip and then the dragon created a strange sucking sound while both her captors gripped her in the sack. The tension of the magic caused her head to spin. Her vision and sound blurred making her want to throw up. Magic was siphoned away from her from all directions somehow cutting off the spells that had kept her safe.

She knew the instant she crossed over to Vankerdale. The air felt different. The small hum of magic vanished, leaving her feeling empty. It was surprising. She had no idea that all of Aralot felt different from Vankerdale before. Kayla got the sense that the magic she was leaving was incredibly angry to have her slip away. Then the dragon below her wobbled and screamed.

Threats

Tristan

"D eath to all who obstruct the heirs of the crown."

The notice hung above Tristan's head as he woke up. He rolled his eyes at his newest death threat. For a message like this to have appeared, it had to mean that Vermelo, the Captain of the Guard, had set it up in his room the day before. Nothing got past Tristan in his sleep. Tristan had been born a Colt, and despite being taken into the castle when he was seven years old as his father gained the stewardship, he had completed his Colt training to earn his wild stallion tattoo.

His father, King Klavian, had cautioned him against turning into a rebel, but what could the steward do? The king of the land was a Colt too. If Jack could be the king with a tattoo right above his heart, Tristan could grow into being the next king with a tiny stallion on his ankle. Nobody ever saw it. Tristan was also a dragon rider, like Jack, and he wore thick boots most of the time. His claim to fame was concealed although known by everyone in the entire kingdom anyway.

"Someone has been reading too much Gladius," Tristan declared. He pulled down the notice, wadded it into a ball, and tossed it into his unit fireplace. Gladius was known for his hasty death sentences, particularly against anything that messed around with dragons or Aralot. Since Gladius was a past king and his whole life was centered around dragons and the kingdom, everything to him was worthy of such dooming remarks.

"The Colts are prowling today. There are secret missions to learn some sort of information relating to the crown..."

The thought came from Riven, his glorious bronze dragon. Tristan opened up his window and looked outside trying to spot those prowlers. He saw the tree line, the dragon ware, the town, and the monastery. He had the best view, but he didn't make out any Colts. Ritz was usually fantastic at predicting early complications. Colts crawling near the castle could only mean one thing. Something was going to happen, and it was going to be important.

Tristan scanned the air looking for one of Queen Tia's dragons. She was the real queen of the land, even if she lived with her husband in the north and visited the castle sporadically. She was here less than Jack was. If the problem was going to be dragon related, Tia often felt prompted to be around to help, showing up days in advance before anyone else had identified the troubling situation.

Queen Tia was a keeper with magical blood that called on her to protect the scaly creatures. Old King Gladius was her grandfather. He had ruled with magic and malice. Her father was Herb Felding who ruled without ever being crowned king. The fate of the kingdom of Aralot ran through the Felding bloodline. Now it ran through the Brixton bloodline since Tia had married Jack. The lack of the queen's wild dragon army out the window said that the issue wasn't dragon related. At least not yet.

"You totally missed it!"

Bummer. Tristan leaned out his window searching the area. His dragon knew that he liked discovering things on his own without being

Pg. 88

told them directly. Despite that, there were times when he did need to be told. He thought over the two hints he had gotten this morning. Vermelo was crying about the real heir to the throne again. That would be Kayla Brixton who couldn't hear anyone tell her that she was a princess or that her parents were the king and queen.

Whenever Kayla came up, Tristan got annoyed. It wasn't like she deserved to rule Aralot. She did nothing to help the kingdom. She hadn't joined the Colts. She hadn't bonded a dragon. She didn't do service projects with the monks or travel the land helping the needy and poor. The only thing that girl did was rock climb and hide. She wasn't fit to rule anything. Her mother had years of farming and a love of dragons under her belt by Kayla's age. Her father had been one of the best spies in all of Aralot, despite never working directly with Ritz. Kayla was the wisp of their shadow in comparison. She was so rather unimportant, Tristan often wished that she wasn't born at all. It was the kings that mattered most inside of Aralot. He'd do such a better job than the shadow puppet.

"It's something to do with Kayla, isn't it Riven?" Tristan asked as his eyes settled back on the town. He stared at a villager for a while before he realized the problem. The person was frozen in the act of hanging up a washed shirt. The woman didn't move. Not one inch.

Kayla! She had been practicing spells since she was eight. With her father missing perhaps she had decided that she was going to do something to claim her role as princess. How did she know she was the princess!? There was no way that Jack could destroy the spells on his daughter. He had tried and tried. He would never guess where the source of the spell was located or the condition of the spell that he needed to satisfy before it could be destroyed. If he had guessed where the spell came from, he'd venture into Vankerdale to find it. That would leave Kayla to be the spellcaster while he was away. She couldn't do that! She was a girl!

"I want to congratulate you for noticing the immobilization, and roll my eyes over your accurate description that Kayla is a girl."

Tristan slammed the window shut. Kayla had no right to take over the kingdom even if by law it was already hers. There had never been a female spellcaster sitting on the throne.

"Aralot hasn't seen this many people using magic at one time either."

On that note, there were way too many people that used magic. Fewer people touching the blue glow would be nice. The immobilized town could have been caused by quite a few people that could have messed up a spell they shouldn't have touched. Tristan ran out of his room and down the hallway in search of his father. King Klavian should know about the illegal magical use. Tristan rounded a corner and nearly crashed into Vermelo who was running the opposite direction. Since the guy always knew where King Klavian was located, Tristan turned around to follow him.

Vermelo was a man who looked like your best friend. He had gray hair that used to be black, and he had perfected his friendly smile over the years. He was perfectly loveable unless you knew him. Behind his charming exterior was a scheming mind that outsmarted spies and kept the king alive. Since Tristan wasn't the king—yet—Vermelo didn't care if he lived or died. Tristan knew who kept leaving him death threats. However, Vermelo was yet to act on them, so Tristan was fine with the unwelcome hints. Vermelo suspected that Tristan was messing with the guy's favorite Brixton family. He could speculate all he wanted. He couldn't prove anything.

Despite being the steward of the land, Tristan's father acted as the king and was called the king by all his subjects. Likewise, Tristan's mother, Aria, was called the queen. Tristan was called the prince, and it was a minor formality that Jack, Tia, and Kayla were invited to yearly celebrations in the castle.

Vermelo looked behind him as Tristan caught up. "This had better not be your doing," Vermelo spoke.

"Frozen town? Isn't it Kayla's doing?" Tristan asked.

"I will not be warning you again," Vermelo replied.

Tristan shrugged and kept running after the captain, still wanting to know what was happening. He wouldn't find out until Vermelo told King Klavian. While the captain made no attempt to hide that he preferred Jack to Klavian, he took his job of protecting Jack's steward seriously so that Jack could go traipsing around the kingdom at will.

Tristan watched as Vermelo reached the king's door and shoved it open without knocking. They both slipped inside at the same time to find the steward. King Klavian was a stately man with a keen mind for scholarly subjects. He had gone through many different hairstyles over the years, but he always returned to the classic clean shaved look. He had also spent five years starving and rotting in a dungeon so his favorite shirts were tight to show off how much muscle he had managed to put back on his arms and chest.

As Vermelo entered the room, King Klavian shook his head perturbed. He was halfway through getting dressed for the day. Tristan noticed that his mother was up and out no doubt two or three hours before. She wasn't the type of person to ever sleep in. King Klavian finished pulling his shirt down as he spun around irritated.

"Sorry," Vermelo told him. "All the people in the town beside us have been frozen."

"That must be a sight. It's already hot in here," King Klavian replied as he put on his shoes.

Vermelo shook his head at the calm nature of the king. He didn't get more tragic words out because Klavian was already coming up with a solution.

"Go have Charles's Ware dragons thaw them out. I'll talk to Tia about controlling her ice dragon. Sparkle hasn't been problematic for—"

"They are not frozen in ice, sire. They're just frozen. They don't move and they don't blink. I hope it's a timed curse or that you can fix it because otherwise the town beside us is frozen in time."

"What?"

Tristan nodded at his father's look and the man jumped to the window to see the town for himself. He pulled the shutters open to lean outside a little bit too. This couldn't have happened too long ago because the commotion over the spell wasn't loud yet.

"*Spells,*" Riven sighed. "*No one was aware of anything being wrong until the cause started to dash away.*"

"*Who did this?*" Tristan asked.

"*I'm only going to spoil it if Vermelo gets it wrong,*" Riven answered.

Tristan rolled his eyes at the wrong time. Vermelo looked at him and gave him a glare.

"It wasn't me! I just woke up," Tristan declared. "But Riven won't tell me who did this yet, so I hope that you have a good idea."

"Was it Jack?" Klavian asked. "Maybe he's been messing around with a few of those hidden magical artifacts that he and his wife hide from us all. Jack doesn't usually make public protests. All he needs to do is show his face around here and everyone disregards everything I've ever said for the last eleven years or more…" His father wisely trailed off as Vermelo's glare turned onto him.

"This was not Jack. This morning we failed to stop a kidnapping attack. Kayla Brixton has been carried away into Vankerdale. I don't think Tia knows yet. Her dragon guard is frozen along with everyone else."

Pg. 92

Vermelo folded his arms and gave Klavian a meaningful look as he explained this. Klavian grunted indicating that he acknowledged what Vermelo wanted. Living with the man for so long didn't make it hard to guess. Vermelo wanted King Klavian to do something to get Kayla back. Tristan caught the next look from his dad and heard himself copying his grunt. Then he smiled about it.

He knew what his dad was thinking. Klavian had been after Tia and Jack to betroth Kayla to Tristan since the girl was born. If they merged their two ruling family lines, then the unsettling, unspoken, family feud they had going on between them would end. Klavian hardly ever talked about it, but Tristan had picked up enough to know that his father both loved and hated the Brixtons. He hated the way they ruled the kingdom instead of him, even if they gave him control most of the time. He loved them because they were his best friends, never mortally against him even if Tristan was certain that his father had planned out a complete overthrow of the kingdom a time or two that included their death. Klavian hadn't ever been able to act on his angry thoughts because Vermelo was always there in the way.

In any case, Kayla wasn't allowed to date anyone until she turned sixteen. Tristan tried to recall the girl's exact birthday. It was sometime this month. That meant that his father had no doubt already planned their first date. Since Kayla couldn't hear that it was her duty to date him so they could get married and cool the tension, Tristan expected this whole date thing to be a disaster. They were not going to get along. Kayla was always lost inside her own head, ignoring people, conversations, and dragons. As self-centered as she was, Tristan was hoping that Vankerdale would take care of her for him permanently. That's not the way he phrased it though.

"It can't be that bad," Tristan remarked. "Kayla might be the worst Colt there ever was, but she was still born to one. She knows that she has to solve her own problems. She'll do something."

Oops. He shouldn't have said that. Vermelo gave him an even worse glare. The Captain of the Guard loved the Brixtons because he loved the Feldings ruling. He read the ancient laws of the land stating that a keeper had to be the one sitting on the throne for Aralot to function. If it wasn't for laws like that, Tristan was certain that his father would have gotten rid of Tia and Jack long ago. That, and Klavian hated dealing with dragons. He let Tia and Jack handle all the dragon problems. They were a well-seasoned team of enemies who were friends.

"Perhaps you are indicating that the way for Kayla's curses to be removed is for her to remove them herself?" Vermelo asked with narrowed eyes.

"How should I know?" Tristan shrugged. "I just meant that despite her being reclusive, she has to have some sort of backbone."

She didn't really. Kayla's favorite thing to do was walk around with her gray hood up. She ignored everyone. She brushed aside every dragon. Tristan didn't think the girl had any friends either. She spent her time studying, rock climbing, jumping, and hanging out with Anvil.

That was why Tristan never felt bad that Kayla couldn't hear anyone tell her to take over the throne. Kayla had Anvil wrapped around her desires and his was the strongest ware. He had three keepers at his fingertips, and despite what everyone said about Anvil not being "infected," Tristan knew that Anvil was inside of Tia's keeper bond of mentally linked dragons. It had been so obvious the day that Kayla was born and Anvil had rushed to the rescue.

If Kayla said jump, Anvil would jump. So Tristan blocked Kayla from learning that she could come to kill him. He was like his father, hating yet unable to kill off his rivals. Despite his negative view of Kayla, Tristan had also cast out spells to stop her from being kidnapped. He had cast spells to make Kayla fireproof from dragons and waterproof from the ocean. She couldn't set foot on a ship without becoming instantly seasick and wanting to return home. Between Jack and Tristan, the girl should have never been able to go anywhere. Tristan wanted her where he could see her. She was his largest threat.

On that note, Kayla had not revealed herself as a keeper yet, but she was nearing the customary age to do so. Her Aunt Rosa had shown her keeper abilities when she was fourteen which was considered really young. Tia hadn't shown anything until she was eighteen, but speculation said that Tia had spells on her preventing her from bonding dragons so that could have been why. According to Anvil's all-inclusive keeper research, sixteen was the normal age that a keeper started to hear dragon thought without being bonded. It would not be good if Kayla's kidnapping jump-started that keeper trait causing her to bring over a mind-linked host of Vankerdale dragons to overtake the throne.

Kayla knew more spells than Jack had when he started to be the spellcaster. It would be so characteristic of the magic on the land to push Kayla at Tristan, even if Tristan could work magic too. Aralot's magical laws dictated that the king was a male, keeper, spellcaster, Felding. So far those four things didn't exist anymore inside a single person, but Aralot warped things around to make them fit.

Tristan had taken steps to prevent any other kings coming against him. Tia had several miscarriages over the years. They got blamed away on whatever dreadful event had happened during Kayla's birth. Then Rosa had gotten engaged to Clark, and Tristan wasn't an idiot. He knew what came after that. If Tia could be made queen without needing to be crowned, Rosa could be too. They could very easily produce a baby boy that would rise up against him, and that child would have been a male, keeper, Cluster, spellcaster. One more step closer to the right requirements of true heir.

Thanks to magic from the ice dragon Bantin, Rosa and Clark couldn't have any children either. The spell would have worked against Tia forever as well, except someone had gotten around him and caused

Tia to have Kayla born. Tristan wished Tia would talk about it. She refused to ever say what really happened. Jack had admitted that the event had terrified her and left her possessive over Kayla for months. Tia wouldn't let anyone hold that baby until she was a few months old. Not even Jack could hold his baby.

Kayla's birth still bothered Tristan. Whoever found the way to cause Kayla's birth could figure out who had cast the initial curse. Vermelo had brought the issue up once. He worried that Tia and Rosa couldn't have children. Klavian had sighed and started talking about a report Tia had written where she admitted that her father Herb had told her that the line of keepers should end with her. Klavian believed Herb had cursed his daughters. Tristan was not one to contradict him, but Vermelo didn't believe it. He was such a pain.

However, Vermelo couldn't pin anything on Tristan. Jack had never been able to, and if anyone was going to find the way to end the Brixton's strange curses, it would be Jack. Jack had been to the spot where Tristan kept his curses, although the cursed objects used in Tristan's condition were not kept there at the time. Tristan had picked that spot a year later. It was a great hiding spot.

Tristan cast his mind back in time to see the wooded location. He had first been to Vankderdale back when he had first used portals. He had no idea what he was doing. He only knew that he had to tap the corner block with magic to turn the thing on. He had gotten himself lost for nearly a week wandering through portals trying to get back home. It was Jack that rescued him.

"Tristan!"

Tristan had scrambled for cover when he heard the sound of a dragon exiting the portal after him, but the voice was one that he trusted—at that time. King Jack was there come to tell him off for using the portals. Since Tristan had been lost for a week already, he came out of his hiding place to face the man.

"What are you doing here?"

"I'm lost." Tristan gave Jack his best pout face. Jack shook his head at him, but that was the end of his chiding.

"Your mom's been looking for you. What do you say we get you back?"

"Swell!" He had meant it. That would coincide with Jack letting him up on his dragon. Pyro was a red dragon king, regal and brilliant. "Where am I anyway?"

"Vankerdale," Jack had answered. Tristan had gone back to that portal plenty of times, amused that he could get into Vankerdale so quickly. That was where he buried any item that he didn't want to be found inside of Aralot. His mother had never found out. Jack had spun her a story and gotten him out of his portal disaster. Queen Aria had sighed about it all and made Tristan wash dishes for a week but that was it. That was when Tristan learned that Jack was really good at keeping secrets and telling lies if the man wanted to be. He trusted Jack less after that, even if he would still trust the man with his very life.

Jack had the calling of the king upon his shoulders. The magic of the land demanded of him that he save all his subjects if he could. It was that stipulation that Tristan's father had schemed about, dreaming up ways to get Jack out of the way in some elaborate accident where he tried to save hundreds of people and didn't make it out himself. There was one problem with all those thoughts. Jack was the spellcaster and had his own magical protections. Plus, he wasn't stupid. He would save himself even if he did have to watch close friends die around him. He'd done so before.

"Not thinking of placing curses on Jack, are you?" Riven asked him, concerned.

"*No,*" Tristan answered. He still liked Jack. He didn't mind that Jack was the king, only that Kayla was the princess. Jack was a fabulous king. He worked hard to keep the peace between all the fractions in the land. Everyone could count on Jack for help. No one could count on Kayla for anything.

"Did Kayla cast the time spell in her attempt to not get swept away?" Klavian asked Vermelo, bringing Tristan back to the present. "She's smart. She's a good backup option if anything ever happened to Jack, but giving Kayla access to magic—"

"Your son has far more access to magic than Kayla does, and he has no limitations," Vermelo cut off. "Kayla can't curse an entire town. She can't use that much magic at a time. It is my belief that the spell came from the spellbinding dragon that was spotted fleeing the scene. It was not King Peyton's dragon, SilverWings. This was a dragon we have never seen before."

"Are you certain she was taken to Vankerdale?" Tristan asked.

Spellbinding dragons were usually born in Wisteria. The only reason why King Peyton had one was because he stole the egg before it hatched. The man stole lots of dragons in the past because their kingdom had been cursed in winter and their dragons couldn't reproduce. They couldn't get into Aralot to steal dragons, so they stole from Wisteria.

"She is in Vankerdale," Vermelo assured.

"I thought Kayla had spells on her that prevented her from getting kidnapped," Klavian stated as he started to grow frustrated.

Tristan could already see the problems piling together. If they didn't get Kayla back, Tia was going to throw a fit. Vankerdale would be sending a ransom note or news of Kayla's horrific death to start a war. Then there was the town. Did they have any spell strong enough to undo what a spellbinding dragon sent out? Their spells were binding. If they could take apart binding spells, they would be able to unbind the documents that made Jack the king and Tia the queen. Klavian would have done so years ago even if he never intended to harm the two of them, and since those spells were still in place, Tristan doubted they could save the town.

"She does have spells preventing kidnapping, but perhaps Vankerdale found a way to get around those spells. Kayla could have gone willingly."

"What would cause her to go willingly?" Klavian asked.

This was one of those questionable moments with Vermelo. Tristan knew that Klavian had given Vermelo the task to understand Kayla's character as well as he could. Vermelo's spies were also to know everything there was to know about Clark, Rosa, Tia's six adopted siblings, Jack's parents, and Jack's four brothers. Vermelo was an excellent person to consult on what would drive each of these people. It was sometimes up to debate if he told the truth or not.

"If Kayla was told that Vankerdale had Jack, I could picture her trying to rescue him. That would get around her thoughts of being kidnaped. Hers would be a mission to save."

"Does Vankerdale have Jack?" Klavian pressed.

Tristan looked at Vermelo intently for the answer as his father started sweating. Tristan didn't really care if they never got Kayla, but Jack... Tristan would go into Vankerdale to get Jack. Despite his legal status and last name and family feud, Jack and his spells were the breath of Aralot. To have him outside of the kingdom would start tipping magical notes that Klavian had been trying and failing to fix for ages. Jack was the only thing appeasing a lot of unseen magical rules.

"Where's Tia?" Klavian asked, when Vermelo didn't answer him.

No one knew where Jack had gone. Vermelo had searched. Tia

had searched. Kayla had searched. Tristan had searched. All the dragons, riders, and Colts had searched. Tristan had started to believe that Jack was walking around invisible and odorless to avoid everyone, but now that Kayla was in Vankerdale, he was getting new ideas.

Jack wouldn't crack under pressure if Vankerdale had him, because he was the best Colt that ever lived, besides Ritz who led them all. However, Jack might crack if Kayla was tortured in front of his face. Tristan suddenly felt unsettled.

"I already sent a message to Tia asking her to confirm where her daughter was," Vermelo told Klavian. He straightened up taller as he said this and put his hand on his sword by his side. Klavian scowled at him. Tristan didn't do anything because he expected Vermelo to act without authorization when it came to the Brixtons. The man was predictable. He would turn to Tia and Jack and Kayla when he felt panic.

"Thank you, Vermelo," Klavian replied without a tone of real thanks. "Tia will show up soon demanding action on our part."

"Don't be so sure," Vermelo replied.

Klavian eyed his Captain of the Guard with dread. Tristan didn't know why. If Vermelo said Tia would be incapable of action, he was going to believe him. The woman was overprotective when it came to Kayla, but she was also nonconfrontational when it came to Vankerdale. The topic of war had come up many times over the years since it was obvious that Jack and Tia did not trust Vankerdale. But the couple had never pressed war charges. Tristan could see that playing out yet again. If something was going to be done, it might be left to the Clusters this time. They could finally take charge over the queen and be the real heroes of the land.

"I take Kayla's security seriously," Klavian said. "If she's been taken into Vankerdale, I will do what is necessary to get her back. Come on, Tristan."

"We don't know a spell that will take apart anything from a spellbinding dragon," Tristan reminded his dad as the man started to move toward the door. "Why waste magic when we know it won't work? We're going to need that stuff."

"We must do something. I'll search the magic library again. I could use your help."

"Why don't we send a spy into Vankerdale to find Jack?"

"We need to find Kayla," Vermelo insisted. "Her going missing will anger Aralot beyond anything you can imagine."

Tristan ignored the man as he followed his father out of his room. He could imagine quite a lot, and what he was imaging wasn't pretty.

"Let's say that Vankerdale found some way to trick Jack into crossing the border. The guy charges across and his faithful dragon charges after him. In an instant, their mental bond is shattered, broken." Tristan theorized. "Jack has lived with a broken bond before, but even I know that it's the man's worst nightmare. Pyro is not in Aralot, therefore, it's fair to assume that they are both across the border. Assuming Jack escapes the trap, he is now severed from his dragon. He could be going in circles trying to find Pyro. Or perhaps he is unwilling to take down his spell that prevents dragons from crossing the border because King Peyton has a host of dragons at the border watching the area, ready to break through to start a war. Jack won't leave his dragon broken and alone so he stays. Jack would rather suffer his own nightmares than cause Aralot an unforeseen attack. We need to find Jack and Pyro. We need to know if they are really there."

"If Jack crossed the border, it wouldn't be a trap. He would have gone willingly," Vermelo said from behind them. "He would have been looking for something he couldn't find here."

"And gotten stuck," Tristan replied, without looking behind him at Vermelo. "I'm going to find some spies and see."

With that, Tristan ran past his father in search of a Colt who could cross the border. He crossed through the castle town of Troni, coming to stop amid aged A-frames that had housed the Colts sporadically through the ages. He was looking for a friendly face. Who he ran into was Ritz.

In his early years, Tristan had avoided Ritz. He hadn't changed his attitude toward the man particularly because he believed that Ritz didn't like him at all. From spying on him, Tristan had only come up with two people that Ritz had ever liked in his entire life and those two people happened to be Tia and Kayla. The guy transformed around them into something sweet and sickening. Since they were not around, Ritz was brutal.

He aimed a knife at Tristan's head while Riven shrieked in the distance without enough time to come save his rider should Ritz not like the outcome of what he was after. Tristan didn't even let him start asking his questions. To let Ritz speak was a form of torture in his opinion. Ritz could claim authority over all his Colts, but Tristan bowed down to no one.

"Early this morning Kayla was captured by a spellbinding dragon and taken into Vankerdale. I believe that Jack is there too with Pyro. He will be disconnected from his dragon and reluctant to leave the beast. Know anything about it?"

"You guys are very dimwitted. Tia has known where Jack was since the first week. Kayla figured this out faster than you only she couldn't do anything about it."

Ah, see? That was the information that Ritz wanted to hear. He wanted to know if the castle was going to do anything. They were not dimwitted and Tristan didn't like being called such.

"If you'll excuse me," Tristan said, moving as if the knife was not aimed at his head.

"He's out. I know that's why you're off running. Jack is out of the castle dungeon in Vankerdale. He doesn't have human spies over there to help him, but he does have dragon ones. Whatever Jack went over there to get, he's going to find it, and Kayla will help him. They will save you from the catastrophe you had no idea was even happening."

Tristan barely kept himself from mouthing off at his leader. Ritz couldn't act like he knew what was going on everywhere. Ritz did this a lot: pretending to withhold information when he had no idea what was going on either. Then he would play at knowing everything the whole time to make it sound like everyone else was stupid. There was no way he was getting away with it this time. None of the Colts had learned anything about Jack in the last three months. Ritz was guessing because of Kayla.

"I don't need the Brixtons to save me."

"You do. You really do."

The sound of a dragon growl over their heads put Tristan on the verge of shouting for the animal to go away. It wasn't Riven. It was one of Tia's dragons come to snarl at Ritz for being uppity with the prince. Ritz, of course, put his knife away and ran off laughing as if that was all the proof he needed that Tristan wasn't good enough to save himself. Annoying old man. Interfering Tia!

"Go away!" Tristan shouted at the flying animal. He took a few more running steps and then stopped. What Ritz had told him was all that anyone was going to tell him. Jack had been locked up in Vankerdale and it took him three months to break himself out. What sort of disaster did Ritz suspect was going to come from this? Tristan wanted to be the one to stop it.

He hated how the Brixtons got the glory for everything when all they did was swoop in whenever there was an emergency. They didn't do the day to day tasks that was the real reason Aralot was still functioning. It drove Tristan crazy. He didn't need them to solve anything. He could guess what Vankerdale wanted because it was the same thing they had always wanted—magic.

Jack would hold his mouth shut no matter what the cost to himself, but Kayla? She could still very well give Vankerdale the magic it was after. She carried that magical keychain and King Peyton and Prince Evan had a world of spells in their heads that they could use once they reached it. They had no doubt taken Jack's magical wedding ring, and that was what they had used to kidnap Kayla.

Tristan changed direction running for Kayla's uncle's house. He needed to ask someone who knew her better if the girl would crack under pressure. It was hard, but Tristan shoved Ritz's words out of his head as he reached his destination. Just because he was going to talk with Kyle didn't prove that Tristan needed Brixtons to save him.

He ignored the Colts hooting at him as he showed up. They were typical in their teasing, calling him shaggy, laughing about his dad, etc. They stopped talking when they realized that Riven was over their heads. Tristan found Kyle Brixton in the middle of playing one of his kids at a marble game. The kid looked at him but Kyle didn't. He was one of those Colts that hated dragons, but Tristan knew that out of all the Brixtons, Kayla liked Kyle best. He was a far cry from Anvil, but he would do in a pinch. He always dressed like a pirate with his medium-length hair pulled back into a manbun. He had a bunch of scars to match his chosen look.

"How well can Kayla withstand torture?" Tristan asked.

"No idea," Kyle answered with hardly a glance up at him. "No one is allowed to torture her. The girl didn't stub her toe until we pulled her away from her house at the age of ten."

True. They were all doomed because of Kayla. They had all been doomed since she was born. She couldn't lead. She couldn't hold herself together. She had no real-world experience. She'd cave. She was going to give Vankerdale magic. Then they would all die. Ritz had it all wrong. The Brixtons brought death, not redemption.

"What about unkind words?"

"They make her cry," Kyle replied. "Why? Still opposed to dating the girl? Good. Take your ego and go. Off with you." Kyle looked up at him with narrowed eyes. He didn't try to hide his dislike. If anything, the guy was doing his hardest to increase it because he didn't like Tristan coming to talk to him.

"Is there anything that she's good at?" Tristan asked, not about to show his real annoyance. He was a better Colt than that.

"Hiding. Kayla can hide in plain sight. You will never be able to see the real person beneath all your prejudice. You won't be able to crack her mind, her heart, or her feelings. She shows what she wants to show. She gives what she wants to give. She hides so well, that no one knows what's really inside. She gets that from her dad. We thought that all Jack would amount to was scrounging up food from playing card games and now he's the king. So really, take your ego and leave. You will get nothing good from me if you pester me about my niece. There's a diamond buried in that lump of coal."

Typical Brixton. Trying to sound tough when they realized they had nothing. Kayla didn't have any good qualities. It wasn't like she was going to surprise everyone by becoming a genius overnight the same way Jack had sprung up from the ground.

"You'll never hear me say this again, but you Kyle, got it spot on for once."

Ritz's voice was most disconcerting. The geezer was following him! Kyle glanced in the direction of Ritz and turned nervous, probably wondering what the guy's angle was for the praise. Tristan couldn't help but laugh. Ritz was in love with Kayla. That's all there was to it. He would see anything he wanted to see about that girl. The man was like Caleb Andrade, only Caleb was in love with her romantically instead of being in love with the idea of gaining power from using a princess. Yeah, Tristan could see that about Ritz. He spent more time with Kayla than he ever did with Jack or Tia. He had plans to use that girl.

"Coal burns," Tristan replied as he walked off. He really had to do something about this because this was a disaster.

Telepathy

Kayla

The dragon yelled again as it landed with enough of a deep tone that Kayla identified it as male from her position inside the tied sack. The sound was answered by wild dragons that told the exhausted beast to be quiet because they had a group of sleeping night dragons nearby. Mr. Exhausted chirped out a sorry as he rolled, knocking the humans off his back. As a Vankerdale dragon, Mr. Exhausted would have a love-hate relationship with people. The dragon would like the smell of them, but he couldn't bond one so he wouldn't be able to hear human thoughts. All his directions would be verbal and the animal was right now proving he was done listening to the humans it had carried.

"Get back here!" Nasty redhead shouted as the dragon's legs carried it away.

"He'll be back. We've got what he wants."

Lackey was the one answering, calming the situation. Kayla listened to the exchange trying to gather everything she could about these people to use it against them. Lackey was by far the more level-headed of the two, but he had to owe the redhead something because he was working for him. He alluded to the reason why the dragon was helping.

"If we had what he wants, he wouldn't run off, Tyler."

"Yes, he would. He might be hungry or need to relieve himself."

"He's dangerous out there with all those spells he's inhaled. At least he's antisocial. He'll curl up in a cave and be easy to get back. I hate MSD."

"He can still hear you," Tyler sighed. "Be careful. MSD can do something about all the times you've screamed at him."

"I'm not stupid. I wouldn't ride that ugly thing without coming prepared. I'm carrying magic with me. MSD can't get away with anything. Don't say it."

"Not going to," Tyler responded.

Interesting. The dragon was MSD which had to stand for something. These two got its cooperation by holding ransom something it wanted. Perhaps they had raided his jewel stash and taken his favorite one. The redhead could cast spells, although he hadn't used any that Kayla had seen. The freezing spell had come from out of sight so must have been done by the Lackey. If Vankerdale was anything like Aralot, only its rulers and spellcasters were allowed to use magic. The redhead had to be the prince since he dressed finer and was bossy. She was taken by Prince Evan and the Vankderdale spellcaster, Tyler. Where was her dad?

Currently, Kayla was plopped over onto the ground still tied up inside the sack. She had given up on screaming. Her cheeks hurt from the gag in her mouth and there was no one around that would rescue her anymore. She would have to find a way to rescue herself. For that, she was doing her best to listen to everything. Apart from the sounds of the woods and resting wild dragons, there wasn't anything here other than them.

"Do you think we could sleep in the Half Moon Inn? We can make it to that. I'll keep Kayla quiet. I promise."

Prince Evan didn't want to sleep on the ground so he agreed. It was far from lunchtime, but the prince was tired and hungry and he gave Tyler a few threats about what he would do if Tyler didn't keep Kayla as quiet as possible. Kayla remained unmoving inside the sack drawing everything she could out of their snippets of conversation.

She mostly learned about Tyler. He had finished a homework assignment for Prince Evan. He had an older brother named Narl that the prince thought would have finished it faster. He was not released from some contract they had made, even though Tyler argued that he had managed to get the prince into Aralot. Prince Evan was still upset that he didn't also have Tia who knew the words to a spell. Tyler pointed out that MSD wouldn't care for Tia and would make no extra effort to drag her from Aralot instead of Kayla.

It was not stated, but Kayla got the impression that the dragon had gone looking only for her. That didn't make her any more comfortable inside the sack, and she squirmed, pressing into Tyler's back trying to locate better air. She considered screaming again, but Tyler got the message and set her down.

When he opened the sack, he looked a little sorry for the state of her as he untied the gag on her mouth. Kayla could already hear the Colt part of her brain drawing upon that one look. Tyler could be used and persuaded if she looked uncomfortable enough. She could poke at his compassion.

Kayla had never seen nightmares of Prince Evan, but she had heard her parents talk about how much they didn't like him from papers that King Klavian sent back and forth between their kingdoms. No one inside of Aralot liked Prince Evan. Kayla looked at Tyler wondering if anyone inside of Vankerdale liked the prince. Tyler was shaking his head, but at least he dumped her from the sack and carried her over his shoulder so she could breathe.

"What are you doing?" Prince Evan asked poking his head over to see. Kayla spent a lot of time wearing sweaters and hoods around in the heat, so she wasn't new to the fact that her face was always red and sweaty. She could tell what she looked like without needing to be told. She was flushed and hot and quietly taking in the fresh air that lacked anything magical about it. The lack of magic around her still had her feeling odd. It was strange to miss something she had never noticed she had before.

"You think we'll get far if she suffocates?" Tyler asked.

Bingo! Kayla held back any retort because she was totally going to make use of Tyler. She could get him to slip in his guard, loosen her hands so she could reach her magic or something. This was going to work. She would get out of here. Maybe she'd even find her dad, or was it better to return to Aralot and send back reinforcements? It was hard to say when she wasn't sure what her father would be over here for exactly. What spell was it that everyone was after?

Prince Evan and King Peyton both spent hours and hours inside the magical library learning spells. If they hadn't found the answer, it had to do with King Gladius. Perhaps they suspected that Tia had found the answer to the spell in Gladius's journal, in which case Kayla would be able to pick it out since she had nightmares of that whole written text.

"Think we can steal her blood and save it for later?" Prince Evan asked stepping away from her as if she was repulsive.

Blood. Kayla did know what spell they were after. Gladius had put a curse on Vankerdale so that their dragons couldn't bond. The spell had been lifted for a short month or so and put back on. The only way to break the spell was to use blood of one of Gladius's relatives. That's why Kayla was here. As Gladius's great-granddaughter, she was going to be bled until her parents gave up the words for the spell. As alarming as it

Pg. 110

should be, she didn't feel very scared. She was rather relieved that she could breathe and see the area around her.

She had been able to smell the woods through the sack, but seeing the trees from this side of the river made them look different. Everything looked darker and more foreboding, and it wasn't because she was kidnapped. The trees were closer together, casting shadows over everything.

Now that she was out of the sack, her human scent was able to spread easier. Kayla was very aware that her father's dragon Pyro put his dragon king protection on everything he liked. Her parents smelled of flame and cinnamon to the vast majority of dragons, and Kayla figured she smelled the same. Dragon's liked that smell. It wasn't always the best of things to be known by a dragon king. She heard the inhale of a curious dragon ahead of them. It chirped. Mr. Exhausted gave off a defensive growl from the left and Kayla finally decided to talk again.

"You're walking right into a wild dragon sleeping camp."

And that would never do. She would have to shut her eyes again to avoid looking at the unfamiliar creatures. Her ears were plenty brilliant, but she did rely on her eyes to tell her when she was going to run into a tree.

"The MSD dragon is to the left."

"I can see what you're doing," Prince Evan claimed. "We are not going to the right. That is back toward Aralot. Nice try, but no."

He had no idea what she was thinking. Escape was in her best interest, but so was not walking through a camp of wild dragons that didn't have any humans around to hold them back. Mr. Exhausted growled again, bringing up more dragon voices ahead of them snapping at him for being too loud and telling him to go away. Prince Evan kept walking forward, but Tyler got the hint that the dragons up ahead didn't want to be disturbed.

"We can veer to the left. Safer that way. Any sleeping dragons that way, Kayla?"

Tyler was already stepping that way while Prince Evan huffed about him being a sissy. Kayla offered up a shrug and kept her gaze on the ground while she grinned. Tyler had asked for her opinion like they were accomplices. She had to get this guy alone and then she could get out of here. She was slung over his shoulder with her hands tied behind her back currently. If she could squiggle the ropes on her hands toward the keychain on her belt, she could reach her magic and blast the ropes off her all at once. Then she could run wherever she wanted. It would be a good indication if she had trained her legs well enough.

She didn't enact her plan just yet. She let Prince Evan get ahead of them again hoping that once he was farther ahead, she could get Tyler distracted. While he had moved her, she had gotten a good look at his face.

Tyler wore thin-framed glasses that rested on top of a rounded nose. He had a square jaw with a dark brown beard that covered his chin and went around his mouth. His cheeks were shaved free of the facial hair. The sides of his hair were cut shorter than the top of his hair which had enough volume to make his dark-brown hair fluffy. Tyler had just enough of an edge to be called handsome instead of ordinary. Kayla tried to spot a magical earring, necklace, ring, or bracelet when he gave a good view. Perhaps Tyler hid his magic down his shoe or it was sewn into his pants leg because nothing flashy was visible.

Kayla scanned his lower attire but couldn't make out anything of interest. He didn't wear boots, but flat-soled shoes that were horrible for dragon riding. He was not wearing rider clothes, but Kayla knew that dragons in Vankerdale couldn't bond so she didn't expect to see any functioning ware colors. In Aralot there were seven functioning wares that trained riders and dragons to work together. They all had different colored stained leather gear to distinguish them from each other. Tyler wore the clothes of middle-class citizens: comfortable and plain.

"Are you Vankerdale's spellcaster, Tyler?" Kayla decided to whisper at him to cause a distraction, although making him think about magic wasn't the wisest thing to do when she wanted to reach for her own.

"We can't have a spellcaster when we don't have magic for spells. Not a human one anyway. Our spellcaster is SilverWings. He's—"

"I know who that is."

He was King Peyton's dragon that had silver wingtips. The dragon was a rare breed. The answer gave Kayla another thing to think about. If Tyler didn't know magic at all, and Prince Evan hadn't been casting out spells, the immobile people in Aralot could have been a result of SilverWings.

"Are SilverWings and MSD the same?"

Tyler shifted her a little bit on his shoulder as Prince Evan slowed down trying to hear them. He was the one with magic, so Kayla needed to watch out for the prince. If she could reach her keychain, she could get anything past Tyler. However, there could be a spellbinding dragon around and Kayla worried that if anything was to stop her, that would be the thing. If only she was her dad, she'd be able to look the beast in the face while she blasted spells back at it to escape. As it was, the dragon would have a large advantage over her.

"Yes and no," Tyler answered. "I don't really like calling him MSD. It stands for Mopey Spell Dragon. He's not all that bad. From what I've heard, Aralot's Mr. Grumpy—your ice dragon—is worse than MSD. I call our dragon friend Valiant. The name suits him better. He valiantly awaits for his redemption. You're supposed to be able to provide it for him."

She was needed to break a curse so the dragon could bond. Valiant was like SilverWings because he was a spellbinding dragon. That's why his sounds were unfamiliar to her. Somehow Vankerdale had gotten another spell shooting animal without anyone in Aralot knowing. Wisteria had to know. The dragon would have come from there. If Valiant was waiting so he could bond, Kayla was guessing that what Prince Evan had captured was the animal's rider.

"Your dragon knows perfectly well how to distract everyone away from you."

Prince Evan had said that before she was taken, and if she was putting together everything that Tyler and Prince Evan had previously said, it made it sound like Valiant was *her* dragon. Another helpful escape buddy or was she getting this wrong? She didn't have a dragon. She avoided dragons. And while she had heard interested creatures ask for her bond several times over the years, she had never been bonded. Sparkle and her mother's wild dragons had seen to that. Valiant couldn't be hers. She was missing something.

Prince Evan was worried that Valiant would take away the magic he carried rendering him useless. He wanted her blood for the bonding spell. Tyler... What was Tyler in all of this for?

"What do you know about the rulers of your kingdom?" Tyler asked her.

Kayla didn't look at him as her thoughts voiced the answer. King Klavian employed the best people in the kingdom. Both of her parents worked for the king. Her mother was the royal dragon tamer and her father was the spellcaster. They had met when Jack rescued Tia from a mountain cliff after Indigo, Pyro's dragon mother, had thrown Tia there. Indigo had since bonded the ware leader Rogan.

Everyone thought Indigo had been born a wild dragon making Rogan the first illegal ware leader ever. It wasn't like that at all. Indigo had been born inside of Gladius's Ware which got her the same criminal record anyway. However, King Klavian didn't mind. Rogan was the king's largest supporting ware leader, and besides, Klavian had married Aria. She wasn't a noble. She was a Colt. King Klavian could easily turn a blind eye to ancient rules that stood in the way of love and friendships, especially if those people would in turn work for him.

Aria had been a school teacher as a Colt, but she had also passed herself off as a noble which is how she met Klavian. She was very good at slipping into unsuspecting roles. Jack had told Kayla that Aria often worked as her own spy for the thrill of it. Kayla believed him. Aria could disguise herself as anything, and with her Colt background, she would find it alluring to trick people. She was informed and stealthy and a powerful force in the king's life.

Prince Tristan had grown up half a Colt and half a dragon rider. The first dragon he had ever ridden was Pyro. Tia had personally trained Tristan into his second year of dragon lessons before he bonded a beautiful bronze dragon and moved his dragon training to the King's Ware. If he wasn't at the castle, the best place to find Tristan was out hunting. He had rooms filled with his animal collections. He had two rooms filled with his bug collection. For some reason, he enjoyed staring at dead animals. It grossed Kayla out. She had viewed his collections before and listened politely as he told her about his favorite specimens. Then she had washed her hands a few times over.

"Can you really not hear anyone tell you that you could rule Aralot?" Tyler asked her before she could think more about the bug collection.

This wasn't working out. She was supposed to be distracting Tyler, not letting him distract her with a lie.

"Rule Aralot? What I can't hear is between me and the person who put the curse on me."

"You heard me?!" Tyler was so excited that he dropped her on the ground grinning. That unfortunately brought back over Prince Evan who didn't look as thrilled with this conversation.

"Vankerdale's curses are rather strong. Perhaps they negate your previous curse or perhaps Valiant took it off you. He was sucking up something when we crossed the border," Tyler continued.

She had felt a bit dizzy, but she didn't want to jump to conclusions like Tyler was doing. This was still all a large lie.

"My parents work for the king. You have the wrong person. Prince Tristan—"

"Tristan is a doormat," Prince Evan said. "He's absolutely nothing."

That was rude. Tristan trained to be the next king of the land. She knew that for a fact. He often bragged about all the lessons he had taken that made him wise and smart and oh so much better than her. He wasn't feeling jealous, was he? No. She was going to discover the lie in this. Maybe what Tyler and Prince Evan were thinking was that her father could magically take over the castle from King Klavian. Since these guys had Jack locked up, they could use the guy to rule both Vankerdale and Aralot. That had to be it.

They were the ones planning the war, and everyone else had been trying to stop it by keeping her out of the way so she wouldn't be used against her dad. She had to get out of here. Her dad could resist a lot of things, but she knew that he loved her. He might give up all of Aralot to keep her safe. She couldn't let that happen! She could keep herself safe.

"We don't have the wrong person," Tyler said. "Your father is the king and your mother is the queen and King Klavian is technically their steward. Aria and Tristan don't have binding legal rights to anything. I just found that out myself. I had never heard of you before. I always thought that Prince Tristan was in line for the crown, but it's you. It makes complete sense if you study history. All of Aralot's past kings were keepers. The kingdom has some strict rules about keepers needing to be on the throne, particularly if they're male. It's set with magic and all that. After Gladius, all the keepers were killed off until your mother came along. She married Jack. so by blood right, Aralot is theirs and yours."

Kayla tried to find the lie in this logic. The more Tyler kept talking, the more she felt that he wasn't lying at all. He sounded certain of his facts. He looked certain too, and Prince Evan's annoyed expression only proved that he didn't think now was the right time to be having a conversation where Tyler revealed that she could be a princess.

It made total sense. One of the first times that words had blurred out on her was when her father had said, "Hello my little..." The word princess could fit into that nicely. So could all the other conversations she had missed over the years with people coming up to talk to her parents. They could have used the word king or queen. Jack and Tia were always out helping King Klavian, but Kayla had thought it was because they had that as their job.

It was their job. It might have been easier for her to have figured this out if her parents had lived in the castle instead of distancing themselves from it, but she knew from her nightmares that they both hated the castle for different reasons. Tia had bad memories of the building from her grandfather Gladius's journal, and Jack had bad memories of Colt friends dying there. They wouldn't want to live in a haunted castle. She could have been getting these nightmares as a subconscious effort from her dad trying to tell her that she could live in the castle. She knew every part of it.

The only thing that wasn't making sense was this keeper rule. If the kingdom was passed along to keepers then Jack couldn't be the king. Jack wasn't a keeper. Her mother was. Therefore, there wasn't a real king of Aralot, and when Kayla married, there still wouldn't be a true king of Aralot. Aralot should really belong to her missing Uncle Conner. He was a keeper and he was descended from Gladius the same as her mother was. Uncle Conner was the closer relation.

Gladius had twin sons. One of them had been Herb Felding and was Kayla's grandfather. The other son was Arvid who had died along with the rest of his family scaring Herb away from dragon wares in his fifth training year. Due to the timing of Conner's birth and his age, speculation would suggest that Uncle Conner was either born from Arvid before he died, or Maslon, Gladius's younger brother, who was also dead. Maslon had been a shoemaker. Why did no one ever talk to Uncle Conner about being the king?

"I don't think you have it right," Kayla said again. "By your reasoning, without a male keeper, there isn't a real king of Aralot."

"No real king?" Prince Evan asked perking up. Kayla shook her head, annoyed with herself for giving him this idea. She should keep her mouth shut! She wasn't allowed to talk about Uncle Conner, and she wasn't going to tell these two greedy magic stealers that there was a king available for this job. Only as it was, Uncle Conner would have a hard time moving King Klavian out of that castle. Maybe that was the war everyone was talking about. There were too many possible wars.

"Jack is the magical binding king of Aralot through magic and paper," Tyler pointed out to Prince Evan. "If he wasn't, your father, King Peyton, would have told you otherwise long ago."

"You're right. Jack signed that binding paper over here and then signed that binding paper in Aralot. You know what this means? We made Jack the king of Aralot. It was Aralots trick to give them the legal authority to smash us down."

Kayla looked at Tyler, shifting as she did so that she could finally get her hands where she wanted them. Surely Tyler wasn't believing this. From what she heard all the time, it was Vankerdale that always tried to come up with tricks against Aralot. Aralot hardly did anything at all to Vankerdale. They had ended one of Gladius's curses for that kingdom and started up trade with them. Aralot helped Vankerdale despite their nasty rulers.

"The first binding document Jack signed was one to open gem trading," Tyler mused. "That made him the king?"

"He wasn't really engaged to Tia at the time, but I believe he already had Aralot's crown," Prince Evan answered.

"Then he was the king if he was already crowned —"

"No one is crowned as the king inside of Aralot. King Gladius figured out that the crown is what was killing off all of the king's wives. Since him, no one puts that crown on their heads. Jack made a fake copy of it for his ceremony. Before him, Herb Felding ruled for fifteen years without touching the crown. They had a cursed spellcaster guarding the thing until Jack took it and hid the item someplace else."

Kayla shifted again as she watched the two men arguing. They could keep it up. This was working out in her favor. She knew where the crown was supposed to be hidden and where the crown actually was. Her father had hidden it inside the cave that led to the magic library portal — the portal she had just used this morning. One of her father's nightmares had been the time he found the crown had gone missing. Kayla never told him she saw that dream, but she had found the crown for him after that.

Vermelo had it. As the Captain of the Guard, it was his job to safeguard the king and, in his opinion, the crown. He had somehow found the hiding place after years of searching and kept the crown inside the castle. When Kayla had told her father that Vermelo had the crown, he had been very relieved that it hadn't gotten lost into evil hands. That was only four years ago.

She was just about there! Kayla felt her fingers brush the edge of her keychain hooked to the belt of her pants, and she stretched her fingers farther feeling her wrists hurt. These ropes were tight! Tyler hadn't made it easy on her to reach anything. Arguing over Aralot was the best distraction these two could give her.

"So Aralot has no legal king that satisfies all of their laws?" Tyler asked. "The only thing keeping them from evaporating back into Vankerdale is the king's magic?"

"It appears to be so," Prince Evan replied. He glanced at her and Kayla drew up the magic into her fingers before she lost her chance. Magic created a blue glow, but she was hoping it would be concealed since her hands were behind her back.

"Once we get magic back, Aralot won't be anything."

Wow, it was always so nice when villains revealed their wicked plans out loud. It wasn't so nice when they discovered that she had plans of her own.

"You!" The prince shouted, and pulled from his pocket a jeweled pen right as Kayla cast her spell to release her hands. She shot two spells out in rapid succession as she jumped to her feet. One was a deflection against anything Prince Evan could cast, and the other was a spell that would bind him stiff so he couldn't continue to move. He didn't get any spell off at all before he was immobilized. Kayla guessed that he didn't have any real-life experience in spell fighting or he might have tried to be quicker.

She turned to Tyler next. He took one look at the prince and held his hands straight up in surrender. He had already admitted that he couldn't cast spells, but Tyler could run off to King Peyton, or even worse

Pg. 120

SilverWings, and bring back something that would have no trouble in spitting out dark magic at her. Kayla cast another spell, but it didn't hit Tyler. He drew in his breath expecting it, but it was stopped by a lurching sucking sound from the left. The dragon!

The MSD-Valiant dragon was closing in. Not wanting to face the beast that could actually take her on, and probably win since his spells were binding and sticky, Kayla ran. If she could get away before Prince Evan was released, that was one less spellcaster coming after her.

"I'll... um... go see if I can catch her?" Kayla heard Tyler say from behind her. She didn't hear the dragon moving, but he would and soon. She kept her ears open waiting for the sound of the dragon casting a spell that let Prince Evan free. It was hard not hearing anything at all but she had to admit that she hadn't heard the dragon cast the spell on the town either. This was a quiet creature. It could get her without her knowing.

Kayla changed up her dash pattern, hearing Tyler grunt behind her as her only indication that there was still anything coming. She ran to the right, fainted to the left. Circled a tree that made Tyler complain when he did the same thing. She jumped over a log and swung from a low branch to get a larger distance. Tyler was falling behind but he was still there.

Kayla dodged a tree and gasped as the MSD-Valiant dragon was suddenly before her. He must have used a spell to make himself ultra-quiet. She should have expected that. She should have done the same thing and added to it a spell to not smell so good to dragons. Even quiet and invisible they could find her by smell. It was too late to think of that now that she was spotted.

Kayla was forced to spot the spellbinding dragon. Her eyes traveled over the animal before she realized what she was doing and her legs kicked up the speed to get away. Even with that short of a look his image was burned into her brain. He looked more like a Valiant than a mopey creature. She had to agree with Tyler on that. Valiant had blue-gray scales. Typical of spellbinding dragons, the tips of his wings were edged in silver that glimmered in the sun. Since he was in the shade, those wings looked dull. The odd part about the dragon was his brown eyes. Such strange eyes. Kayla was used to green and yellow irises on a dragon. Blue was a rare dragon eye color, but she'd never heard of brown. Kayla wondered if Valiant had been born this way or if he had changed his eye color himself.

He wasn't used for breathing out fire or hunting through the dark like night dragons. If he needed to see better in the dark, he could use a spell to achieve the result. The brown made him look more human than other dragons, more trustworthy when the animal could tear her apart faster. That would make for some rather interesting sightsharing.

Valiant hummed at her, and she wasn't sure if it was because he had decided he liked her smell, or he was happy that he had caught her so he could cast spells at her body. Too bad for him. She knew the best shield spell there was, and she used it as she changed up her direction yet again to dash around the dragon. She had to get out of here before that look took her down.

"Don't leave me."

Oh gosh! There was that sadness again pouring through her at such a bad time that her feet stumbled and her legs crashed to the ground so she could have a good long cry. Kayla tried to resist. Fight! Fight! She had to fight it! She was not going to stay here and be used by Vankerdale to destroy all of Aralot. She was better than this. She still hadn't internalized the idea of being a princess, especially hearing that her father wasn't crowned the king, but despite not being legally in charge of the kingdom, she was still going to defend it by escaping.

Except that look was taking its toll. She was on her knees and she could hear Tyler catching up. Still no sound of Prince Evan, but it was

Tyler who had tied her up before, and it was him that would tie her up a second time. Hopefully, he didn't have any more rope.

Then there were those words that had been in her head. Horrible, awful words! Now was not a good time to turn into a keeper like her mother and Aunt Rosa and Uncle Conner. Couldn't she skip that part of her blood and be Brixton completely through instead of part Felding? If she wasn't careful, she would end up with lots of dragons talking directly into her thoughts all the time. It was impossible for keepers to keep out dragon words without being bonded, and she couldn't get bonded. Bonds didn't work inside of Vankerdale.

She was in so much trouble! The act of looking at a new dragon could pull the creature into her thoughts forever! The act of thinking of dragons could do the same thing. Her mother had gained a few dragons simply by knowing them well enough and thinking about them before she was bonded to her first ice dragon Misty.

This was not going to do. Kayla couldn't think back to dragons. She couldn't look at dragons. She was the worst keeper there was. She wasn't even sure if she was a keeper.

"You are the best keeper," the voice contradicted.

Valiant. It had to be Valiant. There was good and bad to this. If he was in her head because he wanted to be, that had to mean that he wasn't going to hurt her bad enough for her to die. However, that wasn't going to stop him from taking her back to Prince Evan and Tyler. She was going to have to fight him.

Could she do that? She was still struggling back to her feet while Tyler caught up. Keepers were supposed to love dragons, not fight them. They were supposed to care for the wounded, clean scales, trim nails, and cure diseases. She never did any of that. In fact, she walked the other way whenever a dragon asked her for help. She was not a keeper. She simply had another annoying mental issue.

Pg. 123

"You are a keeper. You care so much for dragons that it hurts."

"Get out of my head!" Kayla screamed, even if she knew it was impossible. It was too late. She had failed to keep the dragon out. No one should enjoy talking to dragons in their heads. There wasn't anything out there that had the right to know what tormented her the most. The only person that had ever come close to guessing was Caleb. Too bad he wasn't around to help her. He'd save her without her needing to say a single word. She wished that she hadn't let her ire over hand-drawn pictures get in the way of being Caleb's friend. *He* wasn't scared of dragons.

She could remember every single dragon that had ever asked her for help. She knew their names, and if she didn't, it didn't matter. Their names were told to her soon enough. She could see their illness and she knew the cures, but she couldn't help them.

She wasn't going to help Valiant either. His image flashed at her again while Tyler came to a stop beside her. Valiant was so large and tall! He had rows of terrifying teeth, a strong tail that could smash, and penetrating eyes that could see farther than she ever could. He moved, reaching out a massive clawed hand that pulled Tyler toward himself. Kayla's mind jumped through scenarios of Tyler screaming from the cuts those claws placed all along his body. He didn't scream, and she wondered if Valiant had cast out a spell on him to demand silence while he ate the guy.

"I'm not hungry."

Well he might not want to eat, but he could still squish things, and the dragon's other arm was extending next. She had to act! Kayla fumbled for the keychain refusing to go down quietly. This dragon had trapped her before, but it wouldn't do so again. The animal's tail whipped around to act as a scoop, and before she knew what spell to cast, she found herself shoved into the claws of a dragon.

Kayla screamed.

She was too slow! She didn't know anyone else that would be kneeling here frozen before the unfamiliar dragon. Everyone she knew was so much braver. They would have used prongs to turn the beast to their own will. Why didn't she carry prongs?

"You know, his claws aren't sharp at all. He's never used them."

Be quiet, Tyler! She didn't need a distraction from him. She needed to think up a way to get out of the claws. He was correct that Valiant had the dullest claws of any dragon she had ever met. It wasn't from disuse. It was from filing. She could make out the streaks where metal had been pulled across each section turning the nails blunt. That was cruelty to dragons. He couldn't hunt like that. Valiant should cast a spell to fix his claws but only after she got out of them.

"Help!" Kayla screamed.

"I'm trying to help you!" Tyler assured.

Him? Kayla couldn't hold back the snort. He was her enemy. "You're trapped just the same as I am!" she shouted back at him.

Valiant used his back legs to get a running start and jumped into the air slightly premature. Kayla whimpered shutting her eyes as she listened to the sounds of his wings stumble and then drop him back to the ground. He tried again running and beating his wings until she let out a sigh. As if that was his signal that he could rise, he took another leap.

She should not be helping this beast fly. She had to escape! Her parents were legends. She had to know some tricks. She had to know some spells. She was holding magic in her hand. She could cast a spell that would cause the dragon to drop her. Kayla looked down to see how far of a drop it would be and screamed again.

"Do stop shouting. You're attracting attention."

Oh dear, he was right. Valiant had them out of the woods, but he wasn't heading toward the Aralot border. He was heading deeper into Vankerdale. The woods ran up to the side of a field of unkempt grasses that were long and trampled. The trampling had been done by another group of wild dragons, and these ones were not sleeping. Kayla shut her eyes, already hyperventilating as the pressure of her lungs was squeezed out from spotting that many dragons. They could not get into her head! She couldn't look or think about them, but refraining from thought was practically impossible because they were loud and there was nothing wrong with her ears.

"Go away strange ugly one!"

"Do you smell that?"

"My baby can fly better than you!"

"He's got a snack!"

"I don't think he regurgitates."

"That smells good."

"I want to see it."

The pounding feet started up. Then the wings started flapping and they had company. Valiant hissed at them to go away, but they were curious dragons. They weren't going to listen to him. Kayla heard a few of them crash in the air since they were uncoordinated without drills and linked thoughts. They growled at each other and flamed. Tyler screamed this time and Kayla knew why. The heat from the fire was close enough to make human skin bubbly.

Kayla held her breath. It would be horrible if ware dragons in Aralot still flamed each other. Just think of how many more times she could have been killed! She walked past dragons all the time. If she had

Pg. 126

accidentally stepped in the way of a flame session she would have been roasted. Dragons were so scary!

The unruly herd shoved into each other squawking and scrambling, preventing themselves from achieving their goal of reaching her and Tyler. At least she had that to her advantage, but it was only a matter of time before the more aggressive ones turned to fight each other and the more patient ones had room to get close.

That moment came too soon. The flame grew stronger along with the snarls to get out of the way. Then the dragons were upon each other fighting. Valiant tried to rise, but that put him near the top with the patient dragons.

"You are beautiful."

No, no, no. She wasn't. The voice was that of a light green dragon. Kayla didn't even need to look at it to know. Wait! She couldn't think of the dragon. That would be disastrous. If she was lucky, the animal was talking about Tyler instead of her. If she was extra lucky, the green animal was talking to Valiant. A burst of flame got too close again shooting heat right into Valiant's face and all across Kayla's body. Too close!

Valiant swooped downward, but since she wasn't used to his flying style, and he made no warning sounds before dropping, the pressure had Kayla slipping from the blunted claws. She couldn't help but scream as she was forced to open her eyes to find leverage to stay inside the daggered cage. Her hands grabbed at the talons pulling her back to a safer position, but these dragons were tricky. The green dragon swooped downward noticing her open eyes and chirped out hello.

Kayla tried to not look at it. She tried to avoid the sight of its luminescent yellow eyes. She failed and her brain betrayed her. The light green dragon was beautiful too. He had a really pretty pale color although he could use help with the moss on the underside of his tail. In fact, if she was to pick a name for the dragon, she'd call him Reed.

"Back off!" Valiant shouted, hissing and sputtering as if he was a baby and didn't know how to use his flame yet. Silly spell dragon. He had to use a flame spell if he wanted to get heat. Reed hissed back and then laughed. He flicked Valiant playfully with his tail on his belly. Valiant sucked in his breath as if he was going to charge up flame again and then shook his head catching the message from Reed. He had to shoot out spells to defend himself, and for that, he had to use the magic in his stomach that he had sucked up from charging through the border.

It was hard to decide if Reed was helping them or simply clearing away more space for himself when he turned on the closest dragon and started flame attacks to keep everyone away from Valiant. Reed at least knew what he was doing. His swooping was effective. Tyler tried to help by mimicking a few defensive dragon sounds he must have heard before. It made Kayla wonder how often humans in Vankerdale resorted to dragon speech in order to communicate. It was unusual for that to happen in Aralot.

Valiant turned grumpy, and his frustration found itself inside of Kayla's head.

"Humans in Aralot use hand signals. That won't work on these lawless fiends. They only care for themselves and don't consider the toll of trying to talk to you from another kingdom. You thought your mother was good at hearing the creatures, but she's nothing compared to you. You should stay quiet!"

He couldn't know what she thought about her mother! She wouldn't allow it! Her thoughts were her own. They were personal, especially since there were lots of them that verged on resentment. She loved her mom, but she hated being spied on all the time and not trusted. To avoid thinking too much about her mom, and all her mother's dragons, Kayla tried to shut her brain down turning back to her ears.

Two other dragons had started to attack the light green one and all three were now falling behind. Valiant decided to use a spell finally. He picked up his speed, blasting her and Tyler through the clouds until Valiant started panting heavily. Kayla wondered how often Valiant participated in chases. He should be able to fly longer given his age.

The dragon turned shaky. He faltered and they started going down. Kayla tried to not scream again, but she couldn't help it. Dragon's landed by using their feet and claws. The dragon was going to land right on top of her and squish her flatter than an eggshell.

"Am not. I'm going to drop you."

That didn't make her feel any better, but at least she had some warning. When the claws started to separate, she dropped and rolled, jumping to her feet long before Tyler who plumped into the ground with a huff.

"I can't believe I just rode a dragon!" Tyler cheered, spreading his hands and legs out against the ground. He was insane. He was giving Valiant a wider area of his body to squish.

Kayla wasn't going to join the madman. While she had the chance, she scanned the area trying to get her bearings. They had landed in one of those large overgrown grassy fields. By her reasoning, she was a good thirty miles or more from the Aralot border. She needed to head west to go home.

"You did not ride the dragon," Kayla replied to Tyler as he stood up. Kayla kept her ears open trying to hear when Valiant was going to land. "You were kidnapped by him."

"Don't spoil it," Tyler replied. "Since it's just the two of us, let's start over. I'm Tyler Valeron. I am indentured to Prince Evan for the time being, but I'm almost free of him."

Indentured servitude. Vankerdale was seriously the worst place ever. She was so glad that she didn't live here and have to deal with people who were forced to be loyal. Loyalty never should be taken. It had to be earned.

"I promised Valiant that I would help him. That included finding you."

"Congratulations," Kayla said dryly. She turned toward the west and got started on her goal of getting back home. She had to move quickly before the wild dragons found her again. It would be nice if Sparkle was here. Her mother's dragon would defend her against an attack and so would her Aunt Rosa's dragon named Pewter.

It came as no surprise that apart from adoring her mother's dragon Sparkle, she loved her Aunt Rosa's dragon Pewter, even if she ignored them like she did all dragons and pretended to hate them. Pewter was the first dragon that Kayla had ever touched on her own. He was the last one she had ever touched too. Touching him had made her feel so sad. She couldn't ever figure out why.

"You were missing me of course!"

Kayla grimaced at the unwelcome thought in her head. She didn't miss dragons. She didn't have her own dragon. If she did, it would have talked to her a long time ago.

"As if! Your mother has been trying to hunt me down for years! She can be scary. Besides, your brain had to be more developed before you could sustain conversation like this."

"Someone help me," Kayla whimpered.

"I am trying to help you," Tyler answered, trotting along behind her like a stalker. He stopped short of her knife hand and looked around the grassy field when Kayla pulled the knife from her bag to warn him away. She started to back away from him again. Perhaps he was used to following people around being indentured, but he was going to learn soon enough that she didn't want the company. She had no idea who

Pg. 130

Tyler was at all.

"Tyler is a helpful friend who freed me. He reads books for Prince Evan."

"Uh." Tyler held out his hands but it was already too late. She had walked backward right into the face of the mysterious blue-gray dragon with shimmering wingtips. Kayla froze in fear. Valiant hadn't made a sound when he landed! The cheater! She had been listening. So if Valiant hadn't landed what if it wasn't really him. It could be a different dragon that had been sleeping in this field that they had awoken. Kayla instantly imagined the worst—a black-scaled beast angry at being woken during the day. It would have blood-red eyes, sixty tail spikes, extremely sharpened claws, and it could shoot lightning.

"Fascinating. Tia told you the story of the fake lightning dragon when you were two. She doesn't like lightning dragons."

"Get out of my head!" Kayla screamed.

There was no way Valiant could know her timeline like this. Dragons couldn't search through past thoughts. They had to be satisfied with the present ones. Kayla knew what her mother was scared about. Tia often relived nightmares with Misty dying, or Tia being turned into a ghost. The ghost dreams inside Gladius's old castle were bad. Her mother would walk through things with one desire—to touch again. Tia was trapped in a body that couldn't communicate with anyone. It was like she was... well dead, which is what her mother had been at the time. It was horrible feeling partly alive understanding what was happening but not being able to interact with it. She was a shell with no meaning. However, Kayla couldn't remember what her mother had told her when she was two. This was creepy. Her weird dreams were leaking into her reality and they kept getting stranger.

"You don't want a dragon in your head?" Tyler asked mystified. "Everyone wants a dragon in their head. I wish I could hear it. What's it like?"

"Horrible," Kayla shivered. She wasn't a keeper. She had a dragonphobia.

"The first thought I ever heard from you clearly was you telling yourself that dragons were scheming ferocious creatures you could never trust. I've been quiet ever since, even if I suspect that you do like dragons. I had plans to ask you one of your homework questions when were deep in thought so that you'd ramble off the answer and start talking to me when you were not scared. I never did it. I guess I was too afraid that you wouldn't like me. Please like me."

Tyler decided that her knife wouldn't do anything to hurt him and took a gutsy step closer to her. She glared at him.

"Unbonded people who hear dragons go crazy," Kayla answered him because answering the dragon was too difficult. "My granduncle Maslon never had a bonded dragon. His journal is full of random tidbits of dragon thought that made no sense and turned him insane."

"You're already bonded," Tyler told her, looking downcast. "Sure the bond is not exactly active in Vankerdale so the dragon will have to bite you again, but you're a keeper so a broken bond doesn't stop you from hearing dragon thoughts. I'm not an expert on keepers so I have no idea if you'll go crazy, but it can't be that bad if you did have a bond."

"You won't go crazy. I can help prevent other dragons from sending you thoughts now that we're together again."

Kayla shook her head disbelieving. He couldn't. If Valiant blocked dragon thoughts for her that would mean he was her gatekeeper dragon. For that to be possible they would have bonded in Aralot sometime in her past as Tyler had suggested. If she was bonded, she would have a fang wound…

Kayla glanced down at her leg catching her breath. That's what her father had figured out! She had one deep indentation beneath all the knife slashes. It wasn't that her mother had refused other people holding her as a baby because she was scared of losing Kayla. Tia held her until the fang wound on Kayla's leg healed over enough so she could deform the mark and pretend that Kayla didn't have a bonded dragon!

Her mother was horrible! She could have said something! She could have told Kayla the other day in the kitchen what the marks on her leg were for. They were there to hide the truth until Kayla started hearing a particular voice in her head—the voice of Valiant. Her mother had been lying to all of them for the last sixteen years! No wonder her father had turned up missing. He had to be in Vankerdale. He was searching for Valiant only he wouldn't know what sort of dragon he was looking for. He had come to save his daughter from the dragon in her head, and in doing so, he had fallen into Vankerdale's trap. Her father wouldn't be able to communicate with Pyro now that they were here.

"Where's my dad?" Kayla demanded of Tyler. If the man was really trying to help, he could help with that.

Tyler shrugged. "I think he was locked up in the castle dungeon, but he escaped. As far as I know, we've not found him yet. He's out here somewhere."

Lost. Kayla could find lost people and dragons. She scanned the area, glad that Valiant was behind her so she wouldn't have to see him. At least he understood that looking at dragons made her weak. Kayla tried to decide where both Jack and Pyro would go first. They would go where they expected the other one to be hiding and waiting. She didn't know the area well enough to plot out its crooks and crannies, but Tyler could know.

"We're going to find my dad."

"Okay," Tyler agreed, looking around shortly before picking a direction that was not west.

"Just agree with everything I say," Kayla remarked, finding it strange that anyone would do that. She was used to Colts questioning hidden meanings behind everything. Not this.

"And I was told that people in Aralot were not rude," Tyler snapped at her. "You're not in charge of me. I'm here to help Valiant or whatever his name is. You're his rider. I've always wanted to know his name. What is it?"

Kayla felt herself frowning. She resisted naming dragons, but in this case, she probably didn't have a choice. She took half a glance at the face of the dragon waiting behind her and shrugged.

"Valiant."

"I wish you would tell me. I really want to help you!" Tyler insisted.

"I'm not lying. Some names are just right."

"I got his name right!" Tyler sounded far too excited about this. Kayla rolled her eyes.

"That's remarkable! I could be good with dragons! One day a dragon will decide to love me. I always thought that if I could break Valiant out that he could be my dragon. I probably shouldn't say that and turn you jealous or anything. Don't hurt me."

She did not feel jealous. She didn't feel much of anything even if Valiant sent a short burst of warm air in Tyler's direction. Valiant did seem to like him, or at least the idea that Tyler wanted to break Valiant out of things. What had Tyler broken him out of?

"To avoid my avid jealously, I think you should lead me to places man and dragon can hide. Where might my dad and his dragon end up?"

"Right this way," Tyler directed with half a bow.

Kayla didn't step after him as he started to walk. He could lead her right into the hands of King Peyton, and she would have no idea where she was going. She only moved when Valiant did. He backed up so his nose wasn't pressed into her back anymore and started after Tyler. If the dragon thought Tyler was alright, maybe he was. Grr. She was trusting the opinion of a dragon. Gross.

Treason

Tristan

Tristan had spent two full minutes looking at the portal that led to the magic library where his father was trying to find a spell to get around both Vankerdale and spell-bound curses before he had walked away. Only heirs to the kingdom could get into that magical library. King Klavian made it inside since his father had ruled with the crown that killed King Virgil Cluster IV's wife. Jack and Tia made it into there because they were the heirs by Felding blood and marriage. Prince Tristan made it into there on the back of that same stretched heritage, but it was hard for him to linger in the room. Whenever he was in that library, his breath felt squished out of him like a spell was telling him that he didn't really belong. Tristan had never told anyone. He went in there only when he had to, and since he didn't expect his father to find anything new on an ancient search, he had turned away from the portal and went back to the castle.

Despite his earlier resentment over Ritz's words, Tristan had to admit that Ritz usually knew what he was talking about. If he claimed that Jack had gotten out of a dungeon, then Ritz had probably heard the information from a spy that had come over from Vankerdale to tell him this. Ritz heard things way too fast.

That part about Jack being in Vankerdale for a specific reason had to be correct. Jack had blocked people from easy travel between the two locations. He wouldn't go into Vankerdale without a pressing need. Tristan wanted to know what Jack was trying to find, and the best person to ask that was Anvil. Anvil wouldn't tell Tristan unless Tristan had him under a spell, so Tristan was back in his room to change out of his princely garb into his rider leather.

He had to think really hard about casting spells on Anvil. Jack had given that man magical protection just as he had given magic to all the ware leaders so that the job of ware leader became even more coveted. It made it a lot harder for Tristan to come up with how to use a spell on Anvil to get him talking too. Maybe if he claimed to know where Kayla was, Anvil would trade the information about what Jack was after. Anvil would do anything for Kayla.

Tristan moved to his dresser and brushed his light brown hair out of eyes while he examined his sideburns in the mirror. His image did nothing to make him cheerful, not when he realized that the Colts had been right about him. He was getting shaggy and needed a haircut. He usually used the barber in town, but the entire place was frozen trapped in their failure to realize that Kayla was being taken away by a spellbinding dragon.

Tristan pulled open his armoire and jerked backward as twenty knives flew out of it from a previously set rig. The knives smashed against Tristan's magical protective shield, causing his heart to pound against his rib cage so fast it nearly pushed itself out.

"Are you hurt?!" Riven screamed at Tristan, causing him to rock backward on his feet slightly thrown off balance. If it wasn't for the screaming dragon in his head, he wouldn't have moved at all.

"Fine," Tristan replied, keeping most of his annoyance to himself even if Riven could hear it all anyway. This had Vermelo written all over it again. His threats to Tristan were getting worse. Tristan should have

expected it after he had called Kayla reclusive and the worst Colt there ever was. It didn't take much effort to see that Tristan had never liked the girl, or that Vermelo really did. Tristan needed to safeguard his room better. He cleared out the trap and cast a few protective spells on his closet and bed so that they wouldn't surprise him again. Then he grabbed his rider clothes and was halfway into his pants when he heard voices in the hallway that made him hurry up.

He had picked his room strategically. For one, his room had a window with a view toward the town, monastery, and dragon ware. That alone was a blessing, but his location was even better than that. His was the room closest to the conference room that Vermelo used. Anyone that headed toward secret meetings with the man could be heard from Tristan's room. Anyone looking to start a meeting with the Captain of the Guard would be heard too, and that was what Tristan was hearing right now.

"I can't believe that you're still defending him. Well, I can believe it, but seriously," Rosa Felding complained. "I've always thought that you made a good queen. Vermelo needs to stop sending letters asking me to take over. I'm never going to do it, and I certainly am never going to show those to Clark. It's putting a dampener in my marriage to keep secrets from him."

Vermelo was doing what now? Tristan shoved on his boots and jumped to his door so he could listen closer. It sounded like this was a repeated offense of Vermelo trying to dethrone Tia and Jack. Remarkable! Vermelo loved them. What was he thinking in aggravating Rosa and Clark? If Tristan was the king, Tristan would have Vermelo hanged for his betrayal. Unfortunately, he wasn't the king and no one could call for Vermelo's death except for Jack. He wasn't here. Surprise. Surprise.

"You know he only sends those when he wants to talk about something else. He doesn't mean it, Rosa," Tia responded.

"I wish I had permission to punch him, because I'm with Rosa on this. These have got to stop."

Ah, that was Anvil's voice. If he was here this fast then he had taken a portal. Anvil wasn't immune to portals. For him to go through one meant that he subjected himself to feeling fit to die for a full hour while he writhed on the ground waiting for the effects to wear off. He would have eaten a walnut to cut that time down so he didn't have to experience deathly torture for three hours instead of the one. The pain was enough to make any man never want to touch a portal when they shouldn't fly through them. Anvil hated portals, but he would brave the sensation at times if he felt the situation was serious.

Tristan wouldn't be able to find Anvil if he ventured over to the man's ware because Anvil had come here. That was ruining Tristan's plans. There was no way he could get away with using a spell on Anvil with Tia and Rosa both in the room. He'd have to think of something else while he continued to eavesdrop on this conversation. It sounded highly important, and with King Klavian inside the secret magical library, Tristan could picture Tia and Vermelo making large kingdom-wide plans without Klavian's approval. Tristan was going to stick around to tell his father what was happening.

"He's harmless," Tia tried again.

"You call this harmless?" Anvil asked, nearly shouting. "While designated rulers, Tia and Jack do not fulfill the requirements of the land. Written law was changed to allow Jack and Tia to marry outside of the bounds of noble blood, but magical law has never been changed to reflect the same thing. The Brixton bloodline will never be considered fully noble. The Cluster bloodline is a much closer fit, making Rosa and Clark better suited to rule this kingdom. You cannot put your hope in Kayla Brixton for your future. Aralot has other plans for the girl. Take your rightful place, Rosa," Anvil concluded with a huff.

"I wish he would leave Kayla out of this too, but—"

"Gosh, this is not about Kayla!" Rosa screamed at her sister. "This is about me. Vermelo needs to stop!"

"This is about Kayla," Tia stated, sounding hard and commanding. "You don't hear it because you're so stuck in your own fears."

"You take that back!"

"Ladies!" Anvil intervened. "Must you fight over this with each other? The person you need to argue with is Vermelo."

Tia let out a loud sigh. "I like Vermelo, but all this talk of taking Kayla away from what should be hers is driving me crazy. I'm telling you, Rosa, that this is not about you. Vermelo is freaking out because Kayla was kidnapped into Vankerdale. He didn't want to put that in a letter so he picked the next best thing that would rile us all to come storm the castle."

"Kayla's what?" Anvil asked, sounding punched in the gut.

"You didn't tell us until right now?" Rosa asked, sounding angry instead of wounded like Anvil did.

Tristan risked opening up his bedroom door. The three of them had come to a stop standing in the hallway beside the conference room waiting for Vermelo to arrive. Anvil looked as punched as he sounded. His face was white as he worried over the safety of his favorite child. Kayla wasn't really Anvil's child, but he treated her like she was. Some would say that he loved her more than his real kids. He was tall and lean and wore the magical earring that Tristan would like to see go away. Tia, by contrast, looked perfectly fine that she was missing her daughter. Rosa, as blond as her older sister, looked a little sick.

It was Rosa that first spotted Tristan. She gave him a pitying look as if Tristan was supposed to be heartbroken over the news that Kayla was away from him. Perhaps he should play that part, but he really didn't want to. He still had no desire to date the shadow. In all his years of knowing Kayla, she had never once been anything more to him than an obstacle.

Tristan stepped fully into the hallway as Vermelo rounded the corner with a smile on his face and his hands extended outward in open invitation.

"Pleasure to see you all. Did my helpful letter spur you into taking action against Vankerdale?" Vermelo asked.

"No!" Tia snapped, while Rosa demanded that Vermelo explain himself.

"It's clearly obvious. Tia won't do anything against Vankerdale, and since that is the case, Rosa needs to step up to do what Tia can't. You've been avoiding fighting with Vankerdale for over a decade! Something has got to jolt you to realize that it needs to be done."

Now that Vermelo had started talking, he really had fully explained himself. Vermelo was ready to stand behind Rosa taking over the kingdom so that he could get Kayla back. It was astonishing how many people loved that girl and what things they would break apart to reach her. Vermelo was willing to take down the legal king and queen. Tia was right. Vermelo's letter had been about the missing princess. His threat was treason.

Tristan dashed into the conference room with his boots echoing off the stone floor as Vermelo let the others inside. Vermelo gave Tristan a nasty glare, but he couldn't throw knives at him when Tia was around. She wouldn't stand for it. Tristan returned the glare with a knowing smile. He was staying in the room even if he had heard arguments about why they shouldn't go into Vankerdale before. There was always one new thing to learn by hearing them again. Maybe there would be two. It was new to Tristan how far Vermelo would bend for Kayla.

"We can't send dragons into Vankerdale," Tia told Vermelo. "Their bonds will be broken. All our riders will be rendered useless as soon as they cross the border, and they won't be able to fight anything. If you insist on attacking, you'll have to use foot soldiers, which is also rather useless since they are not as strong as our rider teams and Vankerdale will be using dragons."

"You can take the curse off the land so our dragons don't lose their bonds," Vermelo advised.

Tia shook her head. "If I did then we're really asking for a war right now. Don't you think Kayla is smart enough to handle her own kidnapping?"

"No," Vermelo answered.

"Rubbish," Anvil countered. "Kayla is a strong person."

"Unless they put a dragon in front of her face," Rosa sighed. "They'd use SilverWings. Even Jack has trouble matching SilverWings. We should get Kayla back."

"You are not to listen to him," Tia told her sister, trying to stay in charge of the room because to lose to Rosa would mean that she lost her position as queen. "Vermelo doesn't know as much as you think he does. We don't need to send people over for Kayla."

Tia gave Tristan a "sorry" look next, so he made sure that he reflected a remorseful expression over losing Kayla this time. He had to keep up his front with that woman. Tia and Kayla were his worst threats with their blood heritage and dragon problems. Tristan spent a lot of time in the Desert Ware where neither one went. The only person who fretted about the desert was Rogan, but King Klavian had a habit of disagreeing with Rogan about the desert, so Tristan got away with his secrets. If the Brixtons came to dethrone Tristan, he was ready. He had been storing magic up from Bantin inside the desert. All it took was using the ice dragon's real name and the creature would give him glowing magic orbs. It was easy. For everyone else, even Jack, getting magic from Mr. Grumpy was a struggle.

Once Jack wasn't the driving force of magic in the land, Tristan could take on being the spellcaster, and settle all those magical laws that didn't work for Jack. Hopefully. Tristan would need to do a bit more research into what the magical problems even were before he was ready to face Jack. He hadn't changed his mind that right now, everyone needed the rider Colt. Jack took care of magic and Tia took care of the wares. King Klavian was too busy discussing trade laws and funding upkeep to realize that he always forgot to focus on dragons. Just as Klavian feared, dragons would be his downfall if Vermelo got his way and caused a war. Tristan was making sure that dragons wouldn't be his personal downfall as well. He had bonded one.

"We do need to save Kayla," Vermelo insisted. "When I first stood behind you, Jack had the crown. I thought he would be able to satisfy certain forces inside of Aralot, but it's been sixteen years and they are only getting worse."

Tristan felt his blood start churning faster. Vermelo was serious. He wanted to kick Tia and Jack off the throne! At the moment, that would only make Tristan's own life harder. Jack held certain forces back like that demon ultra-dragon king. Herb Felding had been researching how to make an ultra-dragon king to take over the kingdom, and when the man died, his infected dragons were left unchecked and alive.

Normally infected keeper dragons were hunted down and killed. Tristan had ended a few of those infected dragons himself, but only after discovering that they had continued Herb's work and hatched that dragon. Demon tore through everything he fancied, from wares to villages. From wild dragons to sleeping deer. Demon's talons had slashed them all. Jack had spells to keep the dragon out of certain locations, and Tristan hadn't looked into those to learn how to copy them yet.

Why was Vermelo acting like Jack was already dead? They would know if Jack had died. Tia would have told everyone already... or maybe not. Tia might be telling everyone that Jack was fine because she didn't want to lose her place as queen. This conversation was raising too many questions. Was Jack even still alive? Why did Tia not want to defend her own daughter?

"Jack has been missing for three months. We both know that he's in Vankerdale, and we both know what that means, Tia," Vermelo said, ruining Tristan's idea that Jack was already dead. "He is incapable of stopping the force that truly plagues us. What Aralot needs is Rosa and Clark to take the crown—"

"Tia and Jack are the rulers of Aralot," Anvil burst. "If you keep up with your treason—"

"It doesn't matter that Jack is not noble," Tia cut off Anvil instead of letting him carry out his rage.

Tristan was agreeing with Anvil. Vermelo turning against the king he usually favored would only spell horrible trouble for the rest of them. Vermelo needed to be stopped. It was a shame that Tia never learned from all her past lessons. She forgave people who tormented her too easily. This was going to slap her in the face.

Tristan looked at the closest guard in the room. They normally stood around impassionate and bored. Vermelo always had a few milling about the conference room, and they had been there when Tristan and the others had stepped inside. The guards today were looking back at him just as nervous as Tristan felt. It made him wonder if the guards were fidgeting because they already knew of Vermelo's shift in loyalty or because this was their first time hearing their commander's evilness too. This was the worst coup Tristan had ever heard of. Tristan wasn't looking forward to bringing this up with his father. King Klavian would sound off about it for months.

"I am doing what is best for the future of Aralot," Vermelo replied. "Crowning Clark would take a lot of pressure off of Kayla."

"She's fine!" Tia burst.

"She was taken away by a spellbinding dragon into Vankerdale. The girl is not fine."

"Yes, she is," Tia argued.

Anvil started to sputter, but Vermelo and Tia were not done having it out against each other.

"This is the worst thing that could have happened. Kayla knows absolutely nothing about what she is. No one has been able to take that curse off her. We have to consider that Kayla will never be able to hear about her lineage. She won't be able to rule a kingdom that she can't hear about. In her current state, she's not fit to rule Aralot. It needs to be given to someone else. I'm not talking about you." Vermelo glared at Tristan.

"Didn't think you were," Tristan shrugged, even if he wanted to toss Vermelo out a window already. This was very confusing. Vermelo was against Jack and Tia. He was against Kayla ruling although he wanted her back home. It sounded like he was trying to put Rosa and Clark on the throne even if they didn't have an heir. Vermelo was leading them all in circles trying to protect Kayla from what?

Tristan gave Vermelo a short smile. Him probably. Vermelo didn't want Kayla to be married off to Klavian's son. He didn't want Tristan cursing the girl. It was just like Vermelo to think ahead of everyone and try to save Kayla from being cursed to death on her wedding night. If Tristan didn't know that Vermelo wanted Kayla back where he could see her, Tristan would have wondered if Vermelo was in league with Vankerdale to capture Kayla away from him in the first

Pg. 146

place.

"Crowning Clark is not helping Kayla any. We'll find some way around this so Kayla can lead. We always do," Tia argued.

"We'll mount an invasion to get Kayla back," Anvil spoke up. It sounded like he had already passed over the Rosa, Clark, and crown thing now that he had heard about where Kayla was. "I can have men here in three days. Between the three of us, we can get them into Vankerdale past Jack's spells."

"I'm telling you that Kayla is fine." Tia ground her teeth. "We are not sending dragons into Vankerdale to break their bonds. Not everyone is like Jack and can live with that. *Jack* can hardly live like that. Breaking dragon bonds is cruel."

"And yet we keep that spell up against Vankerdale," Vermelo complained.

"Yes, we do. You can't make me take that spell down. Not for anything."

"I am not leaving Kayla out there on her own!" Anvil screamed.

"She's not helpless, Anvil," Tia reminded.

"She was taken by a dragon. Perhaps you haven't noticed her ability with dragons. She won't stand a chance regardless of the number of spells you've taught her. That girl still trembles when dragons get too close," Rosa cut back in.

"I won't argue about this all day," Tia declared. "I understand that the both of you spend way too much time worrying about Kayla's abilities, but she has it covered. We won't mount an invasion to bring her back. We have to consider the toll this would take on our dragons. I am not injuring all our dragons leaving them with broken heads."

"And I understand that you're a keeper and feel compelled to protect dragons from anything, but you're also this girl's mother!" Anvil screamed. "You have to consider *her* safety."

"Don't you dare treat me like I haven't thought this through." Tia's voice wasn't forceful anymore, but strained as if she was holding back a fountain of tears. "Kayla is the future of Aralot."

"She won't be for long," Vermelo muttered under his breath. Tristan rolled his eyes as Vermelo cast him a furtive glance. Tristan had never hurt her—yet.

"Her current safety is a little strained, but I assure you that she is in good health and well. She will get herself through this. Her father has to be close by. There is no point in sending anyone else into Vankerdale which will harm dragons. It will be pointless to torture them like this. Jack and Kayla will find each other."

Ouch. Tristan shook his head. That was the calling of a keeper. Tia would strand her own daughter, subject her to death and worse, in favor of caring for dragons. That had to strain the relationship between mother and daughter. Tristan wondered if Kayla realized how little her own mother cared for her.

"I cannot accept that answer," Anvil replied, now sounding like he was starting to cry too. "You might have decided that you can live brokenhearted, but I can't. Not a second time. I already lost you. I'm not losing her too. I'll go over there myself."

"No, you won't."

"I love that girl!" Anvil screamed, as his tears started to trickle out. He wiped them away. Tristan leaned his head against the wall. What was there to love about Kayla? He'd loved bugs more than her.

"I love her too. She has to do this on her own. She has to find her own feet," Tia stated.

"The princess of Aralot is kidnapped!" Anvil stomped his boots hard into the ground after saying this as if that would make Tia change her mind. It was amusing how the ware leader threw fits. Anvil had always been one of those young at heart people. He was great at keeping the younger crowd cooperative, but sometimes he picked up a few of their whiney habits.

"Promise me that Jack is still alive," Tristan spoke, so they could return to that instead of this Kayla issue. It was a vague memory, but Tristan felt like he had read before that if the king of Aralot died outside of the kingdom, some horrible spells would activate. Ancient curses were the last thing they needed. Jack had been taking strange magical spells like that down, but Tristan would rather not find out if he had destroyed that one.

"Pyro promises that Jack is alive and that he's out looking for him. They will be reunited soon and Kayla will probably be found sooner. Vankerdale's dragons will be talking about her. We all know how dragons get when she's around. Finding her will be easy. There is nothing to worry about."

That seemed to calm down the moods in the room a little too well. Anvil wiped at his face and wrapped his arms around Tia. If only it was that easy to make everyone change sides, Tristan would have everyone deciding that he was the better choice to rule Aralot. That would take all the stress off Kayla that Vermelo was concerned about.

Tia let her head rest against Anvil's chest while Anvil closed his eyes like he was dying. He probably was. He had never stopped loving the woman in his arms even though they both married other people. Most of the time Anvil was able to pull off that he and Tia were really good friends. Tristan had heard about Anvil's earlier flirtations, but he'd never seen the man get personal. With Jack gone, all sorts of things were slipping. His wife was hugging an old lover, and his Captain of the Guard was trying to dethrone him. Tristan made a note to himself to never be gone for three months.

"There's a younger audience present if you don't mind," Tristan said. Anvil didn't budge, but Tia got the hint. She wiggled her way out of Anvil's arms to face Tristan, looking slightly guilty. Yeah, well, she was guilty. She was the one choosing Jack over Anvil. She shouldn't be in Anvil's arms like that.

"Where would you look for how to break a binding spell?" Tia asked Tristan, as if he could help the trapped town nearby.

"What do you think?" Tristan asked his dragon.

"I think that if I wanted to find a way to break a binding spell, I would ask a spellbinding dragon."

"We can't do that. King Peyton will demand something huge from us if we ask to borrow SilverWings. He's been looking for a way to get us in his debt. Looks like he found it, so we can't give in."

"There are two spellbinding dragons," Riven reminded.

"I'll go look into it," Tristan replied to Tia as he headed out of the conference room. He was done watching this. He didn't think that they were going to say anything else important. If they started talking again, it would only spiral back to their same points. Tia wanted to preserve dragon bonds regardless of what it did to her family. Rosa and Anvil wanted to charge Vankerdale. Vermelo wanted Tristan dead, and if he couldn't kill him, he was going to do his best to keep Kayla safely out of Tristan's reach. It was all so typical that Tristan had to shake his head.

Unbonded

Kayla

Kayla knew that everyone had a hidden agenda. Tyler, the indentured servant, wasn't taking her to King Peyton as she had thought at first, but his chosen location was equally nasty.

"I asked you to show me where my dad might go to hide," Kayla said stopping a good distance away from the wild dragon herd that she had just started to hear. They, of course, would have heard and smelled her coming long before now. Valiant hadn't done anything to tell her what she was approaching, even though he would have known. She almost sent him a scathing look because he was being so quiet. Then again, he was probably quiet because she had spent a good amount of time thinking about how much she hated creatures talking into her head. Now she was sounding bipolar both wanting and not wanting the thoughts to come. Warning thoughts could be nice though. What about a warning sound or even dragon speech? Valiant could have verbally told her that they were headed toward a herd of dragons and she would have understood him.

"You asked to be taken to where your dad's dragon is."

Tyler pointed in the direction of the herd. Kayla took a step back. Somehow, Tyler was missing that she wasn't a dragon fanatic even after that comment she had shared with him that she didn't like the dragon in her head.

"Pyro is not there." She could already tell. If he was there, he would have hooted at her by now. Besides, he wouldn't join up with any wild group in Vankerdale. He'd go solo, probably turning himself invisible to the naked eye and scourging the far corners of the kingdom as a secret spy.

"I need to find hiding places like valleys and gullies and caves. That sort of thing. That's what I asked you to show me. I don't know the landscape."

"Has anyone ever told you that when you're lost in a large area the best thing to do is stand still?" Tyler asked with a grin. She didn't return his sudden humor because that was the last thing she needed to do. Standing still would allow King Peyton to find her.

"Kayla, you're a keeper," Tyler shook his head at her like she should have accepted this already. Maybe he would like to trade heads or perhaps blood types. "Valiant didn't tell me how many dragons you have, but the thing you are good at is talking to dragons. All you have to do is go over there and ask the dragons if they have seen King Jack and King Pyro. You probably won't even have to bribe them for the answers. I read that dragons love interacting with keepers."

Ugh. This was the worst thing ever to be walking around with a book reading guy who loved dragons and didn't understand her past history. If she was with anybody else from Aralot they would have never suggested this to her.

"This is your grand moment. Go over there and build up an army to take on King Peyton. Then he can't kidnap you anymore. While you're at it, you can put in a good word with the dragons to like me."

Kayla grabbed the edge of her hood and pulled it further down over her face even if it was really hot in the middle of summer. Her answer was no. Tyler was a rather bad servant telling the enemy to build up an army against his king. He probably saw himself as helping her escape so that Valiant could be free, but he stated his alternative goals rather clearly. He wanted her to get him a dragon. That was never going to happen. She couldn't even look at the animals. Tyler was going to have to find someone else to help him achieve his dragon dreams. Dragons weren't that great. They interrupted thoughts and stood around asking for things like sheep and hours of labor to make their scales shiny.

"If I have the right spell, I would shrink for you. Then you could clean my scales in ten minutes with a simple brush of your hand and not complain so much."

See? Valiant was proving her point right there, although, in his favor, he was trying his best to stay quiet and out of her way. Kayla was trying to not admit that she felt rather bad about that. She had a dragon that was scared to talk to her because she was mean to him. She wasn't Gladius-type mean who tortured his dragons physically and mentally, but she was still causing Valiant pain.

"We have a broken bond. I don't blame you, Kayla. Your ambivalent feelings are justified."

This was not justified. It was an excuse he had told himself over and over because she wasn't a nice person. She couldn't keep friends. She couldn't keep dragons. She couldn't keep herself put together. Her eyes were tearing up. Kayla pulled at the hood again and looked around trying to spot a place to go to ignore the thoughts in her head.

"I have learned that no one can outrun themselves. The inner self has to be confronted."

"Yes, but on my own," Kayla snapped.

Behind her, Valiant whimpered. While not privy to the conversation, Tyler was still adding to it.

"Valiant would love to go with you. He's been locked away inside the same room for the last sixteen years with his only sanity being the thoughts in your head and sparse visitors. He got so large that he couldn't fit through the door that he was brought inside as a baby. Whenever I saw him, he had his eyes closed and laid around being lethargic, just waiting for you to come save him. We had to blast part of the castle open to get him out. He was blinking like he had never seen the sun before."

Well, now she knew where Valiant had been, and why he seemed to know things from when she was two. He had been with her through it all. That was a cruel way to live through the eyes of someone else that never wanted to look at you.

"I am not getting a dragon army," Kayla declared, trying and failing to not think like a Colt right now. They would try to see everything from all perspectives. She did not want to empathize with Tyler as he tried to solve dragon problems by using more dragons. Feeling sorry for Valiant was just as bad. His wings had to be aching from not flying for his entire life.

"*I'm not that much of a wimp,*" Valiant snorted, even if he had been wobbling and straining himself before.

"Why don't you like dragons?" Tyler asked as Valiant set his head on the ground. Kayla heard him curl up too as if his version of shrinking before his rider was to contort into a ball. Normal dragons only shrunk down to the ground if their riders were furious. Valiant seemed to be rather susceptible to sadness. Maybe he felt sad that she didn't like his wings or something. Then again, his life was sounding rather depressing.

"Dragons are scary," Kayla answered Tyler.

Kayla wished she hadn't said it when Tyler turned around from staring after the dragon horde they could hear but not see. The crazy dragon lover. He was the one that should be scared of them. He lived in Vankerdale. Dragons here were even scarier than the ones in Aralot.

"You're scared of dragons?!"

There was no way to pull her hood any farther down so she shut her eyes instead. She wasn't going to see anything she didn't want to see. Right now that was Tyler. She hoped Tyler would be able to keep that to himself and not tell anyone else her fears, like her dragon loving parents. No one else understood except the Colts, and she wasn't going to share dragonphobias with any of them. They would make fun of her. There wasn't a single person she knew that would understand how brave she had to be to walk past dragons. No one else understood how looking at them made her want to cry, especially if she spent too long staring at Sparkle, and too long was usually under twenty seconds.

"Wow. I've never heard of a keeper that was scared of dragons. Maybe you're still cursed. How long have you been scared of them?" Tyler asked, stepping closer to look at her pinched face. She sensed him looking between her and Valiant, studying both of them.

Behind her Valiant slowly reached out his tail and tapped the back of her shoe as if testing to see if she would come back to the present instead of be stuck inside her head with her fears. He even hummed at her, a sound that was supposed to instantly overcome her own feelings and push her to experience his happiness. Bonded riders were instantly washed over with their dragon's happy hums. Kayla wasn't.

This dragon thing couldn't be a result of a curse. She knew all of her curses. She had learned the spell that would tell her what she was cursed with. There was the curse about the topic she couldn't hear, the one that made her instantly seasick on a boat, the one that prevented her from eating too much candy, the one that prevented her from using an excesses sum of magical energy at one time, the one that would cause her to turn around if she tried to not do her homework for an entire week…

Did she need to go on? Her parents were overbearing and perfect. They couldn't understand.

"Forever. It's not a curse."

"So you haven't tried to befriend a dragon. How do you know if you will stay scared of them if you don't give it a try?"

"I can't. I physically can't," she told him.

She wasn't going to elaborate either. She crossed her arms to prove it. Tyler didn't need to know what she was thinking about. She was remembering the time four weeks ago while she was ignoring her homework. It was the first of summer break and she wanted her break. So she had left the house to wander their large property and maybe build a treehouse.

A wild dragon had shown up. Its face was bleeding where a scale had been ripped out. Kayla had screamed. She started to go through all the things she needed to do to help the dragon. Cover the wound to stop the blood and then apply scale paste. She had all the tools with her to pull the task off. She even felt like this could be the time she got over her fear of helping dragons. Except that one step toward the beast changed everything. Her fear and sadness came over her so strongly that she couldn't even move. She had crumbled to the ground and her mother's dragon guard of the day had chased the dragon off. Her mother had helped it instead. She was a horrible keeper. Why would any dragon ever want her?

Valiant hummed at her again, but it didn't help. There was too much guilt from everyone expecting her to love dragons and her not even being able to look at them.

"What physically happens if you try to befriend a dragon?" Tyler asked. "I think it was the result of a curse, and as I said before, I'm pretty sure Valiant took your curses off."

Kayla turned her back on Tyler, annoyed that he was trying to help her. She shouldn't be talking to him about her dragon fears. She'd not been able to talk to Anvil about them. He was usually the first person she told secrets to. She hadn't told him this because he had his own dragon, and she knew that if she said anything, he would tell her parents. Tyler, however, didn't know her parents unlike the rest of Aralot.

"I get so sad and scared that I can't move. I can't help dragons. I've tried before."

"If you are certain that this is not a curse, then I think the reason for your sadness is Valiant," Tyler puzzled out. "Your emotions are connected, right? He kept you away from other dragons out of jealousy. You were all he had and he didn't want to lose that. There's a simple cure for that. Turn around and meet your dragon."

She couldn't do that! She'd fall to the ground and become useless! She would start to cry! To turn around would be to acknowledge that everything she had learned so far was true. King Peyton had stolen Valiant from Wisteria somehow knowing that he would be her dragon in the distant future. Then he had taken Valiant away so he could start a war with Aralot. His war had failed the first time and she was going to keep it from starting this time too.

"Valiant stop making Kayla sad," Tyler continued. "If you want her to be with you, she's going to need to interact with dragons because you are one."

Kayla opened her eyes back up and looked to the open air. Tyler didn't know what he was talking about. This was a fear that hit her every time she tried to interact with a dragon. That wasn't going to go away simply because Tyler wanted it to. She wasn't going to turn around.

"Good. I don't want you to look at me anyway," Valiant snorted in dragon speech.

That was interesting because bonded dragons couldn't lie to their riders if the bond was intact. If the bond was broken then lies could be shared. Kayla was guessing that this was a lie because all dragons asked her to look at them. This proved that Valiant was scared that she'd find him lacking if she turned around. So, her fears about dragons were not really her own fears. She was afraid because Valiant was. She had never thought that her inability to be around dragons was because of a dragon before. She had taken the blame for it.

"How did you come to that conclusion?" Kayla looked down to face Tyler.

"Easy. Both of you try to hide all the time. You close your eyes and try to shut out the world, try to shut out the complicated pain of being unbonded but still mentally connected. The riders here in Vankerdale have broken bonds and they get angry every now and then. I'd imagine that if thoughts can still be sent, the missing bond would cause you both intense sadness because you miss it."

In that case, it wasn't Valiant's fault and it wasn't her fault. It was the fault of the missing bond. It was King Peyton's fault for taking Valiant away. It was her mother's fault for never telling her that she had a dragon of her own.

Kayla frowned and tried to think like her mother. Queen Tia would have come up with a good reason for her silence. Perhaps her reasoning was that King Peyton might kill Valiant and then the broken bond wouldn't be able to hurt Kayla anymore so there was no reason to bring it up. Perhaps she thought that Kayla wouldn't be a keeper and the broken bond would go unnoticed for the rest of her life so why worry over a spellbinding dragon that King Peyton had?

"What do you think?" Kayla asked, spinning around to look at Valiant.

He had his brown eyes closed, breathing softly as if he was nearly asleep. All this sudden exercise out in the sun was taking a toll on the normally immobile dragon. The dragon's tail was still stretched out toward her. Kayla looked at the strange tip of it. Ice dragons could split their tails into three blades. Water dragon tails were flat and wide to help them swim. They could fan them outward if they needed to. Dwarf dragon tails were like snakes made up of coils that could strangle and open doors.

Spellbinding dragon tails were split into two flanges that touched at the end. The whole of the shape looked like a flame, but the inside of the tail looked like a petal on the mystique, which was the unreal flower on Aralot's flag. Aralot didn't have a spellbinding dragon to learn this, but it seemed strange that no one had remembered this detail and passed it on. Valiant's tail looked like their kingdom's flag. She wondered what he used his tail for.

Valiant gave a short laugh and Kayla wasn't sure what part of her thoughts he found funny, or if he was laughing at something entirely different. He didn't open his eyes regardless, so she scanned the rest of him, surprised that looking this long hadn't frozen her solid. Valiant reminded her of slate. His blue-gray scales were dull right now, but given a little attention, they would have a soft pleasant glow to them that wouldn't blind anyone in the sun. His silver-tipped wings would do that if the sun hit them just right. They were tucked into his sides currently so he wasn't revealing anything flashy.

He wouldn't shoot fire out of habit so she couldn't be scared of that. In fact, if Valiant had been within her thoughts since she was born, he would know all the magical spells that Kayla herself knew. She wasn't scared of her magical knowledge, so she couldn't be scared of what Valiant knew either. Kayla had memorized a spell to make herself feather-light so Valiant would know it too, and she wouldn't need to be scared of him squishing her if he thought to use it. He would need magic in order to fill satisfied, another thing he was missing in his life since

Bantin was the only dragon producing magic and he lived far away. While most people claimed Bantin to be mean, he had only been nice to Kayla when he came around. He hadn't called out to her. It was the opposite. He had told dragons to leave her alone. There was a creature that understood when others needed space. Valiant was really good at being quiet and patient. He would make a great friend for Bantin and then Valiant could get his magic.

Valiant wasn't too bad. If she did have to have a dragon in her thoughts, there wasn't much she could complain about where it came to Valiant. He already knew all about her. He remembered more about her earlier life than she did. He would give her the space she needed — hopefully.

"So," Kayla said again. "What is my mom's reasoning?"

Valiant opened his brown eyes to look back at her. His mouth turned up into a grin before he hummed at her pleased with her assessment of him. He raised himself up on his forearms to nod his head at her. It had been some time since Tia told the story of meeting SilverWings, but she had said that the dragon bowed to her. It had to be a spellbinding dragon's way of giving respect if Valiant did this too.

"Your mother would consider the answer to this question a betrayal. She would pry up my scales if I told you," Valiant vocalized in perfect dragon.

Beside them, Tyler tried to mimic the sounds. Kayla glared at him and told him sharply not to repeat those dragon words. They would make dragons mad at him and he wouldn't get a dragon that way. This proved though, that Valiant had it more figured out than she did. He laughed again and hummed at her rolling over, trying to look cute and playful.

That was enough of looking at the dragon. She could only take so much at once. She wasn't going to play with Valiant. Kayla turned her

Pg. 160

back on him and looked again to the air and across the fields, trying to decide where her dad would go. Behind her Valiant curled up into a ball again.

"Tired?" Kayla asked him.

"Listening," he answered. "I'm trying to decide if we need to be worried about the dragons flying this way. I'm guessing there are at least twenty. Maybe fifty. They sound coordinated."

It was time to go! Standing still was the best way to let dragons catch her. Kayla picked a direction and started running. Tyler complained about her speed as she dashed off. Not a moment later, she heard Valiant offer him a ride. It nearly made her stumble. She was supposed to be Valiant's rider and yet he was letting Tyler ride him. Kayla pushed the stab of jealousy down, seeing very well why Valiant might have a hard time watching her around other dragons. It was the force of shattered expectations that was getting her now. At least Valiant didn't leave her wounded for long.

He caught up to her and Kayla grabbed Tyler's hand to get onto the back of Valiant. She mounted in front of Tyler. It wasn't a moment late either, because she could hear the dragon's catching her scent and she could tell what they were saying. Her parents would be so amazed right now! She was actually riding a dragon!

"Cinnamon and flame! Oh, how I've missed that smell!"

"You know what this means, don't you?"

"Freedom!" another dragon shouted back.

Yeah, no. She wasn't pleased to hear any of these dragons. She wasn't going to save them from anything. She was going to escape and find her dad!

Uncle

Tyler

A keeper that was scared of dragons! How Tyler wanted to write this all down, to tell future generations what a broken bond did to a keeper. There was plenty of information on what broken bonds did to normal people. He didn't have much information on keepers since Vankerdale didn't have any, so he really wanted to record this someplace. Wishing he had paper with him had him eying Kayla's bag as she sat before him on Valiant. There had to be something in that bag that he could use to write on. However, he didn't feel like she liked him much, so he wasn't going to ask.

She was a bit stiff, adamantly set on her goals without wanting to change. She did have the hint of a hero in her, asking after her dad and trying to find him instead of ordering Valiant to take her directly home. The dragon would brave the border again if she asked. Tyler was a little hesitant about not charging through already, because the longer they took, the longer it gave King Peyton to find his frozen son, unfreeze him, and come charging after them next. Tyler could picture the border being blocked to prevent Valiant's escape, and it wasn't going to make things easy.

Valiant was holding his breath, waiting for Kayla to give him a kind word. Tyler had never seen the dragon express himself so much.

When she wasn't looking, Valiant was staring at Kayla's back, taking in her gray hoodie and bag. It was hard to make out her auburn hair with it hidden, but she was a rather beautiful girl. Valiant had hummed at her. He'd laughed at her. He had spoken to her until she answered him. He had rolled over in a burst of happiness only to have it all squashed on him as he curled back into his defensive lump. Kayla must have thought something that put him off. It had turned Tyler's insides sour.

This whole thing wasn't right. He had to get Kayla to fall in love with the dragon. Tyler couldn't stand for his friend to be so miserable. He didn't know how to change the girl's mind apart from encouraging interaction. Valiant and Kayla were very similar, both shrinking from themselves, but with that inner fire to endure and succeed. He'd seen it in both of their eyes now. There was a very strong drive to never give up.

It sounded contradictory that a keeper would turn scared of dragons with a broken bond, even if that was what Kayla and Valiant resorted to. Maybe he hadn't gotten the answer right. Perhaps the better way to view the emotion was as a defensive mechanism. Kayla hadn't known about Valiant, which meant that the dragon hadn't talked to her before, even if he knew about her. Valiant probably saw his silence as his only way to protect his rider from coming to find him and getting trapped by King Peyton.

At some point in her life, Kayla had noticed that something was wrong with her. The silence from her dragon resorted her to fear. She inwardly felt like she had lost something she loved only she couldn't put words to this because she had no idea that she had Valiant to begin with. Her response to dragons, added to by the silent Valiant, was to turn away from the animals her keeper blood told her to protect. She wasn't protecting her bonded dragon, and so she had distanced herself from the feeling of failure. That brought on the sadness. Valiant brought on the fear, and the combination sounded deadly.

How would Tyler get a dragon of his own traveling around with a keeper that shoved dragons away? Her first response wasn't to turn to the creature that shared her soul but to run from it. Tyler wanted to run at a dragon that wanted him back. He wanted the experience of always having a companion with him through thick and thin, through the boring homework, through the exciting moments of changes.

This was one of those moments of change. Just like when the last snowflake fell in Vankerdale, and rain started pouring down upon them, the atmosphere in the air riding on the back of a running dragon felt like a brand new start. A scary start. Wind rushed past his face, and jolts rushed through his bones. He had left Prince Evan behind, frozen in a spell that Tyler couldn't break, and joined up with the princess of Aralot. The prince would kill him for that if they caught him, so Tyler was all about escaping too.

Regardless of Kayla's personal struggles, Tyler had always seen the rulers of Aralot as far more influential than anyone in Vankerdale. He was going to be part of this change even if it meant turning on King Peyton and Prince Evan. He had already come to accept that he would be considered a traitor for the way he was going to approach curing the land. Instead of intensifying the fear, aggravating magic users until Vankerdale became so trapped that their only escape was to lash out, Tyler was going to reel Kayla in slowly. She would see him as a hero if he got her to like her dragon. This girl needed to become his friend. He had to get Kayla and her mother to save the dragons of Vankerdale through friendly means instead of force because the latter had never worked.

Tyler placed one hand on Valiant's hide and his other one on Kayla's shoulder to hold on. It had been a bumpy ride entering Aralot. Once Kayla was captured Valiant's flight had evened out probably due to Kayla's thoughts on the way he approached getting into the air. Kayla was exactly what Valiant needed. It was going to be harder to convince Kayla that she needed him back.

Tyler glanced behind him at the incoming dragons inwardly moaning because he knew a few of these ones. They were nasty creatures, cunning, crafty and always in the way. These were the dragons that picked on King Peyton the most, disrupting his plans, interrupting outings, burning his progress. Individually, SilverWings could take them on, but when they grouped together like this, there was nothing stopping this particular herd of dragons.

"Can you go a bit faster?" Tyler asked Valiant. "These ones are not to be taken lightly."

"Dragons are never light. They weigh ten to fifteen tons you know," Kayla muttered at him.

"I just meant that this herd is the worst. They get past SilverWings all the time led by that large green dragon right there."

Tyler turned in his seat a bit more. He could see the dragon leader, male, green, full of temper and wit. He didn't know how this creature did it, but this guy could smash through other herds and leave them laughing even after destroying everything they had been working on. He was responsible for all the burnt bridges, lost cargo, and broken equipment in all of Vankerdale. The worst of the worst had found them.

"He reminds me of a storm after he hits," Tyler sighed.

There was good and bad about this. They had not been found by King Peyton yet so Tyler didn't have to worry about being seen as a traitor before he got Kayla on his side. The downside was that the green dragon already saw him as an enemy. Tyler heard the dragon's voice start up, calling out directions and hoots. Kayla groaned when a few of the other dragons answered. She pulled at her hood again wanting to escape the dragon sounds as if she could understand them all.

"Hey, what are they saying?" Tyler asked.

He wished to know even more when Valiant gave off a short

scream and started running them in circles. Kayla reached over and checked the dragon's wings as if trying to determine if she should ask him to fly. She didn't ask. Instead, she stood up on Valiant's back, causing Tyler to lose his grip on her shoulder. His fingers strained to find something to hold. Valiant was kept rather clean and he was too slippery for easy flying. Tyler grabbed onto Kayla's shoes instead. She didn't say anything to him for disrupting her perfect balance. She only looked to the air after drawing a knife into her hand.

Valiant continued to circle hissing out protective snarls. He was heaving, fighting with himself as he sucked in air and tried to decide what spell he might shoot out to protect the one girl he cared about. That's when Tyler saw the reason for the circling. They were already pinned in before they knew anything was coming. The green devil had his team dropping in around them on all sides. Tyler started counting. Normally this herd attacked in fives, but this time they had come in three groups of six.

"We can't break out on our own. This is a level two formation," Kayla said. "That's so weird. I didn't think Vankerdale had dragon wares."

"We don't," Tyler answered. "It's hard to train dragons and riders together when they can't talk."

He looked up at Kayla, confused by what she said. These dragons knew Aralot formations. They shouldn't. No wonder this herd was so hard to stop. They had come in from Aralot to attack the king and no one had known their origin because none of them knew the formations. Tyler wondered if King Jack was responsible for this secret group, because these guys had been around since Tyler was a baby.

Kayla looked down at him just as confused. She tilted her head to the side and fingered the keychain attached to her side. He had seen her use the magic before, and it caused him to tighten his grip on her shoes.

This girl knew what she was doing with spells. King Jack must have been tricked to give up his magic or Tyler couldn't picture the man ever being taken down. Aralot would be one fascinating place to visit. Tyler hoped he could get away with his final intentions. All he needed to do was stick to Kayla like glue, and he could sneak back into Aralot with her. He'd get a dragon bond. He'd get Kayla's respect for helping her, and she would free the cursed dragons over here.

"Did you say that the green dragon reminds you of a storm?" Kayla asked him. "Like a tempest?"

Valiant came to a sudden stop at the question. Tyler slipped over the side of his scales and would have dropped to the ground if it wasn't for his arms holding onto Kayla's shoes. How she hadn't shifted at all on the running creature was beyond him.

"That's why no one can find him!" Kayla lowered her knife, but she kept her hand on her magical gem that granted her unforeseeable power. Leave it up to the princess of Aralot to personally know all the lost dragons her parents couldn't find. Tyler looked at the green beast as it winged its way so close that Tyler could have felt its breath if it chose to blast it out. Kayla didn't look up at all. She kept her eyes on Tyler as he pulled himself back up. Her not looking at the beastly animal was making him sweat. Kayla didn't think she could look at dragons still even after finding Valiant. If no one had sent this green beast into Vankerdale to cause havoc, Tyler feared that the animal would stop his attacks for no one.

"Have you seen my dad?" Kayla asked. "Pyro is missing too. He's here someplace. Have you seen him?"

To Tyler's surprise, the green stormy dragon stopped snarling. He hovered in place and hooted something soft to Valiant, which caused the dragon to sit down. The teams landed on the ground sucking in air as they gently pressed their brown, red, green, and bronze heads into each other and toward Valiant in the middle to catch his scent. Even in a well-organized herd, there would be shoving, but not with these creatures. Their only indication of wanting a better spot was a snort. It had the hairs on Tyler's neck standing up. They were too coordinated even in this.

"They are going to eat us," Tyler whispered.

"Tempest," Kayla spoke, still not looking at the leader. She was now focusing on a spot on the ground. Tyler watched as the large green dragon shifted a little uncomfortable to be addressed without real attention. "Where did you lose Conner? I've been waiting years to challenge him to a foot race. My name is Kayla—"

She didn't get much farther which was a shame since Tyler had no idea who Conner was. The surrounding dragons erupted into a shout of victory. He heard the dragons from the other nearby herd scream back warnings to keep away, wanting no part in anything that would rile Tempest's herd into such a commotion.

"Great. You distract them and I'll—"

Tyler stopped talking when Kayla's eyes turned onto his in a glare. Tyler contemplated scampering off her dragon's back. She hadn't attacked him with anything yet, but she easily could. He had attributed her earlier leniency to Valiant's display of saving him from the spell his rider shot. But with Valiant starting to tremble as if contemplating all the horrible things this team could do, Tyler didn't think Valiant was going to be much help. Instead of charging up a spell, he slumped even further and curled up into a ball as if waiting for Kayla to save them all.

Kayla didn't look like she was going to help once Valiant sat down. She dropped the keychain and grabbed for the hood. Oh yes, this was going to be very problematic. This broken bond thing had them both down. Tyler let out a short whimper as he realized that he had to be the one offering up the rescue from dragons he had held at a great distance his whole life. Here he went. He moved his weight around so that he had a firmer seat on Valiant's back.

"Esteemed lost dragons of Aralot, I congratulate you on yet another victorious catch. As you can see, we share common ground upon which we can come to a favorable solution for all of us."

Tyler looked right into the face of Tempest as he spoke. The dragon had been watching him warily, but now he chirped out something to his comrades and all of them became consumed with the dragon giggles. Even Valiant gave out a few chuckles, unable to help himself before a sigh from Kayla had him turning ridged again. It caused Tempest to prance on his feet and growl. Tyler found himself reaching toward that keychain Kayla had, even if he had never cast a spell before in his life. It couldn't be that hard right? He'd simply grab at the gem and pray that somehow they would all get out of this alive.

Instead of reaching the keychain, Kayla slapped his hand away with a force that stung. He shook his hand out and glanced toward her face. She was just the same as her dragon, eyes tightly shut, but with tears flowing out, focused on breathing, blind to the world, but not deaf. He could tell that she was still listening. Valiant, in contrast, looked to be trying to hide his ears. His head was shoved to the side pressing an ear to the ground as he inhaled as if the only sense *he* would acknowledge was that of smell. They made a strange pair.

Tempest thought so too because he gave off the dragon bark for "talk" and pointed to Kayla and Valiant with his tail. Then the green dragon moved his head in really close. Tyler's own breathing picked up yet again as he pictured Tempest chomping him so that the beast could have the princess all to himself. Kayla wasn't very hard to capture when he thought about it. All anyone needed to do was surround her with dragons and she and Valiant both would become statues. They could have had Kayla long before now if anyone else had ever realized this. Tyler had to do something to get her braver.

Pg. 170

It was on that thought that Tyler stopped cowering. He straightened up determined to set the example and started to explain his thoughts.

"Kayla and Valiant are suffering from a broken bond that causes them to be overcome with fear and sadness in the presence of other dragons. I don't think that all keepers will react to such a situation in the same way, but since these two were separated at birth, they have developed the habit of hiding from emotions they didn't know how to control."

It was remarkable when Tempest sat down, curling his tail up around him in a rather humbling posture. His team of dragons copied him, dropping battle stances and stares to offer whispered hoots of encouragement for Valiant. Then again maybe they were talking to Kayla because she snapped open her eyes. With more tears flowing out she screamed back at them.

"I am not letting it take me!"

More dragon words were the result, followed by a growl from Valiant as he lashed his tail out toward Tempest's face. Tyler scrambled closer to Valiant's neck where it was safer before the fight broke out. With Kayla in tears, he would feel safer being able to balance on his own. Tyler looked over his shoulder when Tempest let Valiant's tail hit him. The dragon didn't even growl.

Tyler's mouth opened on its own. He had seen dragons attack Tempest before. This guy never let an insult get past him. He was a rage of fire, a force so hot that weapons could be forged upon his breath. Tyler had never seen the animal so placid. Maybe it was talking about bonds that did it. Coming from Aralot, these dragons would have known what bonds were like. They would have suffered the effects of being broken. Where was Tempest's rider?

"Kayla," Tyler nudged her with his foot. "Information please."

"The only part that sounds good is the part about the house," Kayla said. Tyler wasn't sure if she was talking to him, Valiant, or Tempest. Valiant didn't move and Tyler could only shrug. "Okay. Let's go," Kayla concluded. "There won't be anything he can do to help me, but I have always wanted to meet him."

"Who?" Tyler asked, still greatly confused.

Kayla took her eyes off the ground again to look at him. The direct focus of her gaze, and the pulling in of her hood to block out the sight of the other dragons, made him want to weep for her. This couldn't be easy on a keeper to handle. He'd read that their bodies screamed at them to watch dragons. Resisting so much was a large struggle.

"We found my Uncle Conner, but we've not found Pyro or my dad yet. Are you staying here?" Kayla asked him.

Tyler shook his head no and tried to come up with some excuse to remain with her and Valiant. He didn't need to say anything, however. Kayla tapped a scale on Valiant's back and the dragon obediently stood up in compliance with her mental wishes.

Tempest gave the orders and his herd took to the air. Valiant sat back down psyching out the other dragons that he was actually coming. He gave a yawn to Tempest when the animal called to him. The spellbinding dragon's defiance wasn't met with enthusiasm. Tempest didn't growl, but he did look at his comrades and spoke with his tail. Pretty soon the team of dragons shot downward again shoving against Valiant to get him back up. Tyler was in the front, but he found himself reaching behind him to grip at Kayla when the other dragons managed to toss Valiant into the air with their combined efforts.

"I would rather not get flattened, Valiant," Tyler told him. He wasn't sure what Kayla was thinking but Valiant at least responded. He spread out his wings and then did nothing to fly himself. It was a rather clever trick once Tyler stopped being scared to think about it. Tempest and his herd were expending themselves to move Valiant by ramming into the bottom of the dragon and flapping extra hard to keep him airborne. All Valiant did was keep his wings open. He even shut his eyes a few times being exceptionally lazy. He was weakening the stronger team with his stubbornness and no one was getting hurt.

Kayla wasn't sleeping, but Tyler could tell that her mind wasn't on the flight either. Every now and then she would mutter half answers to mental questions as if she was reviewing for a test. She wasn't helping Valiant fly like that. She was miles away, refusing to pay attention to what was around her. Tyler kept looking at all the dragons trying to judge when the next shove would come. He wished that his dragon riding was taking place under better circumstances. All his life he had wanted to go up on a dragon to soar through the sky, regal and grand, administering help to the wounded, keeping in check the squabbling wild ones, and being praised for his mercy and justice. Instead, he got to be the homework boy, overlooked by everyone. He doubted that anyone except for his family and Prince Evan even knew his name.

They crossed over two different dragon herd territories. Neither one did anything more than tell Tempest to go away. But each time they were directly overhead another group, Kayla tucked her head down. Tyler tried to tell her that it was going to be alright, but he really wanted to ask her if she had a plan to escape, because from where he was sitting, they were still captured by the herd of coordinated dragons. He expected to run across this Uncle Conner person soon. He was the reason that Tempest was in Vankerdale. Tyler wondered what sort of relationship Tempest and his old rider had now that they had a broken bond, because Tempest never had a rider on his back.

When Tempest started circling a house hooting at it, Tyler groaned. He knew this place. He avoided it like everyone else, except for the people who lived there and those who delivered packages. This was the home of the grumpy merchant. This guy always knew where the best deals were, and he would get on your case if you didn't give him the discount you had offered to someone else. He wasn't the type of person anyone wanted to mess with. Anyone who tried ended up having something bad happen to them, as if karma or magic came back around to smite them.

Tyler now knew that it wasn't either of those things. The trader had a horde of dragon eyes and ears that gave him information and distracted other people so he could sneak in and turn homes upside down. Tyler had never guessed that Tempest would be associated with this man. The merchant was never seen around dragons in the market or at the castle. Tyler and the rulers of Vankerdale should have paid more attention to this guy's home. The wide open area around his house coupled with the trampled grass and mud pit for dragon rolling was a large give away.

The trader walked out of the house with blond hair shaggy to his shoulders, worn leather pants, thick black boots, and a smile. He jogged into the flat dragon field. The dragons started hooting, talking all at once and laughing as they warily landed. Some ran up to the trader, Conner, and hummed at him as they nuzzled him with noses or warm air. Conner greeted each one with a warm hand and affectionate words. It was strange to watch the normally guarded man so pleasant around dragons. Tyler wanted to nudge Kayla to tell her that she should take notes, but once Valiant landed, she was off his back in a heartbeat, despite him opening up his eyes to whimper at her to come back.

"You did a great job tuckering them out," Tyler whispered to Valiant as he clumsily slid down the dragon to reach the ground. Kayla ran out ahead of him casting some sort of arm signal into the air as she did so. Tyler wasn't sure exactly what it meant, but the dragons knew. They all looked at Conner before a nod from him had them walking away out of Kayla's sight.

Tyler wanted to learn things like that. Controlling dragons with the slightest movement of his arms would be remarkable. He tested out the arm signal and then was forced to jump out of the way as a brown dragon landed before him with a dead carcass. It was placed before Valiant with a chirp. Adult dragons didn't usually get free handouts unless they were too injured to hunt for themselves and those handouts only came from a family herd. Valiant was at a disadvantage not having learned how to hunt, and being distanced from his family, but Tempest's herd was surprisingly considerate for all the terror they had caused. Valiant looked between the food, the brown dragon, and Kayla, seeking permission. Kayla gave her dragon no visible attention as she came to a stop before the merchant. Tyler wondered if she had thought something to her dragon when Valiant gave the brown dragon a short hum of thanks and dug in.

His slobbering chomps mixed with the smell of blood had Tyler leaving Valiant behind as he inched toward the two humans. He didn't make it far before Conner's sharp eyes brought him to an uncomfortable standstill. It was impressive how commanding a pair of eyes could be when the rest of the face wasn't expressing any hostility. Tyler was relieved when the eyes of the trader turned off him and back onto the still shrouded Kayla.

"Mom and Dad are going to be so excited!" Kayla cried out. "Unless you don't want me to tell them that you're here. I'm good at keeping secrets. Honestly, I am. I've not got anyone to spill them to apart from Uncle Anvil although Ritz tries to get things out of me. He's running a losing battle because what he wants to know I'll never say."

"What does he want to know about?" Conner asked with a short chuckle and shake of his head. "How's he looking?"

"Ritz? I doubt he can age. That guy is just as cursed as I am. He was wanting the secrets to portals, but it would do him no good even if he learned them."

Conner nodded as if he understood exactly what Kayla was talking about. Tyler crossed his arms. Tyler knew about portals, but no one in Vankerdale could use them because they didn't have magic to waste on opening up the doorways. He knew who Ritz was too. While that wasn't the man's real name, everyone clear to Wisteria knew of the ageless leader of the Colts.

"You're cursed?" Conner pried. "Can we back up a little?" Kayla took a few steps back and he laughed at her. "Not like that. We've never been introduced although I believe that I'm your Uncle—"

"Conner!" Kayla's excitement was far greater for this man than it was for Valiant. Tyler heard the dragon whimper behind him as Kayla jumped the last few feet, flinging her arms around the stranger. Tyler would have turned around to look at Valiant to offer sympathy, but he didn't want to see the bloody carcass again. Conner wiped at his eyes a few times as if he couldn't believe that he had the princess of Aralot in his arms. He hugged her back.

"Actually you're my great uncle or my grand uncle, but I think of you as a normal uncle as well. I always knew one day I would meet you. I'm so glad it was here because the only supportive person around is Tyler and he's got ulterior motives."

"I do not," Tyler replied, but his words were not acknowledged even if they were heard.

"He's a castle boy, part of a long line trying to repay the king for some slight that no one can remember. The king won't let the Valerons go because it gives him free servitude. There's not enough Valerons to lead a revolt but they could. I've traced their family name as far back as it goes, and similar to how Aralot's founders were Feldings, Vankerdale's true founders were the Valerons. The Peyton's took over the throne from them two generations before the Clusters stole the throne in Aralot from the Feldings. One could say that it was because the

Peyton's got away with their overthrow that the Clusters even staged theirs. In any case, the Peyton's have done a grand job hiding the Valeron name. No one mentions them anymore. You have to actively look to find that information."

There had been exactly four Peyton kings since Tyler's ancestors had held the throne. During that time, Aralot had gone through nine kings because the Feldings often fought back to gain control. None of the Valerons ever had. Tyler uncrossed his arms in favor of shoving his hands into his pockets. If things had been different, he wouldn't be the homework boy but the ruler known for creating peace with Aralot so that they could get their dragons freed. He'd have access to all the old documents he wanted to read, access to the rules, access to those monthly letters sent to Aralot that asked for redemption. Tyler guessed that it was the same letter copied out each time since they had been sending them for so long. Aralot probably no longer read them. But if they did, would he be able to sneak a message through?

Tyler looked over at Kayla and Conner and shrugged. Any message would go straight to King Klavian and not to the person he was trying to reach. The person everyone wanted to reach was Tia. Lucky for Tyler he currently had access to the woman's daughter. All he had to do was get Kayla to start the conversation of saving dragons with her mom. Maybe he was wishing too hard. Kayla still wanted nothing to do with dragons, not even her own. He didn't expect a lot of empathy out of her.

"I need to meet you properly," Conner said, tugging Kayla's hood off her face. He gazed over her features commenting on his favorite ones—her mother's eyes, her father's hair color. Kayla gave him a shrug when he called her adorable. Conner pinched his lips together as if judging something about her before giving her a smile.

"I've been waiting sixteen years to meet you. In that time, I've failed to get your dragon out of the castle. I'm terribly sorry, Kayla. King Peyton thought that Tia was alone when he attacked her, but she wasn't.

I was there, only I couldn't think of a way to get your young dragon away from SilverWings. I thought I could defeat Vankerdale given time, but the only way into that castle is to get an invitation. I've gotten a few through trading and the like, but despite King Peyton telling everyone that magic doesn't exist over here, it does. He's got spells around his walls. The magic must know that I'd take something large out with me if I got inside. You should have heard Tempest screaming when we learned that your dragon was out and we had missed the whole thing. We've tried to save Valiant at least once a month for the last sixteen years.

"It's that magic stuff that has me stuck. Magic was Jack's thing. I must admit that when I first heard Jack was reading magic books and had the authority to cast spells, I spent a good three hours laughing. He was so amusing back then, outcasted from every social circle but accepted by them all nonetheless. Brilliant man, your father. There was a time where I thought we could be good friends."

"You *are* good friends," Kayla informed. "He spent years looking for you but back up a minute. What attack from King Peyton on my mother are you talking about?"

It was probably better to ask *which* attack actually. Tyler had heard of new plans for getting at Tia hundreds of times. They sent in merchants who were to sell Tia items that would then try to snag her. They had tried spells, smoke signals, letters, spies, assassins, and religious monks. Nothing worked. There were times when Tyler would hide himself away from King Peyton and Prince Evan as they screamed and threw things, angry over how they had seen Tia again and not gotten her to acknowledge their existence. They always met her in some kind of library. Tyler hadn't figured out where that library was, but he was still on the lookout for it.

"She didn't tell you!" Conner blinked at Kayla amazed before he looked over at Tempest and shook his head against some angry thought he must have had. It was probably the wish to communicate mentally with his dragon that was getting to him.

"Why didn't you figure it out!?" Conner turned his grumpy nature onto Kayla. Tyler was just about to explain to her that missing a mental dragon connection made even the most docile people act out, but Kayla didn't need his words. She had the perfect sentence that changed Conner's mood.

"Give me a good hint so that I can."

Instead of screaming again, Conner gave Kayla the hint. "Your parent's wedding date versus your birthday."

Tyler had no idea what day Kayla's parents were married or when she was born, but if the two were linked, he was guessing that King Peyton had not only stolen Kayla's dragon but messed with her birthday.

"Oh!" Kayla took a step back as she thought over the dates. "I always assumed there was at least a year between the two."

"Five weeks," Conner said. "You were born five weeks after your parents were married. No one saw it coming. Tia didn't even know she was pregnant. She was hunting for bugs with Sparkle when King Peyton came for a visit, tossed spells at her, and left a bloody mess. He stole her child and shoved you onto the pointed fangs of that dragon behind you. Then he took the dragon and left you all to suffer. I've thrown everything I've had at him over the years."

A forced bond. The hairs on Tyler's arms prickled upward. Kayla grabbed at her hood and pulled it back over her face. Tyler could only imagine what Kayla might be thinking right now, especially when he heard Valiant whimpering behind him, curling up into a ball, and then humming out the "I love you," message until Kayla gave him some sharp hand signal that cut him off. He was utterly silent again after that. Tyler couldn't help but look backward at his friend. The carcass, bones and all, had been devoured, leaving only the faintest trace of bloodstains on the ground. Even those looked like Valiant had tried to cover them over with dirt by swiping his tail over it.

Tyler didn't think it was possible for a human to reject an already bonded dragon, but if anyone was to do it, it was going to be Kayla. No wonder Valiant wasn't doing more to impress her. There was something very special about dragons choosing their own rider. It created a more loving connection when both entities looked forward to the bond. If only Kayla hadn't been in the picture, Tyler might have found himself adopted by the slate dragon himself.

Furthermore, if Kayla wasn't a keeper, their broken bond would mean that they didn't have to be together, because once broken the connection was gone. In this case, Kayla would always hear Valiant in her head due to this keeper business, but keepers sanctioned dragons in their thoughts that had other riders beside themselves. Perhaps Kayla would be like that, giving up Valiant in favor of some other dragon that she actually liked. Could Tyler get her to distance herself more from Valiant or was this thought pointless because Valiant obviously loved her?

"Don't go working up a tizzy," Kayla huffed, as she turned around. She may have given him a glare, but Tyler wasn't sure since he couldn't make out her facial features when she hid them beneath that hood. That hood was a menace.

"I didn't say anything," Tyler replied trying not to fidget. There was no way she could hear his thoughts. He had been wanting to help her, but now he was thinking of his own form of sabotage. He should stop like she suggested before he lost any and all good repertoire with the princess. Going back to his first plan was still the better one. Creating a friendship was much safer than creating an enemy.

"Your breathing pattern changed," Kayla stated, scaring him with how well she could hear things. "No need to feel sorry for me or think Valiant and I are dysfunctional. The very first keeper bonds were created like that. Uncle Anvil told me, and he's spent his entire ware leader career researching and studying keepers. The first bonds were made by taking a child and lashing them with the bonding fangs of an older dragon. Then the keeper would have access to years of dragon wisdom right away. It wasn't until more dragon wares opened up that bonding occurred as a dragon hatched.

"In fact, the first bonded hatchling created a scandal. Everyone was so upset that the animal had claimed a rider when it was so young. These days everyone expects the dragon to be young as if the dragon can magically make such a large decision of who they want to spend the rest of their life with before they have learned anything at all. Some dragons can't make up their minds that easy, especially off-breed ice dragons. They take a while. It's almost a shame that they feel pressured to bond anyone actually. Some dragons really should have their heads all to themselves."

And there it was. Kayla hadn't said it exactly, but with another whimper from Valiant, Tyler was fairly certain that she was thinking of how she would like her thoughts all to herself.

"I really want to get ahold of Anvil's research, but what makes him your uncle?" Conner asked. "For Anvil to be your uncle he would have married your Aunt Rosa."

Kayla spun back around to look at Conner and laughed. "Rosa married Clark! From their stories everyone should have seen that coming ten miles away. You were there long enough to get those early hints. Anvil married Annaliese and has three kids, but he told me just the other day that he still has the hots for my mom, which was oddly disturbing. However, on my part, it's also forgivable since Uncle Anvil's really like my second dad. Speaking of which, Jack's lost over here. I'm trying to find him. You haven't seen Pyro or my dad, have you?"

Conner shook his head as he looked over at Tempest again. The dragon swished his tail as if he could understand his rider's silent gaze. Tyler rolled his eyes at the sight. It was so unfair that Conner had been bonded before. It must have been a powerful bond if years later rider and dragon could guess each other's thoughts. Then again, it wasn't all that great. If he wasn't careful, Conner was going to fall to the ground holding his head in agony if he really tried to send thoughts to his unbonded animal. It happened to King Peyton a lot and gave him horrible headaches.

"Haven't seen Jack or Pyro. I would love to though. If they're here, we'll find them. We know every place either one of them can hide." Conner gave a nod to a few of the dragons in Tempest's herd and they took off into the air, heading out to search with such a short request. Tyler had never been fond of Conner before, but seeing this side of him, Tyler was starting to feel impressed.

"Perhaps you're a bit young to know this, but your Uncle Clark had a crush on your mother as well."

Tyler watched as Kayla flinched. It wasn't in her face but in her shoulders. Ha! He could still get a few good reactions out of her even if she was trying to hide them.

"Most people find my mother impressive because she's not overbearing on any of them. She never gives *me* a moment of peace. There's always a dragon staring at me."

"Hence the hood," Conner mused out loud, watching as Kayla gave him a shrug. Then he looked at Tyler and started to verbalize his thoughts to him which was super weird.

"I'm starting to put this together. She finds herself under constant scrutiny so she seeks to hide. The only Annaliese I remember in Anvil's circle didn't like dragons, although she was born in a ware. She would have moved out giving Anvil plenty of room to stare after Tia without his wife noticing. He couldn't have Tia or Rosa so he snagged up Kayla. Did you detect that fondness in her voice? That was no lie about that second father thing. That's got to grind against Jack like a needle in his sock."

Tyler looked behind him trying to decide if Conner was talking to him or someone else, because the man was staring at him, but Tyler hadn't detected any sort of fondness in Kayla over anything yet. He needed to learn how to pay better attention to these sorts of things, because so far, he was the one not making many new connections.

Conner let out a loud laugh and wiped at his eyes. To Tyler's right Tempest started laughing next and Tyler looked sharply between the two. It was almost like Conner and Tempest were really mind-speaking to each other, but that wasn't possible given that bonds couldn't work.

"Can you imagine a needle in Jack's sock?"

Yet again Tyler wasn't sure that the man was talking to him or not.

"He keeps pointed objects all over himself. Knives were his specialty. A needle would be harmless against that guy. Do you guys want to get dinner?"

Tyler blinked back still confused over Conner's intended target. Kayla at least didn't react the same way. She took a step toward the house. No. She stepped between Conner and Tempest to block their view of each other and brought up something that left Tyler squirming.

"Have you ever considered being the king of Aralot?" Kayla asked.

Tyler had just learned that Kayla was inheriting the throne, but here was Kayla being quite literal with her uncle comment. Conner was related to her by blood which would mean that he was a keeper and could mind-speak to his dragon. If King Peyton knew they had an Aralot keeper living in Vankerdale, he'd have Conner killed off in a heartbeat! Conner was living a very dangerous life on the other side of the border. The thought left Tyler terrified, because he had never liked the way Conner destroyed things and couldn't be blamed for it. Tyler wished Kayla hadn't asked Conner this question, because it was going to be hard enough setting Vankerdale right by becoming Kayla's friend. He had no idea how to gain Conner's cooperation. He held his breath waiting for Conner's answer.

Crowns and Cousins

Kayla

Her Uncle Conner was standing right in front of her! Kayla had tried to picture him over the years: strong, blond, with brown eyes, and the sleekness of a runner. He still had all those characteristics with an added few. He stood with the nonchalance of a Colt and had added to his speech a slight elongated "a" sound, similar to the way Tyler spoke. It must be a Vankerdale thing. Seeing him here, and hearing how he had been trying to rescue her, had Kayla wishing that Uncle Conner would save her from her castle dilemma. She was going to have to face off against Tristan for the title of ruler of Aralot similar to the way her parents had divided tasks with Klavian. However, Tristan wasn't the kind of person to share things. Kayla already knew that he wanted the whole thing, which would mean some sort of battle or complicated trickery was in her future if she wanted to keep the land. There was that, or Conner could save her and take Aralot instead.

"Have you ever considered being the king of Aralot?" Kayla asked again.

"Me? Of course. I've heard the tales too. Aralot will prosper with a male keeper on the throne who wears the crown. I considered taking over the kingdom when Herb was at large. I thought I could do better than him since he was killing off all the Colts and harassing all the riders.

I considered taking the crown from Jack or even pushing Jack aside to get it first. I was with him when he retrieved Aralot's crown you know. I lulled Jack into a sense of security and nearly attacked him for that crown. I had him thinking that we were friends the same way that Klavian had him thinking they were friends. I highly considered tossing Klavian off my dragon when Jack had me fly him back after he collected the crown.

"People whisper that the magic of Aralot is a living thing, pushing against the people inside its borders. I believe it. I felt compelled to follow after Jack and Klavian that day, even if riders could spot me riding Tempest and know who I was. It's no coincidence that the three people who could have used that crown were all there when it was retrieved. We went together. We all desired it, and it left with your father because Klavian and I were too afraid to attack Jack. We were too scared to take on the enchanted spellcaster who had the crown. Jack's nerves are like steel. If he gets his mind made up, nothing stands in his way.

"My head spun around and around trying to figure out what I should do. My main drawback to me plotting my own coup was that I'd have to explain Tempest. Jack got away with Pyro from the very start, but I hadn't. No one knew I had a bonded dragon, and if they ever learned that Tempest had been inside of Gladius's bond when he was a baby, there would be people trying to kill us both. Back then, Anvil hadn't shared keeper secrets with the rest of the world. Everyone called these people infections and to be one was super bad; so bad that questions wouldn't be asked before the death hunts started. It wasn't safe for me to say anything about myself. I hid it with everything that I had.

"Despite that, I couldn't hold back from letting Jack and Tia figure me out. They learned about Tempest and his connection, and while neither threatened me with revealing the information, they might have changed their minds and told the world in order to get me to drop the crown, assuming I could first take it. Taking it would not have been easy," Conner continued as if he had been holding back all of these words for a very long time and couldn't hold them back any longer now that he was talking to a person who would understand them all.

"Jack had all this pressure on him to clear his name from being the most wanted criminal in the land. He had pressure to get Tia to marry him and pressure to stop Herb from destroying people and dragons. He was determined to succeed and he had proven that he could escape the impossible already. Not only that, but both Jack and Klavian held magic. They became this strong force together and apart.

"Even with Jack liking me, he would have taken me down if he suspected my interest in the crown. He hinted it to me once telling me that every time he suspected me coming against him, I always checked out. It was a large warning to not make a move against him because I was on his watch. I had to be where he could see me so he wouldn't suspect I had these feelings. I gave him information. I tried to keep Herb off of Tia. Instead of stabbing Jack in the back, I held him up from behind.

"I had my glorious moments, spots where I felt like I could be the one to take the evil king down and claim the throne. I broke through Herb's dragon spies to destroy the orb he created that immobilized all bonded dragons."

Technically it was Kayla's grandmother, Alice Felding, who had created the enchanted orb spell, not Herb. Alice's name remained hidden since Rosa took part in stopping her own mother, and she didn't want anyone else to know. Kayla knew the information from her nightmares. Her father had not enjoyed battling Alice who was using Tia's possessed body at the time to fight him.

"I snatched away orders to destroy The Pits where the Colts were enslaved. Then I helped Jack free them when he rushed in. He didn't know that I was there at the time, but I was. And then when Herb went after the Colts again using Tia's possessed form, it was me sending Jack dragons when he needed help to clean up the mess.

"It was really hard at their wedding. Oh gosh, it was insane!" Conner rubbed at his blond hair ruffling it up. "Jack had me hold the real crown so he could switch it up and be crowned with a fake one to avoid curses on the relic that would kill Tia. I had the thing in my hand, Kayla! The crown knows it's kings, and it wasn't a slug wreath for me. It was solid silver. I was so close to running off with it, claiming my role right from under Jack's unsuspecting feet as he handed the power trustingly over, but whenever I started to inch away, Ritz was there blocking me.

"Jack and I had passed off the object behind a plume of magical smoke, but nothing gets past Ritz. I feared he would intercept me for the item and try to take it from me to become the king himself. We were both watching each other while pretending to watch everyone else, and then Ritz did something that I still hate him for. He got Tia smiling at him as if he was someone that could be trusted, and I felt horrible for my thoughts of betrayal to the one girl I had looked up to for half my life. I had no problem taking anything from Jack, but from your mom? I couldn't. So I stayed around and when Tia went to say bye to Anvil, I passed the crown back to Jack. I got the thing away from me before I could do something stupid with it, like shove it on my head, dooming myself to accept its curses. Jack has a talent for avoiding curses."

Conner sighed, and Kayla gave her missing uncle a short smile. He most definitely had been waiting a long time to unload all of that. Jack still saw Conner as a close friend having never known that Conner wanted so badly to betray him. Conner was now staring off into space contemplating everything he had gone through. It was true that her dad avoided curses really well. Kayla wished that she had inherited that aspect of his life, because she soaked up curses like a rag.

"He's here someplace," Kayla said, bringing her uncle out of his stupor. "I miss my dad so much. Are you going to help me find him so we can bring him home?"

Pg. 188

"We? As in you trust me after I just told you that I contemplated stealing from your parents and killing off your father?"

Oh, um... She shouldn't, but yeah, she still did trust him. There wasn't an easy way to explain it, but she was just like her dad in regards to trusting Conner. She'd hand him anything for safekeeping and not worry twice about it. Except perhaps the crown. *That*, she was going to keep away from him. Kayla gave him a nod and Conner shook his head at her like she shouldn't be so willing to have him around. She was never going to share his secret. He had the choice to betray his friends and he hadn't. So yes, she still trusted him greatly.

"I've never trusted you," Tyler said.

Kayla rolled her eyes. It was nice of Tyler to keep quiet while Conner divulged his evil life secrets. That's all she ever got was other people's nightmares. It was as if she had one of those faces that made people share these sorts of things with her because they thought she would keep silent. Maybe they were right. She wasn't about to harm anyone's future because of their past, but she was going to watch Conner closely if he ever returned to the castle. Thinking of which...

"Did you ever go back to Aralot? Tempest can't fly through the border spells, but Tyler said that you're a merchant and merchants can get trade goods through the border."

"Yes," Conner answered. "I took up my current job for that very reason. I've been back to Aralot."

"But you never said hello or anything! My parents haven't seen you in years. You could have asked my mom to take down the curse or had my dad fix your bond. He knows a bonding spell that—"

"Stop right there. When you go back over that border, Kayla, you're going to need to take some very happy thoughts with you because being unbonded in Aralot is far worse than it is here. Every time I got over there, I couldn't make it very far. I had all these grand plans of establishing a dragon spy network in Aralot so I'd be kept up to date with the Felding news, but it never worked out. I told myself that I'd go visit your parent's plenty of times only to fall to my knees as the spells tormented me. I wanted to see you. The closest I ever got was collecting pictures of you hidden behind a hood. Your pictures sell for a lot. Let me tell you."

Caleb. Kayla shook her head at how far his pictures spread. She wondered if he knew that people had sold them into Vankerdale. What if her face was all the way in Wisteria as well? Grr! Pictures could be the worst!

"Magic is stronger in Aralot. It's in the air. It's in the ground. It's hard to tell the difference but—"

"No." Kayla cut him off. "I get it. When I came over here, I felt the air was different."

"Exactly. It's hard for me to stay in Aralot because it hurts too much, and there was no sense asking Jack to fix my bond when I couldn't reach my dragon. The bond would break as soon as it was fixed because Tempest can't cross over the border. As for asking Tia to stop the curse on Vankerdale, I'll never do that. That would fix King Peyton, and he deserves to suffer for what he's done. I mess up everything he does as best I can."

"You purposely lived a cursed life for revenge," Tyler noted. "That's some strong revenge."

"He wounded Tia!" Conner screamed. "She was everything I aspired to be and he made her bleed! Then he injured her baby and stole Kayla's dragon! Let me tell you that there is nothing I wouldn't do to King Peyton. Not one thing."

Conner was starting to look a little dark here. Kayla tried to decide how to change the subject away from torturing King Peyton, but she didn't come up with words as fast as her uncle did.

"Besides, I don't live a cursed life all the time. I've managed to get around it. The brain starts finding ways to cope so that you don't always spend your time stuck inside your own isolation."

Kayla usually thought of her feelings as sadness, but isolation worked too. She was alone in them. This probably meant that for Conner, he cried when he felt alone because he wanted to be with his dragon. That was why he had never come back. He couldn't stand to be apart from Tempest. Kayla hadn't known she had a dragon to be with so her brain had called the reaction something else.

"The key is to not focus on what you've lost. You've lost time by being on the ground, you've lost water and salt from crying tears. You've lost friendships because other people can't understand. You've lost peace of mind, your own sanity. That's not the right mindset here. You need to focus on what you still have. What you don't have is hole in your brain that sucks down all thoughts you might think to a dragon. The dragon is still there. You can still live a relatively normal life with the exception that looking at dragons that are not bonded to you messes with your emotions."

"So you're fine looking at Tempest?" Kayla asked as Conner agreed. It hadn't hurt to look at Valiant. That made one safe dragon out of thousands. "What about your other dragons that are not bonded to you? Can you still hear them? Does looking at them bring you to tears?"

"I can still hear dragons that I was connected to before, but I can't make any new connections. There are a few dragons in my current herd that are from here that I can't talk to mentally. I would if I could because you're right. Those dragons are harder to talk to and look at. I get around it by pretending that it's not me doing the talking. I've fooled myself into believing that I'm all sorts of people. Check this out."

"Can you move the sign up a little higher? I can't fix the roof tile like that."

Kayla stared at her uncle. She had watched his mouth move and say those words, but it wasn't his voice at all that had spoken and she knew voices. She was all about hearing voices to know people and dragons without looking at them. Conner didn't have magic to make his voice change on him, so she couldn't explain how he had changed his voice so well.

"That was weird."

Uncle Conner laughed. "I can do four different people. After that though, I'm out of luck."

"I can sound like myself," Kayla said, still amazed at her uncle. "Do another one!"

"Dinner is ready!" A female voice hollered to them from the direction of an open house window. A curious face peeked out too, but Kayla missed the features as her hood blocked them. She looked across the short distance of the field they stood in toward the house and hoped there was enough room to work up some speed.

"Can we race?!" Kayla cried. "I've been waiting practically my whole life to race you. I hear that you're unstoppable."

"I'll give you a head start," Conner laughed at her. That was all she was going to wait for before she dashed toward the house. Conner, unfortunately, ran in the opposite direction toward Tyler so Kayla stopped moving so fast. She heard her uncle start talking to Tyler and knew she would have to ask for a rematch later, because Conner wasn't coming. He wanted to threaten Tyler into silence.

"If you stay out here, Tyler, the dragons would love their own tasty snack. Something around six foot two with brown hair and the plumpness of a castle diet would be highly nutritious."

Behind her, Kayla heard several of the herd dragons lick their jaws. Tyler started running, but Conner must have grabbed his arm or something because she heard his feet tumble to a stop and Conner hissing something, most likely nasty, into Tyler's ear. Kayla left them to it as she reached the house.

She gave off a polite knock before opening the door to meet the woman who had already spied on them. She didn't see the woman right away. Conner had kids! Three blond daughters had been playing with a set of blocks, bored, but they changed their expressions when she came in. The older one stood up scanning Kayla over with interest. Given her height above Kayla's knee level, Kayla was guessing she was around five. Her younger sister was about eight inches shorter and around three. Then there was the youngest girl who still looked like a baby, but was currently standing so had to between a year and fifteen months. The baby of the bunch sat down as the older two jumped toward the door. She crawled over to the abandoned blocks to get them all to herself.

"Hi! Want to play?" the oldest asked.

Kayla managed to give off a nod before she was tackled. The five-year-old grabbed her around the legs, declaring loud and clear that she would take Kayla down. Her accomplice jumped at Kayla's arms telling her to drop all her weapons like they were rehearsing a bedtime story they had heard recently. Kayla had to smile. She had actual cousins on her mother's side! Seeing Uncle Conner had been a thrill, but there was something special about his kids that had her play growling and rolling with them on the floor.

"Girls! Manners!" The woman screamed from an adjoining room.

"But Mom!" the older child voiced, "Dad said that someone had shown up to play!"

"He didn't mean with you. You might be too young to understand, but he meant that our visitors are here to play with him or

Pg. 193

perhaps with those stomping dragons outside. Keep them out of our hair for an hour," the woman mumbled the last sentence.

Kayla cringed on the idea of playing with a horde of dragons. She'd take playing with her cousins, thanks.

"I really don't mind," Kayla called back to ease some of the tension.

From outside the house there was another knock on the door. It was probably Tyler. Kayla glanced at it, but it wasn't her home, so she didn't feel inclined to let him in, and he wasn't rude enough to open it for himself.

"You'd better not be playing that game over Tova!" the woman hollered again without showing up as if she was too busy spying out the window at Conner trying to determine what sort of visit this might be if Tyler was there. She sounded worried, and it wasn't all because of the sounds of roughhousing from the front room.

"She's fine, Mom!" the oldest of the three called back.

Tova. That was the cutest name for a little baby. Kayla regarded the three girls again and made a mental note about how Conner had no sons. There were still no other male keepers for Aralot's throne. It had to be the result of a curse that Jack hadn't found yet. She would need to look into it. As it was, Kayla was a little busy escaping the small holds that her cousins tried to put her in. It was a welcome distraction from her thoughts concerning her birth.

Not only had she been born into a broken bond, but her parents hadn't even planned on her. She had surprised her mom right after Tia had lost her first bonded dragon, lost both her parents, lost her sanity, and lost part of her self-confidence. That was the real legacy of Kayla's birth. She was magically born. The cynical part of her mind asked if her parents had wanted her at all, but the more rational part knew that they loved her regardless of her birthday.

"If you would just stop moving, I'd have you down for sure," the younger of the two attackers told Kayla. Kayla laughed at her and that seemed to be the last straw for their mother. She stepped into the room with her hands on her hips now more assured that Conner had things outside under control. Kayla wondered what the woman thought of the stranger hidden in a gray sweater tumbling with her children. It would be hard to make Kayla out.

Conner's wife had medium-length brown hair that curled at the ends. Her brown eyes sat beneath purple eyeshadow and accented her white and purple dress. Her lips were lightly pink and her face slim. In one glance, Kayla had already decided that this was one of those fun, popular, pretty girls that all the boys chased. It wasn't too surprising that her Uncle Conner had won the race on this one. Kayla gave the woman a smile as she wiggled her legs out of the older girl's belly hug and let the younger girl clamp down on her arm.

"If you would stop attacking, we could be good friends," Kayla said.

Had that sentence really come from her mouth? Since when did she decide to be someone's friend that fast? She questioned everyone, although she had to laugh again at her cousins when the oldest started inching up her legs telling Kayla to pretend that the girl was a rope tying her up.

"Does this rope have a name?" Kayla questioned, watching as Conner's wife stepped further into the room. She had a rather socially aware baby, because one look at the fear on her mother's face had Tova wailing as if she was the one in trouble. Her mother didn't come to pick her up though. The sound went ignored as the woman glanced toward the door, as Tyler knocked again, and then she looked toward a closet. Hopefully, she wasn't contemplating locating a weapon or anything.

"I'm Sashi and your royal bracelet is Ruth," the five-year-old informed Kayla.

Ruth continued yanking on Kayla's arm while Sashi clung to her leg. Sashi, Ruth, and Tova. Could those names get any sweeter?

"Very royal indeed. My name is Kayla," Kayla replied tugging off the hood and giving each of them a disarming smile. She had practiced that one against Colts a lot and it had her feeling smug when the two girls let her go and jumped backward.

"Dad said that he fell in love with mom right away," Sashi told her. The oldest girl looked at her mother fondly and then back at Kayla. "So sparks can fly fast, and I think I've already fallen in love with you."

"No," Ruth said. "It's my turn for that line!"

They were funny. Kayla couldn't help but laugh again for their imagination while she wondered what sort of role she was playing in their pretend game. It appeared that the heroes were very quick at tying up an intruder and then falling in love with them. But if it wasn't a game, she felt it too. She really liked her cousins. Anvil said that keepers could sense an instant connection with each other. Since Kayla had known all the other keepers from birth, she had never understood what that really meant until now. That had to be what had her trusting Uncle Conner so fast.

"Did you know that we're cousins?" Kayla asked as she stood up and gave another smile to Conner's wife. The woman's mouth dropped open on the word and then she paled. She continued to ignore the crying Tova as she moved to the front door with a look of determination.

"Dad says not to lie," Sashi said, "but he does it. He tries to make us believe stupid things. One time he tried to make me think that if I didn't brush my hair it would turn green."

"It did turn green!" Ruth shouted. "It was freaky!"

"Mrs. Jones told me that it had to be hair dye put there by Dad not the missing comb."

Kayla giggled. Conner was great. She knew she already liked him, but now she liked him even more. His wife yanked open the door and glared as she let Tyler inside. Conner was right behind him, and the tight smile that he gave to his wife was enough to get Kayla off the floor. From the looks on their faces, no one was going to help Tova, so Kayla swooped up the child herself instantly cutting off the crying.

"That's remarkable," Conner noted using Tova as an excuse to step into the house around his frustrated wife. "Tova won't let anyone hold her except for us. She screams like a banshee."

Kayla nodded. She hadn't missed his remark that he was left out on all the tidbits of keeper lore that Anvil had picked up over the years. As a keeper himself, all of it would interest him.

"It's a family thing," Kayla told him. She was also good with kids. In fact, whenever she stopped by for a visit Annaliese took it to mean that she got an unexpected break. She would venture out to run errands or visit friends or work in her garden while Kayla became the babysitter. She didn't mind at all. It was another way to help Uncle Anvil with his busy lifestyle.

"If you were to talk to Uncle Anvil, he'd give you a full sermon on what he believes about our family. We're going to share an instant respect. Anvil says that there's always a clear leader that emerges from the family group that takes charge in a council to break ties even if that person isn't the oldest. The others seek to protect that spokesperson because of magical ties. Since that person tends to be my mom, and she hardly ever fights with her sister, there's not been a real need for that council thing. They see each other all the time and they see me way too much. We've lost everybody else. If Anvil's rule is true that there has to be at least five of us at a time then we're still missing someone."

"I know," Conner nodded. "Sometimes I wonder if I have a little brother."

Kayla shook her head. They had never found another male keeper. There was Tia, Rosa, Conner, and now Kayla. Whoever the missing keeper was to create five of them, could be hiding away in Wisteria or in Vankerdale as Conner was doing, ignoring the pressure to take over the throne. However, Kayla didn't think any other male keeper would keep away for so long.

"If you haven't noticed, apart from my grandfather and you none of the rest of us are male, and my mom and aunt miscarry all their other kids so there's just me besides…"

Kayla trailed off because she wasn't sure how much information Conner had shared with his young children yet. The younger generation of keepers included Kayla and Conner's kids. His children might not know that they had the tendency to hear dragon thought without being bonded. They still had a while before they had to worry about it, and Kayla was going to give them all that extra time worry free. It would have been nice to grow up without feeling like she was a disappointment for never hearing dragons she didn't want to communicate with.

It looked like Conner's wife hadn't heard what her children and husband were because she grabbed Tova away from Kayla with a glare and asked Conner to explain.

"It's nothing, Esmay," Conner tried to sooth. He didn't manage his chosen task fast enough.

"That had better not be the girl you've been waiting for. The one that will take you away. We've talked about this! You said that you were happy here."

"I am," Conner agreed. "And I never said a young girl would take me away, only that if I found her, I'd take a vacation—"

"You're running away!"

Oh, dear. Kayla had started a marital conflict even if she had been very careful not to say the word "keeper" in her explanation. She glanced toward Tyler who had chosen to stare at his shoes to avoid eye contact with anyone.

"She needs me!" Conner pointed at Kayla and Kayla felt like hiding away again herself.

"I need you. We all need you. You are not taking the kids. I won't have you disrupting their lives with tales of secret Colt missions. They don't need that, Conner. You send Kayla away."

"No. She's just a girl and she's not here to take me away. She's here to find her dad who got a little lost."

"You don't need to get involved. I can recognize Aralot garb even if I've never been there. The only thing those people bring is trouble."

"Actually, they're the ones that remove our curses so we can be happy again," Tyler said.

"You be quiet Tyler Valeron," Esmay ordered him.

Tyler clammed back up looking surprised that this woman knew his name. Kayla wasn't shocked. Conner would have married someone just as savvy as he was. Esmay went back to complaining to her husband.

"This is exactly what I'm talking about. Your obsession for castle affairs is bred into you by being a Colt, but please don't breed that into our children. They—"

Conner grabbed his wife's arm and marched her into another room. The arguing voices got quieter, but Kayla still felt bad for causing it all the same. Even if she had said nothing about being related, Esmay was going to be against her because Kayla wore a rider's backpack. At least she didn't wear leather gear all the time like her parents to look like a dragon rider.

"I still like you," Sashi told Kayla, noticing her discomfort.

"Thanks, honey. I still like you too, but maybe I shouldn't have said anything."

"Like cluing me in that you really meant Conner was your uncle?" Tyler asked. "Everything keeps getting more and more twisted."

"I heard that," Conner called from the other room poking his head back over. "You keep a tight lid, Tyler, or you'll find something you don't like."

"What about dinner? Can we help set the table?" Kayla asked, grabbing at Tyler's arm so he came with her to the kitchen. Adults appreciated volunteers. Maybe she could help Tyler not get so many threats if he was volunteering to help, even if it was forced volunteering. She didn't know why she was even trying to help him at all, but there was just this happy connection in the air by being around her cousins that she didn't want to burst. That, and she had to find some way to get on Esmay's good side.

Search Warrant

Tristan

Vermelo was certain that Kayla had been taken away into Vankerdale. Tristan was going to verify that with a magical mirror. It had been a full day and a half since those claims, and too many important things could have happened in that time frame. Since hearing Vermelo's treasonous thoughts, Tristan wouldn't be surprised if Kayla's absence was partly Vermelo's doing. He could have conspired with Wisteria to get a spellbinding dragon to start a war with Vankerdale. A war would be just the thing to locate Jack if he was there. King Peyton would surely say something about having Aralot's king if they started clashing.

Jack was probably in Vankerdale. That Tristan believed, but Kayla had been taken by a spellbinding dragon and could have been carted back to Wisteria. She could be on a boat in the ocean. In which case, she would be feeling incredibly seasick with that curse that Tristan had put on her to prevent her from fleeing oversees.

Tristan made his way into the game room where he knew Vermelo had hidden one of the ancient artifacts from Aralot's founding days. It was a mirror in a thin tin frame, unremarkable in appearance, but gorgeous in use. The thing had been crafted to find lost people; particularly lost dragon riders who had gone missing after invasions.

King Klavian had taken the mirror away from Vermelo before, but Vermelo had gotten it back from him when Klavian accidentally left it out in the parlor. Klavian was yet to find it a second time to take it away from Vermelo, but Tristan had found it, and he liked to leave it where it was so that he could also use it. If his father got the mirror, it could very well end up back in the magical library and Tristan didn't like going there. The game room was a much nicer location to spy on anyone he wanted to see.

Tristan walked past a puzzle that some of the servants had been working on during their lunch breaks and pulled down a box that no one ever touched because the game inside took players around in a circle and led to utter boredom. Behind that was the empty box with no markings and inside that box was the magic mirror. Tristan got it out of the box, set himself up at a table with the box in front of him to block the view of anyone who might enter the room, and watched the magic work.

"Show me Kayla Brixton," Tristan told the mirror. The device turned instantly dark which caused Tristan to shrug. King Peyton had messed up the mirror when he found it in the magical library many years ago. No one could use the mirror to see anyone that was inside of Vankerdale. So that meant that Kayla really had to be there if he couldn't see what she was up to. He tested out Jack's name next generating the same result. Then he tried for Dani, his girlfriend.

The dreamy girl was currently inside a sandstone building, listening to a lecture. Tristan couldn't hear the lecture because if the mirror was held upside down sound wouldn't come out. It was hard to tell which was right side up, so sometimes it took Tristan a few tries to get the thing working properly. Given the time of day, no sound was better. Dani was twirling her curly black hair on her fingers looking a little bored. Tristan watched for a few more moments before he shut the mirror off. He hid the item again before anyone could enter the room and catch him using it.

Okay, enough spying. He had work to do. Not only did he want to locate a spell that could break binding magic, but it would be helpful to find a spell that would get around King Peyton's shield of darkness on this mirror. Tristan knew that Jack had used a similar spell to keep King Peyton from spying on the inside of his house, because if Jack, Tia, or Kayla were in their northern home, the mirror likewise wouldn't work.

When anyone tried to spy into that home, they got a message telling them to mind their own business. The first time Tristan had read the message he had laughed. Why not turn the mirror black? No, Jack had to tell you that he acknowledged your desire to pry. Tristan took that to mean that prying eyes would find something worth seeing. He'd always wanted to see into that house. If Jack could find a spell to shield them, Tristan was certain he could find a spell to take down shields. He just had to think like Jack. Where would the man hide his knowledge about spells?

Most likely inside his own rather protected house. Even with Tia at the castle and Kayla and Jack inside Vankerdale, Tristan suspected that getting into that house would be a problem. Tristan had tried to get into it before only to be stopped by the bark of protective dragons. He had tried to gain an invitation inside, only to have the location of his requested meeting moved on him to the castle. He had gotten himself invited to Kayla's birthday party a few times over the years. Those were always fun. Kayla spent the whole time hiding from everyone under her hood while the rest of them ate Tia's remarkable cooking outside. Always outside.

Tristan sighed as he thought about Kayla. Wherever that girl was, he pictured her wandering around with her hood up over her head pretending to be unconnected to the rest of the world. Maybe the only thing she was good at was magic, which was disconcerting. Jack's daughter knew most of the spells he knew so she could probably give Tristan the answers he was looking for. However, talking to her was always a struggle. She never looked him directly in the face, and when she did, he was certain that she was challenging him over something. The only person she really buddied up to was Anvil.

Ah. He was back to Anvil again. Tristan couldn't attack Anvil to get him to squeal on what Kayla may have taught him over the years, but Anvil was still at the castle leaving his home base undefended, and he wouldn't have as many hard spells to take down like Jack's place did. Anvil performed spells under the table because he had never liked the idea of only the king holding all the power. Maybe he had left something open that would help Tristan.

This could work. Tristan would go to Anvil's Ware and see what he could make of it. He hadn't sleuthed through there in ages, but first, he had better check to see that Anvil really was still here or he was going to ruin his own genius. Tristan glanced toward the hiding mirror again, but he heard voices moving through the halls and didn't want to risk exposure. He had to find Anvil on his own.

Given the time of midday, Tristan checked the dining room first. It was empty except for a wooden cutting board with bread crumbs on it. Tristan knew exactly who had left that on the table. When his father got busy, he often forgot to eat meals and grabbed things he could nibble. Tristan hadn't seen his father at all last night at the dinner table, and he hadn't seen his mother this morning at breakfast. He had heard whispers that they were mounting forces for war, and he had heard that they were not. With all the given speculation, he expected his mother had taken up the job of spying. His father would be hovelled up around a pile of books.

He was just about to pass the music room, but a quick glance inside changed that. The room was empty of musicians, but Tia and Anvil were in there. Bingo! Anvil was still here. Time to get a search warrant from his dad so he could rifle through the man's things. What to say to get it though...

Pg. 204

Tristan thought over his options as he cocked his head at Tia's profile. It looked like Tia had been crying. Anvil told her that Kayla would be just fine, having now taken up Tia's own battle cry on the subject, and Tia rushed into his arms causing him to grin larger than was appropriate. Tristan found himself staring at the unfolding scene.

"Don't tell anyone, but I'm not that worried about Kayla. I'm incredibly stressed out over Jack. You know he'll try to do everything on his own whatever it is."

Anvil pulled Tia in closer still smiling. He was not thinking about Kayla or Jack at all. His arms were wrapped around Tia and his mind was miles into the sky. Without knowing that anyone was watching him, he wasn't about to hold back.

"It's been a long time since we've been in this position," Anvil whispered.

Tia smacked him on the arm, but it was a rather soft hit as if she was starting to yield to all his peer pressure. Tristan considered coughing really really loud.

"I need to find Jack," Tia complained. "It's not like I have to stay here to watch Kayla."

"In case you're forgetting, you can't leave," Anvil reminded her. "You'll never make it out of Aralot, just like you won't make it out of these arms."

"Anvil!" Tia cried.

She moved in to punch him again and Tristan missed the interaction because Vermelo came out of nowhere to pull him out of the way. He could still hear the scuffle though. A few of the chairs in the room were pushed around and Tia started laughing, claiming she was going to get Anvil for what he said. If Tristan hadn't already used that mirror, he could make himself believe that Anvil had Jack locked up.

Once Jack was out of his way, Anvil couldn't help but flirt. Tristan could picture Jack refusing to let Pyro tell Tia where he was if Anvil was the one who had him. He'd be too embarrassed.

"You have a problem with friends helping each other through stress?" Vermelo asked Tristan.

Tristan yanked his arm out of his enemy's grip and returned his challenge.

"That was *very* friendly. It's nice to see this kingdom is in good hands. Good day, Vermelo."

One day Vermelo would be sorry that he was still employed. The man's eyes followed Tristan down the hallway as Tristan looked for his dad next. At least his father was predictable in location. Magic library, castle library, or his room. The room was Tristan's first choice and his last stop.

King Klavian was spread out on the bed reading a book. He looked up briefly to wave Tristan inside before finishing the page. Tristan closed the door softly behind him as he tried to remember his exact wording to get what he wanted.

"Did you happen to pass Vermelo? Is he distracted?" Klavian asked. He put a bookmark in the book as he sat up and crossed his legs on the bed.

"He's a little distracted. Why?"

"Something needs to be done about him. He's been working behind my back. He's been trying to entice Rosa and Clark to take over the castle. Did you know that?"

"Yup," Tristan replied. "I was going to mention it to you only I hadn't seen you until now."

Tristan had been busy moving fresh magic orbs to his chosen

secret hiding place at the Desert Ware last evening. While he was there, he had spent a lot of time flirting with Dani. She was very distracting.

"I don't know if I can afford to fire Vermelo," Klavian moped. "He's got all the spies and guards on his side. We have the wares but they wouldn't get here fast enough if he took action against us. Kayla going missing is worse than I ever expected it to be. She shouldn't have been able to break through the border spells. I've been giving it a lot of thought, and I think that dragon is to blame. Spellbinding dragons suck up magic. It must have eaten everything in its path."

"What are you doing about Vermelo?" Tristan asked, before his father got sidetracked talking about dragons eating magic. He still hoped that Kayla would stay in Vankerdale so that Tristan didn't have to worry about her anymore.

"Maybe nothing. I wanted you to be aware that Vermelo could be dangerous."

"He's been sending me threats for months. I know he claims it's not him, but who else could it be? I hope you have protection spells. Vermelo doesn't want us here."

Klavian clicked his tongue together instead of contradicting him as Tristan expected. Maybe his father wasn't being so naïve after all. He just didn't want to voice his concerns around Vermelo, who was always near.

"I found this." He passed Tristan the book he was holding. "I wrote it on the bookmark."

The bookmark featured a spell that could force Vermelo to be super loyal to anyone. It used a ton of magic though. Forcing wills was not an easy thing to do, and if it ever came off, Vermelo was likely to get mad and take revenge.

"I know you get magic from Mr. Grumpy," his father told him.

"Could you take charge of this problem with Vermelo? I don't want him dead. He's too valuable alive, but we need to make sure he doesn't take us down."

Tristan stared at the bookmark thinking of how close a loyalty spell came to actual possession. Tia, Jack, and Kayla were always on the lookout for possession spells, but this one might sneak past them. His father wasn't half bad. Klavian hadn't been around for the first seven years of Tristan's life, because his love to Aria had been forbidden and then he had been locked up by the monks, but since coming back, his dad had proved he was awesome plenty of times. Here Tristan thought that Klavian was trying to find a spell to end the lockdown on the nearby town, but he had really been finding this to use against Vermelo. Awe aside, Tristan brought up his own desire from his father.

"I would like a search warrant for Anvil's Ware."

"You'll take care of Vermelo?" Klavian double-checked. "I'd do it myself except he would catch me. What's the search warrant for?"

"Yes, I'll take care of Vermelo. The search warrant is so I can get in there and analyze the threat Anvil poses. Rosa and Clark are both at his ware. Kayla's there more than half the time too. Anvil has the strongest dragons in the entire kingdom. If they're preparing to turn on us, we need to be aware."

Klavian nodded and started to write one up. Ha! Tristan was using Vermelo's tactics against him. He was going to comb over that ware with a magnifying glass.

"Tia is still being knuckleheaded over Vankerdale, but she won't leave the castle to sit at home alone. We sent more spies into Wisteria in search of information on spellbinding dragons," Klavian said as he wrote. When he finished, he plopped back on the bed. "And your mother is missing. She might have gone into Vankerdale. She gets everywhere."

Pg. 208

Yeah, but Tristan didn't think she would cross the border for Kayla at all. He gave his father a shrug. Queen Aria had to be conversing with spies and merchants trying to get the good information that way.

With the search warrant in his hand, Tristan thanked his dad and walked outside to see Riven. The gleaming bronze animal shook his head at him for being so late coming out today. He couldn't help it! He was up to his knees in trying to stay one step ahead of Kayla coming to dethrone him, and up to his shoulders keeping Tia and her dragon army from crashing down on him first.

Tristan ran his hand over the dragon's leather gear, checking it for tears and scratches since he'd not done that in a while. Riven was a large animal reaching up to eleven feet. His tail and wings were as strong as they could be for a bronze dragon since he had forced himself to practice a few ice dragon techniques. He couldn't launch into the air from a standing position, but his about-face turns were incredible.

Riven had these gorgeous yellow eyes that had sunk into Tristan's soul the first time he had seen them. He also had a few scales that were growing back. Those were gifts from the last time he and Tristan had tried to take down the demon ultra-dragon king that Herb had created. Tristan made sure they were coming in well, replaced the scale putty that acted as a bandage, and climbed up.

They took the portals to Anvil's Ware so Tristan wasn't surprised when they were immediately surrounded after stumbling through the magical device. Since finding the portal, Anvil kept scouts here constantly. Most of the time the only person they ever saw was Kayla, and they let her climb down the rocky surface without pestering her. Everyone else got engulfed.

The scouts circled around Tristan and Riven demanding to know why they were there as they flew in closer to the ware. He asked to be taken to the man in charge. Tristan noticed two squadrons of scout troops in the air. One was older and more established and the other one younger. Looking at the place from above, the ware was packed with riders and dragons. Anvil wasn't one to lie about his number of dragons, but seeing them in person made a large difference from seeing the numbers on paper. This ware would swamp the Desert Ware without sending half its riders over.

Tristan was brought down in the northern field where George was the section leader. At last, the heavy escort faded back, leaving Tristan beside George and Octavian, who was the west side section leader. They were discussing a group of individuals trying to decide how best to split the team up now that they had transferred out one of the other students and didn't have the right number of riders for formations. If Tristan thought he needed a haircut, George always did. George had a full red beard that was just as long and shaggy as the hair coming down to his shoulders. Octavian was the polar opposite with a shaved head. He got his glamour out there by wearing decorative pins along the collar of his rider uniform. Both men greeted Tristan with short bows.

"What brings you by?" George asked with a slight frown. George had wanted the position of ware leader his whole life, but he had to keep giving it up. He first lost to Rogan, and then to Anvil, but he got in his share of duties as a section leader, and Anvil always let him have full control when he was away.

"I'm searching the ware," Tristan informed him. He handed the paper to Octavian who shoved it at George. Neither looked thrilled with the announcement although both read the paper.

"You can follow him," George volunteered his other section leader.

Follow him he did. Tristan walked into one of the bunkrooms and riffled through anything left out. He turned down Octavian's help for finding what he was looking for. He wasn't exactly sure what his aim was, only that he needed to know every inch of what Anvil was keeping around here. Anything could be used against him should Rosa and Clark or Kayla incite the call to battle. By looking at everything, hopefully, it would tucker Octavian out before Tristan went and searched through Anvil's things directly. If he took long enough, Octavian might stop being his shadow.

Octavian followed behind Tristan replacing anything that he didn't put back exactly as he had found it. Several times Octavian shooed people away, directing them to talk to George. Tristan searched through every bunkroom and all the tool sheds. He walked the perimeter of all the fields. With the size of the ware, daylight had already fled, forcing Octavian to carry around a torch for them.

Tristan stepped into the poison shed, after picking the lock on the room that contained such things as venom to break dragon bonds, and toxins to lug at enemies. He rummaged around, picking up dusty containers and moving beneath old shelves only to have his eyes notice a large old coin. No, not a coin. When he bent to pick it up and rubbed off the dust, he found that it was a medallion with a bear printed on each side. Tristan had looked for hidden secret magical artifacts before, but as his father had noted previously, Tia and Jack kept the best ones missing so no one else who hunted for them could pick them up. Ice dragons loved treasure hunts, so Klavian had been excited that they had a controllable one that would look for lost magic until he realized that everything Sparkle found Tia hid again. This coin could be magical. One way to tell.

"Reveal." Tristan cast his spell on the item to determine what it was. He felt the magic, warm and comforting, trickle down his arm and out past his hand. Unlike Jack and Kayla who let their magic be visible, Tristan never let his magical gems get seen. He had several of them, plain and unadorned, pushed into seams of his clothing so that if he lost one magical token, he wouldn't really lose his power.

An image of walking from one place into another showed up in the air above the medallion. Every ancient artifact had been recorded inside the castle, and having read the list, Tristan was pretty sure that the medallion in his hand was supposed to have a second half; a connecting medallion that had to be active in order to use either one. With both, he could move through space jumping between one coin to the other, similar to using a portal but without all the extra headspace. A dragon wouldn't fit. Tristan expected using the medallion to leave him feeling woozy, but he was still going to try it out once he found that second half.

He cast another spell to see who had used it last and an image of Vladimir appeared. The man was a past ware leader, famous for his ability to create ice dragons and infamous for dying on the same day he killed off Tia's first ice dragon named Misty.

"That Leech!" Octavian shouted.

"Looks like you guys don't search through here very often. He's been dead sixteen years already."

"Is that what you were looking for?" Octavian asked, tilting the torch a little too close so that Tristan had to back away from the flame.

"Among other things."

Tristan pocketed the medallion for later. This was super exciting, but he had to control his glee with Octavian around. Tia and Sparkle had never found this artifact due to the overpowering smell of poison that had been around it. Tristan had an ancient relic!

He continued to pluck through the ware. When he reached the south, the section leader there, Roman, wasn't very happy with him when he woke up people in bunkrooms and had them turn their trunks inside out. Roman's side of the ware featured smaller bunkrooms because this was the side where married people lodged. Tristan was impressed with the number of children around. Anvil didn't have to list children on his roster, since they were not bonded. He had a small army in underage kids that would rally to his words. Spooky.

It was extremely uncomfortable for Tristan when he ran across Rosa and Clark's room. Rosa had returned home, and she emptied out several unused baby outfits from her trunk. Tristan tried to not feel bad for her inability to have children. Clark glared at him. He had a few contraband items in his possession, but Tristan didn't comment on them. Clark wasn't allowed any rings that could let him use magic, or the magic books that talked about dispelling dark magic spells. He also had fireworks and a bunch of other people's letters among his stack of illegal items. Tristan didn't dare ask why he had those. Roman looked the other way too.

"How's my sister doing?" Rosa asked as Tristan watched her pack her items back up.

"The last time I walked past her she had been crying," Tristan told her honestly.

"What's this search all about?" Clark asked.

"You have a good night Clark. Rosa. Good to see you again," he lied before he stepped out and continued his search.

He found interesting clues about Kayla, which looked to be harmless. She had her own trunk shoved underneath a bed on the eastern side. No one would open it for him or tell him whose it was when he asked. He picked the lock on the chest and dumped everything out. The extra gray hooded sweater gave him all the clues he needed. She also had a few questionable items like the half-eaten bars of candy, broken tools, and one of Anvil's monogrammed letter stamps. The trunk contained a book about identifying rock types, unfinished homework, and a crumpled note that came from her dad reminding her to take the trash out. Tristan was more careful to put her things back in order as he packed it back up, replaced the lock, and left the room.

"When are you going to be done?" Octavian asked him, when Tristan reached the middle section for his fourth time. He was joined by two of Tia's connected riders. Tristan identified Ruthfort and Achilles, the riders of Duchess and Fang. Maybe he was taking a little bit too long if Tia was being notified of his activities. It wasn't like she could do anything about it though. He had a search warrant and wasn't harming anything more than sleep and time.

"When I've looked everywhere," Tristan replied. "Only a few places left."

He looked toward his next target, one of the rooms he had really been itching to get inside—Anvil's office. George would have a key to this place so Tristan didn't think Anvil would keep anything too incriminating in there, but he would keep notes and records of invasion plans inside. Tristan picked the lock much to Octavian's dismay and stepped inside.

Octavian stood directly in front of the files, blocking Tristan off from searching through them. Suspicious? It looked like it, but Tristan regarded the behavior more as defensive than anything else. Octavian was trying to stick up for Anvil even if he had to block off a prince.

Tristan decided to be specific in his requests to get what he wanted. He asked to see the ware roster which was something that any rider could ask for. Octavian fetched it out with narrowed eyes. It had been a breeding year and Anvil had added twelve new dragons to his ranks. The year before that had been similar. It was always similar. Where was Anvil finding room to expand? Nothing had attacked his dragons the entire time he had been ware leader. He was getting too large.

Tristan poked around the rest of the room slowly, finding small hints and reminders that Tia and Anvil were friends. There were stacks of their letters that were double locked and placed inside a protection

Pg. 214

spell. Tristan thought he had found another secret magical token when he reached the second lock and the spell, but when he riffled the letters, he got disappointed and put it all back.

"Why are you here?!" Octavian demanded. Tristan gave him a short smile and hid again a drawing that Tia had created for Anvil that had been slid between two untouched books. It was a picture of Clawson with Misty.

"One room left," Tristan informed him. Octavian was all glares behind him because the last room was Anvil's special study. The room Anvil secretly performed magic inside. It was also the place where he kept all his really good books. Tristan avoided looking at Octavian which might rile him into an attack, although Octavian couldn't hurt him. The worst he could do was attack Riven, and if they did, he might as well declare war on the king right then.

There were a few spells on the study door that Tristan took down before he shoved at the handle. There was no keyhole, but the door was nevertheless locked. Tristan grinned at the fortifications and had fun knocking on the door to learn what was blocking it further. There was a crossbar pushed down on the inside. He used magic to pull it up and heard the wooden item thud to the ground on the other side. Nice. Anvil had to use magic to get into his own room.

Tristan ventured inside, finding the study well loved. There were items left open on the long narrow desk that ran the entire length of one wall. Most of them related to magic spells that Anvil had been practicing. The other walls were filled with crowded bookcases. Octavian stepped into the room after him looking nervous to be in the place.

Tristan already knew that Anvil studied protective spells, but the books on his shelves showed way more than that. He actively practiced advanced magic while hiding away in this room. Tristan guessed he got his magic supply from Tia. Who else would give him the stuff? He glanced at the open spells and a note that had been left beside one of the books.

"Page seventy-four answers Kayla's question," it read.

Tristan picked up the book and flipped to the page. What was Kayla asking about? The page talked about how to summon a school of fish to make fishing easy. Was this her homework? She couldn't set foot on a boat without feeling seasick. Tristan grinned at the note wondering how often Kayla's homework was really her parents sending her off to hunt for spells they wanted to use. This did make Anvil look more frightening to magically attack though. He was the one providing the missing answers. Tristan set the book down as he found it and skimmed the rest of the room before stepping out.

He replaced the spells, thanked Octavian for his time, and found Riven sleeping. Tristan didn't let his smile cross his face until he was out of sight of Anvil's night scouts. It was a productive search. He had learned that Anvil was overpopulated, that Tia and Kayla both half lived with Anvil, and that Vladimir used to have access to Anvil's poison shed. Tristan pulled the medallion out of his pocket and ran his fingers along the bear. It was going to be really hard to find the second medallion. Not only could Tia and Sparkle have it especially hidden, but right before Vladimir had died, his entire ware had been blazed to the ground. If he had his connecting medallion inside his ware at his death, it could be buried really really well beneath new construction.

"Too bad we don't know a spell that would locate the other half," Riven thought to Tristan sleepily, as he flew them back to the castle. Tristan rubbed his hands along his dragon's neck one step ahead of him.

"But we do know a dragon that would love to search for it," Tristan replied.

He would let Riven rest and then they would go see Bantin again. Tristan couldn't entice Sparkle to find him things, but Bantin was starved
Pg. 216

for entertainment. He wouldn't mind searching for a lost artifact that had belonged to Vladimir. Maybe Tristan would use Jack's strategy and entice him with a few sheep.

Monolith

Tyler

Tyler slipped out of the house so he could go watch the dragons and get away from Conner and Kayla. Kayla had kept everyone up last night even after Conner had picked her up and moved her into another room that had better sound control. She hadn't stirred at all while her nightmares were shared by everybody. It wasn't very hard to tell what she had been dreaming about. Even Conner's kids were picking up on her fears as she screamed about them.

"Stop! She doesn't need the tar. He doesn't need the acid. You do realize that the suffix -ious means to be full of. You should be full of gladness, not this."

Kayla was having a nightmare about her great-grandfather Gladius torturing his dragons. Conner had tried to wake her up and then gave up on her to pass out earplugs. Tyler hadn't been able to sleep with the earplugs so he'd heard more.

"Of all the stupid things. You do this every single time! Don't give Wisteria that curse! And he does it again."

All night long her comments were about torture and pain and war. Tyler wondered if it had something to do with her being unbonded, except that Conner said he never got dreams like this. They had all gone outside to look for Valiant to get him to make Kayla stop screaming, only Valiant had taken off to get away from it. Unlike the dragon, the people didn't have another place to sleep, so they were left to suffer through the screaming. At least Tyler couldn't see what she was seeing.

Then came morning and Tyler thought he might finally get a few hours of rest. Nope. Conner was up, and he was proving that he had his keeper qualities down tight. Conner was everything Tyler had read about in a keeper with the exception of his bond being broken. He got information about events happening hours away from him in an instant.

"There are dragons being outfitted for war at the border. You're going to tell me what King Peyton plans to do with those. Also, Prince Evan was found immobile in the woods. Know anything about that?"

Tyler wasn't sure how he got out of explaining hours and hours of overheard war strategy with Conner. All he had told him was that Kayla had put Prince Evan in a spell to get away from him and the dragons were probably there to catch her should she run back home. He could recall Conner's own war strategies too well. Tyler would take Kayla's freeze spells over turning into a pastry for the cleverest dragon herd in all of Vankerdale, especially since their herd master had placed him on the menu. Now Tyler was trying to sneak away to get some peace and quiet. He closed the front door softly behind him glad that Kayla had stopped being so loud.

He sat down on the porch steps and looked out toward the dragons noticing that Valiant had come back finally. Tyler normally made a point of spying on the dragons that regularly came to the castle. That was where the ones who had once been bonded came so they could chat with each other and commiserate that the king had not fixed their bonds. There were several of them in particular that Tyler fancied more than others. He wondered how different it would be to watch dragons wake up that were part of a keeper bond.

He wouldn't admit it to Kayla, but he was jealous of keepers. He watched as the first of Conner's dragons woke up. It was a brown female dragon if he was correct. She blew a blast of hot air onto the sleeping green dragon beside her. The dragon covered his face with his tail and ignored her.

Tyler watched as she tried to wake up a few other dragons. The largest green one, Tempest, yawned from the other side of the sleeping herd before telling her to stop bothering them. The brown dragon snorted about everyone being lazy and took off on her own. Tempest yawned again and went back to sleep for half a minute before jumping to his feet and calling out a warning that got all the other dragons instantly awake. The dragons leapt to action as one.

They were so impressive but what was the warning? The brown dragon circled overhead coming back moments after leaving. She chirped out the same warning and then snorted her annoyance to find that the rest of her herd was already awake now that Tempest had given his command. The female dragon landed in the group and all the dragons watched the sky.

A few minutes later a pale green dragon flew over them, giving out a friendly hello. Tyler recognized the dragon. It was the same one that had circled around Kayla earlier that had chirped to her and then helped Valiant escape the wild group they had flown over. It had found her and come alone.

Tempests herd watched the dragon circle around them. It was fascinating how none of them started to attack. Dragons that were strangers to each other often did that. Tyler knew from his extensive reading that this wasn't the case before bonds were broken. Dragons were friendlier back before his parents were born, and it looked like these ones were rather friendly despite the havoc they always threw at the castle. Tyler gained a whole new respect for Conner's dragons. They didn't do anything mean. One of them said hello back. The light green dragon circled a few more times before taking the risk of landing.

"Friend?" it chirped out as it tried to judge the other dragons that were around. A few dragons of various colors walked farther away from the newcomer and curled back up to sleep behind the rest of the watching crowd.

The green dragon looked toward the sleeping house and loudly called "come out!" Tyler knew the green dragon was trying to get to see Kayla again. Tempest leapt through the rest of his herd and started to growl at him.

"He's looking for Kayla," Tyler said. He didn't bother to say it very loud. The dragons would be able to hear him from his distance on the porch steps. None of the dragons had time to react to his words because they were all suddenly reacting to a display of magic.

Tyler jumped to his feet with his heart hammering against his ribs terrified that King Peyton had sent a trap at them in the form of a large, well-muscled red dragon. The light green dragon screamed in terror and skid away from the red beast over his head. Tempest shrieked, jumped behind his herd to protect him, and then started laughing. His herd went from defensive growls to happy hellos.

Tyler glanced over at Valiant. He had woken up to look at the red dragon. He gave the beast a short snort and closed his eyes again as if there was nothing scary going on at all. Yes, there was! This red dragon had materialized out of thin air! The other dragons hadn't been able to see him or smell him. Tyler hadn't heard him and the red dragon wasn't that far away. This dragon had magic placed upon him. That was scary.

Tempest jumped back to the front of his heard humming happily. He gave the red dragon a bow that had Tyler stepping off the porch steps to get closer even if he was scared of the magic that had just been there. Only spellbinding dragons bowed when they wanted to impress others. Other dragons didn't do that sort of thing unless they were showing respect to a king. Was this a dragon king? Tyler had never seen this dragon before, but since Tempest had and Valiant wasn't worried, Tyler was guessing that the red dragon was Jack's unbonded animal, Pyro.

The dragon herd started to talk to the red dragon after that. They resembled a group of school children trying to show off for a surprise guest. A few of them came to nuzzle Pyro like they were best friends. All the while the light green dragon inched backward heading towards the other side of the house where it could see windows.

Tyler glanced behind him at the door, waiting for Conner to come out and see Pyro for himself, but he didn't. He probably didn't need to with all his other bonded dragons telling him that Pyro was there. Tyler suspected that Pyro had followed the light green one to learn where Kayla was hiding.

Pyro finished greeting Tempest with the friendliest of dragon hellos. He bonked his head into him and curled his tail around Tempest's legs. Then his large eyes turned themselves onto Tyler. The sudden commanding stare reminded Tyler too much of looking at Conner tell him to never say anything about him being a keeper. The eyes were so intense! Pyro scratched some large letters into the ground and looked back at Tyler.

"You can write?" Tyler asked him. Gee, dragon's in Aralot were so much smarter, well cared for, and overall brilliant than the dragons here. Tyler wanted to get over there even more to bond one, but he still had the problem of getting Kayla to like him enough to let him, not to mention that there was now an army that King Peyton had organized to stop them. Tyler looked at the written message reading it easily. It was Kayla's name.

"She's asleep. You should let her sleep. That girl had nightmares all night long. Don't wake her up."

Tyler's comment was too much for the light green creeping

dragon. Hearing that Kayla was nearby, it howled at the windows for her to come out again. Pyro jumped on him. Tyler ran back to the porch to get out of the way of the dragon battle, but there wasn't much of a battle. No flame. No snarls or scratching. Pyro gurgled out a message and shoved the green dragon over. He flamed the moss off the underside of the dragon's tail before telling him to be quiet. The green dragon sat down after that and waited.

Nothing could stop Tyler's jaw from dropping. Pyro was a dragon king, sure, but he'd never seen a dragon surrender that fast before. Even Tempest gave up control of his entire herd when Pyro looked over and started giving out demands. Tyler could only understand simple dragon words and phrases, so he couldn't really interpret the message Pyro spoke until dragons dashed into the air in groups. He guessed that Pyro was telling them where he had looked to find Jack and was now enlisting help to find his missing rider.

"You're Pyro, aren't you? I'm Tyler." He couldn't help but talk to the amazing dragon. Unlike Valiant, Tyler had no desire to make Pyro his own. Pyro's demeanor was too intimidating. He looked like the kind of dragon that was used to ordering things about, and Tyler felt like he'd be over powered if he ever had a dragon like this.

At his words, Pyro returned his gaze and wrote Tyler a new message answering yes.

"It's a pleasure to meet you, Pyro. Have you visited the dragon king stone yet? There's a monolith here that ancient dragons wrote on. Humans have been trying to interpret it for generations but they say only a dragon king will be able to understand it."

"Show me," Pyro wrote on the ground.

"Uh…" Tyler stepped back as Pyro turned sideways to him flashing more magic. One minute he was red-scaled all around, and the next, Pyro had a leather saddle on. That was one neat trick! Vankderdale

Pg. 224

dragons refused to put on saddles, and it was strange to see one on the animal. It was even stranger that Pyro could conceal it on himself without the help of Jack. Tyler found himself wishing that he kept his mouth a little more closed. Those large commanding eyes held no argument. Pyro demanded that Tyler ride him to the monument, causing him to gulp. Riding Valiant was one thing because Valiant was his friend. Getting on Pyro felt scary.

"Hey, Valiant?" Tyler asked, looking at the dragon and hoping that he was mostly awake so that he would answer. "Is this safe?"

Valiant thankfully cracked one eye open to look at him. He chirped out a yes and then curled into a tighter ball trying to go back to sleep. The poor dragon. Tyler wondered if he had heard all of Kayla's unsettled thoughts last night. They were enough to make any dragon feel exhausted and scared. It caused Tyler to frown. If Kayla had nightmares a lot, that would only be one more reason that Valiant didn't want her around other dragons that could be unsafe for her. Fixing their emotional imbalance looked complicated. He couldn't change up what Kayla dreamed about!

"I have to stick around to help Kayla," Tyler tried against Pyro. The growl that followed wasn't enough of a warning to avoid the tail that Pyro shot out. Perhaps if Tyler had trained to be a dragon rider, he would have known what to do about a tail shoving into him, but he hadn't gotten any of that kind of training. King Peyton was the only man that could get his dragon to answer his call on the first shout. SilverWings would let him ride him whenever he wanted to as well. Everyone else stood around on the ground and bribed and cried to get those dragons to come to them. Tyler had never managed to get any dragon down, although he'd tried a few times to call out to the ones he fancied.

Tyler had no idea how Pyro did it, but the tail deposited Tyler onto the saddle. Tyler plopped against it and then grabbed at the leather horn and the ropes to hold on. Yup, he was no match for a dragon like

Pyro. This dragon had commander and servant completely down. Before Tyler could complain, Pyro had him up in the air and was chirping out more commands. Tempests herd of dragons encircled the house guarding it. Kayla would be trapped there until the dragon king returned.

"Alright, well the monolith is west of here. I've never been there myself. It's on the other side of the great lake."

Tyler fixed his grip on the rope that was connected to the dragon's neck and tied in a knot at the top of the saddle. He wondered if he was supposed to untie the rope, but he wasn't feeling brave enough to do that.

"Would this be okay with Jack?" Tyler questioned. He'd watched riders brawl with each other for calling out to each other's dragons, even if the dragon had never made any indication that it liked a particular human. Tyler had always held a large respect for Jack, so he really didn't want to make the man mad at him.

Through yes and no questions, Tyler got answers. Pyro assured him that Jack would be fine with Tyler riding him. Pyro expressed that he loved Jack very much and that he wanted to see the old writings. A few times Pyro tried to communicate something else to him by talking but Tyler couldn't understand. He could understand basic dragon words like hello and goodbye, but most of the other words escaped him.

"It would be amazing to be a keeper," Tyler replied. "Then I could understand you."

Below him Pyro laughed and kept talking. After a while, Tyler got the impression that Pyro wasn't really talking to him. He was wishing to talk to Jack and his chatter was things he would like to tell his special friend. Tyler could understand the slightly sad intonation. Dragons here used it all the time when trying to talk to their riders who no longer could hear them. It was usually followed by the dragon

Pg. 226

screaming at the rider and fanging them trying to bond again.

While Pyro talked to himself, Tyler took in what it was like to be riding a trained dragon. He had never ridden one before. It was far different than riding inside of Valiant's claws or even on his back. Pyro didn't jostle him about. He moved through the wind currents easily going up and down to keep the wind beneath him so Tyler was not blasted with cold air. Tyler kept looking around trying to spot other wild dragons but he never did see any. Pyro had to be avoiding them. Dragons here would be offended at the sight of a saddled dragon with a rider on his back. The ones who were friendlier to humans would be jealous. Tyler was already jealous. The ride was so smooth! The flight was better than his dreams.

The saddle made staying on the dragon rather easy and Pyro was very polite with him. When Tyler admitted that he had not had breakfast, Pyro agreed that he could look in the saddlebag for food. Tyler opened the bag and started to search through it. There was food right on the top, but he was curious to see what else would be there. There was a whip and prongs and an entire case of knives. There was a pack of playing cards and a canteen of water. There was a document listing Aralot's price range for trading with Wisteria. The price of silk was circled a few times and the paper was smudged on the side. Tyler smiled. Wisteria tried to swindle their silk prices with Vankerdale too.

Tyler also found gloves and a hat and a first-aid kit. There was an extra sweater and change of clothes neatly rolled and tied together with string. There was a magic book that he opened up and smiled at it. The inside pages refused to be read by him. They were blank except for when he turned to the first page and then it told him to stop messing with the book. Slid into the back of the book was a picture that Tyler stared at for a while. It was Kayla and her parents. Hand sketched, the image had Kayla about five-years-old, swinging from between her parent's arms.

"Did you know there's a picture of Kayla in here?" Tyler asked

Pyro, as he checked their direction by looking down. He made sure the items were put back neatly into the bag, and he only ate what he needed to stop his stomach from rumbling.

"Yes," Pyro chirped, and started talking again this time about Kayla. Tyler couldn't understand him, but he could make out her dragon name. Valiant had used it too. They crossed over the great lake way faster than Tyler expected since he'd never been here. His days were filled with serving Prince Evan, and if he did get a rare break, it was spent at home feeling like he was missing out on the lives of his family that he never got to see. Sometimes it was nicer to head back to the castle to get away from the feeling of not belonging anywhere else.

Tyler didn't say anything when Pyro located the monolith, because he didn't want to get off. If he was quiet Pyro might forget he was there. No such luck. Pyro shoved Tyler off his back with his tail and then he circled the large stone on foot.

"I wish people in Vankerdale could hear dragons," Tyler mumbled, as he got back to his feet. He looked at the monolith too. It stood taller than a dragon, with writing etched in magical blue. Pyro stared at it. Then he stared at the monolith's shadow. Then he stared at the writing again. He blew on it. He licked it. He smashed his head against it, and hit it with his tail.

"Explain," Pyro wrote into the grassy ground. His claws dug the letters in deep, tearing up the grass as he did so.

"I don't know what it says. It's been there for centuries. History records it...well about the same time that Aralot was created into a kingdom." Pyro gave off a curious chirp so Tyler kept going. He had been reading way too much about Aralot lately anyway. The information came easily.

"There were two twin brothers born to a king back when Aralot was part of Vankerdale. We used to be a single kingdom. The twins both wanted to rule so the king divided up the kingdom and one son founded Aralot. He named his kingdom after his dragon. The other son kept Vankerdale. A little while later the two sons started fighting, breaking the king's heart. When the king died, his dragon king started attacking the castle in Vankerdale, and the monolith showed up. Of course, Vankerdale fought back. The distraught and wounded dragon fled into Aralot where he was nursed back to health. You might know the rest better than I do. The dragon king granted man the ability to be a keeper and Aralot has been stronger than Vankerdale ever since."

Pyro walked around the monolith again before he started to use the ground as a drawing pad. He copied the symbols and studied them from every side moving around them in circles until he grinned and cheered.

"You understand it?" Tyler asked. "Will you tell me?"

Pyro didn't tell him what the stone meant. He grabbed the monolith with both hands and bit the side of it. When he pulled back there was a new symbol glowing dark blue on the stone. One of the old symbols flashed orange and vanished from off the face of the monolith as if Pyro had changed the nature of the spell somehow. He clawed through his writings on the ground to erase his thought process. Then without warning, Pyro shoved Tyler over and scratched his left arm. The cut seared and then healed over with a blue line.

"Ow! What was that for?" Tyler asked him. Pyro blew on him to answer his question and then he gave him a short hum as if saying sorry. "You could have warned me."

Pyro didn't warn him for what he did next either. He stared at the magical wound proudly and started chattering again. He gave up eventually and slashed at the ground angry that he couldn't fully communicate.

Tyler looked at the odd bumpy blue line on his arm and then

looked back up at the dragon king. He knew that dragon kings had special abilities, but this was just weird.

"Yes, I think so too," a strong voice entered into his thoughts. Tyler scrambled backward away from Pyro wondering what the beast had done to him. Something had happened for sure. Pyro was in his head!

"That insults me. Pyro would be insulted too. He is exceptionally loyal to Jack and Tia. He would never do anything to put himself in your head. Who are you?"

"Who are *you?*" Tyler questioned back.

Pyro hooted into the air watching Tyler talk to no visible living thing. He started dancing. Tyler had seen dragons dance before but not like this. Pyro had his wings up as high as he could go while he pranced on his feet and raised his tail.

"That's not dancing. That's bragging." The voice laughed at him. *"Clearly you need to spend more time around ice dragons. You should have seen Pyro during his treasure burying phase. He got really good at his bragging swagger."*

This was just too weird. Tyler shouldn't be hearing voices. The only people who heard voices in Vankerdale were crazy people. The voice in his head was most likely a dragon since it interpreted dragon moves without looking at them and seemed to know Pyro well. So, Tyler had to tell himself that Pyro had somehow amended the monolith and turned him into a dragon keeper. He didn't want to go with the insane theory.

He rushed back to the monolith running his hands on it, trying to figure out what it had made Pyro do.

"Aha! A clue!" the dragon voice trumpeted across his brain. It was so loud! Tyler pressed his hands to the stone to brace his body up. *"The small human voice hails from Vankerdale. Pyro said he would find me a rider*

one day. He must have bypassed some ancient magic blocking the rightful bloodline heirs in Vankerdale from hearing thought."

Tyler pulled his hands away from the stone as if he'd been electrocuted. This was an evil thing he was touching. He should stop touching it. It had been constricting his brain, stopping magic from connecting with his blood. Keepers hadn't ever existed inside Vankerdale. That had always been Aralot's pride and joy. It was rather frightening how quickly Pyro had decided to change what made his kingdom great to allow for this to happen. What had the dragon been thinking? Tyler had wanted to hear dragons, but Kayla had just told him that unbonded people who heard dragons went crazy. She had sited her great-granduncle as her example for people who turned insane.

"I like keepers," the voice continued to talk. *"Particularly Kayla Brixton, although I'm sure to like you too. You met Kayla?"* A very happy hum moved through Tyler's head, flooding the rest of his body with the thought that he should probably love Kayla.

Oh no. He couldn't have the hots for that girl. He did not want to change his opinions about her. She was nothing more than scared of her own skin. She didn't like dragon thought. Tyler looked around as if to spot the dragon in his head and frowned. The only thing he could see was that it looked like Kayla had a few things right. Dragon thought could be scary in a way. He had no idea who was talking to him, shoving him with emotions that were not his own, whispering to him things he'd never thought of like how an ice dragon bragged. The scary part came into play knowing that he couldn't stop the voice. He couldn't make it talk and answer when he wanted it to. He had no control over the force that had stolen his body.

"That is incorrect. Stealing only happens with sightsharing, and even then, it's trading. Besides, you don't have my full range of emotions. Last I checked, which was right now, we are not bonded. You have no idea what being flooded with dragon emotion is like. The real stealing of a bodily form comes with

possession which is a spell that can't attack Kayla. The lucky adorable girl. I wish it couldn't take me either."

"Are you possessed?" Tyler questioned, feeling even worse now. He had a dragon that could send him some evil person's thoughts.

"I attack things without remembering anything about it. Whoever does it is good at fighting with dragons. I've searched the wares and stared at the ware leaders to no avail. Most people in Aralot now detest me. Most dragons fear me except for Pyro, but even he wants to kick me out. Looks like he has plans to send me to Vankerdale."

This was really bad Tyler decided. Not to mention incredible at the same time. He was picking up clues about this voice. The dragon lived in Aralot, but it could trick him and send him dark thoughts, making him do something disastrous if the possessor realized that Tyler was there. Tyler wasn't safe from his own mind all of a sudden. Why had he gone anywhere with Pyro?!

"You don't like dragons, do you? How could Pyro release into the world a keeper that doesn't like dragons?"

Tyler had to laugh at the question. He loved dragons. Kayla was the one who didn't like them.

"I take it you've met. She's lost so I find it amusing that you know where she is. It's a shame she's so far away. I had my next attempt all planned out."

"Attempt at what?"

"Bonding her. Anyone who tries to bond her is chased away. A guy tries more than once and he gets beaten up. It's never a fair fight either, particularly if Sparkle gets into it. Boy, that ice dragon needs to let go of Kayla. She's not the animal's baby."

"Why would anyone want to try bonding Kayla more than once when she's already bonded?" Tyler asked the voice. Beside him, Pyro snorted trying to say something. Tyler had no idea what.

"Probably warning you that you're talking out loud without being bonded. Just a guess. That will get you in trouble you know. And who wouldn't try to bond Kayla is the better question. Apart from smelling incredible, being exceptionally willful, brilliant, smart, kind, and influential, having her with me would guarantee that I would be fixed. No more possession. Kayla is the master of possession spells. Her parents made her that way. Why is she already bonded? To whom?"

Pyro snorted again, causing Tyler to look over at the dusty red scales and realize how much he was paying attention to the thoughts in his head instead of paying attention to what was around him. Tyler glanced around not seeing anything that would get him and went back to trying to figure this out.

"Did you promise a dragon in Aralot that you would find it a rider?" Tyler asked Pyro. "Some creature that is being possessed and attacking things?"

Pyro made a lot of sounds, but Tyler had no idea what he was saying. Who was this dragon? And if Kayla was an expert on possession why had she not done anything about this before?

"You think I'd tell Kayla and her parents that I'm possessed? They would send Pyro after me and he would roast my scales. Have you ever seen a dragon king's protector flame? It's the hottest blue fire. It can shove beneath scales it's that bad. I don't need Pyro coming at me with that. Thanks to you he now might. I'll blame it on you and let you hear me scream about it the whole time."

Oh, help. Tyler had to do something or he was going to be mentally tortured!

"Why did you do this to me?!" Tyler shouted at Pyro. The dragon used both his tail and words to talk, but Tyler had no idea what he was saying still.

"You could translate," Tyler ordered the voice in his head not too kindly.

"You try it. I will tell you the random sounds that an animal makes in another language and ask you to tell me what it's saying. If I can't see or hear him, I can't translate for you. It's your thoughts I hear. If your mind doesn't know the words, I don't either."

"Take me back to Kayla!" Tyler ordered the dragon king. Pyro growled at him, but Tyler didn't let that stop him. He still mounted the dragon regardless.

"Most likely he's upset at you for telling him what to do," the voice interpreted the look it couldn't see.

Tyler felt frantic. There was a dragon in his head! Since Tyler had already dug through Jack's bag before, he did so again to pull out a bandage to hide the strange blue bump on his arm. He didn't need other people questioning him about it. What was he supposed to do?! Accept the dragon, of course, but the animal needed help that he couldn't provide. Is this how Kayla felt all the time? Completely helpless?

"Kayla is never helpless. She could help me. I was hoping for someone smart. Shucks. I ended up with you."

Tyler cringed. He wasn't bonded to the dragon so that meant the animal could ruin his inner concentration with mean comments. The animal had no magic forcing him to be polite.

"Clearly you have a lot to learn. Bonded dragons can think mean things too. Their only restriction is they can't lie. I haven't lied to you."

"Who are you!?" Tyler screamed. He covered his mouth when Pyro jolted him in his seat for screaming. Right. He had to keep this quiet. How could he keep a voice in his head quiet?! Apart from the fact that

Pg. 234

no one else could hear it at all except for him. If he thought too hard about that, he started to sound mental.

"Panicking will help. No one will think you're crazy if you run around screaming things into the air."

"Stop!" Tyler screamed. Pyro jolted again, this time pulling to a stop in the air as he moved into a hover and chirped out a question. "Sorry. Not you. The voice. The dragon. It's not being nice."

Tyler did understand the reaction he got from Pyro that time. The red dragon started laughing at him and tried to explain something. Pyro had to know who he was talking with. If only Tyler could get Kayla to tell him everything he didn't know. How was he going to do that? He didn't have a good enough connection with her to have her hand him the answer on how to end a possession spell.

"Well lucky for you, I know a few things. You need to find the object that is being used to possess me. I lost a scale right before all this started up. Alas, I have no idea where it is. I'm not small enough to find it. You find that and you can stop the spell."

The pressure to save the dragon was pounding through him and Tyler knew that it was something that would never leave him ever again. That was the calling of a keeper: the pressure to aid dragons. Maybe things had been a little bit nicer when he couldn't hear any dragon at all. That had to be what rumbled at Kayla too. She didn't like the pressure to help dragons that she refused to look at. It wasn't only Valiant being scared of everything; it was so much deeper. A force that pounded through her bones, her very soul. He'd thought she was exaggerating before, but gee, he had nothing but sympathy in this present moment.

Tyler was all too glad when Pyro landed back at Conner's house. He wasn't happy for the questions that sprang into his head from the mysterious dragon about Conner's last name, his kingdom of birth, what he looked like, and a host of other things that Tyler refused to answer.

He couldn't tell when the dragon was being possessed or not. This was going to be really hard to not think any confidential information inside his own head. It sounded impossible. He needed that help fast.

"Kayla!" Tyler screamed as he burst into the house, ignoring the light green dragon that was still sticking around. He watched Kayla pull a pile of blankets up over her head. She had been moved out of the closet and was back in the front room on a mat. Tyler glanced back toward the window at the late time of day and started to shake her, disregarding the fact that he knew she needed her rest.

"I can't understand what Pyro is saying. Do you know a dragon that—"

"*You better be careful with what you say about me,*" the dragon growled into his head.

"A dragon that has attacked places inside of Aralot?"

"Be quiet, Tyler," Kayla mumbled, tugging the blankets back around her further.

"I really need to—Oww!"

She kicked him! This wasn't going to work at all. Tyler felt his hope for getting the answers he was seeking take a sharp turn. Kayla could tell him. She was right in front of him and all she wanted to do was sleep.

"*Oh, the frustration!*" The voice laughed hysterically into his head. "*I've been there so many times with Kayla. I still think she's marvelous though. A real cutey. It takes a lot to get her to tell you anything at all. She only talks to a handful of people. Good luck with that.*"

"It really is Pyro!" Kayla suddenly shouted, as if Valiant had confirmed this for her. She jumped from the bed. "He'll be able to find my dad!"

Pg. 236

"No," Tyler moaned, at the distraction he had created by revealing Pyro. He scrambled backward when Kayla glared at him. "I mean yes, Pyro will help find your dad, but I don't think he's found him yet so he won't be much help." Although Pyro had already sent out more dragons than Conner had in search of Jack. They had to find him eventually. Jack would probably recognize past Aralot dragons and come out to chat if they got close. Maybe Pyro had given the dragons some code phrase to use to make Jack reveal himself.

"So you're going to tell me where to look," Kayla demanded.

Tyler was about to complain but then the light of opportunity came to him. If he kept Pyro's antics under wrap, he could use Jack being hidden to his advantage. "I sure will. Just as soon as you answer some questions."

"Oh good one. I never had anything I could use to make her grovel."

"Will you be quiet!?"

This was way harder than he expected it to be. Hearing dragon thought was supposed to be a happy exciting event.

"Only if you're bonded. Otherwise, I guess it's like this."

Tyler closed his eyes wanting to scream at the dragon to stop talking so he could think. Maybe if they were bonded, he would feel better about all of this because then the dragon would feel the need to keep him happy. Never mind. He would feel worse because then the person possessing the dragon might be able to sightshare with him and possess him too. This was downright terrifying.

"Ugh, Tyler. Is this a dragon question because you shutting your eyes is not going to help me want to answer anything," Kayla sighed. "What is it? The dragon that attacks things? He's a black ultra-dragon king bred by my grandfather Herb Felding, with the intent of controlling all other dragons around him. He's been called many things including

Reaper, Demon, Devil, and Night Terror. Sparkle calls him Dirt Face."

Tyler opened his eyes back up as part of his fear moved away from him. She was answering the questions except it only brought up more questions. Kayla didn't know the dragon's name.

"See the hard part about names is that dragon ones don't translate to human. Once I'm bonded, it will finally make sense what my name is. I've been waiting a long time to hear it. Presumably, Tia knows, but she never says."

"If there are no other questions…" Kayla trailed off as Tyler stood there trying to concentrate on everything at once. He rushed out the first question he could.

"How close does a keeper need to be to hear an unbonded dragon?"

He couldn't keep the burning question away. If he put more distance between himself and this night terror would he get his mind back?

"I will try to not take that as an insult," the night beast said.

Why was the dragon even awake right now? The animal should be sleeping. Tyler could have been talking with the evil possessor this whole time.

"Nope. You got me. You woke me up."

"Please go back to sleep," Tyler begged.

"No. I've been waiting ages for this."

In front of him, Kayla let out a long sigh and pulled at the edge of her hood. The poor girl tried to hide from thoughts about voices in her head too, and she couldn't keep them away either. Her head had to feel invaded. Tyler's sure did even if he felt the sense of loving the dragon that was there. It was complicated.

Pg. 238

"I wish I could tell you that I don't know," Kayla answered. "But I kind of know. For most keepers to create the first connection with a dragon, they have to be next to the animal. However, I've always gotten the sense that with certain dragons like Pyro who is a dragon king, the connection can be created without needing to be so close. It all depends on the keeper's mental capacity and the dragon's mental capacity for that first thought. Most people don't know this, but two of my mom's first dragons, Blare and Fern, were added to her keeper bond without her being near them at all. They were good friends beforehand though. My mom's first dragon, Misty, described the connection as a web where certain dragons already felt connected so it wasn't hard to add them to her thoughts. After that first connection, no matter what the web feels like, distance has no effect."

He was not going to get rid of the dragon. It was stuck with him forever because they had that first thought. The rest of his life he was going to get thoughts from a night terror. He had to end the possession or he was never going to be able to trust himself or that voice. It didn't help that he felt in his heart that Kayla had told him the truth. Kayla had called the night beast an ultra-dragon king. They were super rare, harder to find than dragon kings like Pyro was. They were supposed to be stronger too, and they had their own kind of magic.

"Are we good now?" Kayla asked, being impatient.

"How does one find an object being used for a possession spell?" he asked next.

Kayla pulled her hood over her head further. "You'll get nothing about magic from me," she declared and walked out the front door.

Tyler watched her from the window. One minute she was trying to make it off the front porch toward Pyro, and the next she was falling to the ground grabbing at her hood unable to do anything but cry. Tyler sighed. Here they went again.

Down to Dust

Kayla

Possessions spells. Kayla gave a shiver as she tried to contain the flood of tears that were splattering onto Conner's front porch. She could see where this one was going. Who did Tyler want to possess? Sure, his question had been on how to stop one, but knowing that would help a person defend the spell they had cast to keep it from being stopped. Of all the evil things that Tyler wanted it was that. Even stranger, when he had walked into the room, Kayla had the sudden urge to like him regardless of the crabby mood he was in this morning. So she'd shared a few keeper secrets and this is where it led her. Possession was one of the evilest spells around. It made people do things against their own will. It was a spell that had been used on Tia to cause her to destroy dragons and Colts, so naturally, Kayla had been well quizzed on the matter by both her parents.

"Does a possession spell have any qualms with distance," Tyler asked her as he walked outside after her and looked directly at Pyro. Kayla wasn't looking at the dragon, but she knew where he was because the animal was breathing. It really was Pyro. She wanted to run at him and hug him only she had never touched him before, and he would probably scream in wonder if she did.

"You'll get nothing about it from me, Tyler," Kayla told him again, as she tried to hold back the leaking eyes. They were bad this morning. Last night was horrible too. Her dreams were normally a bit more random than the oddly specific place her dreams had taken her. It was as if her subconscious was trying to make her leave Vankerdale before she found her dad.

Each dream had featured the same portal—the one that was closest to Turid's Ware. She got a full history of the magical stone structure starting with the keeper Troy who, by Kayla's reckoning, was her third great-grandfather. He had the portal created in the exact location he had bonded his first dragon. Troy had a son named Shane who used the portal more than his father did. Kayla had heard Shane's views on the structure calling his father a proud man for putting the portal where he did in a spot that wasn't hidden. Try as she might to wake up, the dreams were a harsh force succeeding in breaking through her mental defenses to teach Kayla history that was lost. Kayla couldn't avoid the nighttime history lessons.

She had watched Shane travel out of the portal, wounded and hurt after battles with Wisteria. Then there was Gladius rushing into Turid's portal to toss tar on his animals after he tricked them to come to that location. There was Herb stepping out of the portal holding his baby Tia. He had nearly killed Tia but decided against it at the last moment, begging her to be normal and not a keeper like he was. Each dream showed the portal surrounded by soft green grass out in the open, begging Kayla to run back to the location to create her own better memories there.

Kayla had used that portal a hundred times since it was the one closest to her home. Her dreams were trying to bring her home, and she refused to leave without her dad. Besides, she had no idea where to find a portal inside of Vankerdale to link to the one by her house. Her father would know. He had stepped through a portal to enter Vankerdale in the first place. Searching for him was still her best option, and now that Pyro was nearby, she expected to see her father soon.

"Don't say my name…" Tyler whined at her bringing her back to the present. She wiped at her eyes careful to keep her gaze only on him and not directed out toward the dragons. It was a shame that even the thought of looking at Pyro brought her to tears. She hadn't even glimpsed him yet, just knew he was there. She feared that Tyler was starting to see her as a weakling with the way she couldn't stand in the face of dragons.

"I can talk to Pyro for you," Valiant offered.

Kayla logged the thought away because right now her attention was on Tyler. Tyler trailed off pinching his eyes tight as if something inside his head was pestering him about his name. His tone this morning, strained and troublesome, was more than him being tired from lack of sleep. His questions about possession were unsettling.

Kayla shot him with a spell so fast, she didn't have time to contemplate her reaction. King Klavian hadn't acted fast enough against her mother when Tia had stood right before him and told him that her head was doing something strange. Then her mother had died. Tia was turned into a ghost as her soul split from her possessed body and SilverWings had to put her back together. Kayla did not want to see King Peyton's dragon at all. That would be the absolute worst thing that could happen. Hopefully, Tyler's questions about evil spells didn't mean that he thought he was being possessed.

It didn't hurt to check though. Tyler crumbled to the ground so Kayla crept closer to him and waited for him to get back up. He was slow at this. She waited and waited. Maybe she had been a tad too strong… He got up. His expression was even worse as he glanced around wondering why he was on the ground.

"You are not possessed," Kayla told him. "I shot you with a spell just to be sure. If you were possessed you would not have fallen. I knocked out the mental you for a moment so if someone else had any control of part of your body you would have stayed standing."

"You did what?" Tyler asked, reaching to grab her. Kayla scrambled away from his arms, shrugged, and then let Tyler cling to her leg. His face was red and his eyes were darting everywhere, trying to spot something that wasn't going to be there.

"I checked to see if you are possessed because you asked that question. It's not a pleasant question especially with you looking like..."

Yeah, something was weird about him this morning. Where had this instant like come from? Just yesterday Tyler was a person that she followed hoping that he would help her find her father. Tyler did look like his desire to gain a dragon was larger than his loyalty to King Peyton. Today, Tyler felt the same way Uncle Conner had; he was to be trusted for no reason at all. Odd. He was up to something. She would have to keep an eye on it, but it wasn't possession. Something else. Maybe King Peyton had cast a spell on Tyler. It could be anything, and if it was a pressure spell on his head, Tyler might be reacting as he was right now.

"You made me feel a whole lot worse," Tyler declared. His hands got tighter as if he needed her near him to stay sane.

"Describe your symptoms," Kayla tried to help him.

"No way! I'm not sick. I had a few questions and instead of answering them, you knocked me down and made me feel like I was possessed for a moment. You can't tell me that you didn't possess me."

"I didn't," Kayla answered, and pulled her leg away. If Tyler claimed to be fine, she had other things to focus on. The sounds of dragons had gotten quieter which meant that more of them were away from Conner's house. She hadn't seen Uncle Conner since last night, but she was sure it was him that had moved her onto the mat she had woken up on. There had been a lot of clothes on top of her as if Conner was trying to dampen sound.

"You were screaming a lot last night," Valiant told her. *"I tried out hunting while most of the day animals were sleeping. I thought it would be easier to grab something if it was asleep but it's still hard."*

"I'm not an expert on dragon hunting. Sorry. Perhaps you can ask Pyro," Kayla answered Valiant while she found a sneaky way to talk to Pyro at the same time. It worked. Uncle Conner had told her that looking at her previously bonded dragon wouldn't hurt, so talking to him wouldn't be a struggle either. Maybe she could overcome this knee falling thing after all. She could have Valiant be her voice.

Pyro had been quietly waiting for her to get over her fright, but now that she was attempting to engage, he started rambling. Pyro wasn't talking about dragon hunting, and his sentences were split as if half the things he said he thought into an empty void. That was the sign of a broken bond. Dragons would attempt to be heard in any way possible. Kayla listened to only part of what Pyro was saying. He was giving out the story of Jack asking to go into Vankerdale to look for Valiant. Their thoughts were disconnected at the border. Her father had cried and not been in the best frame of mind when he reached the castle. He was taken. Pyro couldn't get inside the castle to get his rider back out.

"My dad is out of the castle," Kayla replied, looking at Tyler so she could avoid looking at Pyro, "and you said that you'd help me find him."

Tyler looked at her rather defeated, and she had no idea why. Something other than her own problems was occupying his mind today. She didn't know him well enough to decide if the problem was something commonplace or something of tragic proportions. She cast another spell at him to check another possibility, and he screamed jumping away from her. His jumping was what made him fall over that time, not her. Kayla didn't see anything flash around him, so she shrugged.

"Well, you have no magical curses on you at all," she declared. Tyler was fine. He was mentally miles away, but there was nothing wrong with him otherwise.

"My dad?" she tried yet again, but all Tyler did was sit up and stare into space as if he couldn't respond to her because he was too busy responding to the thoughts in his own mind. That was weird. He was acting like a rider that was just bonded, only bonds didn't work in Vankerdale. Maybe this was a trick. Yes, he was trying to act like a bonded rider so that she would think he had a dragon. Then he could get her to tell him all sorts of secrets that she would normally not mention. She had already told him that distance had no effect on a keeper's mental linking. Solution: ignore Tyler. It shouldn't be too hard to do. She ignored lots of things.

Kayla closed her eyes still determined to reach Pyro. He was not as good as her dad, not at all, but he was still rambling half his words out loud and the sound was so pitiful that Tempest was starting to answer him trying to get him to stop thinking with her dad because Jack couldn't respond. Pyro growled and the anger was so intense that Kayla gave up on doing anything to assist him herself. That was the sort of sound that said Pyro was ready to attack something and his attacks were harsh. The growl brought Conner out of the house and he started trying to ease the wounded dragon with soothing words about Jack being fabulous and their bond being fixed shortly. He tried to distract Pyro by mentioning that he had to be strong and protect Jack's daughter. Pyro rumbled a ball of fire in his throat and Conner gave up on him too.

"What's up with Tyler?" Conner asked her.

"Not sure," Kayla shrugged. "I already checked to see if he was cursed in any way and he's not. I think he's play acting so that we start to like him and tell him secrets that he shouldn't know. He had strange questions."

Tyler lost his blank gaze to shake his head at her. He now looked super annoyed that his first gimmick hadn't worked as well. Kayla did need to be careful here. She had already answered a few of his questions, and he hadn't given her a single location to where her dad could be hiding. Round one to Tyler. The thing with mind games was that more than one person could play. If she could distract him from them maybe he would forget that he wanted to play them in the first place. He was supposed to be some brilliant scholar for Prince Evan, so she had just the thing.

"He knows all about the universe. In sleep he calculates inverse. He knows prose, transpose, compose, and throes. His every sentence comes out lyrical. He's a modern genius miracle. He's well versed in all the 'ologies, from cosmo to anthropology. His written word is aesthetic. His noble form is cosmetic. Thoughts are always mathematical. Perfect, right, and oh so statical."

"Are you sure that statical is a real word?" Tyler asked her. "Why are you rhyming?"

"To prove a point," Kayla grinned at him. "You're smart enough on your own."

"Forget I ever asked, Kayla. I'll figure out the answers myself. It will just take longer."

Much, much longer. It wasn't easy to come across information on possession even inside of Aralot. Hopefully, Tyler wouldn't be able to find anything in Vankerdale either. Who did he want to possess and why? Or in the event that he wasn't trying to cast the spell himself, did he think that she was possessed because she had spent the night screaming?

Tyler let out a long sigh, but he did stop pretending that he had something talking into his head. To his credit, he was rather convincing that he had a bond especially for a person who would not have seen such a thing in his entire lifetime. On that note, Kayla eyed Tyler again, suspicious of the information he had been able to research about dragons. What did he know?

"Most of the things that Tyler is told to read relates to Aralot. Prince Evan had him find a way to get through the border," Valiant told her. *"Did you know that Aralot's flag was invented by a dragon and crafted by man?"*

She wasn't really surprised. Men had the tendency to think that they were the ones in charge of the kingdom but often times it was really a dragon behind everything. Dragons helped ware leaders decide who to transfer and who to keep. They helped with laws and taxes and safeguarding produce and trade goods. Through the eyes of a dragon, they were in charge of everything. They were the protectors of the land, the helper to man as they safeguarded his soul and eased his burdens.

Valiant hummed at her causing Pyro to stop growling and churning flame inside his throat. Pyro chirped out a question that Valiant was all too happy to answer. Kayla was thinking about dragons being in charge of the world. The conversation starter worked like a charm as Pyro started to tell Valiant a few of his greatest achievements. He was particularly fond of getting magic out of Bantin, and Valiant was particularly interested in how he did it. Kayla stilled to listen to the conversation because Valiant and Pyro had never once met each other and yet they were talking like they were good friends already.

"Should I not? He's in your thoughts so often that Pyro feels like a brother to me."

Kayla supposed that could be true in Valiant's case, but Pyro wouldn't have heard all about Valiant over the years. He should have said hello instead of jumping right into a conversation like he was picking up with a friend he'd not seen in a few days. Pyro was usually

Pg. 248

more cautious about meeting new dragons.

"*But I'm* your *dragon*," Valiant pointed out. "*And since we were once connected wouldn't it feel like Pyro was talking to the other half of you?*"

Except for the fact that she never talked to Pyro so why would Valiant feel so comfortable in doing so?

"Dragons radiating outward from one central location and one of them happens to be Nebula. I'm thinking that I finally found a lost friend," an amused voice said from behind the area of the house.

Kayla wasn't the only one who recognized the tones. Dad! Her dad was here! He had spotted Nebula, which was Conner's water dragon, and backtracked the animal's path to Conner's house! The day had started out in tears, but it was now going to get incredibly better.

"Dad!" Kayla screamed, while Pyro belted out Jack's dragon name.

Kayla jumped from the porch to run toward the voice only to be blocked by Pyro's tail taking a swing at her. Oh no he didn't! Nothing was going to stop her from reaching her dad! Unfortunately, Pyro was thinking the same thing so when Kayla cast a spell on him to slow him down, he sent his tail at her again to impede her progress. The rage that filled through her chest was something she wasn't used to. It was said that there were three cures to fixing any regularly broken bond. Those happened to be the love of a friend, numbness, and anger. Kayla had never had a reason to be that angry at a dragon before, not even to the ones that had picked on her over the years, until today. She was incredibly angry at Pyro. She had been missing her father longer than he had. She wasn't letting Pyro get in the way of her reunion with her dad!

Somehow the anger was strong enough to overcome the feelings she got when she tried to look at other dragons. Kayla yanked the hood off her head and gave Pyro a glare that was all business. He might be a dragon king, but she was a princess, and he wasn't going to get in her way!

Pyro noticed. He shrieked at her look, stumbling backward a step before his own brokenness got the better of him. He wasn't going to yield over Jack either. He sent her a growl and charged right at her instead of around the house toward Jack. Valiant screamed. Conner screamed. Even Tyler screamed. Kayla ignored them. She had seen way too many examples of how to effectively take a dragon down. She didn't have the best tools for the job, but she had spells and she had a knife. She pulled out the knife facing Pyro head on while her father's voice started to issue a new command.

"Plant the blue thorn bush!"

Her father and Pyro had established a language all of their own for times when they had to communicate verbally and didn't want others to know what they were saying. Kayla didn't understand the message that was sent at Pyro, but she could guess what it was—move. Valiant had jumped into action ready to land on top of Pyro's head to pin him down before he reached Kayla with anything harmful. Pyro growled out a bad word at Kayla and then rolled away from Valiant.

When he got up, he snarled at Valiant and raised his hands ready for battle. Kayla blinked at them well aware that she was staring at two dragons with her own eyes and not doing anything about trying to see her dad. She had caused this. She was making the two dragons fight, but the anger inside her wasn't about to give up yet.

Even worse, she didn't want it to. With the anger in place, she had found a way to look at dragons. If she was her mom, she would have been scared that the feeling would lead her down the same road that Gladius and Herb had traveled when they went about torturing dragons. Kayla was too familiar with their work to think that she would ever be them. Her anger was embraced for a different reason; for healing rather than hate, and she let the thoughts in her soul pour out of her mouth.

"You wait your turn!" she screamed at Pyro. "He's my father! You get him first all the time! Why is it always the dragons coming first? Why? I'm always left behind flattened to the ground and forgotten when it's a choice between me or a dragon. I'm getting him first!"

Pyro roared back at her, gargled some words to the out of sight Jack that only made sense to them, and slashed his tail at Valiant who hadn't adopted the same battle stance that Pyro had. Valiant kept his arms and wings down although his tail was out to the side. Kayla had never watched him fight, so when Valiant heaved with his stomach and shot out a spell, she had to stare in wonder at how the magic didn't start out blue before shifting. The entire spell was already complete before it came out of his mouth. Valiant shoved Pyro backward with a gust of wind. Not to be outdone, Pyro flapped his wings rising above the spell before he headed back toward Valiant with a burst of flame.

Arms circled around Kayla forcing her eyes off the dragon battle to see who was getting in her way. Oh. No one. It was her dad! Her heart jumped in her chest and her face lit up to see him. It didn't last. Jack was looking like he hadn't seen a bath in those three months he was missing. His red-brown beard was unkempt and scruffy, his hair was getting long enough to tangle, and his eyes blazed his own frustration.

"The first thing you do when you look at my dragon is to fight him?!" Jack hissed into her ear. "We'll talk about this later."

He let her go and ran toward the commotion, leaving Kayla to stare after him with her breath cut off. No! It was always like this! She was second best when it came to dragons. Her father might have greeted her first, but that wasn't the greeting she had wanted. She was always looked over. Her father should be rejoicing to see her, but there was no gladness left when Pyro was facing off against a spellbinding dragon. Pyro had probably started the fight on purpose so that Jack would run straight to him and no one else.

"He started it! He swiped at me first!" Kayla screamed. Then she wiped at her eyes as the anger started to be replaced by hurt.

"Dad!"

That was all she had wanted and he was running away from her. She had lost him yet again! Kayla tried to hold onto the hate so she could continue to watch the display of battered feelings. It was getting harder to do. Conner had mounted Tempest and they appeared in the air above Pyro as if they were picking his side over Valiant's. All Valiant had done was tell Pyro off for being a bully. Pyro should not be getting away with this and yet he was. Both her father and Valiant dodged the blast of flame that Pyro spat. Above them, Conner was screaming words of reason trying to make them all stop.

"We should have expected this. Everyone stand down! You can't resort to anger to fix your broken bonds if you're taking that anger out on each other! What a mess we are. All of us torn apart on the inside and fighting! Let's take the opposite approach to friendship. Pyro don't flame Valiant. That's Kayla's dragon! Jack don't scream at your daughter! She's been beside herself trying to find you. Valiant stop shooting spells. It will only make everyone madder. Kayla stop shouting at everyone to get your way."

Nobody was listening to Conner. Kayla sent him a glare as did the rest of them even if he was right. They all had the exact same problem right now and were trying to overcome it by fighting each other. They really did make one large mess, and it kept getting worse. Valiant yelled at Pyro to yield. Jack screamed at Valiant that they would flame his scales. Pyro screamed at Kayla calling her a little devil. Conner screamed at Tyler to not move away from the porch steps. He must have been inching forward either to see better or attempt to help even if there was nothing he could do.

Pg. 252

Valiant shot another wind spell directed at Pyro right as Jack jumped at his dragon. The spell launched Jack into the air. If their thoughts had been linked it would have worked out because Jack would have used the spell to reach his dragon faster. However, Pyro couldn't hear the plan so he had already launched upward to get out of the way sending Jack into a void with nothing to stop his movement except for gravity. It was going to be one really hard landing when he fell.

"Dad!" Kayla shouted, listening to Pyro yell out his own fear. Pyro dove earthward to catch him only to be battered out of the way by Tempest who was saving Pyro from his foolhardy move that would have smashed his face into the ground. Pyro was too close to the ground for such a steep dive. He was knocked upward as he screamed furiously. Kayla waited for her dad to cast a spell to save himself, but he didn't do anything at all. He should have done something by now!

Valiant rushed forward lashing out his tail and casting a spell that pulled Jack to him before he could break an arm on the ground. It was strange looking at her father being set on the ground by her dragon like he was a blanket. Kayla wondered if he was okay. That was the last thing she could see before her anger dwindled away. Watching fighting dragons didn't leave her feeling angry. It usually left her wishing that she would wake up, and since there was no way to fight already being awake, she felt defeated.

The tears reached her eyes and she pulled up her hood trying to find a way to stop the fight now that she couldn't use anger to view dragons. She should have looked at more dragons while she had the chance. Maybe it would have made her father proud of her if she could tell him that she was taking steps to not push the animals away so much, but she hadn't, so the only thing she had to look forward to was his disappointment.

Kayla dropped to the ground listening to the sounds hoping that no one got hurt as they continued to fight. Pyro shot more flame at

Pg. 253

Valiant. Tempest screamed at them both. Kayla heard Tyler sneaking off the porch. Why wouldn't they surrender? Pyro had already won the love battle. Jack had run to him first and here she was left on the ground alone again. The loneliness made her cry more than the sounds of Conner's team jumping to the air to separate two battling dragons.

Kayla didn't know what formation they were using, but she heard Pyro snort over it not wanting to stand down. Valiant didn't snort. He started walking backward. Tyler started blotching dragon sounds trying to mimic things he'd heard before so that the dragons would look at him wondering what his problem was and forget their own.

And there she was still on the ground doing absolutely nothing to make anything right. This was all she amounted to—to be left in the dust. Kayla tried to get angry about that but couldn't. The tears kept falling, making her think that Conner had been right. It really was loneliness that got to her the most. Nothing could stop the pain until she got the will power to stand up to it and fight against it.

She had to find the strength to get up and run. That always worked out. She gave it a go. She shoved with her arms against the ground trying to get herself back up. Her arms shook. Her body refused to move. She tried harder only to find her arms give out. She tried her legs next. Fight! She had to fight it. She always fought it!

No. What really happened was another person came around and chased away the dragon that had made her fall down. It was either that or a human voice would say something to distract her. Where was Caleb coming to distract her with his random comments? Where was her mother or Rosa or any of the keeper-linked riders that showed up at the right time to give her a new passion besides the loneliness? She had left them all behind, and Kayla had no idea how to get up without them. Her dad was going to be too distracted by Pyro to help her. Tyler and Conner had no idea what she needed. She cried even harder and curled into a ball when a dragon's breath brushed over her. No dragon could help.

Pg. 254

Not one.

"*Not even me?*" Valiant's voice asked. He hummed at her next, but Kayla couldn't feel it. All she felt was abandoned by the one person she wanted to see.

"*Are you sure I can't help?*" Valiant asked, nudging into her with the tip of his nose. "I thought the problem was that you miss me. I'm right here. You don't need to cry."

"He left me," Kayla whimpered.

Valiant plopped down beside her letting out a defeated sigh. She wanted to glare at him for that. He couldn't give up. He had to stand up and fight through the darkness because he could still stand. She tried it again with her limbs trembling and her mind screaming at her to get up. Help! She didn't know how to get up! The Colts would tell her that all she needed to do was have enough will power and she could accomplish anything. She could take an old life and rewrite it. She could scratch out the parts she didn't like about herself and glue together something new. But no. There had to be something else that was going to work.

"Not sure what to say?" Tyler asked, drawing in close. She assumed he was talking to Valiant and not her. His intention was to help Valiant help her, but see, that was the problem. It was always the dragons coming first. She didn't know how to make her mind see it differently so that she had the power to rise.

"You can try some positive comments. Tell her how you feel about her. You know like, Kayla, you are a beautiful person with a loving heart that just happens to get trampled on…"

Kayla shook her head as Tyler trailed off realizing that he had messed up his comment. Valiant sighed again before he wailed for Jack.

"I am too mad to help," Jack's voice rang through the air. "I spent three months breaking the lock on my dungeon door with a broken fork after I knowingly tore myself apart for her and what I come back to is my daughter holding a knife toward my dragon's face."

"Oh, Jack," Conner reprimanded. "Go toss some knives until you feel better. Don't talk to her like that. She's only a child, one that has been suffering way longer than you have. Tell me. How often have you seen her like this? Does it even bother you anymore or is it so commonplace in your mind that you have numbed yourself at the sight of it. You have nothing left to give her when she's down?"

"I don't know what to do. Nothing helps. You help her," Jack retorted still angry.

"I have devised a new theory," Tyler said, risking lightly touching her back. Kayla didn't hear Conner move, but she pictured him staring at her dad in disappointment as if Jack should be better with his daughter than this. He usually was. It was just that all of them had the same torn conundrum.

"The anger didn't last very long," Tyler continued as the only one without a messed-up head. "You refuse to turn numb to the world and feeling abandoned won't help you feel like you have any friends. So perhaps you can fight the thoughts of sadness with thoughts of joy."

He was actually talking to her that time! That was nice, but she couldn't think up anything happy. Tyler decided to give her a few hints as if he had somehow stepped inside her life and could tell her what things she enjoyed doing. It was a little freaky because she had never told him any of this.

"Picture a tall cliff with these challenging handholds. You stare right up, toss your rope and just go. The climb is hard, it kicks up your breath, tests your reach, but for each backward step you manage to get higher until you reach the very top. It was hard, but you conquered it just as you'll be able to find a way past this."

There was no way he knew that she loved rock climbing. He started to talk about rocks next. She was to picture finding a unique one that she was going to tuck into her pocket as if the compressed mineral was a glowing treasure worthy of extreme care. Then he moved onto watching plants grow and helping others understand a particularly challenging homework problem. She had to stop him when he started talking about Colts and how she could slip around them knowing where they were before they could detect her.

"Tyler you are creeping me out," she admitted. He couldn't understand dragon speech. It wasn't like he had heard all of these things from Valiant telling him about her life.

"Great," Tyler shoved his hand beneath her and found her hand, which he used to drag her to her feet. "You are now standing, my lady." He gave her a bow that she had to laugh at. Despite calling herself a princess just a moment ago, she felt far from that royal status now.

"Did it help?" Valiant asked. *"I'm going to try that next time. I want to help you, Kayla. I can talk to you about happy memories. Lots and lots of them."*

Kayla turned around still determined to fight herself. She spread her feet outward so she could look at the dragon. Valiant had tears swimming around his pupils. His fear of him not being able to help her was too much. Kayla looked down and pulled her bag around to the front of her so she could search through it to the very bottom. Valiant had helped. He was the only dragon she could be safe with no matter her mood. She gave him a smile and he let his tears dry up.

Her fingers brushed over the only picture from Caleb that she had ever saved. It was them on that boat playing pirate as if they were still young enough to believe that they could have very different lives, and young enough to believe that they could be anything they wanted to be. She didn't pull out the picture, just touched it, wishing that she could still believe that she could be somebody else. Kayla gave Valiant a hug and turned to face her dad, ready to take his moods now that her own had been settled down.

"You're the king of Aralot?" she asked.

Jack's mouth dropped open. His hands stopped tossing the set of knives he had been chugging through the air like a juggler. He communicated something random to Pyro whose face was way too close to Jack's shoulder to mean anything good. Pyro wanted to fang him. Kayla looked over at Valiant who hadn't once done anything to scare her into thinking he was going to bite her. Huh. He was very patient. He had to be suffering too, and he never once acted up because of it. Valiant hummed at her like he wouldn't do anything to scare her.

"You know I'm the king?" Jack asked, stepping away from Pyro. "You can hear it?"

Kayla nodded. "Valiant ate my curses off."

"Well, I'll be. Your mother is entitled to the throne through the inheritance in her blood. Klavian used me to fetch Aralot's crown for him because he suspected I'd get hitched to Tia and that made me in line to be the king. But the crown has a curse on it, so I gave Klavian a fake one. He was crowned with the replica and the abbot found out and forced me to marry Tia by a certain date or he was going to harm your Uncle Kyle. That was right when Herb was terrorizing everything and I had no idea if I'd ever get your mother before he did. Then she was turned into a ghost and I plain out broke down. I managed to end her possession—"

"That was Rosa, Dad," Kayla corrected. "I know the stories and I know the truth. Rosa was responsible for ending my mother's possession. I just didn't realize the crown thing. SilverWings came to save mom because you came here and asked King Peyton for help. Then you married Mom and have been ruling everything behind King Klavian."

Pg. 258

"That's right." Jack agreed. "When you turn sixteen you have to go on a date with Prince Tristan because Klav has this grand idea of ending our family fued that we've already ended."

"What?!"

Date Tristan! He did nothing more than hunt and collect dead bugs. If he wasn't doing that, he was pestering people, stealing from them, and delighting in being the largest pest all of Aralot had ever known.

"Just a few dates, Kayla. Maybe I should have saved that news for later." Jack made a face and then gave her a smile. "I missed you terribly. I kept thinking that if I could break your dragon out that you wouldn't have to suffer through anything King Peyton could hit you with. I should have known that you could take him on. Here you are not locked up at all. If he had you, I might have broken down and handed over Mr. Grumpy, giving up our only magic to keep you safe."

"Dad, no!" Kayla glanced sharply at Tyler. Prince Evan and Tyler had devised that the only thing holding Aralot together was that very magic. It would fall apart if Jack gave it up.

"I know, but you're my kid. There isn't a dragon or kingdom around that can stand in the way of that. What you just said isn't true. You're always first. You come before the sunrise, before the roll call, before kindling, before the shoes, before my every breath."

That was her dad alright. He liked to come up with word games where he listed things out. Pyro was especially good at giving him various categories to amuse their minds on.

"Forgive me for being short with you before. I wasn't in the best of places, and I don't turn a blind eye when you fall down. I fall along with you. So I want to tell you something. There's nothing wrong with being scared of dragons. Not being scared of them would be far more foolish. They are powerful creatures. Conner and I both started out scared of dragons and look where we are now."

"Oh yeah. Just look. You've got one and I've got more," Conner bragged. Jack glanced at Conner and had to laugh.

"I ride Pyro everywhere and Conner is hardly ever seen riding so there's that too. There's no right or wrong way to love a dragon. There's no rush to get over your fears. You take your time, Kayla. Do what's right for you."

This was so much better than the fighting they had going on a little bit ago. Kayla gave her father a smile and then ran to hug him. She'd found her dad! Well, he had found her, but still. He felt wonderful to have in her arms, and she didn't even mind the musky smell that came off him or the whiskers on his face. He was safe! Her dad was safe! She was so happy. Happy enough that Kayla decided to risk another look at Pyro. He blinked back surprised that she would try it out. It didn't make her fall down and Kayla wondered if it was because Valiant was close and there was no room for loneliness in her heart when she knew her family was well.

She took it a step farther letting her eyes travel to Conner's dragons. Conner was still sitting on Tempest, although he was cross-legged and resting an elbow on the dragon's neck. He had about ten dragons left after the rest had spread out in search of Jack. Still, the ten were a formidable bunch, strong, intelligent, and mindful enough to know that when she looked at them, they should smile and preen. Kayla rolled her eyes and moved on.

"I am so proud of you," her father whispered to her. There wasn't another phrase he could have said that would have made her glow more. She'd done it! She had turned around the situation, overcoming the sadness now that she understood it. She could look at dragons!

"Be careful where you look. Some dragons are not the friendly sort,"
Pg. 260

Valiant mentioned. *"And don't expect an instant recovery."*

Kayla looked at her dragon and gave him a smile. She knew a few demons already and she agreed wholeheartedly to avoid them. With her heart warm and happy, she had to test her boundaries. How far could she make it? How far could she push?

"Do you want to play?" she asked Valiant.

Barrier Between

Tyler

Tyler stood up with his hands in his pockets, feeling as though everyone could see through him right now. His crimes were so translucent! He'd told himself not to trust the voice in his head, and there he was telling Kayla about happy moments that the night terror had seen her accomplish. Jack would have no idea how much Tyler had talked to his daughter already, and Conner wouldn't either, but when Kayla said that he was freaking her out, he felt like they would all pick up on the reason why he knew so much about Kayla Brixton. It wasn't him. It was the dragon in his head.

The night terror had promised that it would help with Kayla's condition so Tyler had started talking. Judging by the way Kayla had slowly stopped crying to listen to him, the dragon had been right. Which brought Tyler to the uncomfortable place he was in now. When should he trust the dragon's words and when should he not?

Kayla was continuing to shock her dad and his dragon. She was eyeing the host of large reptilian creatures around her while King Jack stared at her as if he'd never seen his own daughter before.

"Are you alright?" he asked her. "You don't have to move that fast past your fears you know."

"Dad, I have to fight them," was her reply.

She stepped away from him and it was like the largest switch had clicked in her head. Valiant was all for it, or perhaps he was taking advantage of it because he hooted loud and excited. It was the happiest that Tyler had ever seen him yet. Kayla laughed at something in her own head and started to ask her father for a particular spell while she proudly waved at Valiant and introduced him to her father.

Tyler started racing through his own thoughts now that the night terror had stopped adding to them for a moment. He had once wondered how many other dragons Kayla had in her keeper bond. The answer to that was none. Valiant didn't have any other friends to keep him company through his previously isolating existence. Tyler had also wondered what it would be like to stand before Jack Brixton, who had his utmost respect. Jack continued to keep it. There was something about his demeanor that oozed out kindness on top of justice. After he admitted that King Peyton had stolen his wedding ring, a theft that had Jack's face turning dark and angry, Jack flashed back to his happy self even though Pyro was behind him whining something at him.

"I missed you more than anything, Pyro," Jack told him, right as Kayla plowed into him from the side with another hug. "I was not going to leave Vankerdale without you."

"Not that you could anyway," Kayla was quick to point out, "since your magic is gone."

"You know sometimes I wonder who raised you. You always look like you're not paying attention and yet you see everything. Except for this," Jack laughed holding up Kayla's keychain and dangling it in the air above her head. She jumped to grab for it, but her father only laughed and continued to keep it away.

"Now your magic is gone," he teased her.

"It probably is. I've been using it so we're both out."

"Good thing we have Valiant then."

Jack looked at Valiant with a smile so that Kayla's attention moved back to him. The dragon gave Jack a bow, making Tyler take his hands out of his pockets to cross them in front of his chest instead. That wasn't fair. Valiant had bowed to Tyler before, and he had loved the honor of being considered the dragon's friend. Valiant was going to be picking up friends all over the place now that he was out of the cage. Tyler was going to be pushed to the back of the dragon's mind.

"I've never known a dragon to forget a human friend," the night terror tried to ease his jealousy and Tyler tried to ignore it.

Then Valiant started showing off. He used the spell that Jack had just told his daughter and shrunk his own size so that he looked like a newborn. Kayla blinked at her small dragon staring as if she'd never once looked at Valiant before. He performed a dragon's happy dance and rushed toward her to scoop her up onto his much smaller back so he could race her around. The effect was interesting. Kayla didn't fit as well when he was that small, so she stood up, spreading out her arms and squaring her feet to work on her balance. Tyler guessed that was the dragon playing.

Pyro wailed some more, shoving his head into Jack. Whatever it was that he said, it had Conner coming down from Tempest so that both men moved over to where Tyler was standing. He felt himself gulp. These two men had such a large advantage over him. Conner had a dragon army all his own and Jack had his daughter's magic. Pyro kept mumbling, shoving his claws into the ground trying to say something that he wanted to desperately communicate. Jack looked sadly back at him and shrugged.

"I'm sorry. Either I can't remember what that stands for or we've never talked about that before because I have no idea, Pyro."

Pyro growled. Jack clenched his fists together at the sound, equally frustrated, but he didn't let the emotion take over him again. He extended his hand to greet Tyler. Tyler gulped again. He could guess what Pyro wanted to communicate. He was going to tell Jack that he had made Tyler a keeper and that Tyler was already hearing dragon voices. Once Jack and Pyro got their connection back, there wasn't going to be anything in the way of Jack knowing what was going on behind Tyler's eyes. Tyler hoped that Jack wouldn't be upset with it. He had been stifling magical properties inside of Vankerdale for years and Pyro had let one loose.

"I hear that you're Tyler. Nice to meet you. I don't want to assume that you know who I am, but I'm Jack."

Not even King Jack or spellcaster Jack. He didn't use his full name of Jack Brixton to demand that Tyler offer a bow instead of a handshake. No. Jack was nothing like King Peyton at all. He was up close and personal and Tyler found his hand reaching back to shake Jack's own feeling as though he already knew Jack like a close friend. It was so weird!

"Not really. Jack's like that. Got to love him despite his temper and his fears and his rough edges."

"I think I like those rough edges," Tyler replied. He didn't elevate himself.

"You really shouldn't stay long," Tyler told Jack after shaking the king's hand. "Conner said that King Peyton was putting dragons at the border to block off Kayla. King Peyton will learn where you are sooner or later and then you'll be facing a battle right above Conner's house. I have no doubt that Conner would take him on, but that's going to hurt."

"Tyler works for Prince Evan," Conner stated. "He's the spy in our midst and I'm not sure that he's a good one."

Pg. 266

Tyler opened his mouth to refute Conner's claims and then closed it again because he had no idea what Conner really meant. Did he mean that Tyler was going to betray the Brixton's, or did he mean that Tyler wasn't smart enough to mess up the keeper's plans because he was horrible at spy work? Tyler was one of these guys! They didn't see it yet, but they would one day. They'd see him for who he was, and he'd be standing right before them staring them down demanding that they free Vankerdale from the plagues they had cast them into. This was his domain and these two were trespassers.

"Ooo, you see that spark of fire?" Jack chuckled at Conner. "Tyler doesn't like being called a bad spy."

Tyler narrowed his eyes at them. He wasn't a spy. He was the backbone of Vankerdale, even if no one else would ever realize it. He was the one telling Prince Evan everything he ever wanted to know, and it was Prince Evan telling King Peyton. Tyler was the one getting into Aralot. The one who solved all the hard to handle issues. That was probably the real reason Prince Evan had told him that he wouldn't release Tyler from his service. To lose Tyler would be to lose his own brain. As far as Tyler was concerned, he was the same as King Jack right now. Level in brilliance. Level in status. They both ran things behind the scenes. Tyler wasn't going to let them push him under.

"Are you really?" A rather amused and happy dragon hum rang through his head. *"Very well, I agree to stick with you."*

"I thought you didn't have a choice," Tyler answered. They were stuck with each other already. Tyler was old enough to handle dragon connections, so when he was cut and that monolith spell altered, his head had reached out. At least he was doing a much better job at not talking to the dragon in his head out loud anymore. No one but Pyro and himself knew anything about the connection.

"Does Valiant instantly remind you of Kayla or what?" Jack

asked, shifting his eyes away from Tyler as if Tyler couldn't hold his attention for more than a few seconds. "Magic is the one subject she won't complain about doing homework for. It makes sense. She has a spellbinding dragon. I bet Valiant knows everything she knows already. You can see the evidence of it in Valiant's use of weather magic. Kayla isn't that good at wind spells yet. She doesn't get the force and acceleration right. I had no idea that Kayla even had a dragon until three months ago. Tia lied to both of us about it..." Jack trailed off and then looked back at Pyro who blew Jack with warm air to soothe the painful expression Jack let flash over his face. "How is she? Is Tia alright? Is she worried? I didn't plan for any of this to happen," Jack asked Pyro.

Pyro shook his head and started chattering again, giving the answer that Jack wanted to know. He probably told him that Tia was fine.

"She is well, yes. Queen Tia is at the castle with the ware leader Anvil and her sister Rosa. From the flashes of guards rushing around the outside whispering to each other, the guards don't like the discussion taking place inside."

Um. That was something that Tyler would never know without this extra voice. So his dragon was close to Aralot's castle right now. That would mean that he was relatively close to the border as well.

"I am considering running at the barrier between us," the dragon answered.

"But should you? We can't bond over here." Although getting that bond so he didn't go crazy still sounded like a good idea. A complicated idea, because Tyler would return back to Vankerdale after bonding in Aralot and the bond would break on him. He could start finding himself down on the ground consumed with emotional turmoil so large that he couldn't stand back up like Kayla and Conner. That was the plight of a broken bonded keeper.

"Bond? You won't let my fangs near you until you believe you can't be possessed through me. Bonding can wait. I want to charge the border to get Kayla back. The other option is to wait until you send her back for me."

Tyler looked back at Kayla too. It suddenly felt like everyone needed her to rescue them, but she was too absorbed in fighting her own mental battles to hold up anything but her own body. Even then, she had trouble getting off the ground. She had pushed herself against the dirt and hadn't been able to get up.

"You'd better pay attention, Dad. He's going to fang you," Kayla said without looking at any of them. She was off Valiant's back now and was chasing him through the legs of other dragons that were trying to catch them. Tyler looked back over at Jack just in time to see him roll out of the way and Pyro smash his face into the ground hard as he missed his target. Pyro wailed.

"Stop it, Pyro!" Kayla shouted at him. "You can tell my dad your secrets later."

Pyro raised his head off the ground and stumbled backward, looking scared of the young girl for talking to him. He wailed at Jack again. Then he took to drooling all over the patient man's shoulder to satisfy his need to bite him.

"I don't know," Jack replied. "I had no idea that she could understand dragon speech. It's like... like I don't know my own kid anymore."

"Oh seriously," Kayla stopped playing to look at the rest of them. "I've known dragon speech since I was eight. Pyro said that he discovered a secret you should know about. He's going to feed you a roast every day for a month. He claims that Mom won't stop asking him about you, and he wants to tell you that Rosa, Anvil, and Mom are at the castle discussing war options. Pyro estimates half a week before the border defenses fall against King Peyton and SilverWings. Pyro also said that he wasn't going to leave Vankerdale without you either, and that Anvil hugged mom...well never mind."

Jack looked between his daughter and Pyro vexed. His eyes gained a dangerous edge that Kayla turned away from.

"She knows about Anvil." Jack shook his head. He pinched the bridge of his nose and Conner gave Jack a hug. Tyler felt like he was missing something so he waited for the dragon in his head to provide him the answer. The animal was silent; however, so he had to pick it up from what Conner said. Thankfully, Conner didn't make understanding the topic complicated.

"It was weird seeing the way Kayla looked when she talked about *Uncle* Anvil. He couldn't get Tia from you so he takes her."

"Don't say it like that. Kayla adores him." Jack sighed. "I'm going to have another talk with Anvil about not putting moves on my wife, but I can't very well tell him to not be friends with my kid. Kayla needs a good friend."

"And you blame yourself," Conner mused, as if he could see through Jack's expression.

"If I was less busy, I'd be where Kayla needs me. Instead, I always have a large checklist of things to do so that when Kayla needs something, she goes right to Anvil for the answers. He's always in the same place and easy to find. It's gotten so bad lately that Kayla won't even tell us where she's going. She heads right for Anvil's Ware every single day to see him. If I want to find her, I go ask him where she is.

"It's not all bad, Conner. It bothers me that I'm not the largest force in her life, but Anvil is great with her. Besides, we both know that at her age a parent is the last person she wants to hear from. I can have Anvil tell her the same thing I just told her, and she'll take the answer if it comes from him. It's a phase. Kayla would be far worse off without

Pg. 270

him. I've come to accept that Anvil is around to keep Kayla's head up. Hugging my wife though…"

"Good luck with that," Conner said, shaking his head as he released Jack from his hug. "Kayla said Anvil was married with a few kids."

Jack nodded and Tyler looked away from them, not wanting to be in the way of this personal conversation. It sounded like there was a bit of a love sandwich going on here. If this had been King Peyton with another guy hitting on his wife, the guy would be dead. Then again, King Peyton's wife had died in childbirth. Still though, any offense would be met with harsh punishment. It wouldn't be handled in the same manner Jack met his problems. Jack had found a way to accept the man he didn't like. Wouldn't it be nice if Tyler could use Jack's same compassion to help Vankerdale get better?

"Maybe you could find a way to modify the antibonding spell so that King Peyton is the only one not able to bond and the rest of us—"

"Tyler wants a dragon and he's got his eyes on Valiant," Conner cut him off. "Don't you dare drop that curse until you can beat King Peyton down with the softness of a pillow."

"Valiant and I are friends! He's Kayla's, but I'll take a good word with a dragon," Tyler replied, because Jack had cast him a glare as if to warn him to not interfere with the one dragon that Kayla had.

Gee, he was standing around with the king of Aralot! There had to be something he could do that would get Jack to help them. So far, Tyler had devised that Jack didn't have anything against Vankerdale as a whole. It was only King Peyton stealing Valiant away and trying to destroy Jack's entire kingdom by devising plots to steal Aralot's magic that had Jack on the defensive.

Maybe the answer was as cruel as looking into dethroning King

Peyton. But then Prince Evan would still be there and he was often worse than his father. That would require taking down Prince Evan too, which would leave this empty gap of no one on the throne. War inside of Vankerdale would be the result. Tyler was going to have to puzzle this out more. He was going to need to find a new king or their dragons would never get the relief they sought. If their dragons suffered, he was only going to suffer, because he was a keeper now and dragon problems were now his problems.

Thinking of relieving dragons, the light green Reed was still around, sitting with his head on his arms, looking sad as he watched Kayla. He had whined at her a few times and she had stopped to listen so she had to know what he was after, but she hadn't answered anything back other than she didn't know.

"I want to see Kayla play. Tell me what she's doing, please."

Kayla was laughing at something as she cast a surreptitious glance into the air over their heads. Tyler looked above him and had just enough time to jump out of the way before a water dragon released a blast of water that would have soaked him through.

"Conner's water dragon is named Nebula," the wise voice in his head informed him. The more this thing talked to him, the harder it was to not trust the information.

"Conner probably thought that Jack could use a bath with all that dirt from the dungeons and drool on him from Pyro."

Tyler was in so much trouble if he couldn't save the dragon in his thoughts from being possessed. He already felt like he had known this dragon forever, and the animal would be this brilliant aid in patching things up with Aralot. Tyler knew the ins and outs of Vankerdale, and while he had studied Aralot more than anything else, the night terror had valuable insights like this that could fill in all the little gaps Tyler needed.

Pg. 272

Nebula was now laughing so hard that he had to land. Jack was trying to brush the water off, and Conner was shaking out his hair congratulating Nebula on a shower well placed. Nebula shot a stream of water toward Valiant next who got hit and then returned to his normal size so he could charge after the water sprayer. Kayla charged after them both to make sure they didn't get too aggressive with each other. In the process, she ran across the top of one of Conner's dragons that was sleeping and woke it up.

Jack stopped shaking the water away when Pyro started to blow him with warm air. "She is touching dragons. She's not done that since she was five. That was eleven years ago. Tia is never going to believe this or that," Jack said as Kayla ignored her father's words in favor of jumping on the back of his dragon to use Pyro's tail as a bridge so she could reach Valiant who had launched into the air. Pyro let Kayla climb and then flicked her up with the tip of his tail so that she could shoot above Valiant in the air and land on his back. Tyler found himself feeling envious. People over here didn't play with dragons like this. It was way past time to get their connections back.

"Jack, what is stopping you from ending the curse on our dragons? I'll help you solve the problem. Whatever it takes."

"Are you sure that Tyler is a bad spy?" Jack asked Conner. It looked like a struggle for him to pry his eyes away from Kayla to look back at Tyler, but he did so. Unfortunately, Jack didn't trust Tyler with anything. He gave Tyler a tight assessing smile and didn't give him any additional clues.

"*His wife has to end the curse,*" the helpful dragon voice told Tyler. "*Either her or Kayla. It has to be someone that will touch magic and has Gladius's blood in their veins. Focus on Kayla. We can get her to do it. Bring her back here, Tyler.*"

"Can I go to Aralot with you?!" Tyler blurted out. He had to see this dragon that was talking to him. Tyler turned in the direction of Aralot and tried to make his eyes wider so that he could see across all the trees and miles and miles of fields that held them apart.

"I have black scales if that helps. What do you look like?"

It didn't help. There were too many variations of dragons with black scales. They had different head sizes and muscle mass and tail spikes. Tyler had brown hair, a beard that only ran under his nose and around his chin missing his cheeks. He wore glasses and usually thought of himself as an average height and build.

"What do you smell like?"

To a dragon? He had no idea, and if he asked that question that would only give Kayla more reason to suspect what he had become. It would help everyone guess that he had every intention of using Kayla Brixton to save himself while he stole away one of the dragons in their land. He couldn't let them know what he was really after. He didn't want to end up messing up everything as King Peyton had. Stealing dragons from other people made them angry even if they didn't particularly like the dragon in the first place. He was going to steal this dragon that Herb Felding had bred. That made him sound evil.

"Tyler, I appreciate everything you have risked to help us, but if you come with us now, King Peyton will know what you've done. You should return to the castle. You still have his trust that way," Jack told him.

He didn't want King Peyton's trust. He wanted a dragon. His dragon! At this rate, he wouldn't get that dragon until Aralot had come through and destroyed half the dragons in Vankerdale with their war.

"Do you have to kill off all our dragons? Couldn't you just…I don't know…eat King Peyton?"

Pyro stopped drooling on Jack's shoulder to hum at Tyler. Jack punched his dragon in the face surprising everyone. Tyler didn't think Jack had it in him to be cruel and Conner jumped between the unbonded pair to break it up.

"It's a communication error, Jack. I'm sure Pyro isn't deciding to like Tyler in the way you are thinking. Maybe he was agreeing to eat King Peyton."

"No, he wasn't," Jack snapped. He pulled out a knife that Conner was quick to get out of the way of. Jack threw it towards a tree stump that was fifty yards away and the knife struck true. Pyro snapped something at Jack and flew away from him just as angry. Jack continued to throw a few more knives until they ran out. Then he yanked them out of the stump and threw them all again. So, yes, for the time being, Tyler really should bypass asking for that bond until he got Kayla where he wanted her. He didn't want to end up like any of these emotional people.

"Come play cards, Jack," Conner invited, to snap him from his mood. Jack threw his knives twice more before he nodded his head and stepped toward the house.

"Do you play?" Conner asked Tyler.

Tyler looked at Valiant really quick. The dragon had landed now and had decided to not partake in the rest of the playing that Nebula was still after. Since Valiant was down with his eyes closed, Tyler glanced around, trying to find where Kayla went. He expected to find her with her hood up again, or else sobbing on the ground no longer able to face dragons if Valiant wasn't alert enough to face them with her. Conner pointed into the house.

"Kayla yawned and dashed back inside," Conner said.

Tyler hadn't noticed at all, but apparently, Jack had because he entered the house without a struggle. Without the dragons in the way, Tyler could make his plea again for the curse to be released at a better moment. Tyler stepped into the house after Conner to find that Kayla had pulled a pile of blankets and coats around her like a nest. She was curled up inside of it while her two cousins whispered about poking her to wake her up. Conner had them go play in their room.

"Did she sleep last night?" Jack asked. "She was one of those kids that refused to nap after she passed two. We could put her down, but she'd stay awake and talk to herself the whole time."

"No one slept last night," Conner yawned his answer as he returned holding a deck of cards. They followed Conner over to the kitchen while Tyler hoped he could prove that he wasn't too bad at card games so he could earn these men's respect.

After the third round, Tyler was glad that the only thing they were playing for was a pile of beans. Jack was incredible. Nothing Tyler did could make him lose. He even tried conspiring with Conner a few times when Conner passed him cards beneath the table and Jack still managed to beat them both. He didn't brag about his winning streak even when they hit seven rounds with him far in the lead. The reason why Conner had suggested they play cards had to be to boost Jack's ego. He was unstoppable, and he laughed a few times when he suspected that they were cheating against him without bringing him down.

Conner jumped to his feet when an audible gasp came from Kayla in the next room. Jack stilled and looked that direction but shook his head.

"Kayla's had nightmares since she turned twelve," Jack told him. "They typically come three nights in a row with a single night's break and then two nights in a row with another break."

"You ever ask her why she's so scared?" Conner questioned as he sat back down.

"I thought it was obvious," Jack replied. Conner looked toward the window and nodded. "Maybe the nightmares will stop soon now that she has Valiant. She's probably so emotionally exhausted right now that she's got to sleep off the rest of those fears."

Jack picked up the next card. He put it right back down without looking at it when Kayla walked in with her hood off. She rubbed her hands together excited and kissed her fingers. Conner and Jack both stood up with a single glance at her. Tyler didn't know why they looked so anxious until Jack clued him into the issue.

"Valiant she needs to sleep," Jack told Kayla. Tyler stood up too so he could see around them. Sightsharing wasn't possible unless a rider was actively bonded. Valiant shouldn't be able to take over Kayla's body and walk her around at all. Either Valiant was using a spell to achieve his desired result, which in this case would be possession, the very thing Tyler wanted to learn about, or sightsharing functioned differently for keepers. He was making a large mental note to look into this and find out, because if Valiant could walk Kayla around, that demon dragon could move *him*.

Tyler gripped at the table to steady himself. He had read all about sightsharing. Kayla's eyes were supposed to change color. He tried to note a difference and was surprised to see that Kayla's usual Felding blue eyes were bright yellow.

"Kayla threw away my picture," Valiant told them. He had his rider cross through the kitchen to select a piece of paper and a pencil. He sat down with them at the table and started to draw. Jack gawked at his daughter. Conner gawked too. Tyler wanted to start asking his many many questions.

"I seriously thought I'd seen it all," Jack told Conner. Then he started to talk to Valiant again. "Is this your first time sightsharing? You've not made her move in an atypical way. I've seen riders wetting themselves, doing cartwheels, and trying to fly. You look way too comfortable. How are you drawing?"

"It's not hard. Kayla took drawing classes from Rosa. Have you seen Rosa draw? She's remarkable."

Jack admitted to watching Rosa draw before and Conner asked him to send him a picture. Valiant was amazing at drawing too. He had Kayla draw a picture of himself in his shrunken size. He was crouched down with his rump in the air and his wings stretched out looking for all the world like a lovable puppy. Beside him was Kayla realistically standing with her hood up but she was holding a ball ready to throw it.

"Can I keep that?" Jack asked when Valiant had finished. Valiant gave him the picture and then had Kayla give Tyler a hug. Kayla had never hugged him before. It was super strange. He awkwardly patted her shoulder knowing that it was Valiant controlling the person before him. Valiant still liked him which was nice, but it wasn't comforting knowing that the dragon could move Kayla like this.

"You've sightshared before, yes?" Jack pressed again. "We're leaving in the morning. We can't do that if Kayla's head is exploding."

"Oh, she won't notice," Valiant assured her father. "She's sleeping. She's been begging me to let her sleep for over twelve hours. I don't see how I'm supposed to provide that unless she's not herself."

"So you hide her from her nightmares?"

"Wouldn't you? They are horrible," Valiant told Jack before leaving the kitchen.

Tyler pushed open the kitchen's revolving door to watch Kayla head back to the pile of blankets she had been sleeping in. She fixed the arrangement of the circular nest and then curled up inside them again. So, if Valiant was being Kayla to block out her nightmares, that had to mean that the dragon sleeping outside the house was really Kayla unaware that she was being a dragon.

Pg. 278

"I'm creeped out," Jack said, looking at the picture in his hand. "Do you think that Valiant's been sneaking around in Kayla? I know she wakes up at night sometimes but..." He shivered. "How I wish I could hear Pyro! Do you think Valiant has drawn lots of pictures? Kayla used to draw a lot but then she stopped keeping images and started tossing all her work in the fireplace. I have no idea how long this has been going on."

"How is it possible?" Tyler asked in a voice that begged an answer. He had to know. "They're unbonded!"

"Yeah." Jack shrugged. "But Tia can sightshare with all her linked dragons regardless of the closeness of their bond."

"It's a keeper thing then?" Tyler asked to confirm. Jack looked at Conner who wasn't commenting if he could do the same thing. Tyler wished he would say something. This was either a trait specific to Tia and her offspring, or to all keepers. Tyler didn't need his body moving off on him. He had to trust himself!

"Are you coming back to Aralot with us Conner?" Jack asked him. He looked at Conner like he couldn't stand to lose such a good friend again.

"No. I can hardly stand up in Aralot. The thing that gets Kayla all the time gets me too. It's easier for me here. I can't return until Vankerdale is no longer cursed, and I won't rush that release. You do what is best for everyone over there. I'm counting on you guys to hold it all together. Besides, I've got this, Jack. All I ever do is mess up King Peyton's plans. I'll get you through his defenses. Don't you worry about that. I'm going to get some rest," Conner announced.

He passed his cards back to Jack. Jack looked through them and grinned as if he knew everything that had been in the hand. Tyler gave him his hand as well. Jack didn't look over his cards. He scooped them all together and then moved into the front room to make himself comfortable in the rocking chair beside his daughter. Tyler headed outside to look at Valiant and wonder how many times he had seen the dragon and had really been looking at Kayla Brixton. This was so unsettling.

Charm

Tristan

Tristan hadn't really meant for the charm hunt to get out of hand but it had. Bantin was super excited to be on the lookout for something Vladimir had used, and he had found the other half of the bear medallion quicker than Tristan had thought possible. He expected the medallion that had once linked Vladimir to Anvil's Ware to be hidden in his secret cave, kept by one of Vladimir's relatives, or buried beneath pounds of stone of reconstructed buildings, but it wasn't. The matching bear medallion had been in Vladimir's pocket, and he had been buried with it. Bantin had dug up the man's grave, and he didn't have small fingers to nab a coin that small. He was respectful enough of his old ware leader to not tear the man's bones apart.

Tristan had jumped into the grave to search the decayed corps himself, and he had been caught being a gravedigger. At least he had already searched the man's pockets where he found the other half of the medallion he was seeking. Then he faced punishment from Vincent's Ware for digging up the grave. He tried to make excuses that he hadn't stolen anything. He tried to talk his way out of being punished. It worked more than half the time since he was the prince, but the ware leader, Vincent, didn't care. He had his current pair of pink *almost* ice dragons surround Tristan, and those creatures were only friends with people they had known from birth. Everyone else was liable to get squished, or chomped, or flamed, no matter who they were. These pests behaved for their riders and of course Shilo who trained them.

His punishment was to replace the grave and scrub the outside of every building in Vincent's Ware to cleanse it from dirt and charred marks. This wasn't a small ware that only trained the newbies. Vincent's Ware was easily the largest one in size even if Anvil's Ware was larger in numbers.

Tristan showed them he could make their ware shine, but he had to break down and use magic a few times on his arms. He also used it on the walls, because he didn't have two weeks to spend scrubbing this place clean. Vincent couldn't take away every magical source he had when he hid them all over his body although he had tried. Luckily, Tristan had been raised a Colt as a child and knew how to pretend like he was picking a wedgie when he wanted to hide coin-shaped items in a place no one would look. He'd kept that coin.

It was very uncomfortable and Riven had spent hours laughing at him and then worrying about diseases he may have picked up from shoving a coin that had been in a grave down his pants. Tristan was too determined to not lose it to care. Just thinking about what Vladimir had used the medallion for proved its high value. Tristan could hide one coin where no one would suspect and instantly get there. Once he had more time to explore its uses, he might even try his hand at tossing it through one of Jack's house windows so he could get inside finally. It was tempting, although, the idea held a certain fear behind it. What if Jack kept the coin for himself? Tristan wouldn't get it back and Jack would no doubt put it in a place Tristan couldn't survive landing inside, like the bottom of the ocean or beneath a pile of boulders.

There was that, and if Jack figured out how to use the medallions, Tristan might find the king appearing inside his pants pocket. That would be bad for obvious reasons, and not just because Jack would show up. No. His pocket couldn't fit the size of a man. His pocket was liable to

Pg. 282

split and with it his pants might decide they wanted to split too and…it was just bad all around.

"*I would laugh so hard!*" Riven was already laughing at him, picturing his pants on the floor and Jack looking surprised.

Riven had been doing a lot of laughing. Tristan was starting to think that they had reversed roles again. He had been older than Riven when they first met, but it was startling how quickly his dragon matured and surpassed him. The creature had already fathered a few dragons of his own, leaving Tristan feeling stricken with the idea that his dragon had grown up so fast. And now he was acting like the child yet again laughing at dirty jokes.

"*I can't help it. Humans are so funny. Have you ever heard your own thoughts? I don't walk around being concerned about pants.*"

Tristan finished walking out of Vincent's Ware, finally, to where Riven was waiting for him. He had a few good comments he could have said back, but he resisted saying them. That didn't stop Riven from his continued laughter.

"*Stop. Vincent's dragons will think you're laughing at them.*"

"*They will not. They know who I'm laughing at.*"

Tristan looked behind him at the almost ice dragons that had been staring him down. Some of them were laughing along with Riven. He gave Riven a nervous glance hoping he hadn't shared the joke because if they knew what he had in his pants, he didn't think Vincent would let him leave. It had been a struggle just to get back everything he had in his pockets. Vincent had tried to rob him of half his cash.

"*That's why you shouldn't carry so much money with you,*" Riven told him.

"*I had plans for it.*"

He really did. He hadn't planned on wasting time washing buildings. In his mind, they would ask Bantin to search for the matching coin and then perhaps in a week or so they would hear back. Bantin had taken less than a day, which wasn't very shocking all things considered. Vladimir had raised him, so Bantin would know what the man carried with him and where the medallion had been put before Tristan ever wanted to find it. In any case, the side trip was worth it even if Tristan was late in delivering his birthday present to Dani.

"She will make fun of you for being so late," Riven thought.

He knew she would, but he still had to show up. Dani was beautiful with her curly black hair and green eyes and warm laugh. She was nothing like the noble girls whose giggles really meant that they had practiced them under the careful guidance of their mothers. They were never honest and Tristan felt it. Dani was honest.

"Too honest."

She was honest about only being half interested in him: unsure of her feelings. She was also at the Desert Ware, and Tristan needed to head down there to cast the loyalty spell on Vermelo. She was going to love her present.

"Has any of your bribery ever worked against a girl?" Riven asked him.

"It's flattery," Tristan grumbled. *"You have it easy. All you need to do is hoot and you have female dragons enchanted with you. Human's aren't like that."*

"I did more than just hoot to get Holly to love me," Riven defended. *"Come to think of it, I haven't flattered her with any gems lately. Got any for me?"*

"Bribery?" Tristan snorted. Riven always asked him for gems around mating season. Tristan never questioned his motives. He helped

Pg. 284

his dragon out. Why couldn't Riven do the same for him? What was wrong with wanting a girl to wrap her arms around him and make him feel wanted?

"It's bribery if used on humans. It's flattery if used on a dragon."

Whatever. Riven was a dragon. He would always be a dragon, and he would always think like a dragon. Humans were flattered by gifts too, even if they came late for their birthday. Tristan told Riven to stop bothering him as they approached one of the two portals near Vincent's Ware that would connect them to the desert. He pulled out the necklace he had bought to make sure that Vincent hadn't damaged it. The creation had a dragon with a blue sapphire eye.

He had flattered, not bribed, a few of the noble girls before. They were not very good at keeping their opinions off their face if they didn't like what he gave them, even if they thanked him sweeter than anyone. He had flattered Colt beauties too, but they usually kept coming back trying to trick him into giving them things they could sell for a large profit. Dating was hard. He just wanted one girl to understand him.

"Abbie understood you," Riven reminded him.

"And then she married Elliot," Tristan reminded him.

They had gotten along really well, but Abbie didn't like the idea of ruling the kingdom someday. He needed to find someone who would love him for everything he was. Wanting to rule Aralot was part of him. He couldn't take that part away without losing his identity. He was yet to meet a girl that was worth walking away from Aralot. As he saw it, everyone knew who he was. If the girl was going to really love him back, she should respect him.

They reached the Desert Ware and its strange outcropping of stone buildings. It was hard building in the desert where the sandstorms threatened to knock down and bury dwellings. The Desert Ware had been built with the storms in mind. There was a large stone slab underneath each building to provide it with support. Each day one of the riders was in charge of walking around it and adding or subtracting sand to keep the structure in place. There was also a stone wall that encircled all the buildings. That was to prevent some of the sandstorms from bashing up against the training structures. It was not a perfect solution, and everyone now saw the flaws in the building design, but no one had fixed them.

Tristan and Riven easily found Dani. She was sweeping sand off of one of the slabs. Her black hair was covered over with her head wrap but they knew it was her. For one thing, Riven could smell her. For another, her brown dragon was sitting nearby lazily flicking her tail. Dani looked up when her dragon announced their arrival, and she pulled the head wrap off. This was followed by a large inhale of fresh, albeit dry, air. Dani had not been born in the desert, and she didn't appreciate the stuffy headgear that kept her hair and eyes free of sand. She had every intention of transferring to a different ware one day.

"How was your birthday?" Tristan asked. He pulled her out of her bow by grabbing her hand and kissing it.

"Oh, dear. She spent it kissing Glen according to her dragon. Do you think she will tell you something different?"

"Shut up, Riven."

"It was fine. I hardly remembered it was my birthday until they lit the birthday bonfire and everyone started singing. Then they pulled out the punch and boy was it good punch! You should have been here Tristan. What were you doing?"

Tristan gave his dragon a harsh signal behind his back. Riven wasn't going to tell Dani's dragon, or anyone else, why he had missed the birthday. He didn't like spreading castle news or his confrontations with other wares.

Pg. 286

"Relax. I don't share your secrets."

"I got tied up, but I didn't forget your birthday. I really wanted to be here. I got you something."

He passed her the present wrapped in colorful paper and watched her eyes light up when she pulled it out. She had him hook the necklace on for her, and he caught the scent of lavender in her hair along with the musty smell of sand that clung to everyone in the desert.

"Tristan it's beautiful! Thank you so much!"

Tristan beamed. It was easy to pick out items for dragon riders. He could have bought her a pair of boots and she would have been thrilled. He had almost gotten her a pair of really nice gloves but the necklace had sounded better.

"It was more expensive."

Dani giggled at him. "Riven's bothering you, isn't he? You just rolled your eyes."

Tristan apologized and turned around to wave his dragon away. Riven returned his gesture with a sneeze that covered him in large wet drops. He never did like dragon sneezes. It wasn't so bad if they came from his own dragon, but if it came from someone else's…

"I've got a clean cloth. I'm sorry," he told Dani. He fetched the cloth from the bag on his back and helped dry her off.

"Tristan," Dani tugged on his arm questioning. "I heard a rumor the other night about Kayla."

Tristan felt his gut churn an uncomfortable rumble. Anything about Kayla was always unpleasant. He hadn't thought news of Kayla being captured would have time to get here so fast. There wasn't any way for it to travel that quickly unless someone took a portal. Otherwise, they were looking at at least a week or two of communication delay.

"What about her?" he asked, working his way up to asking Dani who she had heard the rumor from. Had her ware leader started using portals? Usually getting sick going through them discouraged most people from attempting the trip more than once, and only a few ware leaders discovered how to use them. Those ware leaders, namely Rogan and Anvil, didn't make frequent use of the portals either.

"Glen said that you have to date her when she turns sixteen and that would mean in four days you'll be actively dating the king's daughter. What would that make us? I mean... I'm not saying that we have to be anything, it's just... I don't feel comfortable being your girlfriend when you're off flirting with someone else."

Oh, darn. She had heard *that* rumor. Dani even knew the exact day of Kayla's birthday. Four days wasn't enough time for freedom. Her words hung around his neck like a child that wouldn't let go. The desert had not heard that they were on the verge of war with Vankerdale yet. He wasn't going to tell them either. The Desert Ware forces might not even be asked to join in the battle. Charles's Ware was the closest to defeating the threat if it reached the castle and after them was Vincent's Ware.

"Kayla doesn't mean anything to me. My dad got her parents to sign this addendum that we would go on four dates. There's nothing to say what counts as a date. I could buy her a piece of bread four times and call it a date."

"You won't because your dad would get mad if that's how you approached it. I think for the time being that we need to take a break in our relationship until you've handled your business with Kayla."

Tristan wanted to scream. Right when he thought he was getting closer with a girl something always came up that related to his role as the future king. It had never been Kayla before though. The fact that Kayla was now getting in his way when she wasn't even inside of Aralot tormented him. He could never get rid of the effects of that girl being born.

"Dani, really, there won't be anything between me and Kayla. She's nothing more than a shadow."

"She's pretty," Dani told him and dug out a picture from her pocket. "Isn't that her?"

She passed him the picture of Kayla. Tristan could only glare at it while behind him Riven hummed. Someone had done a really good job drawing her with her hood off. She was even smiling. Imagine that. The image wasn't signed, so Tristan knew automatically that Caleb Andrade had been the creator of the work of art. Tristan didn't like Caleb. The guy needed a new hobby apart from drawing the king's daughter.

"She's only pretty if you happen to be a dragon," Tristan retorted, even if this picture was actually pretty. Kayla's face was shaded to make her look gentle. Her shoulders had wrongly been left as a single line as if the artist might come back and fill in the details later. This had probably been stolen before Caleb had finished it.

"Tristan when you're done buying Kayla four pieces of bread you can come back and talk to me."

And in that amount of time, Dani would be completely smitten with Glen. That's how it always went. All the amazing women were snatched up fast. Life wasn't fair.

"Thanks for being honest with me," Tristan told Dani. "I have some other business to do so…"

He started to back away and ignored the half sorry look he got from Dani. "Happy birthday again," he told her before he turned the rest of the way and kicked sand through the ware on his way to the extra nest that he had taken over.

A dragon nest was the best place to store magic. It came equipped with a fireplace where he had placed an emerald cauldron that would melt the magical ice balls he kept in the room. This helped him tap into the magic at the center of each sphere. The guard, covered head to toe in his desert gear, stepped to the side as he neared the door.

"*I hate Kayla!*" Tristan shouted at Riven.

He stepped into the room that he unlocked with magic and glanced at the frozen ice balls that covered the floor. They varied in size but most of them reached up to the top of his boots. In the center of each one was an unearthly blue glow that made this room the brightest place he ever stepped into.

"*So I should assume that you will not buy Kayla any dragon necklaces?*" Riven quizzed.

"*Kayla ruins my life. I'm not buying her anything.*"

"*Besides bread.*"

Tristan kicked a few of the ice balls watching them knock into each other. Four real dates with the worst threat to his life. He knew it was coming, but it had always felt farther away. As soon as he could, he would take her out for breakfast, brunch, lunch, and dinner. That totaled to four dates and took less than a day. He would be able to get her out of his life. Kayla wasn't going to like him. He already knew. He kicked another ball of ice and pulled out the spell from his father that he was to use on Vermelo.

It needed a lot of magic so he was going to need to melt a few orbs. He hefted one up and dropped it into the emerald cauldron, careful to replace the lid so magic didn't seep out. Melting these always took forever, so he lit the fire to get started wishing he had brought the magic mirror with him so he could spy on people while he waited. Instead of being able to spy, his thoughts swirled back to Kayla.

Pg. 290

He didn't want her to like him, but if she didn't, what then? The kingdom was hers. He would have to start trying to kill her and Vermelo already suspected him enough. There was also the issue of her parents and their control over the kingdom and dragons. He had control over the Desert Ware, but it wouldn't be enough against Anvil's gang. Then there were people like Kayla's uncles and cousins who liked her. There was the scary presence of Ritz.

If Kayla declared that she hated him, he could be in for the worst fight of his life. Even worse than taking on the demon ultra-dragon king. His safest path was to make her abdicate. How would he get her to do that? He didn't know her well enough to know what would push her to walk away from the throne, which meant that he needed to actually date her and not just slough off the duty to get to know her.

"I seriously hate her!" Tristan shouted. He was going to stretch himself to the limit getting Kayla out of the way.

Nightmares

Kayla

It wasn't enough sleep even if she had tried to lay down in the middle of the day to get some rest. Her mind knew somehow that she wasn't active, so it was doing the best it could to shove through her every thought and tell her everything it wanted her to know. But she already knew it all! Right now, she was hearing her mother's words on repeat and it was annoying.

"Every night they scare you. Kayla, dragons are so much more than these events. Scary things can happen to everyone, but if you only dwell on the fear, you forget how to live in the joy."

She didn't try to escape from her own joy. She had impressed more than herself by playing with Valiant today. Her father had been put into a stupor trying to figure her out. Well, she was too. She'd never felt freer than when she had played with the dragon she had never known. However, feeling free for once had transformed her into this. Trapped. She felt incredibly trapped like she was outside of herself stuck inside a vice grip that refused to let her mind rest even if her body got to. Even stranger, she was getting a new dream. She had never seen this one before, and it left her edgy wondering where the terror was going to come from because it started out so sweet.

She was looking at something that surrounded her entire body. It wasn't exactly leather, but it reminded her of leather. It was dark with striated lines and she could see through it. Maybe it was a wing? However, wings didn't circle all the way around.

There was a deep humming sound that filled her entire body with excitement. Oh. The sound was the largest give away she could ever get. It was the dragon birthing song. She was a dragon inside an eggshell and she was being born. This was weird.

The humming continued and Kayla could feel the baby's excitement as if it was her own. There were other dragons out there excited to see him or her. The baby tried to move to the sound only to be stuck by the shell. That baby clawed at the calcium carbonate crust and then chirped that it was coming. Kayla congratulated herself on knowing dragon voices because she was able to pick up on this one. Valiant. She was being him, which posed an important question. Was this dream given to her from Valiant, or had she suddenly stolen his memories without trying to just as she stole the memories from all the other keepers in the past? How did she get these dreams? She still couldn't explain it to herself.

Valiant continued to scratch at the shell until he broke a hole. The humming sound got louder and Kayla tried to pick out the different dragons she could hear. There was a red dragon nearby. That louder hum had to be from a night dragon. Valiant used his tail along with his claws to bust the rest of the way out. Light poured in around him as the hums made him feisty and happy.

"I'm out!" Valiant shouted. He popped his head up among the hums.

"It's blue-gray! We got one!" came the shout of a creature that was not a dragon.

Valiant looked around confused. Where were the dragons? He could hear them. There was a funny creature there instead. Whatever it
Pg. 294

was, the animal was looking at him intently as Valiant finished smashing down the gray shell.

He was in a funny place. He used to dream that the sun was yellow, but it was coming through the walls looking green. There were other dragon eggs around him but when he sniffed them, they didn't smell ready to hatch, and when he listened, he couldn't hear any clawing. A loud excited hum came from his side, and he perked up as his eyes to focus on a dragon.

"Here I am!" Valiant hooted, as he tumbled around the other eggs toward the dragon.

"It has silver wingtips!" the not-dragon shouted next.

Valiant got close to the dragon he could see, a bronze, and jumped at it trying to say hi. He smashed his face against a hard, slippery, strange substance. The dragon smiled at him.

"That's glass. You're in a greenhouse. Be careful about that human. He steals eggs."

Valiant turned back around to look at the human who was following after him. The guy smelled really good, but Valiant wanted a dragon.

"Mom? Dad?" Valiant asked.

He rushed the other direction back around the eggs that were not ready to hatch and smashed into the glass on the other side. There was a different dragon there that was a bright red color.

"Good luck little one. You're going to need it," the red dragon told him.

Valiant chirped back confused. Shouldn't other eggs be hatching with him? Where was his family? The red dragon stopped humming and started to walk away. Valiant tried to bring it back. He rushed to the other sides of the greenhouse chirping, confused. He smashed into the glass again.

"Easy there," the human told him. There was that good smell again. This time it made his stomach rumble. Valiant looked down at his rumbling stomach and laughed. He was hungry.

"Come get it," the human told him backing away with the food.

Valiant gave the man a bow. *"For me?"* he chirped.

"Did you see that?!" the human called out. A blast of cool air swept through the building as the door opened and another man walked in.

"He's perfect."

Kayla had never seen this guy before, but she knew who he was. He had red hair that resembled Prince Evan's. The red hair also wrapped around the man's face to form a beard. He had broader shoulders and his voice wasn't as deep as his son's. She was now looking at King Peyton who had taken Valiant away from where he was supposed to be and created the scandal that Kayla was living inside. Now that she had found the source of the terror, Kayla tried to fight back against it.

"Valiant!" she screamed at him. Where was he? He couldn't leave her alone to this. He couldn't abandon her to the nightmares now that she knew he was there with her always. She desperately wanted him to be with her to hold her hand when King Peyton got scarier.

"Valiant!" Kayla yelled again.

"If you could make your mind a tad quieter…" Valiant's voice sounded miles away as if he was in a tunnel going backward away from her. Kayla tried to wake herself to reach him. Only she couldn't. She found herself plunged back beneath the grip that shoved her back toward her fears instead of away from them. Enough with this! She

wasn't scared of dragons! She could stand up to them! Except it wasn't a dragon that she was currently trying to hide from.

"You know what to do, and you had better do it," King Peyton's voice was whispering into her ear. Well, not her ear. She was still being Valiant. He gave off a short hoot for yes as his stomach rumbled with fear. Kayla didn't know what it was that King Peyton had said previously to make Valiant work for him, but she already didn't like this next nightmare.

Valiant opened his eyes startling Kayla with the view. Valiant was inside of Aralot in the woods near Anvil's Ware. Kayla had been in this exact same location hundreds of times! He could currently hear the sound of a person coming closer. Kayla's veins filled with dread because she knew the sounds of those feet. Both of them. One person was her mother Tia, and the other lightly walking footsteps belonged to Sparkle. Valiant didn't shut his eyes when they stepped into view although Kayla wanted to.

Sparkle was the youngest that Kayla had ever seen reaching shoulder-high to the blond human beside her. Not that Kayla was trying to compare, but Sparkle was the absolute cutest baby dragon. Her white scales gleamed, her nails were painted pink, and she laughed at the sounds of bugs she could hear coming to stop at a bush so she could tell Tia all about it.

Valiant's dragon eyes zoomed in on Tia and looked at her flat stomach. This was the youngest Kayla had ever seen her mother as well. She knew that if she was seeing Sparkle this short, Tia could have already married Jack, but she looked too young for a baby.

The familiar spark of blue magic rose up beside Valiant as King Peyton cast a spell outward toward Tia. Kayla tried to guess what the spell was, but without understanding the king's intention, she had no idea. Sparkle jumped in front of Tia growling. She tried to cough out ice but was too young so only spit came flying back out. Sparkle started to panic. She couldn't defend Tia, and Tia started running dodging in and out of trees. She wasn't faster than King Peyton with his spells. One of the spells hit her and she screamed as she crashed down to the ground.

"No!" Kayla heard her mother shout. Her voice sounded odd against Valiant's larger ears and it continued being distasteful. "I'll do anything. I really will. I swear King Peyton. I will take Klavian off the throne if you just don't do this."

Kayla had never heard her mother so desperate before. She had never heard her talk about dethroning Klavian either.

"I don't need you to dethrone him," King Peyton replied, watching as Tia's stomach grew larger and larger. Kayla got a sinking feeling in her own gut. She knew what baby was coming because her mother had only ever had one child. Kayla tried to shut her already closed eyes and then tried to shout at Valiant to close his. It didn't work, because she couldn't control the past.

"Don't take my baby!" Tia screamed struggling to stand. Sparkle was trying to defend her again. She tried to attack King Peyton but he was defended by a much larger dragon with silver wings that wasn't Valiant. His own beast was there ready to inflict torture. Didn't SilverWings ever feel bad about what his rider did?

"I'm not taking the child. I'm borrowing it."

"Well, you can't! I'll get back at you for this! I'll curse you all again!"

Tia didn't have time to say any curse because she was suddenly screaming in pain. The scene cut to blackness as Valiant closed his eyes and trembled. Kayla couldn't thank him enough. His whole body gave a giant shudder. Valiant didn't open his eyes again until King Peyton gave him a horrible poke underneath a scale. Kayla screamed, angry at the

Pg. 298

abuse. Valiant didn't though. He didn't let King Peyton know how much it had hurt. He would make a really good Colt.

"Hurry up. Her other dragons will be coming this way," King Peyton said.

Valiant opened his eyes again and Kayla could see a naked baby crying. Her. Wow, she had been really tiny! All newborns looked minuscule, but she looked so fragile and breakable and her mother was still screaming.

Valiant opened his mouth and fanged her leg as carefully as he could, but he was still much larger than the baby. The venom that squirted out had an odd tangy flavor. Valiant swallowed the extra venom and then shook his head as a gasp entered into his brain that had not been there before.

"Hello?" Valiant thought. There was a very loud verbal wail that followed a sharp cry from the baby.

"Hello, Kayla?" Valiant tried again, but the only thing Kayla did was continue to cry.

Valiant looked toward Tia, hoping that she could do something to help his baby. That was a bad decision. Knives pierced themselves right into both his eyes. He screamed, writhing down to the ground trying not to blink and make the loss of his eyesight the loss of his life. Kayla screamed along with him. Her mother had tried to kill her dragon!

"Let's go. I'll fix you," King Peyton said, yanking the knives from his sockets as Valiant's screams mixed with Kayla's. A rope was put around his neck and the king started to pull him away. The baby was left wailing on the ground. Kayla struggled to wake herself up. She didn't want to see anymore! She never wanted to see or hear any of this!

"Now we wait. When it's old enough to walk you will bring me the baby," King Peyton declared.

"Never," Valiant growled.

Kayla screamed, and managed to finally wake herself up. She glanced around noting the dark lighting that put her in a sour mood, because it was night and she didn't want to risk going back to sleep. It had been way too hard to wake herself up. Her pile of blankets had been added to and now contained soft sweaters and coats from Conner's closet. There were lots of colors because Conner pretended to be too many different people. Her father was pinching his eyes together trying to get some rest around her screaming. Tyler wasn't trying at all. He was sitting on the floor flipping cards over onto piles playing a single-player game. He looked up at her when she looked over at him, glanced at her dad, and then pulled a face going back to the cards.

"Valiant," Kayla said, scrambling to the window trying to spot him. He didn't make it hard on her. He was awake too staring at the house as if waiting for her to look outside to find him. Behind her, Kayla heard her dad start to shift, Tyler flipped more cards, and the sound of Conner's feet moved down the hallway toward the front of the house.

"There you are. Have I ever told you that you are an exceptionally strong keeper? Sometimes I just can't break through your thoughts."

"Me either," Kayla replied. *"Why did King Peyton send you after my mom? What did he want with me?"*

"He wanted you to bring him magic. Everyone knows that messing with a keeper's bonded dragon will bring instant death upon their own heads, so King Peyton did the next best thing. He decided to mess around with a keeper that couldn't fend him off. He wanted to take magic from Sparkle, not knowing at the time that she couldn't churn up magic along with her ice. So he stole me to lure Sparkle over the border."

"Why didn't he go after Bantin instead?"

"I've wondered that too. Maybe he thought that Sparkle would be the

Pg. 300

easier target. Maybe it was all out of revenge against King Gladius's curses and King Peyton wanted to make the man's descendants suffer as he had. Maybe he figured that taking Bantin wouldn't make a difference if Sparkle was still there to give Tia and Jack magic. Maybe he realized that if he didn't have the best of leverage, he would never win anyway."

Maybe. Kayla caught the gleaming green eyes of one of Conner's dragons and had to shut the curtain. She was in a house surrounded by unfamiliar dragons. That sort of thing was the basis of a few of her nightmares. At least with Conner's friends, they were already in his keeper bond so she didn't need to worry about them. They couldn't get into her head.

"Says who?" Valiant asked her. *"Pewter tries to talk to you and he's bonded to Rosa. I think you can hear everybody."*

She wasn't safe from any dragon? Would that all change if her bond was fixed?

"We can't bond," Valiant reminded her.

They couldn't right now but they could when they got back to Aralot.

"No," Valiant hooted at her from outside causing her to pull the curtain open again to look at him. He didn't want to bond at all? Why not? She needed that bond to stop herself from crying!

"No," Valiant said again, turning his back on her.

"Why not?!" Kayla screamed at him.

"Shh!" Jack came up behind her placing his hand on her shoulder. Kayla started shaking. It was Valiant that had bonded her as a baby. She had seen it! Right when she started to trust him, he decided that he didn't want her. It was her dreams, wasn't it? Or perhaps her constant tears that were already falling again as he refused to be there for her. Maybe it was because she was a horrible rider or because he had decided to love someone else like Tyler.

"I am not turning on our bond. I love you. I will help you with anything, but I made a promise to not bond you until a certain date, and I won't break that promise because it would have horrible consequences to you. You'll just have to trust me on this, Kayla."

Trust him to not bond her? That was a horrible promise. She didn't care what the consequence was going to be. He should break it!

"Trouble in dragon paradise?" Uncle Conner asked, stepping to her other side and looking out the window. Valiant started crying and Kayla shoved away from her dad to glare in the direction of Tyler. Dragon crying was the worst. She always felt compelled to help the poor thing, and she knew that there was nothing she could do to help Valiant even if he was the one dragon she could look at. It was maddening! Every time she heard a dragon squeal in pain all the other injured dragons she had ignored over the years came back to haunt her.

Tyler froze in fear as if she had caught him in some illicit act with one hand on a card hovering in the air. Oh, bother.

"You ever make Valiant promise you anything stupid?" Kayla asked him.

He shook his head. It was probably King Peyton then. He had scared Valiant as a baby, and the man still scared him. How was she going to get around what King Peyton had done to her dragon so she could get that broken bond fixed? Kayla sighed and shut her eyes. Maybe a little faith here was in order; the sort that her father had been talking about. He gave her enough grace to work out her own problems in her own timing. She needed to allow Valiant that same space to work through his own fears. It wasn't very nice of her to be so selfish, wanting the dragon to bite her to stop her tears. She had to consider his needs as well. Kayla hoped it wasn't some nasty spell that would be sent at him

Pg. 302

like King Peyton ruining his eyesight all over again as her mother had done.

"I didn't tell you that," Valiant remarked. *"That wasn't your nightmare, was it? All King Peyton did was have SilverWings cast a healing spell on me, but he only did it after I was chained up and locked away so I was miserable the whole way back to Vankerdale. I'm pretty sure I told you before that your mother can be scary. That's why. She's got good aim. I'm scared to meet her. You'll stay with me the whole time, right?"*

Yes, she would, but this was just stupid. If King Peyton wanted a magical dragon, he could go breed one himself! He had enough time already to do so. If he wanted to torment Aralot why didn't he do so with messing up their trade or stealing from the Wisterian ships that were headed to Aralot? Why did he have to attack *her?*

"Kayla, I know you're very busy over there inside your own head, but if you're up, we really should get going. Conner's dragons are distracting the spies, but King Peyton is close to finding us. What do you make of this?" her father asked her.

Kayla turned only halfway before she flinched at what Jack was holding. It was a picture and it didn't have the same bold outlines that Caleb used in his drawings. It couldn't have come from him. No this was one of those pictures that she couldn't explain. That was yet another reason that Valiant could want to stay apart from her. He wasn't going to bond her until she figured out how to stop moving so much in her sleep, acting against her own will as if she was possessed when she knew very well that she wasn't.

The picture showed Valiant looking small and lovable playing with her. It was cute but highly irritating. Kayla shrugged at it. When she was younger, she used to draw dragons squishing people. She had never shown her mom, but her pictures had been pretty realistic. She wondered if her dad had found a few. The one where a demon dragon was flaming a person into a skeleton had disappeared mysteriously one night. After that, she had stopped drawing her own pictures.

"Let's go. I am so done with King Peyton," Kayla declared.

Her father sighed at her, but he put the picture into his pants pocket and headed out the door, scanning the area for Pyro while he cooed softly to Valiant trying to make him brave and stop his crying. It had to be hard on him to deny himself of something that he wanted as well because of some mysterious promise he had made in an attempt to not hurt her. One hurt was greater than the other. She had nothing left to do but trust him on which torture would be more brutal. He thought her tears were the lesser evil, so she had to go with that. She could do this. She could get over her own tears. She'd been doing it for years.

Tyler was next out the door, moving to Valiant also trying to console the now hiccupping dragon as he tried to stop himself from crying. Kayla wasn't really ready to go out there and face the dragon that had been just denied her. On the flip side, he was also the dragon that had been defending her her entire life. She took in a deep breath and made for the door.

"Hey, before you go," Conner said pulling Kayla back into the house and shutting the door blocking off her dad and Tyler. "I just wanted to make sure that you're still alright with me being your uncle."

"Of course, I am!" There was no way she couldn't be since they were both keepers. She had always liked her Uncle Conner, and now that she had met him, she liked him even more. He was thoughtful, savvy, and willing to risk himself to save them all. Even without the last point, they were family and she would always love him.

"Good. Because I've been thinking way too much about what you said about Anvil telling everyone that there was a lead keeper who broke ties in some ancient council. I understood what you meant when you asked me if I'd ever considered ruling, and it put me through the process
Pg. 304

of trying to decide if I needed to grab that crown all over again. What I concluded was that it's you that doesn't understand your place yet. Not me.

"I've always looked up to Tia ever since I first saw her. Rosa and I felt it in our bones to save her when she was being attacked by her poisoned father. I could hardly sleep knowing Herb had turned on us. Rosa was the same way. She was shattered when she discovered that Alice was Herb's spellcaster and the person she had to destroy. She had Pewter crush her own mother to save her sister. Tia was meant to be the queen. The magic in Aralot declared it. It was her and Jack uniting us together. My job was to help them get where they needed to be.

"That part I already firmly believed. Then you said that everyone seeks to protect the most influential keeper because of magical ties," Conner continued and placed his hand against the door so no one would push it back open to interrupt. "So many times I would have put myself in the way of anything that hit Tia, but you know what I did the last time I saw her get hurt? I turned my back on her and ran after your dragon. It took less than a second for me to change my loyalty. It's bothered me for years. Why go after the baby's struggling dragon instead of help the person I adored? You told me the answer, Kayla. The dissonance you feel between your parents, turning toward Anvil more than them," Kayla pouted at him for the way he already picked up on that, "is because you're the one in charge, only you don't realize it yet. It's hard to look up to the very people who look up to you. Every single last one of us would do anything for you."

"I'm not in charge!" Kayla said, taking a step back at how Conner was declaring her to be the next queen all over again. She didn't have time to deal with all the problems that King Klavian worked through in a day. She'd seen what he lived like and it wasn't something she was ready for. She had plenty of her own problems thank you very much.

"You are the head keeper, Kayla," Conner insisted again. "As for

Anvil, you talked about him so fondly it sent me stumbling. Perhaps the reason you like him is because he gives you all the information you crave. I'd still be there finding ways to get his knowledge too if I was close enough."

"He gives me chocolate bars," Kayla offered and then frowned for revealing that. She shouldn't have said that. She wasn't allowed to eat much candy because of her parents, but Anvil slipped her treats. She'd never snitched on him before.

"When you finally realize what you are, I shudder to think of the changes that will come."

"I'm not going to do anything—"

"Except perhaps enchant all my children," Conner said, glancing not at the front door but at the kitchen where Ruth and Sashi were peeking through. "I saw the way you all looked at each other. Where did your mother go?" Conner asked his oldest as a way of trying to shoo them away.

"What's a keeper?" Ruth asked.

Such a simple question, such a complicated answer. Kayla stepped around Conner to get out the front door before she had to deal with it. She wasn't sure if Conner was going to explain keepers to his children yet. Maybe in another year or two... Oh, why was she trying to shelter the kids? They'd heard the word now. They would always wonder what it was until they learned the answer. They were going to host multiple dragon voices inside their heads. They were going to feel the need to protect and defend creatures larger than themselves. They were going to get a special name all to themselves in the dragon tongue, and in their case, probably love the dragons around them. At least they should.

If Vankerdale wasn't cured of their curse, her little cousins would have the same problems that Kayla currently had. If Sashi really was five that gave her a good ten years before Kayla needed to worry about saving her cousins from her own fate. She tried to not add more pressure on herself as she joined Tyler who was waiting for her on Valiant's back. Valiant had stopped crying, but he was still down letting his head fall to the ground in defeat.

"You're not coming," Kayla told Tyler giving him a slight shove.

"I can be helpful!" Tyler promised.

"We don't have indentured servants, Tyler, and where we are headed you really can't go."

He'd make himself sick stepping through a portal. It hadn't been talked about, but that was the fastest way to get out of Vankerdale and away from the border patrol that King Peyton had out there. Uncle Conner knew about portals and had gone through them before. He'd know the plan without needing to say it either. Kayla wasn't going to take Tyler through a portal and watch him be sick for three hours.

"I told you before that you're staying here," Jack echoed. "Say bye to Valiant. Some friends you have to leave behind."

"That's not true!" Tyler burst. He turned to give Kayla a pleading look. She shook her head. He *wasn't* coming.

"We can still be friends," Tyler said. "I'll write to you. You'll write back, won't you?"

"Conner used to be a mail runner. Maybe he'll agree to risk the tears to step across the border and deliver letters for you. Otherwise, there's no telling who will read them. You should go in and ask him."

That would get Conner out of having to explain what a keeper was to his two clever children. Tyler looked at Conner's house and then gave a nod as he started to back away.

"You'll write back to me?" he asked again. "I'll go to the castle and say I spent days wandering the countryside trying to find where you ran off to so that King Peyton and Prince Evan take me in again and you'll write back to me?"

Kayla had to rub at her eyes with how desperate Tyler looked. She was pretty sure that he was more normal than she was. He would have friends and a girlfriend and a family without complicated bloodlines, so it was strange to hear him plead to be her friend as if he didn't have enough of those. But sure. She could use a few friends. She was adding Valiant to the friend list. She could add Tyler too. After all, Tyler was Valiant's friend.

"I will write back to you," Kayla agreed. She gave him an assuring smile as he folded his arms and gave her a nod. Kayla was certain that he stood right there and watched them leave until he couldn't see them anymore. Tyler was certainly something. If she hadn't spent so much time being stuck in her own head, it would have been beneficial to try to figure out his. It couldn't only be the thought of bonding a dragon that drove him to play traitor to his kingdom. Maybe she'd learn better who Tyler was through their letters. For now, she had to focus on getting through to Aralot.

There was actually more to focus on with that than she realized. Valiant was still new to flying. She kept telling him how to catch the wind so that his wings were softer and quieter against the night air. Despite her best efforts, there were still instances where she held her breath as she heard wild dragons smell out their location and give off soft hoots.

Kayla didn't know where the portal was located, but she knew she was getting close when she spotted dragon blood on the ground. It was fresh, as if Conner had sent ahead a few of his scouts to clear their path. She had to turn her face away when a full dead dragon came into view. She tried to shut her ears off when Valiant whimpered at the sight of another dead beast that she wasn't looking for. Pyro sent Valiant a warning to keep quiet.

Kayla didn't look down again until she heard Pyro start to descend. Her father jumped from his back to press her magical keychain up against the bottom left portal stone, which lit the structure up with blue and purple magic. Valiant was trying to be quiet, but he had to hum at the sight. Most dragons loved the look of portals. Valiant sent her a happy thought and then they were through, safely back in Aralot.

Homecoming

Tristan

The sound of voices had Tristan jumping from his bed even if the sun hadn't come up yet. Odd hours of the day meant that something important had happened. He wasn't going to miss it. Tristan grabbed his shoes only to throw them to the other side of the room because they felt too heavy. There was something in his shoes waiting for him to step inside so it could jab him. Darn! He'd not put his shoes into his protected closet last night. That meant that Vermelo could get past him in his sleep! Vermelo was leaving him presents and Tristan didn't want to take the time to figure out what it was. He could live without the shoes. Everyone would huddle together inside the conference room anyway.

Also giving up on changing out of his pajamas, Tristan flung his door open and looked at the closed conference room door. The guards that normally stood around in this hallway were missing. Tristan ran past the conference room trying to find the commotion. He wished that he had thought to bring a weapon with him, but in his rush, he had left everything behind. No matter. He had this thought before and was prepared to battle at any point in the castle.

Tristan pulled down a picture frame and checked behind it for his hidden knife only to find it missing. Vermelo *again!* Fine. His fists were plenty effective all on their own. He put the picture back and ran the rest of the hallway, finally locating the guards that should have been near his door. They were looking toward the entrance to the castle that was left wide open as they talked of their own version of treason.

"...said he would tell Jack what Vermelo did when he was away," the guards whispered and turned silent when they noticed Tristan there.

When Jack was away. That had to mean that Jack was back! Tristan sprinted past the guards and out the door to see how Jack was doing. Everyone else had beaten him outside and were standing around in the courtyard. Jack was beside Pyro who was very clearly licking away bonding venom that was trickling down Jack's arm and shoulder. To avoid ruining his leather gear, Jack had tossed it off so that his dragon could fang him again. The leather shirt was crumpled on the ground by his feet. His beard was completely grown out again, and he was holding a hand up to Tia to prevent her from saying anything to him while Pyro jabbered away into his head.

Jack bit at one of his thumbs, glanced at Kayla and shook his head. Kayla! She was there too, only she hadn't come alone. Behind her in a sunken posture that clearly said he was trying to hide, was the other spellbinding dragon. The one that had cursed the town beside them. He looked rather wimpy if Tristan had anything to say about it. Sparkle sure had something to say. She was standing behind Tia in battle stance. Tia was trying to explain away the behavior to King Klavian. He had managed to get dressed and was wearing a form-fitting blue shirt that drew attention to his muscle mass and distracted away from his unshaven face.

"She is not going to attack. It's a mood. She will stay right there," Tia ordered her dragon along with a hard stare. Sparkle snapped back at her but didn't move. Jack was the first person to get Sparkle to behave herself.

Pg. 312

"Stop it," he told her, causing Sparkle to sit down and grumble. He tossed a three-inch piece of metal at Kayla that she caught. Her keychain. If Jack had been using that… Tristan dashed closer eyeing Jack's empty hand. He really had lost his magical ring, and Tristan had only one guess to where it was. The magic was left in Vankerdale, leaving Tristan with a sense of foreboding. King Peyton had a source of relatively fresh magic to work with. At least the king had not gotten Kayla's keychain as well. Carrying magic around all the time could backfire on a person if they were not careful to keep it protected.

"Are you done with him," Tia pointed to Pyro as she talked to Jack.

"You know he had some rather important things to say…" Jack trailed off, glanced at Kayla again, and then nodded at his wife that he was done with Pyro. He lowered his hand and Tia flung herself into him, careful to not bump up against his newest fang wound.

"Jack!" Tia screamed letting her joy take over her emotions. They embraced each other amid a bunch of squeals like they were school children come back after summer vacation. Their mouths ran a mile a minute. Tristan noticed that Tia was wearing Anvil's light leather ware colors instead of Rogan's darker tan, but he kept his mouth shut about her choice. Her blond hair was wrapped into a bun but that was normal behavior for the woman.

"We need to discuss something, Jack," Vermelo said while Klavian stepped around the Captain of the Guard to get closer to Jack too.

"He's trying to take you off the throne," Klavian told the rightful king. "If I were you—"

"You are not, thanks," Jack cut off Klavian. "I know what Vermelo's problem is since he has brought it to my attention before. I will talk to him about it later. I think we just found a spell to get around his

Pg. 313

complications."

Nope. Tristan disagreed with that. There wasn't a spell out there that could make Jack noble when he wasn't. Jack looked back at his dragon for a third time, only to cast his eyes yet again toward his daughter who pulled at the edge of her hood while she gripped the keychain in her hand. Tristan cast another glance at the wimpy spellbinding dragon glad that Sparkle wasn't taking the thing lightly. The reason for Kayla's nerves became more obvious when she let herself look at Anvil. He shook his head at her as if she had to wait and greet her parents before she could jump at him. She gripped the keychain harder.

"Woke up really early?" Riven asked into his head. Tristan told the dragon that Jack and Kayla were back and to not distract him.

The courtyard became rather quiet with the sounds of their breathing being carried away on the wind. Tia pulled herself closer to Jack as if she couldn't get enough of him. He gave a soft chuckle as if they were sending flirtations back and forth in their heads through the connected keeper bond. King Klavian couldn't take the silence.

"When will that thing go back?" he asked, pointing to the spellbinding dragon.

"You can't send him away!" Tia burst, spinning away from Jack to face Klavian as if the dragon was hers or something.

"Never," Jack replied, pulling Tia back into his arms while he whispered something sweet to her.

Their daughter exploded. Tristan had never once seen Kayla get mad so he watched her trying to figure out how far she would take something if she got angry. It was good for him to know because they were going to be spending a lot of their time getting angry at each other while they got in each other's way.

"You lied to us for sixteen years!" Kayla screamed. "And you still

Pg. 314

can't face me with the truth. You've not looked at me once!"

Tia went ridged. Behind her Sparkle raised her tail, itching to get back into battle stance to defend her rider from the screaming offspring. Tristan thought that Sparkle had been in that stance because of the spellbinding dragon but maybe he was wrong. Sparkle wanted to attack Kayla. Just what was going on here!? Sparkle always defended Kayla like they shared souls.

"Kayla now is not the time for this. I understand that you are mad. If I were you, I would be upset too. We can talk about it later. Let's focus on the present and not the past. I'm so glad that you're back safely." Tia held her arms out for Kayla to hug her.

Tristan wished he could make out Kayla's face because if his dad did something like that to him when they were fighting with each other, he wouldn't hug him back at all. When Kayla gave off a sound that resembled a dragon snort and went to hug her mother, Tristan felt himself relax again. She was going to be so easy to handle. The girl didn't have any backbone to her at all.

Greeting complete, Kayla pulled back from her mom and then rushed over to Anvil, which caused Jack to cross his arms. Kayla and Anvil paid him no attention as they embraced and Anvil spun her around. Kayla's entire attitude changed in an instant.

"Don't you ever go getting yourself kidnapped again," Anvil told her, holding her close to his tall frame. His blond hair looked like it needed a wash but his protective gem earring glistened with cleanliness.

"Did you see him?! The silver on his wings ripples outward like a flame pattern just like the flame shape of his tail. You have to see his tail! The inside of that flame resembles the petals of Aralot's flower, the mystique. It's super cool. And his eyes! Anvil come see his eyes!" Kayla tugged on his hand while she yanked her hood down from her face and looked directly at the spellbinding dragon.

Tristan felt his sense of unease return all over again. He didn't want to believe what was happening. Kayla didn't look at dragons and she was looking, no gushing, over the qualities of this one. Anvil let her pull him forward, but his confused face turned to look at Jack.

"I told you that she had a surprise for you," Jack said, keeping his voice level which meant that there was still something about all of this that he wasn't happy about. It was probably that Kayla was more excited to see Anvil than her parents.

"Valiant has these charming brown eyes like he's human or something. I'm still trying to sort out his scales. They are close to slate when he's in the shade or it's dark like right now, but I think that if he got a good polish," Kayla pulled Anvil around to yank out his polish from his riders backpack, "that the blue in his scales would be more noticeable. He's not really like slate at all, but more like cordierite."

She had to be talking about a type of rock because Anvil understood what she was saying. He snapped out of his fog, grabbed a polishing cloth to go along with the polish that had been stolen from him, and wiped at his eyes as if he was starting to cry. It was probably relieved tears.

"He's yours?" Anvil asked her. "You found a dragon that doesn't scare you and you just had to pick a spellbinding dragon?"

"Isn't he gorgeous?" Kayla asked. She took the polishing cloth and started to rub at Valiant's scales while the dragon hummed at her, blushed, and bowed to Anvil.

"He's super polite too and incredibly patient. You will not believe how patient this dragon is."

"I don't believe it," Vermelo said, while Sparkle hissed out her customary "my baby" warning now that Kayla was lavishing attention onto another dragon that wasn't her. Kayla ignored the ice dragon as she always did.

Tristan turned back around to look at Vermelo who had gone white, but not any whiter than King Klavian had. They both looked at each other sharing a secret dread that Tristan wanted to be part of. What was wrong with Kayla's dragon apart from the fact that he had frozen the town beside them and hadn't undone his work yet?

Valiant had Kayla who was a pushover. She would tell him to get the town moving again. On the flip side, this played right into Tristan's fears that Kayla had gone into Vankerdale to create a mind-linked dragon army to take him down. He studied her in his mind, trying to decide if she had done that very thing. He didn't think so. Not yet anyway. Kayla had her hood up before proving that she was trying to hide from the other dragons around her. It was only Valiant that she wanted to impress. For now, Kayla still hadn't decided to take him down.

"What did you go into Vankerdale for, Jack?" Vermelo asked.

"Kayla's dragon. King Peyton had him so I buddied up with a few of the locals and fetched him back."

"You found—!" Tia cut her cry of alarm off by covering her mouth as she looked at her husband who gave her a nod. It was times like this that Tristan wished Tia would take his dragon into her keeper bond so he could know what secrets everyone was sharing.

"You make me laugh. Tomorrow you will be back to calling Tia your largest threat and wishing you had nothing to do with her," Riven said.

"Shush," Tristan answered. There was still a chance he could figure it out if he paid really close attention.

"King Peyton has lots of dragons. That doesn't mean that he had Kayla's unless she started hearing the dragon's voice and no one decided to tell me," King Klavian complained, glancing at Tia as he did so.

"Kayla was not hearing voices when Jack left. Valiant was her dragon since she was born," Tia answered.

"King Peyton forced a dragon bond?" Klavian gasped.

Tristan stepped in closer to them. He could see where this was going. At some point, King Peyton had taken Valiant and introduced him to Kayla. The dragon fanged her. He took the dragon back to Vankerdale with him, and no one except for Tia knew anything about it until Kayla got old enough to start hearing dragons.

"She was a baby!" Tia hissed. "I couldn't let King Peyton trick her over the border."

"Don't look mad at me," King Klavian asked her. "This happened sixteen years in the past. It's long been over. The greater question is will there be problems with Kayla because it was a forced bond? You're the dragon expert. You tell me that and then stand really still while I have Anvil tie you up because I don't care what you say anymore. We are going to mount forces against Vankerdale."

"No! We can't send riders into Vankerdale. They will all lose their bonds! Mount a defensive army if you must but don't send them over there."

"Vankerdale kidnapped the king of Aralot and stole our princess along with her dragon. There is no other course of action that can be taken," Vermelo agreed with Klavian. "Jack, please see reason," he said.

Jack didn't answer because he was too busy watching Kayla and Anvil shine up a rather dull looking dragon that hummed louder every time Sparkle hissed. Tristan agreed with pulling together forces too. Even if they didn't charge over the border, King Peyton was going to find a way to tear down the border spell that Jack had set up. They needed to mount battle stations and be on the offensive because the war was coming whether Tia wanted to see it or not.

"I've been so worried about her," Tia claimed. She too ignored the call for action and looked at Kayla.

"I thought you didn't send anyone to rescue Kayla because you were more worried about Jack and the dragons and couldn't care less about—" Tristan's sentence was cut off by his mother who appeared behind him and put a hand on his shoulder to stop him from being rude.

"That's no way to welcome anyone," Queen Aria told him with a smile on her face.

She was by far the most beautiful person around, wearing a pink and green dress. Her brown hair was in ringlets. Tristan wished he wasn't in his pajamas. The cold stone of the courtyard was starting to seep through his toes, and it was making the rest of him feel chilly.

"Have you welcomed her back yet?" his mother asked, looking at Kayla sweetly. He hoped that she was only acting the part of gracious queen right now and didn't really love Kayla like everyone else.

"Mom," Tristan whined. "I'm hardly dressed."

"Don't embarrass me," she said between still smiling teeth. "Get over there."

With a look like that, he didn't have much of a choice. He was going to have to say something nice to Kayla Brixton or his mother would get back at him.

"I have ideas if you need them," Riven offered.

"All set," Tristan returned as he shuffled his feet in Kayla's direction keeping his eyes on the dragon. Valiant stopped humming as he got closer and even with a shine on one side of him, he still looked dull to Tristan. Kayla was wearing her favorite gray sweater with her red-brown hair pulled up in a ponytail. She had pretty hair, but that was all that was interesting about her.

"It's nice to see that you got around King Peyton's trap," Tristan ventured. "Can you ask Valiant to unfreeze the town?" Once that happened Tristan could finally get his hair cut. He watched as Kayla looked at Anvil slightly annoyed before turning to face him with her customary must-we-talk face. Here came the challenge of talking to her. She was looking directly at him, so she was going to say something that might cause a reaction. Tristan had tried to be nice to her so many times, mostly because of his mother, and this is what he got back in return.

"I figured out why you're irritated by me," Kayla said. "Your current girlfriend is going to be mad that we have to go on a date."

Tristan's heart jolted beneath his ribs. Kayla couldn't know that unless she also knew that she was the princess. How had his spell failed?! She'd been in Vankderdale, true, but his hiding location was perfect. Now he'd have to go back there and make sure that she hadn't taken down his spells, and it would be hard to get around the portal location with King Peyton rallying forces to come against Aralot. How had Kayla heard about this? Did she have plans to kill him off so he wouldn't be in her way? Did she want the throne, the kingdom, everything Tristan had trained himself to handle and she had hidden from?

Tristan's eyes strayed upward to her dragon and he scratched at his nose. Dragon. The dragon could have told Kayla about her princess status. Tristan wasn't sure if his spell limited dragon thought. It was either that or it was as his father said and Valiant was sucking up all the magic around Kayla, including the curses that Tristan had set up. Now that Kayla knew her heritage, there wasn't much he could do about it. He was looking at more than one war right now. There was Vankderale and there was Kayla. He gave her a charming smile, but his words reflected his real feelings.

"I'm not going to tell my girlfriend." It was ruined already anyway. He didn't have a girlfriend anymore because of Kayla.

"Nice," Kayla laughed at him. "I won't mention it either, which means we need to do something about them." She inclined her head toward their parents as if they both had a common enemy. Tristan wanted to laugh at her. She was using Colt training against him! They didn't have a common foe. She was his foe and he wasn't going to be fooled by her into believing otherwise.

"All we have to do is satisfy a piece of paper and then you can go back to your isolated lifestyle."

And by that, he clearly meant that she could leave the kingdom of Aralot to him. She could step down quietly without a fight the same way her parents had stepped aside, only in her case, he didn't want her hovering over his shoulder as Jack and Tia did.

"Sweet. I look pretty good on paper," Kayla answered.

She did actually, especially if Caleb was the one putting her there. However... "It's got to at least look like a date. Let's keep this thing short, shall we?" he advised.

"Short? But Tristan, I've never been on a date before. It's got to be the best night of my life at some romantic location with fancy food but no dresses. You're going to have to make it good or your mom's going to know."

How was she doing this to him? She was making him really mad even if her face looked amused. Maybe it was in the tone of her voice, but she was goading him into spending a lot of money on her when he didn't want to. She had made him lose his girlfriend already and all for this date that he was going to hate. If he didn't have to make this fancy, he would make sure that the date was so horrible that Kayla ran away from him screaming. He had wooed plenty of women into his arms before, but he never wanted Kayla there. Kayla got under his skin like no other. She was bringing his mom into this as if she knew why he had come to talk to her in the first place. Humph. He was going to get back at her for it.

"You're going to have to wear a cute dress," he informed her.

"No. I'm not going to look cute for you."

"If you don't, your mom's going to know," Tristan shot back at her. Then he turned away before he had to talk with her any longer. She could stew on that. She was already mad at her mom and wouldn't it be lovely to make the tension even worse?

"I can see this going well," Anvil muttered as Tristan stepped away lightly to keep the cold off his feet.

"Good idea. I'm going," Kayla declared.

She'd dropped her sweet tone now that she didn't have to face him. Tristan rolled his eyes about it all until he caught his mother's short frown. He gave her a shrug. What did she expect? She knew that he didn't get along with Kayla. Everyone knew that. The harder he tried, the more he didn't like her.

"Maybe that's because she can tell you're not being sincere," Riven bravely whispered to him. If it was anyone else but his dragon saying that to him right now, he'd short-sheet their bed. This was going to be the absolute worst date that he ever had to go on.

Impressions

Kayla

Kayla slipped outside to the nearby pond to get away from Tristan and his words that her parents didn't care for her as much as they cared about dragons. They all thought she was too busy helping Valiant to listen to them, but she was never too busy to use her ears. She'd heard it. All of it, and she didn't need to look at Tristan to see his shaggy brown hair, his perfect brown sideburns, or his irritated face. He wanted nothing to do with her other than watch her stay far far away from him. That was hard to do when her parents ruled the kingdom and he lived inside their castle. At least she had Valiant. This was the first time she had ever been able to break away from everyone so quickly. She got on his back and away she went. This whole larger-than-herself pet thing was still strange, but she was quickly getting used to the added company of someone that didn't judge her.

Valiant had been rather scared to see her mom when they landed in the courtyard when it was only Tia and Sparkle out there waiting for them as if they knew they were coming in. Pyro had probably told them to expect the arrival. Kayla could still picture the awe on her mother's face as she looked at Valiant, called him gorgeous, and heard him hiss at her. She had stepped back as if she had never ever had a dragon hiss at her in her entire life.

That's when Tia had decided to leave Valiant with a short "sorry" no doubt for trying to kill him before, and focus only on Jack. She hadn't been as excited to see Kayla as Kayla would have liked, and Kayla's temper got the better of her again. She shouldn't have snapped at her mom, but she had to sit there and watch her dad bond Pyro again knowing that she couldn't have what they had and everything just hurt. When would she get that bond from Valiant? At least Anvil was always warm toward her, but even he couldn't fix her dragon problem, and Tristan only made everything worse. She needed a break already and she'd just gotten here.

The pond outside of the castle grounds was usually a quiet place where people could think. Today it was occupied by a short man who was fishing and a kid hiding in the bushes skipping rocks messing up the calm surface for the fish. Kayla sat down on the far end away from them as Valiant pulled in close and lay down quietly behind her. The kid that had been skipping rocks ran off. The fishing man looked at her, recognized who she was with a short nod and kept trying to get his food. People's reactions around dragons were always so telling. The man who was fishing had to live in the village and the kid must have been a Colt who was scared of dragons.

Kayla pulled her backpack around her shoulders, careful to keep the picture from Caleb out of sight as she tugged out her homework that she had promised her mother she would finish the last time she had left the house. She'd not put a single line on her paper since then.

"He's a handsome one. Odd that he's not growled or anything about me being near. You know they say that first impressions on a dragon really goes to show what the rider thinks of a man," Ritz said, stepping up beside her as she frantically tried to finish one problem so she could get it over with and not have it in the way anymore. It looked like homework would have to wait yet again.

Valiant hummed at Ritz, although he didn't bow to him, which was probably exactly what Kayla thought of the man too. He was to be respected but not fully adopted and trusted completely.

Kayla looked up from her homework, set the late papers aside, and smiled at Ritz. Riders did say that meeting a dragon for the first time would reflect the rider's thoughts and feelings. That had to be why Ritz was braving the dragon right now, to test everything she ever thought about him even though he had to already know.

"I might like you just a little bit," Kayla told him, causing him to smile back at her. He tried to lose the smile as he drew in closer past Valiant, but it stayed with him anyway.

"I knew you'd find Jack in Vankerdale if I gave you a nudge," Ritz told her.

Kayla didn't want to talk about portals again with him, or the strange way that he knew she would end up over the border. She had not elected to go on her own, but she would have ended up over there eventually when Valiant got tired of being a mime.

"It's not true, right?" she deflected.

Ritz came to sit down beside her and also looked out at the water's surface rippling like spiral art.

"Tristan said that my mom wouldn't send anyone after me because she loves dragons more than me, and my dad went to Vankderdale to search for a dragon so he could love them more too. He told me that I'm always first for him, but it never looks that way. Can they really love dragons more? They could have said something to me since they both knew that I'd been bonded to a dragon as an infant, but instead, they both chose to hide from me why I'm sad all the time. They were not protecting me at all, but protecting all the other dragons of Aralot who were not sent into a war to stop King Peyton from abusing my life. I want my parents to love me, Ritz. Instead, I become the sacrifice to their dragon issues."

Ritz was nice to answer her right away, otherwise she might have felt that he didn't like her either.

"I juggle hard decisions all the time so let me tell you that can't assume your parents don't love you because they made a choice without telling you why. It would not have been easy on your mother to sacrifice her only child like this for everyone else. She loves you very much. It would have hurt her constantly. And your father, he elected to break his dragon bond so he could charge over there and try to save you himself without involving others. What they did was out of love."

Love for the greater good of the kingdom. "I don't want to be their political pawn," Kayla huffed.

"Then don't," Ritz replied, causing Kayla to wonder if she really should be sharing this with him. He was good at twisting things when it suited him especially if politics got involved. He was probably around trying to pick up on all the politics as it was.

"Don't be the pawn. Become the leader. That's always worked for me. You have to make others respect you. You get no respect by hiding away doing nothing. Earn it, Kayla."

"They're my parents. They should always love me!"

Kayla wiped at her eyes trying not to be so hard on them. Ritz did have a good point that her mother probably felt guilt over harming her own daughter, which was why Tia had a hard time looking at her when she got back. Kayla knew that nothing scared Jack more than losing his bond apart from losing his wife. So by conclusion, it would prove that her parents loved her because they had both given up things they didn't want to lose for her. However, it still hurt that they had kept the events of her bonding a secret.

"We always love you," her mother's voice said from her right.

When Kayla looked past Ritz to find her mother, the only one there was him.

"You shouldn't fill Kayla's head with wayward thoughts of taking what's already hers."

Ritz made himself sound remarkably like her dad next. That was not only creepy but a rather bad trait for the man to teach himself. He could make people believe anything he wanted if he used the voices of their king and queen.

"Stop that," Kayla demanded. Ritz was too good at being other people. She hoped he hadn't trained others on this particular vocal trick because it was powerful. Then again, Conner had used other voices rather well too. "This is totally where Conner gets this from, only he didn't use it to confuse people."

At least she didn't think he did. She had never asked Tyler what he thought of Conner or if Conner had picked his voices from select influential people. Kayla realized that she probably shouldn't have mentioned Conner around Ritz when his demeanor changed in an instant. He grabbed her arm gripping it hard.

"Where is he?"

From the intensity of the gaze, Kayla didn't think that Ritz was going to let her go until she told him. That was Ritz alright. He wanted to know where his Colts were all the time, and what better mystery to get into than that of a missing mail runner who disappeared shortly after the last king had?

"Conner chased King Peyton into Vankerdale trying to get my dragon back and he got stuck there…" She stopped herself just in time. Only six people (her parents, Aunt Rosa, Uncle Anvil, Tyler, and herself), knew that Conner had a bonded dragon that would have gone with him. She wasn't about to reveal exactly how he got stuck. He couldn't bare to leave his dragon on the other side or leave hers.

"He has a wife and a few kids now."

"I hate Vankerdale." Ritz's face turned dark, but he did let her go. "It's going down. You've been there. How can we bring it down?"

"Why would you want to?" Kayla asked him, returning back to her own Colt training to not panic. It was always better to ask questions first and learn the why before jumping to conclusions that Ritz was trying to take control of some other kingdom because he couldn't have the throne in Aralot. Conner had said that the man was interested in the crown just the same as he was.

"Don't say revenge," Kayla provided, because that wasn't a good enough reason. She wasn't going to help him if he wanted to be a bully. Most of the people in Vankerdale were not the problem. It was their rulers that controlled things by force and indentured servitude that were nasty.

"We'll take it down to stop King Peyton from his continuous attempts to capture your mother, yourself, and all our special dragons. He seeks to create war and chaos, bringing terror and torture to your family and friends. He's only going to get worse, Kayla. He can't help it. He's crazy from his broken bond, and I doubt he's found a way to cope as you and Conner have done."

Ugh! Ritz shouldn't know that Conner wasn't leaving Vankerdale because of dragons. She hoped that she hadn't ruined things for Conner and his Colt status. Colts didn't have dragons. Hopefully, it wasn't her words that told Ritz that Conner had a broken bond. Maybe he had figured it out on his own long before now. After all, he could have guessed how Conner delivered mail so fast the same way Anvil had guessed at it once.

"You can stop this war, Kayla. You can earn your parent's love, be looked up to instead of looked down on."

Grr. He knew how to pick at her weaknesses, but Kayla had been taught well by her father, and she wasn't going to give in no matter how good it sounded to be praised instead of scoffed at.

"I'll think about it," she replied as she stood up.

"Any news from Vankerdale I can work with. I can walk you through a full revolution if that's what it takes. I'll be here for you because I've always cared for you."

Kayla left him more irked than anything that he was telling her he liked her. He could mean it, but the odds were against him that he was trying to use the feelings of a sense of belonging against her so he could get his way. She *had* just told him that she had a broken bond and wanted to feel like she belonged somewhere. Was this all to stop a war with the neighbors, or did Ritz have other reasons to suddenly take interest in messing up Vankerdale?

"In my personal opinion," Valiant said, without moving to follow her, *"Ritz is angry that King Peyton is abusing you."*

"And so many other people," Kayla answered, thinking about all the people that lived in that kingdom that couldn't communicate with dragons or care for them effectively.

"Kayla." Ritz stopped her from walking off on him by appearing in front of her face. She rolled her eyes. Every single other person she could hear except for him. Maybe he was a ghost that just happened to look and feel rather solid. She glanced down at his feet noticing his soft-soled shoes and gave up on that idea. He was just super quiet.

"I really meant what I said. I would love to hear what happened to you in Vankerdale. Please don't shut me out of this. Please don't turn away. There's a darkness that only you can keep at bay."

"What?" Kayla asked, narrowing her eyes at him. He was rhyming at her trying to trick her into telling him something.

"Did you feel any odd pressure on you when you were there?" Ritz sighed, pinched his eyes together, and decided to be more specific. "What did you dream about?"

Kayla stared at him. Her mother had asked her this question plenty of times and Kayla had just barely told her that she had her parent's nightmares. She had never mentioned all the other ones. Her dreams in Vankerdale had all been new and each of them she saw through the eyes of a dragon. It made the hairs on her arms stand up to hear Ritz ask her about it. What did he know?

"What causes it?" Kayla asked him. "How do I stop it? It's not a curse. I've checked a hundred times. I used to be able to wake myself up, but lately, it's gotten harder. Not even biting my own tongue works anymore. I can't get out of it. Please tell me what it is."

"I can't tell you how to stop it, only that if you ever see yourself walking the hallways of the castle to come see me right away."

She shook her head at him. She'd seen that dream over sixty times. She knew every secret hiding place and path in and below the castle. Walking the castle and watching Gladius scream about his dragon issues was one of the very first nightmares she ever had.

"What did you dream about over there? Please tell me."

She didn't have to tell him, but she had never heard of Ritz begging from anyone before. It wasn't in his character to do something like that. This had him extremely worried, which only made Kayla start to feel scared again. He knew about some "pressure" that wasn't a curse that messed around with dreams. Why? Did he have these dreams? When she reached a certain one would she suddenly find herself like him, unable to age or die? No one had figured out what had happened

Pg. 330

to him, but there was a large chance that he was scared of it repeating itself.

"I dreamed about the portal near my house and then about Valiant and my mom."

He nodded. "Then there's still time. Don't be distant now, Kayla. I know how much you like me."

Ritz smiled at her and risked giving her a hug. It caused Kayla to hold her breath. The ruler of the Colts was giving her a hug! Even worse, while she tried to tell herself to back away and that he was only out to trick her, she felt herself warming to the idea that Ritz could like her too. He could be there for her, in the shadows, behind the trees, a voice that helped to pull her up when she fell down. He was the one person who looked like he understood some of her most terrifying nightmares, and he was offering to step in and save her. She felt like she belonged with him, beside him. He could help her find a way through everything that was being thrown at her because he'd lived a long time and seen an awful lot.

"Later dear girl," Ritz said affectionately, before he took off running. She watched him draw away hearing his words echo in her mind that he had always cared for her.

"I want to believe that, but I also don't," Kayla sighed.

"The air smells different in Aralot than in Vankedale. Did you know?" Valiant answered with a question as he took in a deep lungful.

Kayla shook her head at him. What if nobody knew what her problem was and Ritz's words had been designed to test her to see if she even had a problem. She had recovered her dragon, but still, there were too many things that were unexplainable in her life. She still would have the dreams, and the tendency to feel sad because Valiant had promised not to bond her. She still drew pictures in her sleep. She had not only

Conner but Ritz telling her that she should lead over her parents. She was suddenly the princess of Aralot and had to date Tristan. She winced over that one yet again. Then there was that strange sense of trusting Tyler and figuring out what to do to keep King Peyton from stealing away their magic and destroying the entire kingdom.

"Hey," Valiant hummed at her. *"We're together now. We'll tackle those one at a time and win against them all."*

They might not win them all, but they were in this together. Kayla looked over her dragon with his warm brown eyes, his cordierite colored scales, his flashy wingtips, and his still blunt claws. Last week she would have never imagined herself getting this close to being a dragon rider. She gave Valiant her largest smile yet and decided that she would shift out some of her rock-climbing gear for dragon gear.

She did belong somewhere and it was next to Valiant. All those things she had just felt about Ritz could be applied to her dragon without the fear that he was lying to her. Valiant had always loved her and he always would. She hadn't always loved him, but she was going to change that. They were going to be the best of friends. They would be an asset to Aralot, like her dad who fixed spells and saved people. Valiant happily hooted at her thoughts. Then he asked her to get on his back so he could mobilize the town he had frozen. Yes, they were going to do things right and be the best spellbinding team there ever was.

Continue the story with *Connected*

Kayla

Kayla kicked off her shoes really hard. They went sliding across the room, knocking over her mother's newest music composition that had been on a stand. The stand toppled over with a bang that echoed the slam of the front door. Just great. Now Kayla had created yet *another* disaster to her day. If only she never had a birthday, half of her problems would have fallen to some other day. She was all about splitting up the pain.

Kayla rubbed the side of her face. Her dragon, the blue-gray Valiant, had told her that she no longer showed the fingerprints from the slap. She could still feel it. Even worse, the slap could have been avoided if she had been able to sort through her own nightmares last night. She hadn't gotten over the feeling that they could be real, especially since she had woken up to find that she had mysteriously drawn way too many pictures of Sparkle looking adorable.

Those she had tossed in the fireplace as fast as she could, watching them burn with satisfaction as she destroyed the evidence that she couldn't stop sleepwalking. Or was sleep drawing the correct term? Anyway, she was usually good at picking out what her dreams were trying to tell her, but last night's dream had not been one of her normal nightmares. She had learned that the hard way when she got that slap. She had watched Ritz die, and there was no way he was dead because he had slapped her when she finally saw him.

"Mind over the body, Kayla," Ritz's voice had spoken to her in her dream. He was an ageless man with blond hair and stunning blue eyes. Devious eyes. Harsh, unyielding, traitorous eyes. The man led a group of rebels known as the Colts, and he was known to be brutal, but he'd never extended that same harsh backhand to her before. She wasn't a Colt! He had reminded her of that very well.

In the dream, she had been crumbled to the ground inside Uncle Anvil's dragon training ware. It was one of her favorite places to be, not because of the dragons, but because of Uncle Anvil. He was her uncle by association rather than blood, but he was also one of her best friends. She told him practically everything. He was going to hear all about how bad her date had just gone, but even he never got the details of how her dreams made her sweat.

Currently, Ritz was her accomplice bravely facing his enemies since riders and Colts never got along well. He was trying to coach her through this plague that her body had since she had a broken dragon bond and looking at any other dragon apart from Valiant made her physically overcome with sadness so deep it brought her to her knees.

Valiant refused to fix their broken bond due to some promise he had made, so her condition remained. It would have been nice if they had never been broken, but King Peyton of Vankerdale had forced Valiant to bond her as a baby and then stolen Valiant away. Kayla had just gotten her dragon back, having never known that he even existed until a few days ago. King Peyton had planned on using Valiant to trap Kayla so he could then use her to capture Aralot's magical ice dragons. It was complicated and hadn't worked.

Valiant had been set free by his friend Tyler Valeron, who worked in the Vankerdale castle for Prince Evan. In any event, Ritz had died in her dream. The demon ultra-dragon king with his hardened black scales and fire so hot it was almost blue, swooped into the ware and chomped him. The dragon destroyed buildings and crops and everything he fancied. Kayla called him Reaper. Other people called him Demon and a lot of other nasty things. The dragon had been bred by her grandfather Herb's dragons after the man had died. Reaper scared her.

Kayla had screamed so loud that she woke herself up and brought her parents into her bedroom. She normally saw nightmares about past events in her parents or long-dead relatives lives. She had to admit that she had never dreamed of Ritz before, and most people stayed clear of him and his devilish ways, but Kayla had a particular fondness for the man, so to see him die had her scared.

That was how her bad day had started. It kept going south after that. Happy birthday indeed.

Kayla had done nothing but fret over Ritz being dead all day until she saw him. She had been sick with worry. She needed him! He was going to help her figure out what to do about Vankerdale always trying to start wars with Aralot. He was going to help her find a way to earn her parent's love instead of feeling like they used her as a political pawn against

King Klavian, his wife Aria, and his son Tristan. Ritz was going to teach her how to withstand the pressure of her own mind, distancing herself from her emotions. He was the best master of his Colt practices after all. He could fool anyone to think anything. He could help her fool herself to overcome her limitations. He couldn't die!

So when Kayla had seen spotted him on her date, she had run at him and found her mouth talking away the fears she had been holding all day.

"You have to help me escape my own head!" Kayla had shouted.

"I don't owe you anything, Kayla. You are not a Colt."

And she never would be one, because her mother refused to let Kayla take the Colt tests that would earn her a wild stallion tattoo. The tests were often brutal and extremely hard.

"It doesn't matter. You're supposed to help me! You're the only one that cares—"

Kayla's whine had been cut off with a sharp slap across her face. Her date for the evening hadn't done anything to help. Raised as a Colt himself, Tristan had simply stood there refusing to engage with his leader.

"Don't you ever say that lie around me again. This feeling of not being loved is designed to push you out into the world in search of something that could love you, but let me tell you something. You are not to go searching. You have all the love you already need. You just need to open your eyes and see it.

Stop hiding. You can change your fate. If you don't, you're going to lose it. Anything from Vankerdale? It still has something you need."

Kayla had to take a step back and think about that for a moment. She already had Valiant out of Vankerdale, but Ritz knew that Conner was there with a broken bonded dragon. He shouldn't know that Conner was a keeper, but he had expressed interest in getting Conner out of there before. Kayla had assumed that Ritz was talking about him now instead of her. And since she was on that date thing, she had walked off on Ritz without answering him.

"How was it?"

Tia Brixton asked, surveying the damage of the music sheets spread across the floor and the shoes that had caused the pages to get jumbled. Kayla's mother was standing beside her brown-haired husband Jack, who wore his leather dragon-riding pants and a plain white shirt. His starburst brown eyes ignored the thrown shoes to stare at his daughter. Tia's blue eyes flicked away from the pages. She smoothed over her blond bun and tried out a sympathetic smile.

Kayla's parents were not asking Kayla about her nightmares. They wanted to know how her date with Prince Tristan had gone. He was called the prince, but he wasn't really the prince. His father was the steward of the kingdom of Aralot, and the steward handled the affairs like he was the king so he was called King Klavian. Kayla was called the princess. Both of their fathers had been crowned with the same fake crown since Aralot's real crown was cursed. Kayla's father was considered the real king, only he went by his first name of Jack.

Anyway, it wasn't until a few days ago that Kayla had learned she was the princess because she had been cursed previously to never hear of it before. Now to make their parents happy with the friendly feud they had between them and the Clusters, she was to date Prince Tristan. Yuck.

"The date was horrible," Kayla answered.

Both her parents stood there waiting for more. They had sent her out with high hopes. She had left in a bad mood and come back in a worse one. Tristan had been prying at her the whole time.

"Whether you have fun is up to your own attitude, but please don't ruin this whole thing for me. I didn't want to come either. You're the last person I would ever want to date, Kayla, so try to not say anything to ruin my dinner."

If that wasn't charming his "nice dress," comment had nearly made her smack him. He was the last person in the universe that she wanted to dress up for, but she had put a dress on and stepped out the castle door not looking forward to her current reality.

They had run into Ritz before dinner, and the leader of the Colts had slapped her! Slapped! He had never hit her before in his life. Usually Kayla found Ritz to be pleasant to talk with because he was cursed too. He had been alive for a really long time. At least since before her father was born, and he was really smart. The last time Kayla had seen Ritz, he had mentioned her nightmares, making Kayla think that he might know the solution to ending them. It was because of that that she had rambled away to him when she saw him and he'd hit her!

"You keep coming back to that," her dragon, Valiant, sighed into her thoughts. *"No one can trust Ritz. Everyone says so."*

But she wanted to trust him. Grr! She wanted his help. The only excuse for his behavior she came up with was that he was trying to keep up his vile image in front of Tristan. She had no idea how Ritz acted when around Tristan, but he was usually hard on the renegades he trained. They were the group that took down evil kings. The last evil king had been taken by her father, King Jack, and he had been a Colt at the time. Jack was still a Colt even though he was now also the first Colt that turned into a dragon rider, and became the king, so that he could marry the beautiful Tia Felding. Yeah. He had everything. All Kayla had was a headache. She still had to suffer through three more dates with Tristan.

"You won't give us any other hint of what you did?" Tia asked.

"Why pester her? You'll get it all out of Anvil later," Jack said rolling his eyes.

"Jack!" Tia cried, spinning to face him to prove that she wasn't secretly in love with Anvil while he was still in love with her even after he had married Annaliese and had a few kids.

"What? You will. Kayla will tell Anvil who will tell you. You'll tell your dragon, Sparkle, who will tell my dragon, Pyro. Pyro will tell me, and we will all know how lousy a date it was in the end. I think Kayla wants to be alone to mope for a few minutes."

"We are her parents. She should tell us personally," Tia explained.

"Why? We're the ones responsible for her going on the bad date."

"I simply want to know."

"She didn't spy on you," Jack told Kayla as Kayla pulled her hair down and flicked the hair tie across the room next. Kayla hardly ever got a moment's peace because her keeper mother used her horde of connected wild dragons to follow Kayla wherever she went. Kayla had been spied on her entire life. It was nice to know that her mother had given her a bit of privacy, even if it had come at a bad time.

"When are you going to see Anvil?" Tia asked as Kayla silently made her way toward her parents. They were blocking the stairs and therefore her room.

"Right after I change?" Kayla asked.

"Sounds good to me," Tia answered....

Name Bank

Kingdoms:

Aralot	-current location
Vankerdale	-east of Aralot
Wisteria	-north of Aralot across the ocean

Brixtons and Feldings:

Kayla Brixton	-secret princess	Dragon: Valiant
Jack Brixton	-Kayla's father; the king	Dragon: Pyro
Tia (Felding) Brixton	Kayla's mother; the queen	Dragon: Sparkle
Conner Felding	-Kayla's missing uncle	Dragon: Tempest
Esmay Felding	-Conner's Wife	Children: Sashi, Ruth, Tova
Troy and Shane	-forgotten keepers	
Herb Felding	-Kayla's grandfather	
Alice Felding	-Herb's wife	
Gladius Felding	-Kayla's great-grandfather	
Jean (Frizer) Felding	-Gladius's wife	

Mentionable dragons:

Tia's keeper dragons	-Clawson, Pyro, Midnight, Fang, Duchess, Hemp, Darkwing, Lightning, and Fern
Nebula	-Conner's water dragon
Luna	-a wild dragon and Pyro's sister
Slasher	-a wild dragon from Pyro's herd
Indigo	-Pyro's mother and dragon queen

Aralot Castle:

King Klavian Cluster	-steward and son of King Virgil Cluster IV
Queen Aria	-wife of Klavian Cluster
Prince Tristan	-son of Klavian and Aria
King Virgil Cluster IV	-Klavian's crowned father
Vermelo	-Captain of the Guard
Merlock	-a dwarf dragon

| Bantin | -also called Mr. Grumpy; the magical ice dragon |
| Tristan's past girlfriends: | -Abbie and Dani |

Colts:

| Ritz | -ageless leader of the Colts |
| Fenix, Steve, Bret, and Kyle | - Kayla's uncles on her father's side |

Vankerdale:

Tyler Valeron	-Castle servant	
Narl Valeron	-Tyler's brother	
Prince Evan Peyton	-Prince of Vankerdale	
King Peyton	-King of Vankerdale	Dragon: SilverWings

Anvil's Ware:

Anvil	-ware leader	Dragon: Clawson
Annaliese	-Anvil's wife	
Rosa Cluster	-Kayla's Aunt	Dragon: Pewter
Clark Cluster	-Kayla's Uncle	Dragon: Midnight
Achilles	-a rider in Tia's keeper bond	Dragon: Fang
Caleb Andrade	-a rider and artist	Dragon: Warner

| Aiden | -a rider that fights Caleb | |
| Mentionable dragons | Galivant | - a pink fire-breathing dragon |

Vincent's Ware:

Vincent	-a ware leader that tries to breed ice dragons	
Shilo	-the best ice dragon trainer alive	
Vladimir	-a past ware leader	Dragon: Giselle

Other Wares:

Rogan's Ware	-led by Rogan	Dragon: Indigo
The King's Ware	-led by Charles	Dragon: Clipshire
Niles's Ware	-training ware in the west	
Desert Ware	-training ware in the desert	
Turid's Ware	-led by Turid	female ware leader

Treasure Hunters:

Ian	-used to be a street urchin in Wisteria
August	-used to be a baker in Wisteria

Towns and Places:

The Pits	-a stone quarry owned by the Colts
Troni	-the town by the castle
The Castle	
Old Castle	-Gladius's destroyed castle in the south

Don't fly off yet!

There is magic lingering in the air encouraging you to leave a **Spoiler Free** review on Amazon or Goodreads. This is an excellent way to spark the flames of another person's fire so they can enjoy the book as you have. I thank you for your time.

For more exciting stories and content please visit my website at:

amandaheit.com

Or my author page at

https://www.amazon.com/author/amanda.heit

Special Thanks

A very large thank-you to my reviewers Amy Fowler and Adam Morse who have gone through a ton of versions of this story and have encouraged me through every flight.

About the Author

Finding meaning in life—feeling like you're contributing to all of humanity in a good way—is a large undertaking. When I write, it's the task I take on. Sometimes, that task is daunting. Sometimes, it's full of laughter, joy, and fear. Reaching the end of a book can put me on top of the world or cause me endless frustration. But I can't stop myself from trying. I can't stop the inner clock that ticks and tells me that writing is something I enjoy the heck out of and there is nothing that will stop me from writing for long. As one of the quiet people in the universe, my best joy and flow in life comes when I'm creating new worlds and exploring characters. For me, each book I create finds new friends that share with me the intimate tangles of their lives. They cheer and I cheer. They succeed and I rejoice. They fall and I'm there hoping for that happy ending right along with them. I hope that you can find something in the stories I create that will bring you the same type of thrill. Thanks for sticking to the end!

Amanda Heit

www.ingramcontent.com/pod-product-compliance
Lightning Source LLC
Chambersburg PA
CBHW032136190626
46814CB00005BA/1713